Dear Reader,

Many years a[go] [when I was a] kid, my father said to me, "Bill, it doesn't really matter what you do in life. What's important is to be the *best* William Johnstone you can be."

I've never forgotten those words. And now, many years and almost 200 books later, I like to think that I am still trying to be the best William Johnstone I can be. Whether it's Ben Raines in the Ashes series, or Frank Morgan, the last gunfighter, or Smoke Jensen, our intrepid mountain man, or John Barrone and his hard-working crew keeping America safe from terrorist lowlifes in the Code Name series, I want to make each new book better than the last and deliver powerful storytelling.

Equally important, I try to create the kinds of believable characters that we can all identify with, real people who face tough challenges. When one of my creations blasts an enemy into the middle of next week, you can be damn sure he had a good reason.

As a storyteller, my job is to entertain you, my readers, and to make sure that you get plenty of enjoyment from my books for your hard-earned money. This is not a job I take lightly. And I greatly appreciate your feedback— you are my gold, and your opinions *do* count. So please keep the letters and e-mails coming.

Respectfully yours,

William Johnstone

WILLIAM W. JOHNSTONE

QUEST OF THE MOUNTAIN MAN

TREK OF THE MOUNTAIN MAN

PINNACLE BOOKS
Kensington Publishing Corp.
http://www.kensingtonbooks.com

PINNACLE BOOKS are published by

Kensington Publishing Corp.
850 Third Avenue
New York, NY 10022

First Pinnacle Books Printing: August 2006

10 9 8 7 6 5 4 3 2 1

Printed in the United States of America

QUEST OF
THE MOUNTAIN
MAN

1

Spring had come early to the Sugarloaf this year, and Smoke Jensen's hired hands were well on their way to getting the spring branding and separating of the winter calves from their mothers done a month earlier than usual. It had been a mild winter, and the snow accumulation on the lower slopes of the Rocky Mountains was already beginning to melt and disappear under the rays of the spring sun.

Smoke sat on the top rail of the corral, a half-smoked cigar in his mouth, and watched as Pearlie, his ranch foreman, cussed and hollered at the hired hands to get the last of the calves in the corral branded so they could stop for lunch. The wiry young man was working like a dervish, moving from place to place within the corral, kicking and shoving the branded calves into the chute that would lead them out to pasture even before the smoke was cleared from their fresh brands.

Smoke smiled around his cheroot as he glanced upward at the morning sun as it shone through mild cloud cover. He figured it was only about ten-thirty in the morning, and Pearlie was already yelling about lunch. That figured, since Pearlie rarely let more than a few hours pass without putting something or other in his mouth. He was, as Cal, his young protégé, called him, a real food hog, with Cal usually putting heavy emphasis on the word "hog."

Hearing light footsteps behind him, Smoke turned and saw his beautiful wife, Sally, approaching the corral with a metal pot of fresh coffee in one hand and a platter of her well-appreciated doughnuts, called bear sign, in the other. Her long, dark hair was hanging down to caress her shoulders, just the way he liked it, and her hazel eyes were bright and clear and full of life, as usual.

"Hi, darlin'," Smoke drawled, jumping down off the rail. "What's this?" he asked as he took the platter of bear sign from her hands.

She smiled, and it was if the clouds parted and the sun shone brighter to Smoke. "I could hear Pearlie shouting about lunch all the way in the cabin, so I thought a short break for some coffee and doughnuts might help him make it until noon when I'll serve the boys lunch."

Pearlie, who was busy lying across a calf's neck so Cal could apply the branding iron, hadn't seen Sally's approach.

Smoke whistled through his lips and held up the platter for the men in the corral to see. "Hey, we got coffee and bear sign, boys," he shouted.

Pearlie's head whipped around at the words "bear sign," and he jumped up off the calf and literally ran toward the corral gate. As soon as he was up and off the calf, it kicked out with both hind legs and scrambled to its feet, knocking Cal on his ass and sending the branding iron flying.

Pearlie didn't take time to undo the latch on the gate, but just jumped up on top and leapt on over. He didn't intend for anyone else to get first pick of the doughnuts. When Pearlie arrived next to Smoke and Sally, skidding to a stop in the mud that was a result of the spring rains earlier in the week, he ignored the coffee and grabbed a double handful of the bear sign, while simultaneously tipping his hat at Sally.

"Mornin,' Miss Sally," he said just before he popped an entire doughnut in his mouth and began to chew.

"Good morning, Pearlie," she said with a laugh, shaking her head at the way he was making the food disappear.

Cal and three other hands walked up at a much slower pace, showing a good deal more restraint than Pearlie had. When Cal got close enough, he reared back and kicked Pearlie in the seat of his pants with the side of his boot.

"Gosh darn it, Pearlie," he groused, "that calf dang near took my leg off!"

Pearlie juggled the bear sign in his hands to keep from spilling them onto the ground when Cal's kick made him jump. "Dagnabbit, Cal, you almost made me drop these here bear sign!" he shouted, holding the doughnuts in one hand while he rubbed his posterior with his free hand.

Cal pointed at the platter heaped full of doughnuts. "Well, what was your hurry, Pearlie? Miss Sally made plenty enough bear sign for all of us."

Pearlie shrugged. "I just wanted to git'em whilst they was hot, Cal. You know they taste better that way," he answered, looking not at all ashamed of his actions.

"Horsesh—uh, stuff!" Cal rejoined, glancing at Sally as he reached over and took a couple of the bear sign for himself. "You just wanted to make sure you got more'n everbody else, that's why you was in such a hurry."

"There's plenty for everyone," Sally said, stepping between the men. "And I made a fresh pot of coffee to go along with the bear sign."

When Pearlie opened his mouth to ask a question, Sally interrupted him. She pulled out a small brown sack containing sugar and held it up. "And yes, I did bring you some sugar for your coffee, Pearlie."

Cal shook his head as he poured himself a cup of the steaming brew. "I swear, Miss Sally," he said, smiling slightly, "you done spoiled that man rotten."

"What?" Pearlie asked as he dumped the entire packet of sugar in his coffee without asking anyone else if they wanted any. "Just 'cause I like a little sugar in my coffee, you think I'm spoiled?"

Cal smirked. "You mean a little coffee in your sugar, don't you?" he asked. "And what's next, Pearlie? Pretty soon you're gonna be putting cow's milk in it like the ladies in town all do."

Smoke laughed and put his arm around Sally. "You boys finish up your coffee and get back to work. I'm not paying you to sit around on your backsides jawing at each other all day," he said as he walked Sally back toward their cabin.

"Thank you kindly for the food and coffee, Miss Sally," called Pete, one of the hands.

"Yes, ma'am," Pearlie mumbled through a mouthful of doughnut, "thanks."

Cal took off his hat and slapped Pearlie in the back of his head with it. "Don't talk with your mouth full, Pearlie. Didn't your momma never teach you no manners?"

"Hell," Pete said laughing, "if'n Pearlie didn't talk with his mouth full, he'd dang near never get to say nothin'."

Smoke liked the way his men had an easy camaraderie on the job. Out in the High Lonesome, he knew that on any given day their lives might depend on their coworkers, and he reasoned the better friends they were, the less chance there was of anyone getting hurt or killed in the dangerous business of ranching out on the frontier.

He was especially fond of Pearlie and his young sidekick, Cal. They'd been with him for several years now, and after standing next to them in some pretty hairy situations, he knew he couldn't ask for any better men to be by his side or to guard his back. In the parlance of the West, they would both do to ride the river with.

Pearlie had come to work for Smoke over five years before, after he'd found he couldn't stomach a man he'd hired his guns to in a range war against Smoke Jensen. Pearlie had gone to the man, named Tilden Franklin, after Franklin had raped a young woman, and told him he was through. Franklin was enraged, and he had his other gunnies beat Pearlie almost to death, finally shooting him and leaving him for dead. Wounded and near death, Pearlie had made his way to the Sugarloaf to warn Smoke about Franklin, and he'd been a fixture on the ranch ever since.

Calvin Woods, a year or two later, was just fourteen years old when he found himself in Colorado, broke and starving after leaving his parents' hardscrabble farm to try and make a living on his own. Sally had been on her way back to the Sugarloaf with a buckboard full of supplies during the spring branding, and Cal, rail-thin from not eating anything but wild berries for the past week, had stepped from the bushes at the corner of the trail with a pistol in his hand.

"Hold it right there, miss," he'd called.

Sally could see right away the boy was half-starved and could hardly hold the old pistol up, he was so weak.

She slipped her hand under a pile of gingham cloth on the seat, grasping the handle of her short-barreled Colt .44, and eased back the hammer, just in case.

"What can I do for you, young man?" she asked, no fear in her voice.

"Well, uh, you can throw some of those beans and a cut of that fatback over here, and maybe a portion of that Arbuckle's coffee too."

"Don't you want my money?"

The boy frowned and shook his head. "Why, no, ma'am. I ain't no thief. I'm just hungry."

"And if I don't give you my food, are you going to

shoot me with that big Navy Colt?" Sally asked, trying hard not to smile.

Cal hesitated for a moment, and then he grinned ruefully. "No, ma'am, I guess not." He twirled the pistol around his finger and he slipped it into his belt, and then he turned and began to walk down the road toward Big Rock.

Sally, feeling sorry for the boy instead of angry, called out to him and offered him a job on the Sugarloaf, which he eagerly accepted. When they got back to the ranch, Pearlie took the boy under his wing, even though he was just a couple of years older than Cal. They'd been best friends ever since.

Both Smoke and Sally thought of Pearlie and Cal as more members of their family than hired workers, and the boys, who would gladly lay down their lives for either of them, reciprocated the feelings.

As Smoke and Sally approached their house, Smoke heard the sounds of hoofbeats in the distance, and they were coming closer at a rapid rate, as if the rider was in a hell of a hurry.

Smoke's hand went to the Colt in his holster. Visitors in the High Lonesome weren't always friendly, and Smoke had more than his fair share of enemies still walking around.

"Step into the cabin, Sally," he said as he turned and looked down the road leading to their house, "until I see who this is."

Sally, who'd learned never to question Smoke's instincts, ducked into the cabin and took a Henry repeating rifle off the rack next to the door.

She held the gun expertly and waited to see if she would need to use it to back Smoke's play.

After a minute or two, she saw Smoke's hand come away from his pistol and a smile break out on his face as he called out, "Hey, Monte, come on in and have some coffee."

She hung the rifle back up on the rack and went

into the kitchen to get Monte Carson, sheriff of Big Rock, a cup of coffee and some bear sign.

By the time Sally came out onto the porch, Monte and Smoke were sitting on chairs and Monte was tamping tobacco in the pipe, which was rarely out of his mouth.

Monte jumped to his feet and tipped his hat. "Howdy, Miss Sally."

"Hello, Monte," she responded, smiling and waving him back to his seat as she handed him a mug of coffee and put the plate of bear sign down on a table between him and Smoke.

Smoke took the other mug, and watched as Monte grabbed a doughnut and swallowed it in two bites. Cowboys throughout the valley around Big Rock prized Sally's bear sign.

"How is Mary?" Sally asked, speaking of Monte's wife. "We've been so busy with the spring branding, I haven't had a chance to visit her in a while."

"She'd doin' just fine, Sally," Monte said. "Her rheumatiz is botherin' her a bit, but now that warm weather's on the way, it'll soon get better."

"Winter up here does have a way of getting into our bones, especially as we all get older," Sally said, dusting her hands off on the apron tied around her waist.

Monte's face sobered and he pulled an envelope out of his vest pocket. "Well, I guess I might as well get to the reason I came out here. Jackson over at the telegraph office gave me this telegram for you and said I needed to get it out here right away."

"Bad news?" Smoke asked.

Monte gave a half smile. "You know ol' Jack, Smoke. He wouldn't say, but I 'spect it is or he wouldn't have been in such an all-fired hurry for me to bring it to you."

Sally took the envelope and opened it. As she read it, Smoke saw her face pale and her eyes fill with tears. He got immediately to his feet and stood by her side, putting his arm around her waist, waiting for her to tell him what it said.

After a moment, she folded the letter and placed it in her apron pocket. She looked up at him, her face sad. "It's my father," she said quietly. "My mother says he's real sick. The doctor in Boston thinks it might be his heart."

Smoke hugged her. He knew how close Sally was to her parents, and it'd been over two years since she'd been back to see them. He looked over her shoulder at Monte. "Would you make arrangements for us to take the next train out heading east, Monte? We'll get packed and be in town first thing in the morning."

"Sure, Smoke," he answered, and he looked at Sally, "I'm real sorry to hear about your paw, Sally."

"Just a minute, Monte," Sally said. She turned to Smoke. "You don't have to come with me, Smoke."

When he started to protest, she held up her hand. "No, I know how much you hate to go back East, especially when there's still a lot of work to do around the ranch. I'll just go out there by myself and see what the situation is. By the time you're through with the branding and such, I'll know how my father is and I'll let you know then if you need to come."

Smoke hated to think of Sally making such a long trip by herself, but she was right. He hated the big cities of the East, and could hardly stand to visit for very long. The crowded streets and the dudes with their fine clothes and insincere manners grated on his nerves worse than a burr in his boots.

When Sally saw the indecision on his face, she smiled gently. "I'll be all right, dear. After all, I've made the trip many times before."

Finally Smoke nodded, though it was clear he wasn't happy with the idea of her traveling alone. "All right, if you say so."

* * *

Sally prepared a large lunch of fried chicken, mashed potatoes, and several loaves of fresh bread. She had a lot of hungry cowboys to feed before she could start her packing, and she cooked extra portions at lunch so she wouldn't have to cook later for supper.

Even though Smoke was among the richest ranchers in the area and they could easily afford a full-time cook, Sally enjoyed cooking for the men. She'd been a teacher in the local school, and she wouldn't have known what to do with her time if she couldn't make herself useful in this way. At times, even though Smoke hired a cook for trail drives, Sally would ride along and help him prepare the meals from the chuck wagon. When Smoke asked her why, she said it helped keep her cooking skills sharp—and the men all agreed she was right, for she was widely known as the best cook in the county.

After lunch, she went into the bedroom to get her things together, while Smoke went out to the corral to help with the branding.

Some six hours later, Smoke entered the cabin and found their wooden bathtub set up in the spare bedroom, and it was full of steaming hot water.

"What's this?" he said with a grin. "I'm a mountain man—you know it's not time for my annual bath yet."

Sally appeared from their bedroom, wearing a frilly pink nightgown, a half smile on her face. "Smoke Jensen, I'm leaving in the morning and I won't see you for I don't know how long. If you think I'm going to spend my last night with you with you all covered with dirt and sweat, well, then, you've got another think coming!"

Smoke laughed and began to quickly shed his buckskins. "Well, dear, when you put it that way . . ."

2

Two weeks later, on the day Sally was supposed to wire him and let him know what was going on with her father, Smoke called Cal and Pearlie to the cabin just after breakfast. They'd been riding fence all week, fixing up the areas where the winter storms had torn them down. The branding and separating of the calves from their mothers had been done, and there was nothing much else to do around the ranch. They were all just about bored to death.

When they entered the cabin, Smoke looked up from his coffee. "I've got to go into Big Rock this morning to pick up Sally's telegraph, and I thought you boys might like to go along."

"Boy, Smoke," Pearlie said with feeling, "you got that right! I'm so tired of Buttermilk's cookin', I'm 'bout ready to go on a diet."

Buttermilk Wheeler was a local cook that Sally had insisted Smoke hire to cook for them while she was away. "Otherwise," she'd said with a twinkle in her eyes, "I'll come back to find you all dead of food poisoning."

Cal laughed at Pearlie's claim. "That'll be the day when you pass up food of any kind, Pearlie."

"Well, it's true," Pearlie argued, looking at Smoke

with a pained expression on his face. "Now I know why they call his biscuits 'sinkers,' and the coffee . . . well, let's just say it tastes like ol' Buttermilk flavors it with axle grease."

Buttermilk, who was standing over at the stove kneading biscuit dough, turned his head, looking hurt. "I'll remember that, friend, next time you hold out your cup for your third helping."

Pearlie ignored him. "You think we could have lunch over at Longmont's, Smoke? I got me a real hankerin' for some of that there French cuisine," he said, pronouncing it *queeseen*.

Smoke laughed. He knew a day in town with the boys was just the thing to get him over his boredom. "I don't see why not."

"Maybe we can get Andre to fix up some of those frog legs in butter sauce he's always trying to get Pearlie to taste," Cal teased, knowing Pearlie got sick at the very thought of eating any part of a slimy frog.

"And maybe he can wash it down with some coffee that ain't flavored with axle grease!" Buttermilk added from the other side of the room.

Pearlie held up his hands, his nose wrinkled. "Thank you, but I think I'll just stick with a steak about two inches thick, some of those fried taters, and maybe some of that peach cobbler Andre makes so good."

"It's a mite early for the peach cobbler, Pearlie, but I think we can manage the rest of it," Smoke said, standing up and getting his hat.

"I don't know, Smoke," Pearlie said, walking out of the door behind him. "You know, Andre has that greenhouse of his and he's just about always got some fresh vegetables, even in the dead of winter."

"Peaches ain't no vegetable, you idiot," Cal said. "They're fruit."

"Oh, so now you're a gardenin' expert along with

everthing else you think you know, huh?" Pearlie said, swinging at Cal's butt with his boot but missing.

"If you'd ever try and read some of those books Miss Sally gave me, you'd know a little something too," Cal said, a superior air about him.

Smoke stopped walking and turned as if to go back in the cabin.

"What'd you forget, Smoke?" Pearlie asked.

"Some cotton. If you boys are gonna go on like this all the way to town, I'm gonna stuff my ears full so I don't have to listen to it."

Once they got to town, Smoke sent the boys on ahead to Longmont's Saloon while he stopped off at the telegraph office. He picked up a long telegraph that had just arrived from Boston and took it outside to read.

Sally wrote that her father had indeed had a heart stroke and, though he'd survived it, he was extremely weak and the doctors didn't know how long it was going to take for him to recover. Sally said she thought she'd better plan on staying for an extended visit to help her mother cope with her father's illness.

Smoke grimaced, and carefully folded the telegram, stuck it in the pocket of his buckskin jacket, and headed for Longmont's. It was bad enough to be sitting around on his duff bored to death, but to do it without the steadying influence of Sally was going to be almost intolerable. And to make matters worse, he was having trouble sleeping without Sally's warm body next to him in their bed.

He chuckled to himself. It was funny, but when he was camped out on a trail drive or on a hunting or fishing trip to the High Lonesome, he slept like a baby even on the hardest ground. Guess he was getting spoiled, and he missed the feeling of being spoiled by Sally.

He stepped through the batwings of the saloon, and out of long habit learned from years of watching his back, stepped to the side with his back to the wall until his eyes adjusted to the darkness of the room.

Longmont's was a combination restaurant, bar, and poker parlor, with tables for eating situated off to the left, a long mahogany bar against the far wall on the right, and a few felt-covered tables in front of it for the poker players to sit at while they drank and gambled. Louis Longmont, the owner, had no fancy-dressed women or piano players or faro tables, and offered only the simple pleasures of excellent food prepared by his French chef and longtime friend, Andre, honest liquor, and an honest game of straight poker in a dignified, quiet atmosphere.

Smoke saw Louis himself seated at a table off to the left with Cal and Pearlie, his usual spot until the nighttime poker games heated up. He and Smoke had been close friends for longer than Smoke liked to remember.

Louis was a lean, hawk-faced man, with strong, slender hands and long fingers, the nails carefully manicured, the hands clean. He had jet-black hair, turning slightly gray over the ears, and a pencil-thin mustache. He was dressed as always in a black suit, with white shirt and dark ascot—the ascot something he'd picked up on a trip to England a few years back. He wore low-heeled boots, and had a pistol on his right hip in tied-down leather; it was not just for show, for Louis was snake-quick with a short gun and was a feared, deadly gunhand when pushed. He was just past forty years old, had come to the West as a young boy, and had made a fortune due to his sharp intellect and fearless nature.

When he saw Smoke enter the door, Louis waved him over and poured another cup of coffee out of the silver pot on the table. Smoke took a seat and looked at the coffee. "I may need something stronger than that, Louis."

Louis's eyes grew concerned. "Bad news from Sally, Smoke?"

"Yes and no. Her father is doing all right, but he had a heart stroke and the doctors say there's no telling how long he might be laid up. The bad news is that Sally plans on staying up there with him until he's better, and that could be months according to her telegram."

Pearlie's face fell at the news. "You mean we're gonna have to keep on eatin' Buttermilk's food for months?"

Cal nodded in sympathy with Pearlie. "I'm sure gonna miss Miss Sally's cooking," he said morosely.

"Yeah," Smoke agreed. "The place just won't be the same without her around, that's for sure." Though his mind was more on the coldness in their feather bed than on the quality of her cooking.

Louis's eyes narrowed. "You say Sally is going to be gone for some months, and you are finished with most of the immediate work that needs to be done on the Sugarloaf?"

Smoke nodded. "That's just about it, Louis, and I'm going to get real tired of sitting around watching the grass grow."

"Have you thought about the possibility of taking a trip, maybe going off somewhere on an adventure?" Louis asked, a speculative glint in his eyes.

"Why, what do you mean?" Smoke asked. "What kind of adventure are you talking about?"

"Let's order lunch first, and then there is someone I want you to meet," Louis said, a secretive smile on his face as he held his cards close to his vest.

"I thought you'd never offer," Pearlie said. "My mouth's been waterin' ever since we came in here and I smelled Andre's cooking."

While they were eating, Louis went over to the young black boy who served as his waiter, handed him a note, and then returned to the table.

"What was that all about?" Smoke asked around a

mouthful of steak, cooked just the way he liked it, red and bloody inside and charred on the outside.

"I sent Lincoln over to the hotel with a note for a man I want you to meet," Louis answered.

"Oh?"

"His name is William Cornelius Van Horne," Louis said. "He was one of the builders of the Illinois Central Railroad, and he's out here to do a little antelope hunting before heading on up into Canada to build another railroad."

"And he's here to hunt antelope?" Smoke asked. "Why? You can't eat the damned things. They taste like leather."

Louis shrugged. "He says he wants a head to put on his wall, seems it's about the only big-game trophy he doesn't already have."

Smoke put his fork down, a look on his face like his steak had suddenly gone bad. "Louis, you know how I feel about that. I don't believe in killing anything you're not going to eat. I hope you don't think I'm gonna take this idiot out hunting for a trophy to put on his wall."

Louis held up his hand and shook his head. "No, Smoke, it's nothing like that, but I think you'll like this man. And what with Sally going to be gone for so long, I think you might want to hear what he has to say."

The lunch dishes had been cleared away, and Smoke and Louis and the boys were on their third cup of coffee, when the batwings swung open and the sunlight from outside was blocked by a massive figure.

The man who entered was of average height and had the approximate size and shape of a whiskey barrel, with broad shoulders, a thick paunch, and hands as large as hams that looked tough enough to drive railway spikes with. He looked to Smoke to be in his mid-to-late thirties, and had a full but neatly trimmed beard and mustache.

He was dressed in a suit and vest, and when he waved and walked over toward Louis's table, he had that graceful, light-footed gait common to many big men.

When he got to the table and spoke, his voice was deep and gravelly—a whiskey-and-cigar type of voice, Smoke thought. As he appraised the man, he was impressed. The man had an air of authority about him, and of strength. He was used to leading men and to having his orders carried out without hesitation or question, Smoke surmised, and he didn't appear to be the kind of man who has to prove his manhood by killing animals and hanging them on a wall.

"Good afternoon, Louis," the man said, inclining his head, but his eyes were on Smoke. Evidently he too was appraising Smoke even as he was being appraised.

"Hello, Bill," Louis said, getting to his feet. "Mr. William Cornelius Van Horne, I'd like you to meet Smoke Jensen," Louis continued. "He's the man I was telling you about yesterday."

"Ah," Van Horne said, "the famous mountain man." He stuck out his hand to Smoke.

When Smoke stood up and took the hand, he was surprised to find it hard and rough, with calluses on it. This was not a man who rode a desk all day, he thought, smiling as Van Horne squeezed his hand hard enough to make a lesser man wince.

"Hello, Mr. Van Horne," Smoke said. "I don't know about the 'famous' part, but I was a mountain man for a while in my younger days."

"Call me Bill, Smoke. I'm not much one for formalities."

"This is Cal and Pearlie," Smoke said, "my friends."

"Howdy, Cal, Pearlie," Bill said, smiling and nodding as he took a seat on the other side of Louis.

"Would you care for some lunch?" Louis asked the newcomer.

Bill smiled. "I will never pass up a chance to partake of Andre's excellent cooking, Louis. A steak and some of those wonderful fried potatoes would go nicely, I think."

While Louis gave the order, Bill spoke to Smoke. "Has Louis told you why I was asking about you?"

Smoke glanced at Louis and shook his head. "No, but he did say something about you wanting to hunt antelope."

"Pshaw," Bill said, waving a dismissive hand. "That was just something to pass the time while I waited to get in touch with you."

"Oh?"

"Yes. I've heard about you and your . . . rather special relationship with those men who live up in the Rockies who call themselves mountain men."

Smoke smiled. "I've ridden with a few of them over the years, though their numbers aren't what they used to be, what with the coming of civilization to the mountains."

"Smoke, I have been commissioned to undertake a great task. The government of Canada has asked me to build a railroad from Winnipeg all the way to the western coast, near Vancouver Island."

Smoke pursed his lips, visualizing what he knew about Canada. "That's some pretty rough country, Bill. You'll be crossing at least three mountain ranges that I can think of, not to mention forests so thick you can barely ride a horse through them, and that's not even taking into account the various Indian tribes who won't take kindly to your trespassing on their lands."

Bill laughed, a great booming sound that came from his gut. "You do have a way of putting it into perspective, Smoke. Yes, you're right, but the Canadian government didn't say it was going to be easy."

"Easy is the last word I would use, Bill. Danged near impossible is probably more accurate."

Bill's brow knitted. "You don't think it can be done?"

Smoke shrugged. "I don't know. For one thing, I don't know a whole heck of a lot about what it takes to build a railroad, and I don't even know if there are any passes over the mountains you'll have to traverse. I've never been that far north."

"You're right about the mountain passes, and I don't know either. There have been several expeditions through the area, but the men on them haven't finished their journeys yet, so there is no word on where the passes might be, if there are any."

He leaned back in his chair so the waiter could place his plate of food in front of him on the table.

As he cut up his steak, he added, "That's why I needed someone who might be able to persuade some of these mountain men down here in Colorado Territory to come up there and act as advance scouts for my expedition."

He took a bite of steak and rolled his eyes. "This is delicious, as always, Louis. Are you sure I can't hire Andre away from you?"

Louis grinned and shrugged. "Andre is a free man, Bill, so you can try."

Bill shook his head. "No, that would be worse than trying to steal another man's wife, but tell him if he ever has a hankering to travel up north to give me a shout."

He took another bite and said, "The pay would be excellent, Smoke, probably more money than any of your friends could earn in ten years of trapping."

"Money is not important to mountain men, Bill," Smoke said, a half smile on his face. "Their lives center around being on their own and away from civilization, not on earning a living."

"Well, what better challenge than going where few have gone before," Bill said, pointing his fork at

Smoke as he spoke. "I hear there are fewer than twenty-five hundred white men in an area of several hundred thousand square miles in Canada. You can't get much further from civilization than that."

Smoke thought about it for a few minutes while he got a cigar going and drank some more coffee. He knew several of his old friends up in the High Lonesome who thought Colorado was getting too crowded and who might be willing to try a new place, just for the adventure of it.

"I might know some men who might be willing to take you up on such an offer, now that you mention it," Smoke said.

Bill smiled and finished off his steak. He pushed the plate to the side, took a leather case out of his breast pocket, and extracted a long, thick cigar. He struck a lucifer on his pants leg and puffed the cigar alive. He eyed Smoke through billowing clouds of blue smoke. "Louis tells me you have a wife and a ranch to run and that you would likely be unavailable to leave the country for an extended period of time."

Smoke started to nod, and then he thought. *Wait a minute. Why not? Sally's going to be gone for many months, and I'm bored with ranch life. Why not go off on an adventure? It might be the last chance I get to traverse uncharted, uninhabited land in the company of my mountain-man friends.*

"Ordinarily, that would be true, Bill, but as it so happens, my wife is away on an extended trip just now. Let me think it over for a day or so and I'll get back to you."

"Excellent,"Bill said. "Let's have a drink to your making the right decision."

3

Van Horne pulled a gold watch from his vest pocket and glanced at the time. "It's still a little early for hard liquor, but it's never too early for beer."

He glanced around, but the waiter was nowhere to be seen. He got to his feet. "I'll just go to the bar and get us a pitcher of Louis's finest beer."

He walked over to the bar and squeezed in between several men who were standing at the bar.

"My good man," he said to the bartender, "would you be so kind as to bring a pitcher of beer and five mugs to my table?"

One of the cowboys at the bar stepped back and looked at Van Horne, his eyes going up and down. "Well, just listen to Mr. High-and-Mighty here," he said in a loud voice, slurred by too much whiskey too early in the day. He was tall and slim, with a wide leather belt inlaid with silver conchos, and his boots had silver toes. He was wearing twin Peacemaker Colts with pearl handles tied down low on his hips.

To Van Horne, he seemed to be trying to look like the desperados in the penny dreadfuls.

"Pardon me?" Bill asked, turning to look at the man.

"Pardon you?" the man responded sarcastically.

"Pardon you for what? For being so fat you can't hardly get through the door?"

"Oh-oh," Smoke said in a low voice to Louis. "Looks like trouble at the bar."

Louis started to get up, but Smoke put a hand on his arm. "Wait a minute, Louis, let's see how Bill handles this," Smoke said, wanting to see how the big man handled himself. If he was going to be out in the wilderness with Van Horne, he wanted to see what he was made of. Smoke didn't think Van Horne was heeled, so he loosened the rawhide hammer thong on his own Colt just in case the confrontation turned deadly.

Bill snorted and turned back to the bar, trying to ignore the drunk, but the man grabbed him by the shoulder and whirled him around. "Don't turn your back on me while I'm talking to you, fatty."

Bill's hand moved so quick that Smoke could hardly see it as he reached up, grabbed the lout by the throat, and lifted him up until his feet dangled a foot off the floor. As the man's face turned purple and he grabbed Bill's hand, trying to pry it loose, Bill said calmly, "You, sir, are rude and obnoxious, and I cannot abide rudeness." He cocked his head to the side and stared into the man's bulging eyes. "Often rudeness is prevalent in men whose intelligence is akin to a dog's," he added contemptuously.

He gave a final squeeze and without apparent effort threw the man across the room, where he landed flat on his back, still gasping for breath.

One of the man's friends stepped away from the bar and dropped his hand to his pistol butt. Smoke was just about to draw, for he would never allow an unarmed man to be gunned down, when Bill drew back his right arm and punched the man in the face so hard he splattered his nose flat and knocked the man to his knees.

A third man, his eyes wide, let his hand drop toward his gun and Smoke called out, "I wouldn't do that, partner."

The man glanced at Smoke and saw the barrel of his .44 pointed right at his head. "This ain't no fight of yours, mister," the man said uncertainly, but his hand stopped moving and hung there in the air, shaking slightly.

"It is when you're drawing on a man who isn't heeled," Smoke said. "You want to say something to Mr. Van Horne, say it with your fists, not that hogleg on your hip."

Bill squared off with the man, his fists at his side. "Well, sir, do you have something you wish to add?"

The man looked around at his friends, one still blue and gasping and the other with his nose spread all over his face. "Uh, no . . . I guess not."

"Then I suggest that the next time you want to drink your lunch, you do it someplace else," Bill said, picking up the tray with the pitcher of beer and mugs on it. He turned his back on the man and walked back to the table, as if nothing had happened.

Smoke smiled at him. Van Horne hadn't even broken a sweat. "You pack a mean punch, Bill," he said as Bill poured them all beer.

Bill looked at him out of the corner of his eye, a slight grin on his face. "When you supervise thousands of men building a railroad, Smoke, you either learn to be good with your fists or you stay behind a desk." He upended his beer and drained it in one long swallow. As he sleeved suds off his mustache, he grinned. "And I never was one for staying behind a desk."

"How come you don't carry a gun, Mr. Van Horne?" Cal asked.

Bill poured himself another beer. "Oh, I do when I'm out in the field working, Cal, but when I'm in town, I don't usually see the need." He took a swallow, smaller this time, and added, "Of course, I may have to change my mind about that in the future."

"Are you any good with a short gun?" Pearlie asked, impressed by Bill's coolness under fire.

Bill shrugged. "I'm not the fastest gun around,

Pearlie, but I hit what I aim at, and I'm told that's more important than being fast."

Smoke held up his mug. "I'll drink to that," he said, laughing.

After they'd said their good-byes to Bill and Louis, Smoke and the boys stepped out of the saloon and walked toward their horses.

The three cowboys from the bar were waiting out in the street, one of them with his nose still dripping blood onto his shirt.

"Hey, you!" one of the other two called.

Smoke stopped and looked over at him. "Are you talking to me?" he asked calmly.

"Yeah. You're gonna learn not to stick your nose in other people's business."

When they heard the commotion outside, Louis and Bill stepped to the window to see what was happening.

Bill started to move toward the batwings, but Louis stopped him. "But I can't let Smoke fight my battles for me," Bill said.

"Just watch, Bill. I want you to see Smoke in action."

"Oh," Smoke said to the gunny. "And I suppose you're going to teach me?"

"That's right, asshole," the man said, crouching with his hand held over the butt of his pistol. "Me and my friends."

"You want some help, Smoke?" Pearlie said, covering a yawn with the back of his hand, seemingly unconcerned about the men standing before them.

"No, I don't think so, Pearlie," Smoke said. "After all, there's only three of them."

"All right," Pearlie said, and he and Cal moved to the side. Pearlie leaned back against a post with his arms crossed.

"By the way, gentlemen," he said conversationally, "what are your names?"

The man with the bloody nose looked over at him. "Why do you want to know?" he asked angrily.

Pearlie shrugged. "Most people like to have their names on their tombstones, so I thought I'd ask."

Sweat began to appear on the man's forehead, and he turned back to face Smoke.

Smoke looked at him, his eyes as mean and black as a snake's. "Either draw or go back to the hole you crawled out of," Smoke said, his voice hard. "I got things to do."

"You son of a . . ." the man snarled as he went for his gun.

Quicker than it takes to tell it, Smoke drew and fired three times. The man with the bloody nose was hit high in the left shoulder, the slug spinning him around to fall facedown, screaming in pain. The second and third men were both hit in the middle of their chests and blown onto their backs, dead before they hit the ground. Not one of them had cleared leather.

Bill and Louis came out of the saloon, Bill shaking his head. "I'd heard you were fast, Smoke, but I never believed just how fast."

Smoke punched out his empty brass and reloaded his pistol. "Like you say, Bill, it's more important to be accurate than fast."

Bill laughed. "But it's even better to be both, Smoke."

Smoke walked over to stand over the injured man, who was moaning and crying and holding his shoulder, blood dripping between his fingers.

Smoke dropped two twenty-dollar gold pieces on his chest. "Here you go, mister. Use this to bury your friends and to get your arm taken care of."

He started to walk away, and then stopped and looked back over his shoulder. "And do it by sundown and then get out of town, 'cause if I ever see your face again, ever, I'll kill you."

4

Smoke spent the next two days working around the ranch, overseeing his men as they tended fences, worked cattle, and made sure the new calves they'd separated from their mothers were all doing all right. As he worked, he found himself increasingly looking at the snow-covered peaks of the Rockies in the distance, a longing in his heart he'd ignored for far too long.

Finally, he'd had enough. He was bored silly, and Sally's absence just made matters worse. Smoke decided to take Van Horne up on his offer to help with finding a suitable route for the Canadian railroad. After all, he'd been wanting to get back up into the mountains and see his old mountain-man friends for some time, and this would be a perfect opportunity, what with Sally gone for who knows how long.

He rode over to the ranch nearest the Sugarloaf, and asked his old friend Johnny North if he'd keep a watch on the place for him while he was gone. North agreed to ride over every week or so and make sure the hands Smoke had working for him didn't need anything, and to keep a close eye on his livestock in his absence.

Smoke decided to take Cal and Pearlie along for

company, and to teach them a thing or two about mountain living. Both men had long been fascinated with the High Lonesome and had met some of Smoke's mountain-man friends on previous occasions, and were overjoyed at the chance to ride with them once again.

So, when the packhorses were loaded with the supplies Smoke thought they would need, he and the boys rode into Big Rock, ready to travel. Smoke sent a telegram to Sally in Boston telling her of his plans and promising to keep in touch whenever they were near a telegraph, and then they met up with Van Horne in front of Louis Longmont's saloon.

This time, instead of his three-piece suit, Van Horne was dressed for the trail in trousers, riding boots, and a flannel shirt that looked large enough to use as a sleeping blanket. He had a Smith and Wesson nickel-plated pistol in a holster on his belt and a brand-new Winchester rifle in his saddle boot.

His packhorse was loaded down with enough food for a year, and Smoke grinned and shook his head. It was clear Van Horne did not intend to go hungry on this trip up into the mountains to find some mountain men to ride with them.

"Hello, Smoke, boys," Bill called as they approached.

"I can see you've got plenty of provisions for the trip," Smoke said, smiling.

Bill looked over his shoulder at the boxes piled high on the back of the packhorse and nodded. "Yes, of course, I'm packed for two people."

"Two?" Smoke asked.

The batwings of the saloon swung open and Louis Longmont stepped out. "Yes, Smoke. I decided that it was not fair for you to have all the fun this time, so I have elected to join you on your little jaunt."

Longmont had also given up his trademark black suit for trail clothes, though his still looked as if they'd been made by a French tailor. His black pants were freshly ironed and his dark leather coat was as shiny as his knee-high black boots. He wore a brace of Colts on his belt, and had a Henry repeating rifle slung over his shoulder as he walked toward his horse.

"Is Andre gonna come too, Mr. Longmont?" Pearlie asked, licking his lips in anticipation of fine meals being cooked every night.

Longmont shook his head. "Not on your life, Pearlie. Andre's place is in the kitchen, not on the back of a horse."

"Oh," Pearlie said, disappointed.

Louis and Van Horne swung up into their saddles and looked at Smoke. "Ready?" Louis asked.

"As I'll ever be," Smoke answered, and spurred his horse into a slow canter down the main street of Big Rock, heading north toward snow-covered mountain peaks in the distance.

As they swung into line behind him, Pearlie leaned over in his saddle and said to Cal, "I sure hope they ain't expectin' you to do the cookin' on this here trip."

"Why not?" Cal asked, raising his eyebrows.

"'Cause I plumb forgot to bring any stomach salts to ease the bellyache your food causes."

Two days later, as their horses moved slowly up the side of a mountain slope that was still covered with snowdrifts two feet deep, Smoke held up his hand and the procession slowed to a halt.

Bill Van Horne pulled his horse up next to Smoke's and said, "What is it? Why are we stopping?"

Smoke raised his nose in the air and sniffed. "I smell smoke—campfire smoke."

Van Horne sniffed. "I don't smell anything?"

Before Smoke could answer, a loud booming gunshot echoed through the tall ponderosa pines that surrounded them on all sides, followed quickly by several higher-pitched cracks of rifle fire in the distance.

"What the hell?" Van Horne said as his horse stamped and jumped to the side.

Smoke's forehead wrinkled as he stared in the direction of the sounds. "That first shot was from a Sharps, and the ones that followed were from a Winchester."

"Don't most of the mountain men use Sharps?" Cal asked, standing tall in his stirrups to try and see through the forest.

"Yeah, and it sounds like someone's in trouble," Smoke said, spurring his horse forward as he leaned over its head.

As the men road up the side of the mountain, pistols out and ready, they heard more gunshots from up ahead, the sharper cracks of the Winchesters being answered by the deeper booming of a Sharps Big Fifty.

After riding as fast as the horses could run through the deep snow for twenty minutes, Smoke reined his horse in and was out of the saddle before it came to a complete stop.

He jerked his Winchester out of his saddle boot, and crouched down as he jogged up to the crest of a small hillock and peered over the edge.

The others joined him, all holding rifles cradled in their arms. Below, they could see a small campfire with four paint ponies tied to a tree nearby and a makeshift shelter made out of pine limbs piled at an angle against a large boulder, forming a lean-to.

There was blood in the snow around the fire and tracks where a body had been dragged into the lean-to. A long, black barrel was sticking out of the pine limbs and firing at several men who were lying behind logs and rocks in a semicircle around the camp, firing back into the lean-to.

"What's going on?" Van Horne whispered to Smoke as he peered down at the scene below.

"Looks like some mountain men are being fired on

by those fellows over there," Smoke answered, nodding toward the men on the ground below.

"How do you know they're mountain men in the camp?" Van Horne asked.

"They're riding Indian ponies, and they're using a Sharps Big Fifty." He pointed his finger down at the camp. "And see, there's a pile of beaver and fox pelts over next to the horses. That's probably what the men are after."

Van Horne nodded. "I see."

Smoke laid his rifle barrel on a rock in front of him, took careful aim, and fired.

One of the men below screamed in pain, grabbed his leg, and rolled over onto his back, shouting, "I'm hit!"

Smoke levered another round into his Winchester and stood up. "Drop your weapons, or I'll put the next one in your head!" he shouted, pointing the barrel of his rifle at the men below.

One of the men made the mistake of turning his rifle toward Smoke, who quickly fired, hitting the man square in the forehead. As his blood and brains sprayed all over the snow around him, the other men slowly put their rifles down and stood up, their hands in the air.

"Now, come on out from behind those rocks so I can see you," Smoke yelled.

Three men walked out into the open, one stopping to help the wounded man get to his feet and limp out with them.

"Bring the horses," Smoke said over his shoulder as he stepped over the ridge and walked down toward the men, the barrel of his rifle still pointing at them and his finger on the trigger.

"Yo, the camp," he called, not wanting to be shot by whoever was in the lean-to.

"Who be you?" a gravelly voice called from behind

the barrel of the Sharps as it swiveled to point toward Smoke.

"Bear Tooth, is that you?" Smoke called, a grin on his face.

"Smoke? Smoke Jensen?" the voice answered as a huge man, well over six and a half feet in height, appeared in the opening of the lean-to, a Sharps cradled in his arms.

While Smoke's eyes were on Bear Tooth, one of the men in the clearing dropped his hand and went for a pistol on his belt.

Smoke jumped as a rifle went off behind him and a hole you could put a fist through appeared on the man's chest. He dropped like a stone.

"Thanks," Smoke said to Van Horne, who was still aiming his smoking Winchester at the men below.

"Don't mention it," Bill replied, impressing Smoke with his coolness under fire.

Soon, the three attackers still remaining alive were trussed up and tied with their backs to trees.

Bear Tooth disappeared inside the lean-to, and reappeared moments later with his arm around a man with flaming red hair and beard and a bloody left shoulder.

"Red Bingham, you old beaver," Smoke said, grinning. "I heard you were dead."

"Naw, he ain't dead," Bear Tooth said as he helped Red to sit down next to the fire. "He just smells that way."

Red turned his bright blue eyes to Bear Tooth. "You can talk. At least I took'n me a bath last spring, which is more'n I can say fer some."

Smoke laughed. Bear Tooth was famous among the mountain men for never going near water. He was known to say if God had intended men to bathe, he would've given them fins like fish.

Smoke glanced at the men tied to the trees nearby. "Poachers?" he asked.

Bear Tooth glared at the men. "Yeah, seems they wanted some skins to sell and were too lazy or too dumb to trap their own."

Louis knelt next to Red and used his knife to cut away the buckskin over his wound. He looked up at Smoke. "Looks like the bullet went all the way through. Doesn't appear to have hit the bone and the blood's oozing and not spurting."

Smoke nodded. That was good news, for a broken bone was almost always fatal up here in the mountains, and the slow bleeding meant no artery had been hit.

Red gritted his teeth and pulled out a long, wide-bladed knife from a scabbard on his belt. He leaned over and stuck the blade in the coals of the fire. After a moment, when the blade was glowing red, he looked at Louis. "You want to do the honors, mister?"

"Do you want me to pour some whiskey on it first?" Louis asked as he reached for the knife.

"Waste good whiskey on a little scratch like this?" Red asked. "No, sir, but if'n you have some, a little nip'd do me nicely."

Smoke laughed and nodded at Pearlie, who pulled a small bottle of red-eye from his saddlebags and handed it to Red.

Red looked at the bottle and shook his head. "When I said a little nip, son, I was speaking figuratively, not meaning to be taken so seriously." Without another word, he upended the pint bottle and drained it as Louis picked up the knife from the fire.

When Louis put the red-hot blade to each of the bullet holes, Red's face paled and his jaw muscles bulged, but he didn't make a sound as his flesh sizzled and smoked under the knife.

After Louis was finished, Red took a deep breath and said, "Now, if you happen to have another bottle of that there firewater, stranger, I'd be much obliged for another taste."

Bear Tooth snorted. "A taste, he says. That means he'll drink the whole danged thing if'n you're not careful."

He hesitated, and then he added, "Now me, on the other hand, I'm a gentleman. I'd only take a small dollop of a man's whiskey, just to be sociable-like."

5

While Red Bingham was drinking his whiskey, Bear Tooth dumped a couple of handfuls of coffee into a blackened pot that sat next to the fire, and added some water from his canteen before pushing the pot onto the coals.

Smoke looked over at Bill Van Horne. "Bill, you're in for a real treat now. You're gonna get to sample some mountain-man coffee."

Bill glanced at the pot. "I noticed he put quite a bit of coffee into the pot."

Bear Tooth nodded. "As they say, the thing 'bout makin' good coffee is it don't take near as much water as you think it do."

"Yeah," Pearlie said, grinning. "Like Puma Buck used to say, if it won't float a horseshoe, it ain't near strong enough."

At the mention of Puma Buck, Bear Tooth looked over at Pearlie. "So, you knew Puma?" he asked.

"Yes, sir," Pearlie answered, his face sober at the thought of the old mountain man who'd given his life to save Smoke and Cal and Pearlie in a fracas a few years back.

Bear Tooth looked down at the fire, his eyes suspiciously wet and shining. "I miss that ol' beaver something fierce," he said in a low voice.

Smoke nodded. "Like a lot of our old friends, he's gone on to better things," he said.

While the coffee was cooking, Red Bingham struggled to his feet, his left arm held close against his side. He bent over and picked his knife up off the ground, and walked slowly toward the men tied to trees off to the side of the camp.

The men, sullen-faced and angry, suddenly looked apprehensive when they saw the way Red was holding the knife. One of them, in a strong French accent, asked, "Hey, what the hell are you planning on doing with that knife?"

Bill looked at Smoke, his eyebrows raised in question, but Smoke just winked and stood watching Red with folded arms.

Red knelt next to the dead man with a hole in his chest and grabbed a handful of his hair. He lifted the head up and quick as a wink sliced the scalp off, and held the bloody mop of hair up in the air, crimson strings of blood running down his hand and onto his arm.

He glanced over his shoulder at Bill, who had a sick expression on his face. "This one's your'n, mister. You want it?"

As Bill quickly shook his head, one of the French poachers leaned over and vomited in the snow, while the other two just watched with horrified expressions on their faces.

Red carried the bloody scalp over to the body of the other dead man, the one Smoke had shot in the forehead. He poked at the head with the toe of his boot and looked over at Smoke. "I think you just about ruined this one, Smoke. The back of it's all blowed away where the bullet came out."

Smoke gave a tight smile. "Sorry about that, Red. I was aiming for his chest, but he must've ducked."

"Well, no matter," Red said as he sliced the torn scalp from the head and held it up with the other one. "It'll still do to hang from my lodge pole."

He stood up and moved toward the men where they sat tied to trees, grinning as they cringed back as far as they could.

One of the men hollered at the men around the fire, "You ain't gonna let this crazy old bastard scalp us, are you?"

"He's not really going to do it, is he, Smoke?" Bill asked in a low voice, his face pale.

Smoke again shrugged. "According to mountain-man ways, Bill, it's his right. These men tried to kill him and his partner, and they would've taken everything they worked all winter for in the process. If he wants to take their hair, I'm sure as hell not going to try and tell him not to." He glanced at Van Horne. "This is part of the ways out here in the High Lonesome, Bill. There aren't any sheriffs or marshals to call when someone does you wrong, so you take care of it yourself, or you don't live to see too many winters."

Bear Tooth, who was in the process of pouring mugs of coffee for everyone, looked over at Red. "Hey, Red, we done got enough scalps already. You're gonna plumb stink up the place if you take three more."

Red stood over the men, blood from the scalps dripping off his knife and hand. "I guess you're right, Bear Tooth. Maybe I'll just take their balls. We ain't eaten no mountain oysters fer months now."

As the French men's faces blanched, Bill hiccupped and put his hand over his mouth to keep from throwing up.

"I've got a better idea, Red," Smoke said, moving over to stand next to the mountain man.

"What's that, Smoke?" he asked, smiling grimly though his eyes, which had a characteristic twinkle in them.

"Let's take their guns and boots and set them loose on the mountain without any horses. It'll be interesting to see how long they can go before they end up eating each other to stay alive"

Red pursed his lips and nodded. "That's a good idee, Smoke. After a day or two, if they live that long, they'll he sleepin' with one eye open watchin' each other to see who's gonna be the next meal."

Bill looked at Louis, who was watching the proceedings with wry amusement. "Louis, you can't let them do that. It's barbaric."

"Bill, like Smoke said, this isn't a town where you can turn men like that over to the law," Louis explained as he pulled a long, black cigar from his coat pocket and lit it with a twig from the fire. "Justice out here in the mountains is not always pretty, but it is fast and efficient. If these men are allowed to live, sooner or later they'll try to kill some other trapper and steal his skins." He smiled grimly. "At least this way, they have a chance to live, if they're willing to live the rest of their lives knowing they turned to cannibalism to survive."

"That's right, Mr. Van Horne," Pearlie said as he sipped his coffee. "The Indians would've just hung 'em upside down over a bed of coals and cooked their brains whilst makin' bets on who'd die first."

"Of course, they would sing songs in tribute to the man who died showing the most courage," Bear Tooth added.

"That's an honor I think I can live without achieving," Van Horne said, still looking sick.

As Red cut the ropes holding the men against the trees, he asked Smoke, "Should I let 'em keep their knives and flints?"

"Sure," Smoke answered, his eyes flat and hard. "We want them to be able to make a fire and not freeze to death. That would be too easy on them."

"Yeah," Bear Tooth added, again smiling wickedly.

"And human flesh tastes better if'n it's been cooked a little." He hesitated, and then he added with a wink at Bill, "At least, that's what I've been told, never having partaken of it myself of course."

Red stepped back and pointed at the men's feet. "Throw them boots over here and get the hell outta my camp, you bastards, 'fore I change my mind 'bout your scalps"

"You can't let him do this to us, mister," one of the men said to Smoke as he took off his boots. "It ain't right."

Smoke shrugged and turned away, saying, "Well, I suppose you got a choice, just like you had when you decided to kill him. You can take your chances on foot, or you can let him gut you and scalp you and end it all right now."

While the men were taking their boots off, Red went over to their horses, took their flints and striking stones out of their saddlebags, and threw them on the ground in front of them.

"You boys better get a move on. You only got 'bout five more hours of daylight an' then it's gonna get really cold."

"I figger it'll take you 'bout four days to walk down the mountain to where it's warmer," Bear Tooth called to the Frenchmen. "After two days, if' n you live that long, your stomachs will be growlin' enough to keep you awake, which is good, 'cause long about then your partners are gonna be lookin' at you like steak on the hoof."

After the Frenchmen slunk off down the mountain, Bear Tooth pulled a slab of elk meat out of their lean-to and sliced some thick steaks off it with his skinning knife. He threw them into a cast-iron skillet, added some wild onions for flavor and a piece of fatback for grease, and put the skillet on the coals. While the steaks were cooking, he put some water in a kettle hanging from a trestle over the fire and poured in several handfuls of pinto beans.

"Reckon it's 'bout time to eat," he said as he took a squat next to the fire and used his knife to cut a chunk off a large square of chewing tobacco.

As the men sat around the fire, drinking coffee and waiting for the meal to cook, Red glanced over at Smoke. "You gonna introduce us to your partners or not, Smoke?"

Smoke laughed and introduced everyone to the mountain men, who didn't offer to shake hands but merely nodded, as was the mountain-man way.

"Been a long time since we seen you up here in the High Lonesome, Smoke," Bear Tooth observed, speaking around a large wad of tobacco in his cheek. "You up here to do some trappin' or huntin'?"

Smoke shook his head. "No, Bear Tooth, as a matter of fact, we came up here looking for you."

"Me?" Bear Tooth asked, surprised at the answer.

"You and some of the other old beavers that are still up here trapping," Smoke said.

"Not too many of us old-timers left anymore, Smoke," Red said, his eyes sad as he stared into the fire. "It's just not the same anymore. Time was, you could go all winter an' not see nary another white man, 'ceptin' your partner." He glanced off in the direction the French poachers had taken. "Now, you got pond scum like those men crawlin' all over the place." He looked at Smoke. "Hell, it's getting plumb crowded un here now."

Bear Tooth nodded. "He's right, Smoke. A lot of the men been here for years have headed up north, 'cross the border into Canada, where civilization ain't ruined everthing yet."

Smoke looked over at Bill. "That's the reason we're up here, Bear Tooth. Mr. Van Horne, Bill, is planning on building a railroad across Canada, from Winnipeg to the West Coast over near Vancouver Island, and he needs some experienced mountain men to help with the surveying of the route across the Canadian mountains."

Bear Tooth leaned to the side and spat a stream of brown tobacco juice into the fire, making it hiss and sizzle. "That so?" he asked, his eyes moving to fix on Bill.

Bill nodded, leaning forward. "That's right, Bear Tooth. We're going to cross twenty-five thousand square miles of the most desolate and wildest country in the world, making trails through land that hasn't seen more than a handful of white men in the last hundred years. I'm going to need men like Smoke and you and Red to find us a way through mountains that may not even have any passes in them. It's going to be a big job, one of the biggest ever undertaken."

"When you plannin' on doing all this, Bill?" Red asked as he stroked his beard.

"As soon as we can get up there. I've got several thousand men waiting in Winnipeg for us right now to get the surveying done so they can start to lay tracks."

"T'aint possible," Bear Tooth said as he got to his feet and flipped the elk steaks over to brown.

"Why not?" Bill asked.

"'Cause even if we left now, it'd be the middle of next winter 'fore we could get up there on horseback, an' winter in the mountains is no time to be doin' no surveyin'."

"That's right, Bill," Red added. "You'd have snow up over the horses' heads." He shook his head. "Can't be done 'fore next spring at the earliest."

"Yes, it can, gentlemen," Bill said. "I've got a train waiting for us down in Pueblo, just a few days ride from here. I figure the trip from Pueblo to Winnipeg will take only about a week, give or take a couple of days depending on how deep the snow is in the passes."

Bear Tooth and Red both looked aghast at the suggestion. "You mean you want Red and me to ride on one of them iron-horse contraptions?" Bear Tooth asked incredulously.

"Why, yes," Bill answered. "I have my own special cars on the train for us to ride in. I promise you you'll be quite comfortable."

Red stared at Bill through narrowed eyes. "I hear them things go so fast that the wind'll flat tear the skin offen your face if you hang it out the window."

Bill had to bite his lips to keep from laughing. "No, I assure you, Red, riding on a train is quite safe. People do it all the time."

"What 'bout our hosses?" Bear Tooth asked. "I don't plan on ridin' through no mountains on a hoss I don't know."

"There are special cars on the train for your animals," Bill said. "You can take as many of them along as you wish."

Bear Tooth got to his feet and began to serve steaks and beans to everyone on tin plates. "How many of us old coots you plannin' on takin' up there?" he asked.

Bill looked at Smoke, who said, "I'd like at least two more in addition to you and Red."

Bear Tooth and Red were silent for a few moments as everyone got started eating, and then Bear Tooth looked over at Red. "I heard Rattlesnake Bob Guthrie an' his ridin' partner, Bobcat Bill Johnson, was a couple'a peaks over to the south, toward Pueblo, last month. Maybe they'd be willin' to go along."

"Maybe," Red said as he chewed his steak. "Last time I saw Bobcat, he was complainin' 'bout how crowded it was getting up here, so maybe he'd be ready to try some new stompin' grounds."

"You haven't asked me what the job pays," Bill said, smiling at the wonderful flavor of the elk steak.

Bear Tooth shrugged. "Don't matter much," he said. "We ain't exactly up here in the High Lonesome to get rich."

Red nodded his agreement. "That's right. It might be fun to go somewhere's where we ain't steppin' on other men's toes ever time we go for a ride."

"Do you think you can find Rattlesnake and Bobcat?" Smoke asked.

Red looked down his nose at Smoke as if he'd just been insulted. "If'n they're still alive, we can shore as hell find 'em."

Bear Tooth laughed. "That's right, Smoke. Red can track a snake across granite if'n he has a mind to. If they're up here an' still wearin' they scalps, we'll find 'em."

"Then, you're saying you'll go with us?" Bill asked, excitement in his voice.

"Shore," Bear Tooth said as he cut a chunk of elk steak and stuck it in his mouth. "If'n we don't, ol' Smoke there's liable to get you lost, since he's become so civilized lately."

"That'll be the day," Smoke said, laughing.

6

The next two days were an arduous mixture of slogging through deep snow on the sides of mountain peaks and then, when they proceeded lower on the mountainsides, wading through mud and melted snow in the valleys, where spring was already producing myriads of wildflowers and green grass for the horses to munch on.

Van Horne glanced around at the beautiful scenery and said to Smoke, "This country reminds me a lot of Canada."

Smoke nodded. "Sometimes, when I've been away too long down in the flatlands, I forget just how beautiful it is up here."

Bear Tooth harrumphed. "Beautiful? This ain't nothin', men. You should see it 'bout two or three weeks from now when spring is full on an' the snow is all gone. The colors will damn near take your breath away."

Red Bingham slapped at his neck and snorted. "Yeah, an' most of these damned black flies will be gone by then, thank God."

Smoke and Cal and Pearlie were riding the Palouse horses from Smoke's remuda, while the mountain men road pinto ponies like the Indians used. Van Horne was on a Morgan, one of the few horses large enough to carry his 250 pounds up and down the mountainsides without tiring. The group used the horses left behind by the French poachers as additional pack animals, tying them with dally ropes to the packhorses they already had.

By the time the group reached the mountain area where Rattlesnake Bob Guthrie and Bobcat Bill Johnson had last been seen, they were tired, saddle-sore, and covered with bites from the thousands of black flies the spring had brought up into the mountains.

Just after noon on the third day of their search, they made camp in a valley with plenty of grass for the horses to eat. The sun was out and the day was clear, the temperature climbing into the mid-fifties.

Pearlie climbed stiffly down from his horse and rubbed his aching backside. "Damn, boys," he said grumpily, "I think my butt's done grown to this saddle."

The two mountain men, who were used to spending days at a time in the saddle, looked at him and grinned. "Pearlie, boy, I got just the thing for those blisters," Bear Tooth said, pulling a dark brown bottle from his saddlebags.

"What's that?" Pearlie asked.

"It's a liniment I make from pine sap, whiskey, an' bear fat," Bear Tooth said, tossing the bottle to Pearlie.

Pearlie pulled a cork from the bottle and sniffed it cautiously. "Whew," he exclaimed, making a face and holding the bottle out away from his face. "That smells strong enough to peel paint off'n a barn."

"Don't waste it," Red Bingham said, laughing. "Bear Tooth's been known to drink it when we run low on whiskey."

"Works pretty good to tan the hides of the skins we trap too," Bear Tooth said. "It's guaranteed to either kill ya or cure ya."

While the rest of the men set up camp and started

a fire to cook lunch on, Pearlie moved off into some brush nearby, dropped his trousers, undid the flap on his long underwear, and gingerly rubbed some of the liniment onto his sore buttocks.

Suddenly, his skin on fire, he came running out of the brush, his pants down around his knees, jumping and hollering and fanning his butt with his hands. "Good God Almighty!" he yelled. "Somebody help me!"

Bear Tooth laughed as he stirred a pot of beans warming on the fire and winked at Smoke. "Told ya it'd make him forget all about how sore his ass was."

After a few minutes, Pearlie quit shouting and stopped jumping around. He stood there, his eyes wide as a smile slowly appeared on his face. "By gum," he said, looking at the bottle he was still holding. "It does feel better now."

He pulled his pants up and walked over to the fire. "What's for dinner?" he asked as he poured himself a cup of coffee from the pot on the coals.

Red Bingham looked up at him from over the tin plate on his lap. "Fer the main course, we got beans an' fatback, an' fer dessert, we got more beans an' more fatback."

"Yeah," Cal said, scooping a spoonful of beans onto his plate, "you ate the last of the elk yesterday, Pearlie."

Smoke smiled at this, and then he froze, his hand going to the Colt on his hip as he raised his nose and sniffed the air. "Don't look now, boys, but we got company," he said in a low voice as he eased the Colt from his holster.

A gravelly voice came from a copse of trees fifty yards away. "You plannin' on shootin' somebody with that hogleg, Smoke?"

Smoke grinned and let the pistol fall back into its holster.

Bear Tooth made a face and stood with his hands on his hips facing the trees where the voice came from. "Well, I'll be damned. That sounds like a bobcat, boys."

Two scruffy, well-worn mountain men wearing buckskins so dirty they looked black eased their ponies out of the trees and walked them slowly towards the camp.

Smoke got to his feet and waved. "Howdy, Bobcat, Rattlesnake," he called.

The two men nodded without speaking and rode on into camp. As they dismounted, Bobcat Bill Johnson, a short, wiry man with dark skin and sun-streaked blond hair and beard, sniffed loudly. "That coffee and beans sure do smell good," he said.

Bear Tooth sniffed loudly, his face screwed into an expression of distaste. "At least somthin' smells good around here," he said, staring at the two men as they approached the fire. "What happened?" he asked. "You men forgot to take your annual bathing this year?"

Bobcat stared back at him. "Hell, Bear, it ain't hardly spring yet. We usually wait till the snow's all gone 'fore we take a bath."

"Set an' take a load off," Red said, smiling at the byplay. "You're welcome to dig in, we got plenty."

Rattlesnake Bob Guthrie moved to the packhorse he was leading and took a slab of meat wrapped in burlap and waxed paper off the back of the animal. "You boys want some venison to go with them beans?" he asked.

"Here, let me help you with that," Pearlie said, jumping to his feet and taking the meat from Rattlesnake's hands.

Rattlesnake looked at Pearlie, sniffed a couple of times, and grinned. "Don't tell me you let ol' Bear Tooth talk you into usin' that liniment he makes up."

Pearlie blushed as he cut steaks off the venison and put them in an iron skillet to cook. "He said it'd take the soreness outta my butt," Pearlie said in a low voice.

Rattlesnake laughed. "I let him put some on a pony

of mine once that had some saddle sores on its back. The animal took off up the mountain and we didn't find it for damn near a week. It'd run so long, it was two feet shorter an' fifty pounds lighter when we finally found it."

"But them sores were healed, weren't they?" Bear Tooth said haughtily.

Smoke smiled. It was a mountain-man tale in the best traditions of the High Lonesome—outrageous, with just a touch of humor and truth in it.

After introductions had been made all around, the men sat down to venison steaks, beans, and canned peaches that Van Horne had brought along on his packhorse.

While they ate, Smoke outlined the job offer Van Horne was making to the mountain men, emphasizing the opportunity they would have to travel and explore land largely unseen by anyone before them.

Rattlesnake put the last of his venison in his mouth, added a generous spoonful of beans, and chewed slowly, his eyes on the fire as he thought over the proposition. After a few minutes, he looked up at Smoke. He pointed to the pile of beaver, fox, and bear skins they had piled on one of their packhorses. "You see them skins there, Smoke?" he asked, a look of disgust on his face.

Smoke glanced at the skins and nodded.

"That's 'bout half what we trapped last year by this time, an' last year's amount was less'n half what we got the year before."

Bobcat nodded, his eyes sad. "Yep, there's just too blamed many folks up here trappin' an' huntin' nowadays. Hell, it wasn't more'n a month ago we seen some other men up on that peak over there," he said, pointing off to the side at a mountainside ten miles away. "Used to be, we wouldn't hardly ever see another white man in these parts the whole winter.

"Damned place is getting so crowded a man might as

well live in the city—can't hardly turn around without bumpin' into some other sumbitch trappin' in our streams."

Van Horne leaned forward, setting his plate down on the ground. "Well, boys, you won't see that where we're going. To my knowledge, there's only been a handful of men even try to cross the mountains we're going over, an' that was more than five years ago."

Rattlesnake dropped his plate next to the fire and picked up his tin coffee cup. After he took a big swallow, he said, "Well, me'n Bobcat ain't much fer joinin' up with other men when we go travelin', but"—he cut his eyes at Smoke—"we might just make an exception seein' as how we'd be explorin' with the famous Smoke Jensen."

Bobcat smiled. "Yep, ol' Preacher used to give us an earful 'bout how good a man you was to spend time with, Smoke, back when he was still around. Might be nice to give it a try an' see if'n he was right or just pullin' our legs."

"Preacher told me many times, men, that you were all good men to ride with, and even spend the winter with if it came to that," Smoke said, looking at each of the mountain men in turn. "I'd be honored if you'd care to join us on our expedition."

Rattlesnake looked up at the clear blue sky and down at the melting snow all around them. "Hell, trappin's 'bout over fer this year anyhow," he said. "It might be kind'a fun to go see what Canada's like, see how it compares to the High Lonesome of Colorado."

"One thing they didn't tell you, boys," Bear Tooth said, a malicious gleam in his eyes.

"What's that, Bear?" Bobcat asked as he cut a slice off his plug of tobacco and stuffed it in his cheek.

"We gonna have to ride the train to get to Canada 'fore next winter."

"A train?" Bobcat said, almost swallowing his chaw.

"That's right," Red said, smiling at Bobcat's discomfort. Bobcat stroked his chin thoughtfully and shook his head. "Well, now, I don't know 'bout that, boys. I ain't never been on one of those contraptions before."

"Well, if'n you're too scared, Bobcat," Bear Tooth said with a grin, "we'll understand if you back out."

"Too scared?" Bobcat asked, his eyes wide. "Why, you young pup," he said, "I ain't scared of nothin' nor nobody. If'n you're willin' to risk your life on one of them things, why, then, so am I."

Once they'd decided to go along, the men didn't waste any time. They packed their horses, broke camp, and headed down the mountain in the direction of Pueblo, where Van Horne had a train waiting to take them north toward Canada.

7

The trip to Pueblo was uneventful, the mountain men keeping the group entertained with increasingly outrageous tales of life in the High Lonesome, and the group arrived just after noon on the third day of their journey. As they rode into town, Rattlesnake Bob pulled his pony up next to Smoke and glanced over his shoulder at Louis Longmont, who was riding in the rear.

"Smoke," he said, after leaning to the side and spitting a stream of brown tobacco juice at a mangy dog who was running alongside his pony, "I gotta ask ya' somethin'."

"What is it, Rattlesnake?" Smoke answered.

"What is the story on that Longmont feller? He looks awful soft to be comin' on a trip like this."

"Oh?"

"Yeah. I took notice of his hands. The feller don't look like he's ever done a lick of hard work in his life. His hands are soft an' don't hardly have no calluses on 'em at all." He squinted his eyes in an expression of distaste. "Hell, even his fingernails ain't go no dirt under 'em."

Smoke chuckled. He was used to men underestimating Louis's toughness. His fine clothes and refined manner often made men make the mistake of thinking he was soft. "Don't let his appearance fool you, Rattlesnake. Louis is tough as a boot under those fancy clothes, and in a pinch there is no man I'd rather have watching my back than him. He's saved my life on more occasions than I like to think about."

Rattlesnake chewed in silence for a moment, and then he nodded, "I'll have to take your word fer it, Smoke, 'cause I just don't see him as the kind who'll take to the High Lonesome well."

"Like I said, don't underestimate Louis, Rattlesnake. He came out West when he was knee-high to a horse, and he came with nothing but the clothes on his back. He's now one of the richest men I know, and he's earned every cent of his money the hard way. He doesn't have any back-down in him, and he'll put his life on the line for any man he considers a friend."

"If'n you say so," Rattlesnake said doubtfully, but it was clear he was reserving judgment on Louis until he proved himself to the mountain men in the only way that counted, by being as tough and as mean as they were.

From a few places back, Van Horne called, "Hey, Smoke. Why don't we grab some grub before we head over to the train station?"

"I'll second that," Pearlie said with conviction. "My stomach is pushing up against my backbone I'm so hungry."

"I agree," Louis said. "I find myself missing Andre more and more as time goes on."

Van Horne pulled the head of his Morgan toward a dining place with a sign over the door that said simply THE FEEDBAG, and the others followed, tying their mounts and packhorses to a hitching rail in front of the building.

The Feedbag was set up similarly to Longmont's saloon back in Big Rock. It consisted of a large room with eating tables on one side and a bar and smaller tables for the men who just wanted to drink their meals on the other side. It was about three quarters full. Most of the men wore the canvas trousers of miners, but there was a smattering of men dressed in chaps, flannel shirts, and leather vests who were obviously cowboys from nearby ranches.

Van Horne pushed through the batwings and walked directly toward a large table in the front corner of the room, while Smoke, Pearlie, Cal, and Louis spread out just inside the door with their backs to the wall waiting for their eyes to adjust to the gloomy lighting. The mountain men stopped and eyed Smoke with raised eyebrows.

"You expectin' trouble, Smoke?" Rattlesnake Bob asked, his hand dropping to the old Walker Colt stuck in the waistband of his buckskins.

Smoke smiled as his eyes searched the room for anyone who might be paying him special attention. "No, Rattlesnake, but I've found the best way to avoid trouble is to be ready for it when it appears."

When he saw no one was looking their way, Smoke walked on over to the table where Van Horne was already sitting down talking to a waiter, and took his usual seat with his back to the wall and his face to the rest of the room.

As they all took their seats, Bill said, "I ordered us a couple of pitchers of beer to start with while we decide what food to order."

Bear Tooth smacked his lips. "That sounds mighty good, Bill. I ain't had me no beer since last spring."

Before Bill could answer, a loud voice came from a group of men standing at the bar across the room. "God Almighty! What the hell is that smell?" a man called loudly, looking over at their table. "Did somebody drag a passel of skunks in here?"

The young man, who appeared to be about twenty years old, was wearing a black shirt and vest with a silver lining, and had a brace of nickel-plated Colt

Peacemakers tied down low on his hips. He had four other men standing next to him, all wearing their guns in a similar manner, and all were laughing like he'd just said something extremely funny.

Rattlesnake Bob glanced at Bear Tooth and grimaced. "I hate it when that happens," he said in a low, dangerous voice. "Now we're gonna have to kill somebody 'fore we've even had our beer."

"Take it easy, Rattlesnake," Smoke said. "He's just some young tough who's letting his whiskey do his thinking for him."

Rattlesnake eased back down in his chair. "You're right, Smoke," he said, smiling. "If'n ever man who was drunk-dumb got kilt, there wouldn't hardly be none of us left."

Smoke continued to keep an eye on the man across the room as the bartender tried to get him to be quiet, without much success.

When their waiter appeared with the beer and glasses, Smoke asked him, "Who's the man with the big mouth over there at the bar?"

The waiter glanced nervously over his shoulder, and then he whispered, "That's Johnny MacDougal. His father owns the biggest ranch in these parts."

"Well, I don't care if'n his daddy owns Colorado Territory," Bear Tooth growled. "You go on over there an' tell the little snot if'n he wants to see his next birthday he'd better keep his pie-hole shut."

The waiter's face paled and he shook his head rapidly back and forth. "I couldn't do that, sir," he said.

"Why not?" Rattlesnake asked.

"Just last week Johnny shot a man for stepping on his boots." The waiter hesitated, and then he added, "And the man wasn't even armed at the time."

"How come he's not in jail then?" Louis asked.

"Uh, his father carries a lot of water in Pueblo," the waiter said. "The sheriff came in and said it was in self-defense, though it was plain to everyone in the place that the man wasn't wearing a gun."

"So that's the lay of the land," Van Horne said, pursing his lips.

"Yes, sir," the waiter said, and hurried off back to the kitchen before these tough-looking men could get him in trouble, or worse yet, get him shot.

A few minutes later, after he'd downed another glass of whiskey, the young tough and his friends began to swagger across the room toward Smoke and his friends.

Smoke and Louis both eased their chairs back, took the hammer thongs off their Colts, and waited expectantly for the trouble they knew was coming. Smoke eased his right leg out straight under the table so he'd have quicker access if he had to draw.

MacDougal stopped a few feet behind Rattlesnake's chair and made a show of holding his nose. "Whew, something's awfully ripe in here," he said loudly, looking around the room to make sure he had an appreciative audience. "I think something done crawled in here and died."

Rattlesnake eased his hand down to the butt of the big Walker Colt in his belt, and as quick as a snake striking, he whipped it out, stood up, and whirled around, slashing the young man viciously across the face with the barrel.

MacDougal screamed and grabbed his face as blood spurted onto his vest. Before the other men could react, Rattlesnake grabbed MacDougal by the hair, jerked his head back, and jammed the barrel of the gun in his mouth, knocking out his two front teeth.

As MacDougal's eyes opened wide and he moaned in pain, Rattlesnake eared back the hammer and grinned, his face inches from the young tough's. "Now, what was it you was sayin', mister?" he growled.

"Somethin' 'bout somebody smelling overly ripe, I believe?"

As one of MacDougal's friends dropped his hand to his pistol, Bear Tooth stood up and had his skinning knife against the man's throat before he could draw. "Do you really want some of this?" he asked, smiling wickedly at the man. "'Cause if' n you do, you'll have a smile that stretches from ear to ear 'fore I'm done with you."

"Uh, no, sir!" the man said, moving his hands quickly away from his pistol butt.

MacDougal's eyes rolled back and he almost fainted from pain and embarrassment, and he sank to his knees on the floor of the restaurant.

Rattlesnake shook his head in disgust, pulled the Walker out of his bleeding mouth, and pushed him over with his boot until MacDougal was lying flat on his back, crying and moaning with his hands over his face.

Rattlesnake waved the Walker at MacDougal's friends, who cringed back, and said, "You boys better take this little baby off somewheres an' get him a sugar tit to suck on 'fore he pees his pants."

The men all bent down, picked MacDougal up, and helped him stagger out of the batwings, their eyes fixed on the barrel of the Walker as they left.

Rattlesnake stuck the gun back in his belt and turned back to the table. "Now, then, where's my beer?"

After they'd all eaten their fill of beefsteak, potatoes, corn, and apple pie for dessert, Van Horne threw some twenty-dollar gold pieces on the table and they walked toward the door.

Smoke hung hack for a moment and whispered to Cal and Pearlie, who broke off from the group and exited through a side door.

Smoke glanced at Louis and nodded. Louis nodded

back and kept his hand close to the butt of his pistol. Both of them knew the trouble wasn't over yet. Men like MacDougal didn't take treatment like he'd received without trying for revenge, especially when they'd been shamed in front of their friends and neighbors.

Just before Van Horne got to the batwings, Louis and Smoke stepped in front of him. "You'd better let us go out first, Bill," Smoke said, his eyes flat and dangerous.

Smoke and Louis went through the batwings fast, Smoke breaking to the right and Louis to the left, their eyes on the street out in front of The Feedbag.

Sure enough, MacDougal and his friends were lined up in the street, pistols in their hands, cocked and ready to fire.

As they raised their hands to aim and shoot, Smoke and Louis drew, firing without seeming to aim. An instant later, Cal and Pearlie joined in from the alley where they'd come out to the side of the men in the street.

Only MacDougal, out of all the men with him, got off a shot, and it went high, taking a small piece off Smoke's hat.

The entire group of men dropped in the hail of gunfire from Smoke and Louis and the boys, sprawling in the muddy street, making it run red with their blood.

"Damn!" Rattlesnake said in awe. He had started to draw his Walker at the first sign of trouble, but it was still in his waistband by the time it was all over. "I ain't never seen nobody draw an' fire that fast," he added, glancing at Smoke and Louis with new respect.

Smoke and Louis walked out into the street and bent down to check on the men. They were all dead, or so close to dying they were no longer any risk.

A few minutes later, a fat man with a tin star on his

chest came running up the street. "Oh, shit!" he said when he saw who had been killed.

He looked over at Smoke and the group and moved his hand toward his pistol, until Smoke grinned and waggled his Colt's barrel at him. "I wouldn't do that, Sheriff," Smoke said, jerking his head at the group of people standing at the windows and door of The Feedbag. "There are plenty of people in there who will say we acted in self-defense, so there's no need for you to go for that hogleg on your hip."

"But . . . but that's Angus MacDougal's son," the sheriff stammered.

Van Horne moved forward. "I don't care if it's the President's son, Sheriff. These men drew on us first."

"And just who are you?" the sheriff asked.

"My name is William Cornelius Van Horne," Bill said, pulling a card from his vest pocket and handing it to the sheriff. "And if you'd like to send a wire to the United States marshal over in Denver, I'm sure he will vouch for me."

The sheriff eyed the men standing in front of him, and wisely decided not to make an issue of it. "All right, if it went down like you say, you're free to go." He took his hat off and wiped his forehead. "But I don't think Mr. MacDougal is gonna like this."

Rattlesnake bent over and spat a stream of tobacco juice onto Johnny MacDougal's dead face. "If'n the man has any sense, he'll be relieved that we took that sorry son of a bitch off his hands," he said. "If he'd had any sense at all, he would'a drowned him in a barrel a long time ago."

8

Van Horne left the sheriff standing open-mouthed in the middle of the street staring down at the dead bodies, and walked over and got on his horse. After the rest of the men were mounted up and ready to go, he led them down the streets of Pueblo toward the train station.

When they got there and Van Horne had identified himself to the stationmaster, he had them walk their horses to the rear of a train waiting on a siding. The last couple of cars were fitted out as transports for horses, with two feet of hay on the floor and several buckets of sweet-feed and water hanging from nails on the wooden rails of the car.

Men working under the direction of the stationmaster put a ramp in place, and the horses were unsaddled and the packhorses were unloaded and led up into the cars.

Van Horne stepped back and spread his arms. "There you go, boys. All the comforts of home for your mounts," he said, grinning at the mountain men, who were eyeing the car with some suspicion.

Bear Tooth stepped up into the car, stuck his hand down in one of the buckets, and pulled out a handful of the feed, bringing it close to his nose and smelling.

He grinned and looked over at Van Horne. "What the hell is this?" he asked, taking a lick of it with his tongue.

"That's called sweet-feed," Van Horne answered. "It's grain mixed with molasses and corn and oats. It's used to put weight on horses after they've been out eating only grass."

"Damn, this stuff tastes good enough for *me* to eat," Bear Tooth said. He glanced over at his pony, which had its head already buried in one of the buckets. "I don't know if we gonna be able to git our hosses outta here after they've got a taste of sweet-feed."

Van Horne laughed and motioned for Bear Tooth to get down out of the car. "Now," he continued, waving them to follow him, "let me show you where we'll be riding."

He walked several cars forward and then climbed up a small set of steps into another car. This one was evidently fitted out for officials of the railroad, for it was very plush, with Oriental rugs over gleaming oaken floors, heavy brocaded drapes over the windows, and comfortable chairs and couches arranged around the car. A large bar stood in the corner with over twenty different kinds of whiskey and brandy and wine in circular racks behind it, and a plate of sandwiches and fried chicken lying on it. The car even had its own pot-bellied stove in one corner, in case the weather turned inclement.

"Now this is what I call travelin' in style," Pearlie said, moving around the car with wide eyes, pushing on the cushions of the couch to see how soft they were.

"The car just behind this one is fitted out with bunks and curtains in case we want to sleep along the way," Van Horne said proudly.

Rattlesnake Bob and Bobcat Bill stood in the doorway, along with Bear Tooth and Red Bingham, not venturing inside the beautiful car. Rattlesnake whispered something to Bobcat, and he nodded in agreement.

"If'n it's all the same to you, Mr. Van Horne," Rattlesnake said, "Bobcat an' me'll just mosey on back to the car with the bosses in it. This one's too nice fer the likes of us."

"But—" Van Horne started to object, until Bobcat cut him off.

"No, sir," Bobcat said, "we thank you kindly fer the offer, but we'd feel better 'bout it if we just stayed with our hosses."

"All right," Van Horne said finally, shrugging. "If that's the way you want it."

"Howsomeever," Rattlesnake added, moving over to the bar and picking up a bottle of Old Kentucky bourbon and a handful of chicken and sandwiches and stuffing them in his pockets, "we will take a bottle of this tonsil paint an' a little of this here food to keep ourselves warm just in case it gets a mite chilly out."

Van Horne laughed as the two mountain men backed out of the car and moved off back down the line of cars toward the car holding the horses.

"How about you, Red and Bear Tooth?" he asked. "This car seem too fancy for you?"

Bear Tooth grinned, exposing yellow stubs of teeth. "Hell, no, Bill," he said as he stepped over to the couch and sat down, putting his feet on a coffee table that probably cost more than he made in two years of trapping. He leaned back with his hands behind his head and smiled at Van Horne. "I figure it's your money and your play. If'n you want to waste this good liquor and food and furnishin's on the likes of us, then it's all right by me."

"Course, if'n you're gonna let Bear ride in here with the rest of us," Red said as he entered the car and moved toward the bar, "you might want to open them windows a mite." He glanced over at Bear. "'Cause much as I hate to say it, that boy in the bar back there was right. Somethin' does smell kind'a ripe in here."

Smoke and Louis and Cal followed Bear Tooth into the car, and all took seats except Pearlie, who was already over at the bar next to Red Bingham, filling his face with chicken as fast as he could chew and swallow it.

Van Horne moved to a funnel-device on the wall and pulled it down and spoke into it, telling the engineer they were ready to proceed.

As the train pulled out of Pueblo, Sheriff Wally Tupper loaded the bodies of Johnny MacDougal and his friends onto a buckboard and prepared to make the long trip out to the MacDougal ranch.

He looked down at the dead men and shook his head. Angus MacDougal was gonna be plenty upset about the death of his son, and old Angus was not a man who would take such a thing lying down. Tupper sighed. He sure as hell wouldn't want to be in the shoes of the man who'd shot Angus's only son. There was going to be hell to pay, and that was a fact!

As he climbed up on the hurricane deck, Tupper took a deep breath. He just hoped Angus wouldn't shoot him for bringing him the bad news.

As the wagon pulled up to the ranch house, Angus MacDougal was waiting on the porch, already dressed in a black suit. Evidently, word had preceded Tupper's arrival with the bodies.

Tupper brought the wagon to a halt and Angus stepped down off the porch, followed by his wife and his twenty-two-year-old daughter, Sarah.

Sarah was a looker, all right, Tupper thought. It was too bad she was every bit as tough as her old man, and just as good with a gun if the stories about her could be believed. The last man who'd tried to court her had been run out of town with a load of buckshot in his ass for having the effrontery to think he was good enough for Angus's baby girl, or so the story went. Since then, suitors had been far and few between for the pretty woman, though, Tupper thought, if I were twenty years younger and fifty pounds lighter, I might give her a try myself, and Angus be hanged.

Angus walked up to the wagon and pulled back the sheet over his son's body. His wrinkled face showed little emotion, but his eyes blazed with a hatred so intense, it made the hair on the hack of Tupper's neck stand up.

"Who did this to my boy, Wally?" he asked, his eyes still on his son.

"I don't know his full name, Angus," Tupper said deferentially as he took his hat off in respect. "There was a group of men involved in the fracas who worked for a fellow named William Cornelius Van Horne."

Now Angus's eyes shifted and bored into Tupper's. "Van Horne, huh? I've heard of him. A railroad man if memory serves."

"That's right, Angus," Tupper said, nodding his head vigorously. "I checked him out with the U.S. marshal over in Denver, an' he said the man's plenty powerful, all right. Word is he's goin' up to Canada to build a railroad up there."

"He the man fired the bullet that killed my boy, Wally?"

Tupper shook his head. "No, sir. The man who actually shot Johnny was named Smoke, but I didn't get his last name. He was a big man wearing buckskins, and there were a couple of old mountain men with him, but they didn't fire on Johnny and the others."

"Smoke, huh?" Angus said, his eyes narrow.

"That's what some of the boys in The Feedbag heard him called. Another fellow with him was named Louis, who also did some shooting."

"Well, I want you to go back to town and find out if anyone heard anything else, especially that bastard's last name."

"Uh, Angus," Tupper said, "it was a fair fight. Johnny and his friends drew down on Van Horne's men first. They didn't have no choice but to fire back."

Angus's face flamed red and he slammed his fist down on the side of the buckboard. "And I don't have any choice either, Wally! I'm going to make sure the son of a bitch who killed my boy is planted in the ground, and if you don't plan on helping me find out who it was, then I have a feeling we'll have a new sheriff in Pueblo before the snow melts."

"Now hold on, Angus," Tupper said. "I didn't say I wouldn't help. All I meant was Johnny was plenty liquored up and he forced the other men's hands, that's all."

Sarah walked up to stand next to her father and stare down at her dead brother. "I told you Johnny's drinking was going to get him killed someday, Father," she said.

He whirled on her and raised his right hand as if to strike her, but the look in her eyes stopped him. She showed not the slightest trace of fear.

"Go on, Father," she said through tight lips. "Hit me if it'll make you feel any better. But Johnny's the one you should've hit when he needed it, and maybe this would never have happened."

Angus whirled back around, his eyes flashing. "Tupper, what are you still doing here? Do like I said and find out what the man's name was who killed my son!"

9

John Hammerick sat drinking coffee laced with brandy at his favorite café in Grand Forks. Though it was spring in most parts of the country, winter still had a harsh grip on this northern corner of the state, and John felt the brandy would help keep the cold at bay.

Hammerick was what had been called a highwayman in the olden days—a rather romantic name for a thug and robber who had never, as far as anyone knew, done an honest day's work in his entire life. He was, for all of that, a man of many talents, and would prey on trains, stages, banks, and just about anyone or any place that had what he wanted and was too lazy to work for, namely money.

Known as Hammer by the men who followed him in his daily endeavors to extract as much money as he could from anyone who happened to have some, Hammerick had fallen on hard times lately. A two-year-long drought in the area had caused a dip in the economy, with farmers and the banks that supplied them all being extremely low on cash. Hammer was having a hard time finding anyone with enough money to make it worth his while to rob them, and his men were getting antsy, and some had even moved south looking for greener pastures.

Hammer would have done so himself, except for the fact he was too lazy to make the effort to relocate. Also, he rather enjoyed his local status as a man to be reckoned with and one that you shouldn't turn your back on.

He unfolded the *Grand Forks Gazette*, and read it as he drank his coffee, hoping to find some news that would help to enrich him and keep his men happily following his lead. Though he'd been kicked out of school long before he graduated, he had managed to master reading, after a fashion. Long words still gave him some trouble, but the writers of the *Grand Forks Gazette* weren't noted for using fancy language.

An article on the second page caught his eye, and he reread it a second time, his lips pursed in thought. After a while, he smiled and looked across the table at his second in command, Bull Bannion. Hammer didn't bother to show the article to Bull, who'd been kicked out of the only school he'd ever attended for being a bully, because Bull couldn't read. He could sign his name, but he did misspell it more often than not.

"Bull, I think I've found the answer to our prayers," Hammer said, draining his cup and signaling the waiter for a refill.

"Prayers?" Bull asked, his forehead wrinkled. "What are you talking about, Hammer. I ain't prayed since that time the bull gored me in my privates a few years back."

Hammer shook his head. Strength of intellect wasn't one of Bull's strong points. But since Bull was a little over six and a half feet in height and weighed in at almost three hundred pounds, Hammer didn't need him for his mind, but for his ability to beat the living shit out of anyone who happened to question any of Hammer's orders.

"No, Bull. I mean I've found something in the paper that's going to make us rich."

"Oh?" Bull said, putting his coffee cup down. Bull's coffee wasn't laced with brandy, but with the cheapest brand of rotgut whiskey he could find. He always said he didn't care what his liquor tasted like, as long as it got the job done.

"It says here," Hammer continued, "that they're starting to build the Canadian Pacific Railroad up in Canada in the next month or two." He glanced down at the paper. "In fact, they're going to begin the line in Winnipeg."

"How's that gonna put any money in our pockets?" Bull asked. "You ain't plannin' on going to work for the railroad, are you?" Bull grimaced. "You know I got a bad back and I can't do no heavy liftin', Hammer."

Hammer sighed. Trying to have a conversation with Bull was like trying to herd cats—damn near impossible. "No, Bull. But the article says they're going to be hiring over fifteen thousand Chinamen, and another five or six thousand whites to help build the railroad."

"So?" Bull asked, waving his empty coffee cup at the waiter to signal he too needed more. "I done told you I ain't gonna take no job laying track."

"Think about it, if it's not too much of a strain," Hammer said, beginning to get exasperated. "Twenty thousand men, more or less, each of them making about a dollar a day. I hear the railroad pays their men in gold once a month. That means the men that run the railroad are going to be transporting almost six hundred thousand dollars a month through some of the roughest country in the world."

Bull still didn't get it. "You mean they pay them Chinamen a dollar a day?" he asked, shaking his head. "Hell, I never earned that much back when I worked cows, an' I'm a white man," Bull said, clearly feeling discriminated against.

Hammer bit his lip to keep from shouting, for shouting at Bull was a sure way to get your face smashed in. "I don't know, Bull, but even if it's only fifty cents a day, that's still almost three hundred thousand in gold coming through Winnipeg every month just waiting for someone to come and take it."

Suddenly, Bull got the idea. "Oh, I see what you mean." He hesitated. "But just how far is this Winnipeg from here?"

"A goodly ways," Hammer said. "But it's not too far from Noyes, up in the northern part of Minnesota. The sheriff in Noyes is an old friend of mine. I figure if we give him a split of our take, he won't mind if we take the men up there and set up our base there. Then, every month or so, we can ride on up into Canada, pick us up a little gold, and then hightail it back to Noyes and the Canadians won't be able to follow us."

"But Hammer," Bull argued, "that much money is bound to mean a lot of guards. That payroll is going to be a tough nut to crack."

Hammer shrugged. "Well, if it does turn out to be too tough, there's still going to be a lot of Chinamen and other workers who have their pockets full of gold. I imagine they'll be bringing it in by train, rather than stages or wagons, and you know how good I am at robbing trains."

"Still, there's bound to be plenty of men watching that much gold. It won't be as easy as it is down here, Hammer, where they only carry a few thousand dollars."

Hammer gritted his teeth to keep from telling Bull he was full of shit. "Well, even if we can't get it off the train, then we'll just take it off the men after they're paid. Either way, it's still a lot of gold that's gonna be spread around up there, and I don't see how we can lose."

Bull glanced out the window at the gray snow still blowing in the streets of Grand Forks. "I hear it's even colder up there in Canada than it is down here," he said.

Hammer laughed. "Who said getting rich was going to be easy, Bull?"

When it came time for supper to be served on the train, Van Horne reached up and pulled on a cord hanging on the wall next to the large easy chair he was sitting in. A few minutes later, a young black man entered the car.

"Willard, would you please go back to the cattle car and ask the two gentlemen riding there with the horses to join us for dinner?" he asked.

Willard's eyes widened. "They's riding with the animals, sir?"

"Yes," Van Horne answered, smiling. "They thought they'd be more comfortable there." He hesitated, and then he added, "And Willard, once the men have joined us, would you ask one of the porters to gather up all the clothing from the packs in the car and give them a good cleaning while we eat?"

"Yes, sir," Willard said, and left the car.

Pearlie, who was sitting near a window on the other side of the car, looked up eagerly. "Did I hear you mention food?"

"Yes," Van Horne answered. "We'll have it served to us here in this car."

Bear Tooth looked over at Pearlie. "For once I agree with you, Pearlie boy. I'm so hungry I could eat a bear."

"That won't be necessary, Bear Tooth," Van Horne said. "I believe the menu tonight consists of beefsteak, potatoes, corn, and apple cobbler for dessert."

Red Bingham nudged Bear Tooth with his elbow. "That do sound better'n bear, son," he said grinning.

Once everyone was gathered in the car and dinner was served, Smoke turned to Van Horne. "Tell me a little about how we're going to get all the way up into

Canada on the train. I wasn't aware the lines went that far."

As he ate his steak, Van Horne explained. "The man who hired me to build the railroad from Winnipeg west to the coast, James J. Hill, along with some partners, bought the old St. Paul & Pacific Railroad a couple of years back. He then laid some tracks and connected the St. Paul to a Canadian Pacific line from Fort Gary up in Winnipeg down to St. Vincent, Minnesota, and renamed his railroad the St. Paul, Minneapolis, and Manitoba route. The route has been so successful that two of his partners, Donald Smith and George Stephen, got a contact from the government of Canada to extend the Canadian Pacific Railroad west all the way to the Pacific Ocean, and that's just what he's hired me to do."

Van Horne paused and pushed his empty plate away from him on the table. He took a long, thick cigar out of his coat pocket and lit it. As clouds of aromatic blue smoke billowed out, he looked directly at Smoke. "Of course, there are those who think this route cannot be completed since the country we'll be going through is so rough. In fact, they've given our little project the name 'Hill's Folly.'"

Smoke jerked his thumb at a large map of Canada hanging on a wall across the room. "I was looking at that map earlier, and from what I can see you've got at least three mountain ranges to cross, with no guarantee there's any passes low enough for a train to go through." He reached into his pocket, brought out a cigar, and puffed it into life. "And what's more," Smoke added, "I've heard the Stony Indians up there in Canada aren't near as civilized as those here in Colorado Territory. They might have some objections to a railroad being built through land they consider their own."

Van Horne nodded through the smoke. "That's right, and that's exactly why I've hired you gentlemen.

You and your friends are going to have to help us find a route through those mountains, and you might have to do a little convincing of the Indians along the way that we will not be denied our chance to bring progress to the area."

"Getting through them mountains ain't gonna be no problem fer us, Bill," Bobcat Bill Johnson said around a mouthful of steak, "but findin' a pass that ain't gonna be snowed in the entire winter is somethin' else again."

Smoke nodded. "Bobcat's right, Bill," he said. "There's almost always passes in the mountains that a man on horseback can get through, if he knows what he's doing. But even if we do manage to find them and you are able to get the tracks laid, they're probably going to have quite a bit of snow covering them for at least part of the year."

Van Horne waved his cigar in the air. "That's not a problem, gentlemen. We now have snow-trains that have huge plows on the front of them that can keep the tracks clear of snow."

Smoke smiled and went back to his meal. Evidently, Van Horne had never been in a High Lonesome blizzard that could easily drop several feet of snow in the course of a night or two. Of course, that wasn't Smoke's problem. His problem was going to be finding a way through the mountains while fighting off hostile Indians, trappers, and anyone else who didn't want the railroad coming through that part of the country. He smiled to himself, thinking they were surely going to earn the money Van Horne had promised them for the job.

After they'd finished their meal and all the men were sitting around drinking coffee with cigars and cigarettes, Willard came into the car with a large bundle of clean clothes in his arms.

"Here's them clothes you wanted washed, Mr. Van Horne," he said, placing the bundle on a table. "They's still a mite damp, but they's suitable to wear."

Bobcat and Rattlesnake glared at the pile of buckskins on the table. "Them looks suspiciously like our clothes, Bill," Bobcat said.

"Yes, they are, Bobcat. I . . . um . . . I thought that since we're going to be traveling in such close proximity to one another, clean clothes and baths might be in order for everyone."

"You what?" Rattlesnake asked. "Are you plannin' on stoppin' this here train and makin' us get into a river an' bathe?" He glanced out the window. "Hell, it's still snowin' out there."

Van Horne laughed and got to his feet. "Of course not, gentlemen. Follow me."

He went through the rear door, passed through the sleeping car, and emerged into a car with four large copper bathtubs bolted to the floor. In one corner of the room was a large copper barrel hooked up to a stove device that would heat the water.

Van Horne waved his hands. "There you go, men. Each tub is supplied with hot water, soap, and a brush to scrub the dirt and grime off with." He pointed to another wall on which were three basins with mirrors above them. "And there, should you care to shave, are all the necessary implements at your disposal."

The four mountain men walked over and looked at the tubs dubiously. "Well, I'll be hanged," Bear Tooth said. "I've heard of these things, but I've never seen one up close before."

"You mean, we just fill that thing with hot water and get right in?" Rattlesnake asked, running his hands over the copper tub.

"Yes, and while you're bathing, I'll have the porter wash the rest of your clothes," Van Horne said.

Bobcat raised his eyebrows. "You mean we have to take our clothes off 'fore we get in there?"

Van Horne had to bite his lip to keep from laughing, since he didn't want to hurt Bobcat's feelings. "Yes, that is the customary way to bathe," he said simply.

Red Bingham picked up a bucket, held it under a spigot on the copper barrel, and turned the handle. Steaming hot water poured into the bucket, and Red grinned like a child with a new toy. "Damn, this is even better'n those hot springs we usually bathe in. The water don't smell of sulfur at all."

"Enjoy yourselves, gentlemen," Van Horne said as he turned to go.

"Uh, Bill," Bear Tooth said.

"Yes?"

"Could you have that Willard bring us in a bottle of whiskey an' some glasses. If'n I'm gonna dunk myself in one of those contraptions, I'm gonna need some whiskey to see me through it."

"And you might want to bring in a couple of extra brushes," Red said, looking over at Bear Tooth. "If you want all the dirt off'n Bear, it's gonna take more'n one brush to do the job."

Bear Tooth grimaced and threw a bar of soap at Red. When it sailed over his head and into a far wall, Bear laughed. "Red, I bet that's the closest you ever came to soap."

10

The snow that until a few days before had been knee-deep in the center of the main street of Noyes was melting under the rays of the spring sun, and Sheriff Luke McCain stood on boardwalk in front of his office with his hands on his hips, surveying the mess it was making. Main Street was now not much more than a river of mud, and the mosquitoes and black flies were already beginning to swarm.

McCain slapped his neck with a grimace. If there was any time of the year he hated worse than winter it was spring, with its mud, bugs, and temperatures still cold enough to freeze the balls off a mule at night. He vowed for perhaps the thousandth time to move south where he could hold up a snowball and the people would say, "What's that?"

He smiled to himself, thinking that if he did that, he might have to get a real job and work for a living. Noyes, with its population made up mainly of people of Swedish descent, was a very law-abiding town. About the worse thing that McCain had to face was the occasional fight when the farmers from the surrounding area would come to town and get a load of whiskey on, and that, thankfully, was about as rare as hen's teeth. He put his hand on the butt of his pistol as he thought about this, trying to remember the last time he'd had to draw his gun. Not able to remember such a time, he shook his head and decided yet again to stay where he was. After all, when the temperature hit eighty or so, the black flies would disappear for another year and the glorious summer would make it all worthwhile.

As he turned to go back into his office and get a cup of coffee and a cigar, hoping the smoke from the stogie would keep the mosquitoes at bay, he heard the sound of a large number of horses coming into town.

He shaded his eyes from the sun with his hand and cursed softly to himself. Damned if it didn't look like that asshole John Hammerick leading a large group of men into his town. Now what would a lowlife like Hammer be doing up here? he thought. There ain't nobody up here in this godforsaken wilderness with anything worth stealing. And from what McCain remembered about his old acquaintance, stealing from other people was about all old Hammer did other than strut around like the cock of the walk with his chest stuck out.

As Hammer and his men walked their horses through the muddy street and stopped in front of his office, McCain nodded. "Hello, Hammer," he said, his voice flat and unfriendly. "What kind of trouble are you in and is it going to visit my town?"

Hammer gave him a look, his eyes hard for a moment, and then they softened and he grinned. "Now what kind of welcome is that for an old friend come to visit?" he asked.

"Sharing a cell with me in the Tucson State pen don't make us exactly friends, Hammer," McCain replied. He looked around at the group of men sitting in their saddles behind Hammer and he sighed. "Why don't you send your men on over to the saloon for some drinks while you come on in to my office and tell me just what's going on?"

Hammer nodded. "Bull, take the men with you and go get something to cut the trail dust. I'll meet you there in a while."

Hammer got down off his horse, stretched and rubbed his butt, and then followed McCain into his office.

"Coffee?" McCain asked, moving toward the Franklin stove in the corner that had a tin coffeepot sitting on top.

"Don't you have anything stronger?" Hammer asked as he took a seat in one of the two straight-backed chairs in front of McCain's desk.

McCain shook his head, "Not in the office I don't." He stared at Hammer for a moment, wishing the man were anywhere but here. "If it's whiskey you want, you're welcome to go on over to the saloon with your friends." Hammer shrugged, as if the coldness of McCain's welcome didn't bother him at all. "Coffee it is then."

McCain handed him a large cup, and took his with him as he sat behind his desk. "So?" he asked, peering at Hammer over the brim of his cup as he drank.

"I've got a proposition for you, Luke," Hammer said after sampling his own coffee and making a grimace at the bitter taste.

"In case you hadn't noticed, Hammer, I got me a job already, and I'm far too old and too smart to take off riding the owlhoot trail with you."

"This ain't exactly a job offer, Luke. In fact, all you got to do to make yourself quite a bit of change is to ignore me and my men for the next few months."

"Oh, and you'll be doing what exactly while I'm ignoring you?" McCain asked, thinking ten minutes was too much time to spend with Hammer, let alone several months.

"We'll be staying here in your town, behaving ourselves, and every now and then taking a little ride up into Canada. When we come back here, you'll get a full share of any proceeds we've gotten from our trip."

McCain pursed his lips as he drank his coffee and stared at Hammer without speaking for a couple of minutes. "And just how are you planning on making any money up in Canada, Hammer?" he asked. "Hell, the only place big enough to call itself a town within riding distance is Winnipeg, and there ain't nothing up there but trappers and miners who for the most part don't have two dollars to rub together."

Hammer grinned. "I guess you ain't heard 'bout the railroad they're gonna be building up there then."

McCain shook his head. "They've been talking about doing that for the last five years, but I didn't know they were actually going to start on it anytime soon."

Hammer nodded. "Yep. Matter of fact, I hear they've already got over fifteen thousand men shipped in to do the dirty work of laying the tracks."

McCain stroked his jaw and finished his coffee. "I see. You're thinking the payroll for that many men is going to be easy pickings, huh?"

Hammer shrugged. "I don't know how easy it's gonna be, but I'm damned sure gonna find out."

"And all I gotta do is just look the other way while you and your men run back and forth and rob the railroad?"

"Yep, an' for that, my friend, you'll get the same share as all of my men are getting."

A slow grin curled McCain's lips. He couldn't for the life of him see any problem with this arrangement. If Hammer was still as stupid and greedy as he had been back when McCain knew him, he thought, he wouldn't last a week in Canada. "Well, now, I think I can manage that, friend," McCain said, his manner decidedly friendlier now that he knew what Hammer wanted. He reached across the desk and shook Hammer's hand.

"In fact," he added, "I'll do better than that. There's a boardinghouse here that's been closed all winter, and it isn't due to open for another week or two, but I'll put in a word for you and your men and I think I can have you a place to stay where you won't be bothered by a lot of questions."

"Excellent," Hammer said. He looked at his coffee cup, which was still almost full. "Now, what do you say we head on over to the saloon and seal our deal with something a little stronger than this coffee?"

McCain smiled. "One thing I've learned being sheriff. With the low pay and all the bullshit I have to put up with, I never refuse the offer of a free drink."

"Who said I'd he paying?" Hammer asked, grinning.

"It's your proposition, Hammer, so you get to do the buying," McCain said as he grabbed his hat from a rack next to the door.

11

By the second day on the train, washed and scrubbed and with their beards trimmed, Rattlesnake and Bobcat were right at home riding in the fancy parlor car with the other men. No longer afraid they'd mess the place up with their dirty boots and clothes, they, along with Bear and Red, acted like seasoned travelers who'd never been afraid of the infamous Iron Horse at all.

After several days of this luxury, and changing engines three times, the group finally arrived in Winnipeg, Canada. Sore and stiff from sitting down for most of the time, the men could hardly wait to get off the train and stretch their legs.

"I'll have one of the porters take your horses to the livery stable, and another one will take our bags to the hotel we'll be staying in until we get organized for the surveying trip," Van Horne said as they stepped down out of the railcar and onto the wooden platform next to the tracks.

Louis Longmont walked out from the tracks and stood with his hands on his hips staring at the outskirts of Winnipeg, a wry smile on his lips.

Smoke moved up next to him and followed his gaze. "What are you grinning at, Louis?"

Louis raised his nose in the air and took a deep sniff.

"I'm amazed at the appearance of this place, Smoke." He turned his eyes to Smoke. "It takes me back to my first days out West, more years ago than I care to think about."

Smoke looked around and nodded. The streets were full of men wearing buckskins and canvas miners' trousers, and the air was filled with the smells of horse droppings, mud, leather, and wood smoke. The streets were little more than mud baths, but due to the colder temperatures this far north, the mud in places was still frozen patches of black ice.

"You're right, Louis," Smoke responded with a smile. "Winnipeg reminds me of the way towns looked when I first came out to Colorado Territory with Preacher—rough, rowdy, and full of the excitement that comes with knowing you're on the very edge of civilization."

"That's right, Smoke, the kind of place where anything can happen and usually does, especially after the sun goes down and the town really comes to life," Louis agreed. "One of the first gambling halls I owned was in a place exactly like this, and I had the most fun I've ever had in my life there."

Cal and Pearlie were standing wide-eyed just behind them. Neither of them had ever seen a town like this, both being much too young to have been around in the glory days when Colorado Territory was being formed.

"Jiminy," Cal said as he stared at the number of men wearing beards who were moving about the town, all of whom were armed to the teeth and looking like they'd just as soon shoot someone as look at him. There didn't seem to be anyone who had less than two or three weapons arrayed on their persons.

"I ain't never seen anything like this before," Cal added.

Van Horne overheard his comment, and stepped up between Cal and Pearlie. "You're right about that, son," he said. "Canada is the last frontier, that's for sure."

"An' damned if men like us ain't gonna ruin it forever," Bear Tooth said grimly, leaning his head to the side to spit a stream of tobacco juice into the mud swelling up over his boots.

Van Horne looked at him. "What do you mean, Bear Tooth?" he asked.

"He means, once you got that iron horse of yours making regular trips back and forth 'crost the wilderness, it won't be wilderness no more," Red Bingham answered scowling as he stood with his hands on his hips looking around at the swirling bustle of activity in front of them.

"That's right," Rattlesnake Bob agreed. "Pretty soon you'll have pilgrims an' women an' snake-oil salesmen travelin' here on your trains an' crowdin' out all the men like us who like the town the way it is now."

Van Horne shrugged. "Well, gentlemen, you can't stop civilization, and if I don't build the rail lines someone else will." He didn't mention that James Hill's plans were exactly as they'd said, to flood the area with tourists and settlers and in so doing, make himself yet another fortune by building inns and hotels and restaurants all along the hundreds of miles of tracks.

Bobcat Bill put his hand on Van Horne's shoulder. "Oh, we ain't blaming you none, Bill," he said. "It's just that we're old coots who'd like life to stay wild an' hairy a mite longer so's we can enjoy our last days without havin' to put up with what you call civilization."

"Who're you callin' an old coot, you sumbitch?" Bear Tooth growled, trying to look fiercely at his friend.

"For a man who's older than dirt, you're awful touchy 'bout bein' reminded of it," Bobcat Bill said, leaning to the side to spit tobacco juice in the mixed snow and mud at their feet just as Bear Tooth had a moment before.

Smoke stepped between the men, laughing at their antics. "Come on, men," he said. "From what I can see from here, about every other building is either a saloon or a restaurant. What say we try a few of them out while Mr. Van Horne gets our rooms ready at the hotel."

"You think they'll let an old relic like me into one of those places, Smoke?" Bear Tooth said sarcastically, casting his eyes at Bobcat Bill.

Bobcat laughed and clapped Bear on the shoulder. "Hell, yes, Bear. Since you smell so nice and sweet now, they wouldn't dare turn you away."

"Yeah, an' with the amount of that there toilet water you put in your hair, you're liable to be real popular with these miners I see walking around too," Red Bingham added.

With that final comment, the mountain men all licked their lips and hitched up their pants, and began to walk rapidly toward the main street of the town, talking excitedly among themselves about how the town reminded them of this place or that place from the old days.

"Masterfully handled, Smoke," Louis said, smiling as he moved to follow the mountain men.

Smoke turned to Van Horne. "Bill, I think the men need a little time to unwind and get the kinks from the trip out of their systems. We'll meet you over at the hotel after a while."

Van Horne nodded. "That's a good idea, Smoke. I'll just check in with my men at the construction site and make sure everything's on track for starting the surveying, and I'll meet you and the other men at the hotel in a couple of hours." He turned and pointed to a three-story building at the end of the street. "It's the Rooster's Roost down there on Main Street."

He reached in his pocket and pulled out a stack of

bills. "Here's some Canadian money to pay for your drinks and food."

Smoke eyed the bills. "That's a lot of money just for food and drinks, Bill."

Van Horne grinned. "Well, prices are a mite high, this being a frontier town and all. Don't worry, you and your men are going to earn every cent of it before I'm through with you."

He paused and added with a wink, "And if I know men like Bear Tooth and the others, you might end up having to pay for some damages if things get a bit too rowdy."

Smoke laughed and looked at the backs of the mountain men as they walked down the center of the street. "You mean you think gentle peaceable men like those might get into trouble, Bill?"

Van Horne laughed and shook his head as he walked off mumbling, "Gentle, peaceable, in a pig's eye!"

The group entered a saloon appropriately called the Dog Hole, a common euphemism for drinking establishments of the time, and pushed two tables together in a corner to accommodate the eight of them.

While they were waiting for a waiter to come to the table, Louis leaned over to Smoke and said, "It's like I've been here before. Remember that gambling hall I said I owned? This could be its twin."

Smoke nodded. He too had been in hundreds of places like this one back in his early days on the frontier. "I know what you mean," he said, glancing around at the rough plank bar with brass spittoons every few feet along its length, handmade wooden shelves behind it holding a myriad of bottles, many of them without labels, showing they were home-brewed.

The clientele reflected the time and the place, with about half the patrons being rough-hewn trappers and explorers and railroad workers and the other half being miners, with a few well-dressed men who were obviously cardsharps and other characters who preyed on the first two groups.

There were no Chinese in the place, however, probably due to the fact that a large hand-painted sign was on the wall behind the bar saying NO CHINEE ALLOWED!

There were, though, a few men dressed in various types of garb with pistols slung low on their hips and tied down in the manner of gunfighters. Their hard eyes were never at rest as they continuously scanned the patrons and stayed on the alert for danger.

Pearlie leaned across the table toward Smoke and whispered, "I'll bet you at least half those men over there with their guns tied down low are on wanted posters back in the States."

Smoke nodded his agreement. He knew the look of a man on the run well, having been one for several years in his youth himself.

Finally, a young man with an acne-scared face, a pronounced limp, and a dirty apron tied around his waist approached the table.

"What can I get for you gents?" he asked in the flat accent of the home-born Canadian.

"Do you serve any food here?" Smoke asked, realizing it was just past noon and they hadn't eaten yet.

The young man smirked and flicked his head at the bar. "Yeah, if you call boiled eggs and pickled pig's feet food."

Bear Tooth grinned. "Hell with that! You got any bourbon from Kaintuck?"

The bored young man just shook his head. "Mister, we got whiskey, rye, and something the barman made up in his basement he calls brandy. As for where the shit is from, your guess is as good as mine."

"Bring us a couple of bottles of whiskey," Smoke said, and he glanced at Louis, knowing he preferred brandy.

Louis sighed. "And a bottle of the barman's brandy too, if you don't mind."

The waiter shrugged. "I don't mind, but you might," he said, smiling for the first time since he came to the table.

A few minutes later, when he put the bottles on the table, all without labels, Louis asked, "Don't you have any with labels on them?"

The young man grinned again and leaned over to whisper, "Sure, but they cost twice as much and to tell you the truth, they got this same liquor in them as these do. The barman just refills the bottles every night outta the same barrel as these other bottles."

"I take it you don't much care for the barman," Louis said, smiling.

"Not a whole lot," the boy said, looking over his shoulder toward the bar. "He's my father."

"That explains it," said Smoke, being well aware of the anger some boys felt against their parents from back when Sally used to teach school in Big Rock. In fact, he could remember when his father had dragged him out West from their hardscrabble farm in Missouri and how he'd thought his father was a relic from days gone by.

"You think maybe we ought'a order some sarsaparilla or lemonade for the kid here?" Pearlie asked, inclining his head toward Cal sitting next to him.

"Who you callin' a kid, yahoo?" Cal asked, elbowing Pearlie in the ribs as the other men around the table laughed.

"Just kiddin' with you, Cal boy," Pearlie said. "It's just that I know you can't handle hard liquor hardly at all, an' I don't want you getting in no trouble or nothin'."

"I guess if I'm gonna be ridin' out in the wilderness with you fellows, I'm big enough to drink what you drink," Cal said, his cheeks burning red at the laughter.

"Cal's right, boys," Smoke said, coming to his defense. "Cal's old enough to decide when and how much he drinks, just like he's old enough to do a man's work for a man's wages. Besides, if his stomach can take that mountain man coffee Bear Tooth makes every morning, it can stand just about anything."

Cal nodded defiantly and reached over, poured a large jolt of whiskey into his glass, and upended it, drinking it down in one large gulp. His eyes widened and his face turned even redder and he coughed violently several times.

Bear Tooth took a similar drink and grimaced. "The boy's right, fellers. This stuff ain't long outta the barrel, that's for sure."

Red Bingham nodded after taking a sip of his whiskey. "Yeah, but it'll sure get the job done," he said, refilling his glass. "It tastes just like Bear Tooth's horse liniment," he said, and took another long swallow.

Louis, the only one trying the brandy, took a tentative sip and sucked in his breath, his eyes watering. He looked around the table at the men who thought that, being a saloon owner, he would grouse about the local brew. "I've had worse, and in far better establishments than this," he said with a grin.

Cal shook his head, his face still red from the whiskey. He got to his feet. "I think I'll go and get some boiled eggs from the bar to cut the taste of that stuff from my mouth," he said.

Red Bingharn commenced to tell a story about having nothing to eat one winter except boiled quail and dove eggs, while Cal made his way toward the bar.

Smoke was smiling at the story when he heard a commotion from across the room, and looked up just in time to see Cal flying backward as one of the men wearing a low-slung pistol on his hip smacked him backhanded in the face.

The man was well over six feet tall and had about fifty pounds on the slim Cal.

Smoke got to his feet, along with Pearlie, and walked rapidly over to stand between Cal and his assailant. "What's going on here?" he asked, his face neutral.

The gunny, who was standing over Cal with his hand on the butt of his pistol, glared at Smoke. "Who asked you to butt in, mister?" the gunny said, scowling. "This ain't none of your business."

Smoke ignored the man and glanced down as he helped Cal to his feet. "What happened, Cal?"

Cal rubbed his bleeding lip with the back of his hand. "I went to get me a couple of eggs, and this man said they was his eggs and to keep my damned hands off," Cal replied. "And then he hauled off and hit me without any warning."

Smoke looked over at the bar at the stack of eggs, noting there were at least twenty eggs on the platter.

He raised his eyebrows as he turned his gaze back to the man. "You planning on eating all of those eggs by yourself?" he asked.

The man grinned sourly. "What if I am?"

Smoke smiled. "Then I suggest you get to it. I for one would like to see you do it."

"Like I said before, what business is it of your'n?" the man asked, moving his fingers over the butt of his pistol.

Smoke squared around and faced the man from two feet away, his face suddenly going flat and his eyes turning as hard as flint. "If you're planning on drawing that smoke wagon, I suggest you get to work," Smoke said. "Otherwise, I'm going to hit you so hard you'll be gumming your food for the rest of your miserable life."

The man growled and grabbed iron, but before he could clear his holster, Smoke's Colt was drawn, cocked, and the barrel was poking the man in the nose.

His eyes widened and his face paled as he slowly took his hand from the butt of his pistol.

"Now," Smoke said, holstering his own gun. "Let's see you get to work on those eggs."

The man's eyes narrowed and he looked over at Cal. "This is all your fault, you young pup," he growled.

Cal edged Smoke aside and stood in front of the angry man, his face set. "Is that right?" he asked. "Well, why don't you try to hit me again, now that I'm ready for it?" Cal asked, standing with his feet apart and his fists hanging at his sides, his jaw muscles bulging.

The man yelled an obscenity as he made a clumsy swing at Cal's head with his right fist.

Cal leaned to the side, easily ducking the blow, and slammed his right fist into the man's gut, doubling him over and dropping him to his knees. As he knelt there, gasping for breath, Cal squatted in front of him.

"I'm going to teach you to keep your goddamned hands to yourself and your big fat mouth shut from now on, mister," he said. He grabbed the man by the collar of his shirt and lifted him to his feet as if he weighed only a few pounds, and then he marched him over to the platter of eggs, every eye in the place on him.

As one of the gunny's friends, seeing Cal and Smoke were distracted, went for his gun, Pearlie drew quickly and slashed the man backhanded across the face with the barrel of his Colt, knocking him out cold and spreading his nose all over his face in the bargain.

The loud metallic click of the hammer of a Sharps Big Fifty being eared back came from Smoke's table, and the men in the bar turned to see Bear Tooth standing there, his Sharps cradled in his arms. "Anybody else want to dance?" he asked, staring around the room, his eyes narrow. "If'n you do, let's strike up the band an' git to it!"

When he got no answer from the crowded room, he sat back down and laid his rifle on the table, his finger still on the trigger as he watched Cal and the man at the bar.

"Thanks, Pearlie, Bear Tooth," Smoke said. He stepped back from Cal and grinned. "It's your show, Cal."

Cal leaned the man up against the bar. "Start eating, asshole, and if you stop before every egg on that plate is gone, I'm going to beat you within an inch of your life," the young man said.

The man groaned and began to stuff boiled eggs in his mouth as fast as he could, looking out of the corner of his eyes at Cal, his face burning red at being handled so easily by such a thin, wiry young man.

Smoke picked up two of the eggs off the platter and handed them to Cal. "You might want to give the man a break and eat a couple of these for him," Smoke said, smiling.

Cal took the eggs, returned the smile, and then he stuck his face next to the man's. "I'm gonna be watching you from over there, and I better not see no eggs left on that platter or I'll be back."

And then he and Smoke walked back to their table, smiling at the expressions on the faces of the men in the bar.

Bear Tooth put the Sharps back under the table and grinned at Cal. "For a boy without no meat on his bones, you pack a mean punch, son," he said approvingly.

Cal inclined his head. "Smoke taught me and Pearlie how to fight a couple of years back, but I ain't hardly had to use none of it till now."

"I'd say you a good learner, young beaver," Red said, paying Cal the highest compliment he could by calling him a beaver, a mountain-man term of respect.

Bobcat Bill clapped Pearlie on the shoulder. "An' you're pretty quick with that hogleg too, boy," he said.

"Yes," Smoke said, "they do make quite a pair, don't they?"

"I guess they'll do to ride the river with," Rattlesnake said, and then he held up his glass to the two young men and added, "To the young beavers, may they give us old beavers a little more time 'fore they take over the river."

Everyone laughed and joined in the toast, yelling at the waiter to bring more whiskey because they were just getting started.

12

Hammer Hammerick picked up Bull Bannion from the room next to his in the boardinghouse Luke McCain had provided, and told him to get the gang together, they were going for a ride.

Soon, Hammer and Bull, followed by almost thirty men, rode out of Noyes and headed for Winnipeg.

"What're we gonna do when we get there, Hammer?" Bull asked as his horse trotted next to Hammer's.

"We're gonna look the situation over an' see what the lay of the land is," Hammer answered around a long, black cigar stuck in the corner of his mouth. "When the time comes to hit the payroll trains, I want to be sure we know every road in and out of Winnipeg, as well as finding some likely spots to hole up if the posses they send after us get too close."

"Posses?" Bull asked, his eyebrows raised. "You think they're gonna have posses ready for us?" He'd never thought of that, because the trains they'd robbed together before had never had enough money on them to be well guarded. In fact, most of the time they'd had to be content to just take watches and pocket money from the passengers.

Hammer sighed. Bull was a good man with a gun

and he was loyal to a fault, but he was dumber than a skunk. "No, probably not the first time, Bull. On that one, we'll probably get a free ride, since they won't be expecting anyone to try and rob them. But I don't expect the railroad to take the loss of thousands of dollars lying down. After we take the first payroll, I expect they'll have more guards on the second one, so we're gonna have to take different routes to and from the railroad each time we hit it, an' I want to make sure we know the country as well as we can before we start taking the railroad's money."

"Oh," Bull said, "that's a good idea."

Hammer smiled grimly. "That's why I'm ramrod of this outfit, Bull, 'cause of good ideas like that."

They spent the next few days traveling back and forth along the tracks of the railroad into and out of Winnipeg, making notes on a hand-drawn map Hammer had made showing the best trails along the way and where they could stop and set up ambushes against any posses or guards that happened to get onto their tails.

They spent the nights camped out in the open, sleeping under small tents and eating campfire food, with the men complaining bitterly about the bugs and the cold and just about everything else, until finally Hammer had had enough.

Once he had what he wanted, Hammer told the men to divide up and head into Winnipeg. "Go into town in groups of two and three," he said. "Don't act like we know each other while we're in town. I don't want the sheriff or marshal or whatever they have up here in the way of law to know we're all together. Find rooms at different hotels and let me know where you're staying, so I won't have any trouble getting in touch with you when the time comes to hit the train," he told his men.

"What are you gonna be doing?" Bull asked.

"I'm going to be mixing it up with the railroad men in the saloons around town and trying to find out the schedule of payroll payments, so I'll know when to plan to rob the trains coming into town." Hammer smiled. "I wouldn't want to hit an empty train, now would I?"

As the men dispersed, riding off at intervals of five or ten minutes, Hammer lit up another cigar and sat in the saddle thinking of how he was going to spend all the money he planned to take from the men who owned the railroad. Slapping at his neck where a mosquito as big as a bumblebee had dug in, he decided the first thing he was going to do was to move south away from the insects and the cold of the north.

Finally, when only he and Bull were left, he spurred his mount toward Winnipeg, just visible in the distance.

Hammer and Bull reined in their horses in front of a saloon named the Dog Hole just in time to see a large, heavyset man run out of the batwings holding his stomach, his face a pale shade of green. The man stopped on the boardwalk and bent over with his hands on his knees, vomiting into the dirt of the street.

Bull glanced at Hammer as he stepped down off his horse. "Mayhaps we'd better not order any food in here, Hammer," he said, staring at the mess the big man was making on the boardwalk.

Hammer shook his head as he dismounted. He hated men who couldn't hold their liquor. He and Bull went into the saloon, and found most everyone in there laughing and howling.

Hammer made his way to the bar and as he leaned

on it, he asked the barman what they'd missed that was so funny.

When the bartender told him the story of the big mountain man and his young friend who'd made the gunny eat almost two dozen eggs, Hammer turned to stare at Smoke Jensen, his lips pursed.

That might be the kind of man I'd like to have in my gang, he thought, wondering what would be the best way to approach the subject.

As he was preparing to make his way to the table, he saw a large, portly man in a three-piece suit walk into the saloon and join the mountain man at his table.

"Who's that sitting with him?" he asked the bartender when the man brought him and Bull their drinks.

"Oh, that's William Cornelius Van Horne," the bartender said. "He's in charge of building the railroad from here to the West Coast." As he continued to wipe down the bar, the bartender shook his head. "A damn fool idea if you ask me," he said.

Hammer nodded. "Then those men must work for him," he said, glad he'd held off on making his offer to the big man wearing buckskins.

"That'd be my guess," the barman said as he moved off to serve another customer.

As he sipped his whiskey, Hammer thought of another ploy he might use to get the information he needed. "Stay here, Bull. I'll be back in a few minutes."

Hammer finished his drink and made his way over to the table with Smoke and his friends.

When they looked up, Hammer spoke to Van Horne. "I hear you're in charge of building the railroad, Mr. Van Horne," he said.

Van Horne leaned back, his thumbs stuck in the armholes of his vest. "That's right, mister. Are you looking for work?" he asked.

Smoke's eyes examined Hammer, noting the way his gun was tied down low on his thigh, and also noting his hands had no calluses on them. "I don't think he's interested in working on the railroad, Bill," Smoke said. "He doesn't look like a laborer to me."

Hammer cut his eyes to Smoke and nodded. "You're right about that, mister," he said. "I'm more interested in . . . ah . . . security work if there is any."

"Security work?" Van Horne asked.

Hammer shrugged. "You know, like keeping men in line if they get too rowdy, or perhaps guard work if you have anything to guard," Hammer said.

Van Horne pursed his lips, taking in the confident manner Hammer had about him. He slowly nodded. "There might be some way I could use you. Let me talk to my foreman about it and ask me again in a day or two."

Hammer nodded and touched the brim of his hat. "Thank you kindly, Mr. Van Horne," he said, and he walked slowly back to the bar to order another drink.

Bear Tooth leaned to the side and spat onto the floor. "That galoot smells like trouble to me, Bill," he said. "I ain't one to tell nobody their business, but I'd steer clear of that sort if'n I was you."

Van Horne laughed. "Bear Tooth, if I failed to hire men simply because they looked a little rough around the edges, I wouldn't have more than a dozen men working for me instead of almost twenty thousand."

"In this case," Smoke said, "I agree with Bear Tooth, Bill. That man's eyes were dead. I have a feeling you'd be sorry if you hired him."

Van Horne stared at Smoke for a moment, his face thoughtful.

"One thing I've learned over the years, Bill," Louis said. "Smoke Jensen is the best judge of character I've ever met. If he tells you a man is bad, you can take that to the bank."

"You know I respect your opinion, Smoke, so if he does come back, I'll turn him down."

He got to his feet and said, "Now, come on over to the railroad yard. There are some people I'd like you all to meet before we start work on the surveying."

"Uh, Mr. Van Horne," Pearlie said.

"Yes, Pearlie?"

"We ain't had no lunch yet"—he grinned—"'cepting Cal an' his boiled eggs, an' it's way past noon, an' I was wondering if you had any grub over at the railroad yard."

Van Horne laughed, his ample stomach shaking. "Sure, Pearlie. As soon as we get there, I'll have Cookie make you all up something to take the edge off your appetite until we can get dinner tonight."

Cal laughed. "The only thing that'd take the edge off Pearlie's appetite, Bill, is to feed him an entire cow."

When the group arrived at the railroad yard, about a mile and a half out of town, they were all amazed to see over a thousand tents set up and thousands of men milling around a large compound that contained several odd-looking machines that Van Horne told them were used to travel down the tracks as they were laid and bring supplies to the men working the lines.

"Jiminy," Cal said, staring around wide-eyed. "How many men you got workin' for you, Bill?"

"Over twenty thousand so far," Van Horne replied.

"How come most of 'em seem to be staying out here in tents 'stead of in town?" Rattlesnake Bob asked.

Van Horne grinned. "Well, most of the men are of Chinese descent," he said, "and as you saw by the sign in the saloon, the town folk don't exactly welcome Chinese." He gave a slight shrug as he looked around the expanse of tents. "As for the others, most are men like you, Rattlesnake. They're used to living out in the open and feel cooped up when they're in a hotel room."

Louis, ever the pragmatist, glanced over at Van Horne. "You say you've got over twenty thousand men, huh, Bill?"

"That's right."

"And I suppose most of them are being paid about a dollar a day or so?"

"Well, the Chinese don't make that much, but I suppose that's about the average."

"So, when payday comes around, you're paying out almost half a million dollars a month, I guess."

Van Horne nodded. "Probably about that much, but I really don't know for certain, Louis. My job is to get the track laid. Paying them for doing it is someone else's headache."

Smoke knew Louis was trying to make a point. "What are you getting at, Louis?"

Louis shrugged. "I don't know really. It's just seeing that hard-eyed fellow at the saloon asking about security made me think that half a million dollars would make an awfully tempting pie for someone to try and cut himself a piece of."

Van Horne laughed. "Oh, well, you don't have to worry about that, Louis. The payroll train is heavily guarded, and the money is kept in a large safe in a boxcar that is bolted to the floor and is much too heavy to carry off."

"What if some robbers held a gun to the guards?" Cal asked. "Couldn't they make them open it up?"

"Not a chance," Van Horne said. "No one on the train has the combination to the safe, so even if they wanted to, they couldn't get into it."

"That makes me feel a lot better," Pearlie said, "'cause now I know I'm gonna get paid for all this work we're gonna be doing." He sighed. "Now, if we could just get fed, I'd feel even better!"

Van Horne laughed again and slapped Pearlie on the back. "Well, then, come on, men. I'll introduce you to Cookie and see if he can find you all something to eat."

"That's good," Pearlie said with a grin. "If there's one man on a crew I like to know personally it's the cook."

"That's a fact!" Cal said. "And I can tell you one thing for sure, he's gonna get awfully tired of your face hanging around asking him when the next meal's gonna be ready."

13

Later that evening, Hammer sent Bull off to have supper with some of the men at a local restaurant while he went back to the Dog Hole to see if perhaps the man named Van Horne was there. He wanted to see if the man had considered his request for security work.

He stood inside the batwings for a minute, looking around the place, but didn't see either Van Horne or any of the other men who'd been with him at noon.

As he was glancing around, he saw a portly man in a dark suit and bowler hat having a drink at a table by himself. The man had the cold, calculating eyes of a star-packer of some sort, so Hammer decided to approach him and see what he could learn.

He walked over to the table and said, "Howdy."

The man looked up from his drink and turned his black eyes on Hammer, no expression of welcome in them.

"Do I know you?" he asked coldly.

Hammer shrugged and shook his head. "I don't think so, but you have the look of a lawman about you," he said, forcing his lips into an innocent smile. "And since I used to carry a badge myself, I thought if I was right, I'd offer to buy you a drink."

The man's expression softened a little, though his eyes remained suspicious. Lawmen weren't always welcome in frontier towns, and it was wise to be cautious when talking to strangers, especially in saloons. The man leaned back and let his hand drop to his waist, and Hammer could see the butt of a pistol in a shoulder holster under his coat.

"You're partially right," the man said. "I carry a badge, but it's private. I work for the Pinkerton Agency."

"Close enough," Hammer said, signaling to the bartender to bring them another round. "My name's John Brody," Hammer said, picking a name out of the air. "I used to work for the hanging judge over to Fort Smith, Arkansas, a while back."

"Oh, Judge Isaac Parker," the man said. "I met him once. He's as hard as a granite boulder."

"You got that right," Hammer said, grinning. All he really knew about Judge Parker was what he'd read in the *Grand Forks Gazette*.

"My name's Albert Knowles," the Pinkerton man said.

After the bartender's limping son brought their drinks, Hammer said, "By the way I thought the Pinkertons only worked in the States."

"That's changing," Knowles said, upending his drink and draining it in one swallow. After he wiped his mouth with the back of his hand, he continued. "Now that Canada is getting strongly into the railroad-building business, James Hill, who we've done a lot of work for in the States, has decided to use us for his security force." He added, "That's how the Pinkertons got started in the first place, working as railroad detectives."

Hammer nodded encouragingly. "More business is always good, I expect."

"Damn right," Knowles said, and this time he was the one that signaled the bartender for another round.

"I saw all those men camped out by the rail yard," Hammer said. "There must be thousands of them."

Knowles nodded. "Almost twenty thousand," he said, "though most of 'em are Chinee."

"Damn, that must mean a huge payroll."

Knowles leaned forward and said in a low voice, "You have no idea, John."

"That's a big responsibility, guarding that much money," Hammer said in an offhand manner, as if he were just making small talk. "I handled some pretty big jobs as a marshal, but I don't know as I'd want to take that on."

"Naw, it's not so hard," Knowles said, beginning to slur his words a bit as he took another large drink of whiskey. He whispered, "I got ten men hiding in the boxcar with the safe, all armed with the latest Henry repeating rifles and Winchesters, and I got another ten riding in the car behind, with horses all saddled and ready just in case they need to take out after some would-be robbers." He leaned back and grinned. "A few men tried to rob us on the first run last month, but we took care of them."

Hammer grinned, one lawman to another. "What'd you do, Al?"

"The ones we didn't kill outright, we strung up to the nearest telegraph pole and watched 'em dance till they was deader than yesterday's news. Then we brought them into town and set them up in caskets in front of the local undertaker's office, with a sign on them that said this is what happens to train robbers."

"I guess a man would have to be crazy to try and hit one of your payroll trains after seeing that," Hammer said, waving the waiter over for another round.

"Yeah, that's why we haven't had no more trouble since that first time," Knowles said. "And if it was up to me, those bodies'd still be there, though I suspect they'd be a mite ripe by now," he said, chuckling drunkenly at his joke. "But Mr. Van Horne ordered them taken down and buried over in Boot Hill," Knowles added. "Shame too, it was some of my best work."

"So this Mr. Van Horne don't appreciate you, huh?" Hammer asked, trying to get a rise out of Knowles.

"No, no, it ain't that," Knowles said. "It's just that Mr. Van Horne is a real decent man, though he's hard as nails if you don't do your job."

He finished off his drink and got unsteadily to his feet. "Thanks for the drinks, John. Be seein' you."

Hammer nodded as Knowles walked off, veering to one side as he went through the batwings. A slow smile spread across his face. "You're right about that, Al," he said in a low voice to himself. "You'll be seeing me again, and a lot sooner than you think."

Hammer leaned back in his chair and sipped his drink, trying to figure a way around twenty Pinkerton men so he could get the gold they were guarding.

While Hammer was pumping the Pinkerton man for information, Van Horne was treating Smoke and his friends to dinner at the restaurant attached to the Rooster's Roost Hotel.

Van Horne noticed Bear Tooth and Red Bingham glancing nervously around the room and whispering to one another.

"Bear Tooth, Red," Van Horne asked, "is anything wrong?"

"Uh, Bill, it's just that we're not used to eatin' indoors," Bear Tooth answered.

"Yeah," Red added, "it don't seem natural somehow."

"But you ate in the car on the train," Pearlie said.

"That was different," Bear said. "Then it was just us eating, kind'a like being in camp with your partners." He looked around. "Here there's a whole passel of strangers around watchin' us eat."

Louis, who was holding a glass of real brandy in his hands, not the homemade variety he'd had at the Dog Hole, looked up as he swirled the amber liquid around the snifter. "Oh, you'll get used to it, boys. The only difference from eating outdoors is there are far fewer bugs to bother you while you eat."

Van Horne laughed. "Yes, but don't get too used to it, men. We're going to be taking off in a day or two for the wilds of Canada to do some surveying."

He looked up as a tall, slim man wearing buckskins entered the door to the restaurant and looked around. Van Horne held up his hand and waved him over.

As he approached their table, Smoke noticed he had the sun-wrinkled face and observant eyes of a mountain man, but unlike most of those he'd known in the past, the man's beard was short and well trimmed.

"Gentlemen," Van Horne said, getting to his feet and holding out his hand to the newcomer, "this is Tom Wilson. He's the leader of our surveying crew."

"So, you're to be our new boss, huh?" Smoke said with a smile as he got to his feet and held out his hand.

Wilson returned the smile, though it looked like it was an effort. "Yeah, I guess so," he said, taking Smoke's hand.

"I'm Smoke Jensen," Smoke said, and then he introduced the others at the table, who all nodded and then went back to their food and drink.

Wilson's eyes took in the other mountain men at the table, and then moved over Smoke's broad shoulders and muscled arms. "You boys all look like you got some hair on you," Wilson said, and then he hesitated, glancing at Louis and his fancy clothes and at Cal and Pearlie. "At least, most of you do," he added with a half smile.

Smoke took his meaning. "Oh, by the way, Tom,

don't let Louis's clothes or the boys' young years fool you," Smoke said. "They've all been tested by fire, and I'll guarantee you they're up to the job."

Wilson stared at Smoke for a moment, his eyes narrowed, and then he snapped his fingers. "I've been trying to remember where I've heard the name Smoke Jensen before," he said.

"Oh?" Smoke inquired.

"Yeah. It was last year, right after the spring thaw, and I was up in the mountains just north of here checking out the elk herds, fixin' to do some hunting, when I ran across one of the oldest men I've ever met who wasn't sitting in a rocking chair on a porch somewhere."

Smoke's heart began to beat rapidly, knowing what was coming. "He give you a name?"

Wilson grinned. "Yeah, the old beaver said he was called Preacher."

The name Preacher got the immediate attention of all of the mountain men at the table, Preacher being a legend among them.

Wilson reached behind him, took a chair from a nearby table, and pulled it around, sitting on it backward with his arms folded over the back of the chair. "Well, one thing led to another and we made a camp together up there in the High Lonesome. This Preacher, he made me some coffee that'd take the hair off a bear hide, and then he proceeded to tell me he'd come all the way up here to Canada from down Colorado way 'cause it was getting too crowded in the mountains down there. He said you couldn't hardly trap any beaver for tripping over pilgrims and such all the time."

"Jesus," Bear Tooth whispered, staring at Wilson. "Ol' Preacher must be in his eighties at least by now."

"I'd just assumed the old codger had holed up somewheres an' died," Red Bingham said, equally awed by Wilson's story.

Wilson nodded. "You're right, men. Preacher had to be at least eighty, and he looked like he'd been rode hard and put up wet besides. Anyway, some of the tales he told me I put down to typical mountain-man exaggeration, especially the ones about a young pilgrim he'd met years ago who was fast as greased lightning with a handgun and, to hear Preacher tell it, as hard as an anvil."

Rattlesnake Bob nodded. "Well, sonny boy, if'n he was talking about Smoke here, you can take what he said to heart, no matter how outrageous it sounded."

Smoke smiled and shook his head. "I wish I'd been here to see him. We had some fun times in the old days, hairy as hell, but fun nevertheless."

Wilson pulled a canvas pouch out of the pocket of his buckskins and began to build himself a cigarette. When it was done, he screwed it into the corner of his mouth and lit it with a lucifer he struck on his pants leg.

As he let the smoke drift out of his nostrils, he looked at Smoke. "If half of what he said about you was true, Smoke, it's gonna be a pleasure to ride the peaks with you."

Smoke laughed. "And if it's not?"

Wilson shrugged. "Then you probably won't make it across the mountains, and neither will the rest of you." He took a deep drag, leaving the cigarette in his mouth as he talked around the smoke. "Boys, the mountains in Colorado ain't nothing compared to what you're gonna see up here. Besides the Stony Indians, who'd just as soon scalp you and eat your heart as to look at you, we got just about ever kind of wild creature ever born with fangs and claws up here. There ain't been more'n a handful of whites to even try to cross the territory where we're going, an' half of them never lived to tell about what they'd seen."

"If the surveying job is so difficult and dangerous, why did you agree to ramrod the team?" Louis asked, a bit angry at the way Wilson was talking down to them as if they'd never been in dangerous situations before.

Wilson shrugged. "Hell, I was gonna be up in the mountains anyway, since that's what I do, so why not take the railroad's money for doing what comes natural?"

He hesitated, looking around the table. "The question is, since you all seem to have at least most of your senses, why have you agreed to take such a job on?"

Smoke stared at Wilson, wondering why the man had so little regard for others. "Probably for the same reason Preacher told you he was up here," Smoke said. "Colorado's getting crowded and most of the Indians have been either wiped out or beaten into submission. And like you say, we'd be up in the mountains anyway, so why not see some new country and get paid for it?"

Wilson nodded as he stubbed the cigarette out in an ashtray on the table. "Good enough then. I'll see you men 'bout sunup in the morning, and we'll get started going toward the mountains to see if we can find a pass for Mr. Van Horne to drive his iron horse through."

"By the way, Tom," Smoke said, "whatever happened to Preacher after your camp together?"

Wilson shook his head and smiled. "Hell if I know. When I woke up the next morning, the coffee was made and there was no sign of the old man. He'd vanished into the woods as if he'd never even been there. I tried to track him, and believe me when I say I can track a fart in a windstorm, and I couldn't even tell which way he'd gone."

Smoke smiled. "That's Preacher, all right. He once told me he could walk across mud without leaving a print, and damned if I don't believe it."

14

The next morning, Smoke got up and dressed and went to wake the rest of the group just before dawn. After collecting Cal and Pearlie and Louis, he knocked on the doors to the other four mountain men's hotel rooms and received no answer.

Cautiously, he opened the door to hear Tooth and Red Bingham's room and entered, his hand near the butt of his pistol. There was no telling what trouble the men might have gotten into during the night. They were, after all, not used to city life and its many dangers. As he looked around, he was surprised to find that the beds hadn't been slept in. He moved further into the room, and he heard the sound of voices coming in through the open window.

He slipped his pistol out of its holster and eased over to the window and peered out, finding Red and Bear Tooth just getting out of sleeping blankets they'd set up on the balcony running alongside the building.

He shook his head, smiling as he stuck his Colt back into its holster on his right hip. It was just like mountain men to prefer sleeping outside on a balcony under the stars to a soft, comfortable bed inside.

"Morning, boys," Smoke said, leaning his head out of the window.

Bear Tooth looked up, yawning and stretching. "Howdy, Smoke. Looks like it's gonna be a humdinger of a day," he said, peering up at a clear sky still full of stars.

"I reckon it does," Smoke agreed. "Didn't you boys find it a mite chilly out here last night? The temperature must've been well below zero."

Bear looked over at Red and shrugged. "I didn't notice it being particularly cold. Did you, Red?"

Red didn't bother to answer, just shook his head and yawned.

Smoke leaned a little further out of the window and looked to the side. Just down the balcony, in front of the window to their room, lay Rattlesnake Bob and Bobcat Bill. At least Smoke thought it was them. It was hard to tell, for they were burrowed deep in heavy blankets and only their outlines could be seen.

He jerked his head to the side. "Better go wake up those slugabeds down the way, or before long we'll be burning daylight," he said to Bear Tooth.

Bear Tooth grinned. "Them always were lazy layabouts, ever since I knowed 'em," he said as he got to his feet and walked down the balcony.

He stirred the sleeping form of Rattlesnake Bob, and was rewarded with the barrel of an old Walker Colt poking out of the blankets at his face.

He chuckled and pushed the gun aside with his foot, "Don't go pointin' that hogleg at me 'less'n you want it shoved where the sun don't shine, Rattlesnake."

"Then don't go kickin' at me with them dirty boots of your'n, you polecat!" Rattlesnake growled in a phlegmy voice as he struggled up out of his blankets.

"Hell, somebody's got to do it, else you'd likely sleep till noon, an' Smoke says *breakfast is* waiting."

"Did I hear somebody say breakfast?" Bobcat Bill said, jumping up out of his blankets and onto his feet. He was instantly awake, a trait soon learned by mountain men, else they didn't survive long in the wilderness.

As usual, all of the mountain men had gone to sleep in their clothes, as they did out in the High Lonesome.

Rattlesnake grimaced. "Just like in camp, boys," he said to Bear. "Bobcat don't hardly ever stir from his blankets till I've got breakfast on the fire."

Bobcat looked over at his partner and grinned. "An' I do so appreciate the fine cuisine you fix too, podna," he growled. "Especially that stew you make that's just got to have skunk meat in it."

In less than an hour, they were all sitting around a table in the huge mess tent in the rail yard, stuffing down flapjacks and eggs and bacon and beans as fast as they could. Pearlie had even taken a few sinkers and slathered thick white gravy over them, and was eating them as well.

Van Horne appeared, unshaven, his clothes rumpled and untidy.

"What happened to you, Bill?" Smoke asked as Van Horne grabbed a mug of coffee and drank it down.

"This is a mite too early for me, Smoke. I usually wait until at least dawn to crawl out of bed"—he smiled—"but then, I also usually work until after midnight when I'm in the middle of laying track."

"Where's Tom Wilson?" Smoke asked. "I figured he'd have his tent here near the camp."

Van Horne shook his head. "Not Tom. He's not exactly what I'd call the most sociable fellow I've ever met. He usually makes his own camp a ways away from the rest of the crew. Says it's just about all he can do to stand other people's company all day without having to listen to them snore all night."

"You mean he just ups and heads off when the day's work is done?" Cal asked, his mouth full of bacon.

"That's about the size of it," Van Horne answered. "Ol' Tom's a real loner."

"It ain't that I'm a loner," Wilson said from the tent door as he entered and picked up a plate. "It's just that I ain't found all that many people I enjoy being around much is all."

Cal watched wide-eyed as Tom piled on even more food than Pearlie had. When the mountain man sat down, Cal said, "Jiminy, Mr. Wilson, I ain't never seen nobody eat more'n Pearlie here."

Wilson looked up from pouring a half quart of maple syrup on his pancakes. "One thing you learn out here in the High Lonesome, young'un," he said, "is to eat as much as you can whenever you got the chance, 'cause you never know when you'll get your next chance to eat."

Cal laughed. "Heck fire, my friend Pearlie's been following that advice as long as I've knowed him, an' he don't even live up in the mountains."

While they finished their breakfast, Van Horne pulled out a wrinkled hand-drawn map from his coat pocket. He handed the map to Smoke. "I've drawn a rough sketch of what we know about the mountain ranges to the north and west of Winnipeg, and I've penciled in a rough line where I want the tracks to go, with provisions, of course, for any detours we might have to make around peaks or valleys in the mountain range."

Tom Wilson glanced up from his food long enough to pull several sheets of paper from his breast pocket and pass them over to Smoke. "Here's some more maps for you, Smoke. They detail several routes explored by others some years back."

Smoke looked at the maps. They were labeled with the names Dawson, Palliser, and Fleming. "Which of these do you think is the best bet to try, Tom?" he asked.

"Won't know till we get out there, but from what

I've read in the journals of the men involved, I think Fleming's more northern route offers the best chance of finding some passes through the Selkirk and Caribou Mountains."

Smoke grinned. "Then I guess we'll try the northern routes first, assuming we can get through the snow-packs."

Wilson grunted. "And assuming we can find suitable portages across the rivers that dot the area."

"Rivers?" Pearlie asked, looking up from his breakfast for the first time since he sat down. "You mean we're gonna have to cross freezing rivers on this"

"'Less you can fly, boy, that's about the size of it," Wilson replied dryly.

"Just how many men are you planning on taking with us on this little jaunt?" Louis asked as he sipped his after-breakfast coffee and smoked a long black cigar.

Wilson paused in his eating. "Just three in addition to us here at the table. William and Thomas McCardell and Frank McCabe will be good men to have with us, I think. They're experienced surveyors, and if we run into the Stony Indians, we're gonna need every gun we can carry to get us through."

"Do you think there's much chance of that?" Pearlie asked, a worried look on his face.

Wilson looked at him and grinned. "Do you think there's much chance of it snowing up here in the winter?" he asked in answer to Pearlie's question. When Pearlie didn't answer, he added, "It's not a question of whether we run into the Indians, Pearlie, but of when it's gonna happen."

"The trick to fightin' Injuns, young'un," Bear said around his food, "is to see them 'fore they see you, 'cause if'n it's the other way 'round, there won't be much fightin' goin' on, just a lotta dyin'."

* * *

While Smoke and his men were eating breakfast, Hammer Hammerick and his gang were stationed alongside the railroad tracks leading into Winnipeg, about ten miles out of the town.

He'd worked out a plan to deal with the Pinkerton men stationed on the train as guards, and he was anxious to see if it would work.

He had his thirty men lined up in wooded areas on either side of the track. As the rails made a long, sweeping curve to the right, he'd had his men loosen the tracks just enough to derail the train, but leave them in place so the engineer wouldn't see anything amiss. Each of his men had been supplied with several sticks of dynamite with fuses attached.

As the engine made the curve, its wheels jumped the tack and the cars following began a crazy dance, waving back and forth and tipping first to one side and hen to the other as they ran off the tracks and onto the soft dirt alongside. The train soon completely derailed, sliding to the side and plowing twin furrows in the soft earth for over a hundred yards, before the engine and the cars immediately behind it slowly toppled to the side, rupturing the boiler with a loud explosion and great plumes of steam billowing into the chilly air.

When the rest of the cars had come to a stop, Hammer and his men rode their horses out of the woods and galloped toward the disabled train, lighting fuses from cigars in their mouths and pitching them toward the cars containing the Pinkerton men, many of whom could be heard screaming in pain and terror from the piles of wreckage alongside the tracks.

The wooden cars exploded into pieces, and men and horses on the train screamed in further agony as their bodies were ripped apart by the force of the explosions.

Hammer reined his horse in next to the boxcar containing the large iron safe and the dead and wounded bodies of the Pinkerton agents lying scattered all around the ruined car amid body parts, blood, and dead horses.

As he dismounted, he looked around at the men on the ground. There were over twenty men, some still alive, partially buried in the splintered pieces of wood from the car.

He, like all of his men, had covered his face with a bandanna, so he didn't feel the need to execute the wounded men, but he was careful to make sure none were in any shape to take a shot at him with the rifles most had nearby.

"Bull," he called over his shoulder to Bannion, who was just behind him. "Make sure you and the men pick up the weapons, especially from the wounded men. We wouldn't want them taking potshots at us while we get the safe open."

Ignoring the pitiful crying and moaning of injured men all around him, he climbed up on the stack of broken lumber, pulling boards aside until he was standing next to the big iron safe lying on its side in the wreckage.

After examining the safe's door for a moment, he saw that it had a combination lock on it, just as Albert Knowles had said it did.

He reached into the gunnysack he was carrying, and took out a stack of dynamite sticks he'd tied together with a piece of twine. He wedged the dynamite under the door just next to the dial on the lock, and took his cigar out of his mouth.

"You ready, Bull?" he called.

Bull, who was standing nearby with several other members of the gang with their arms full of new rifles, took one look at the large stack of dynamite and began to walk rapidly away from the car.

"Yeah, Boss, just let me get a little bit farther away 'fore you light that bundle."

As Hammer put the bright orange tip of the cigar

against the fuse, a wounded man lying a few yards away croaked, "No, mister, please don't." The man struggled to hold out his right arm, which was bloody and mangled from the explosions.

"Sorry, pal," Hammer said as he began to trot away from the dynamite. "Guess this'll teach you not to work for the Pinkertons no more."

Hammer crouched down behind a nearby overturned car with his men, and covered his ears with his hands, waiting for the explosion.

A few moments later, the dynamite blew, with a resounding clap of thunder that shook the ground and raised a cloud of dust that billowed out and engulfed Hammer and his men.

Broken boards, body parts, and even one of the wheels of the car were blown into the air and rained down around them like hailstones

"Jesus, Boss," Bull said as the heavy iron wheel of the car landed a few feet away from them with a loud thud. "Maybe you shouldn't've used so much dynamite."

Hammer grimaced. Bull was right, but he knew he'd had to be sure the amount was enough to open the safe.

He stepped out around the edge of the car they'd been hiding behind, and walked through the dust cloud toard what remained of the boxcar. Hammer was surprised to see a large crater over three feet deep where the safe had been. The wounded man who'd been near the safe was nowhere to be seen. He'd been blown to bits by the explosion.

The safe was lying open, its door bent and twisted with one hinge completely off. Piles of paper were burning, small bits of the bills rising on heat waves into the air, glowing like fireflies on a summer night.

"Damn it!" Hammer said, running over to try and salvage what he could of the payroll. Knowles hadn't told him the railroad was using paper money to pay the railroad workers their salaries. He'd just assumed it would be in gold or silver coin.

"Where's the gold, Boss?" Bull asked, standing behind Hammer as he knelt and tried to snatch some of the bills out of the safe before they all burned pp. Ignoring the fire, he stuck his hands in the remains of the safe and pulled out several tightly wrapped bundles of hundred-dollar bills.

"There isn't any, Bull," Hammer said disgustedly. "Those assholes are paying the men with Canadian paper money, not gold." He glanced down at the packets of money in his scorched hands and made a quick calculation.

"Aw, shit," Bull said. "You mean we did all this for nothin'?"

Hammer stood up, smiling and holding up the bundles of bills he'd been able to salvage from the fire.

He took a deep breath. "Not exacdy for nothing," he replied. "It looks like we got about fifty thousand dollars here, boys, give or take a few thousand. Not exactly bad pay for one day's work."

Juan Sanchez, one of the gang members, scowled. "*Sí*, but you said there would be over five hundred thousand in it for us," he groused.

Hammer turned hard eyes on Sanchez. "You don't want your share, Juanito, that's fine by me. Course, I'll bet you can't remember the last time you had over a thousand dollars cash in your hands at one time, can you?"

When Sanchez shrugged and grinned, Hammer turned and looked at the bodies scattered around the wreckage, saying to Bull, "Send the man out to search the bodies. Take anything of value, including watches and any guns they're carrying."

Bull made a face. "But Boss, some of them bodies have been torn apart. We'll get all messed up with blood and guts an' stuff."

Hammer glared at Bull. "Just do it, Bull. You've had blood on your hands before, and after all, you're being paid pretty damn good for it." He took a deep breath, trying to calm down and hide his disappointment at the small amount of money they'd gotten. He added, "Pretty soon they're gonna realize this train is behind schedule and they're gonna be sending a posse out here to see where it is. I'd kind'a like to be long gone by then."

"Sure thing, Boss," Bull said, an expression of distaste on his face as he glanced around at the bodies lying all around them. "I'll get the men right on it."

15

Xiang Chang walked slowly through deep forest on top of a hill. His head was bent down and he stared at the ground, searching for the big, brown mushrooms his friends loved so much when chopped and fried in his ancient wok and mixed with rice and fish heads.

So far today, he had found almost three pounds of the mushrooms. Dinner tonight would be special indeed.

In the distance, he heard the mournful-sounding cry of the large steam engine coming toward him. He paused in his search to stand and peer through the trees to watch it approach, billowing huge clouds of steam from the turret on the top of the engine.

Xiang ducked as the engine suddenly lurched to the side and slid slowly off the tracks, plowing up twin furrows of earth with its wheels until it toppled to the side and slid to a stop.

Huge flames leaped from the engine as the boiler exploded and tore the engine to pieces.

His hands went to his mouth when he saw dozens of men rush from the underbrush on either side of the rail tracks and begin to throw smoking sticks at the cars that had followed the engine off the tracks.

Several more explosions boomed across the valley between the ruined train and Xiang as the rail cars jumped and came apart in the air under the influence of the dynamite wielded by the men swarming toward the train.

Xiang winced at the sight of so many bodies being thrown into the air, and he dropped his precious sack of mushrooms and ran toward the mule that had carried him from the rail camp. He had to get back and warn the big boss man about what had happened to his shiny new train.

Tom Wilson had the men lined up and ready to depart, along with several packhorses loaded with supplies, extra ammunition, and tents, when Bill Van Horne came running toward them, waving his arms and shouting for them to wait.

Wilson pulled his horse's head around and sat in the saddle, leaning forward with his arms crossed over the pommel as he waited to see what was so all-fired important as to hold up the surveying party.

Van Horne stopped running when he got to them and leaned over, his hands on his knees, breathing heavily.

"Slow down a mite, Bill," Wilson said with a smile. Van Horne was much too fat to be exerting himself like this. "You're gonna kill yourself runnin' like that."

Two smallish Chinese men were close behind Van Horne, and stood patiently, waiting for him to ask them to tell their story.

Finally, after Van Horne had caught his breath, he straightened up. "We got trouble, Tom. Bad trouble with the payroll train."

Wilson grinned. "What else is new, Bill? There's always something goin' on out here. What happened? Didn't they send enough money from headquarters?"

"It's not that, Tom," Van Horne said, his face serious and grim. "The payroll train is overdue and this man has some information about it."

Wilson and the others turned their gaze to the two Chinese men. One, who looked older than the other, spoke. "This man is Xiang Chang," he said, inclining his head toward the other man. "He speaks no English, so I will translate his story for you. He was out a few miles from town picking wild mushrooms to use in the camp cooking, when he saw a group of men attack the payroll train. He says there was a large explosion, as if many sticks of dynamite were used, and it caused the train to run off the tracks and turn onto its side. Soon, further explosions occurred and several of the train cars were blown up into many pieces."

"Tell them about the men on the train," Van Horne said, his eyes tortured and sad.

The first man spoke to the other in Chinese for several seconds, and then replied in English, "He says there were very many bodies lying on the ground among the wreckage. It was his opinion that few survived the attack."

"How many men were in the attacking party?" Smoke asked, joining in the discussion.

After a few more words between the two in Chinese, the interpreter answered, "He didn't count them, but said more than two dozen."

Van Horne said, "That's enough, Chiu. We won't need you any longer."

After the two Chinese left, he turned to the group. "Almost every one of my security men was on that train," he said.

"Why are you telling us this, Bill?" Wilson asked. "We're a surveying party, not part of your security forces."

Van Horne took a deep breath and turned his attention to Smoke. "Uh, I was wondering if you'd be willing to head out there and see what you could do, Smoke. You have a certain . . . reputation for handling men like this, and since my Pinkertons are probably out of commission, I'm in desperate need of someone who knows his way around a gun to take charge of this mess."

Smoke pursed his lips, thinking for a moment. "How thout if I take Louis and Cal and Pearlie with me, leaving the mountain men to help Tom with the survey until we can get back and catch up to them?"

Van Horne glanced over at Wilson. "That all right with you, Tom?"

Wilson shrugged. "Sure. We ain't gonna get into any hairy areas for at least a week. The first part of Fleming's trail is pretty straightforward until we get up into the mountains, an' I'm gonna be leaving a blazed trail for the railroad workers to follow anyhow. I don't see where it'd be a problem, long as they catch up to us 'fore we get into Stony Indian territory."

Smoke nodded. He looked around. "That all right with you?" he asked his friends.

Louis grinned. "Hell, yes. I'm ready for a little excitement, so this will be a pleasure."

Cal and Pearlie nodded. "We're with you, Smoke, an' where you go, we go," Pearlie said, his jaw tight and set, while Cal just nodded his agreement.

Smoke looked back down at Van Horne. "Get me another packhorse and load it up with plenty of ammunition, some extra firearms, a Sharps if you have one, and enough food and supplies for two weeks. By then, we'll either have them, or they'll be long gone."

"All right," Van Horne said. "You and your men head on out to the wreckage site, and I'll be right behind you with some wagons and our medical people to see how many of the Pinkertons we can save."

Tom Wilson walked his horse over to Smoke's mount. He stuck his hand out. "Ride with your guns loose and loaded up six and six, Smoke," he said. "Anyone who'd kill that many men just to steal some payroll ain't to be trifled with."

Smoke nodded. "I've met plenty of that kind before, Tom," he said, his eyes flat and dangerous-looking. "I know how to handle them."

Bear Tooth called, "Don't give 'em no quarter, Smoke boy. Just shoot 'em down like the animals they is."

Ten minutes later, Van Horne had two packhorses loaded with what Smoke had asked for, and Smoke, Cal, Pearlie, and Louis put their spurs to their mounts, the pack animals following on dally ropes wrapped around Cal and Pearlie's saddle horns.

Van Horne told them to just follow the tracks out of town and they'd come to the ambush site within a few miles, according to the Chinese man.

They rode on the cleared area right next to the train tracks so they wouldn't have to slow down to weave through the forests and woods that were thick in the area.

It took them less than an hour, pushing the horses as fast as they could, before they could see dark smoke rising on afternoon air currents to cover the sky like storm clouds ahead of them.

Smoke slowed his mount and loosened the hammer thongs on his pistols as he pulled his Winchester '73 from its saddle boot and jacked a shell into the chamber.

Cal wrinkled his nose as he checked the loads in his own rifle. "Jiminy, what's that godawful smell?" he asked no one in particular.

Pearlie looked at Smoke before he replied, "That's the smell of burning flesh, Cal, an' once you smell it, it's a smell you never forget."

Smoke and the others walked their horses around a turn in the tracks just in time to see a group of men mounting up onto horses and beginning to ride off in a direction away from them.

Pearlie jumped off his horse, pulled the Sharps Big Fifty from its scabbard on the packhorse, and laid it across the rear of the animal, taking aim at one of the fleeing outlaws.

"Hold on, Pearlie," Smoke said.

"But I can get one or two 'fore they get out of range," Pearlie protested, his eye still on the raised sights of the Sharps.

"Yeah, but then they'll know we're on their trail," Smoke said. "Let 'em go for now. We'll follow them until they make camp, and then we'll be able to set up an ambush and take out more than one or two before hey know what hit them."

"Oh," Pearlie said, putting the Sharps back in its rifle boot. "I never thought of that."

"Smoke's right, Pearlie," Louis said, a pair of binoculars to his eyes. "It appears they have us outnumbered five or six to one, so we're going to have to outthink them as well as outfight them if we're to have any chance of bringing them to justice."

As the robbers disappeared from sight, Smoke said, "Let's head on down there and see if there's anyone left alive that we can help until Bill gets here with the doctor."

Louis moved his binoculars as he surveyed the scene down by the rail tracks.

"I think I can see a few men moving, but they all look like they're in a bad way," he said. As he surveyed the extent of the wreckage, he added, "It'll be a miracle if more than a handful are still alive."

"I wonder why they didn't kill all of the wounded men when they had the chance," Pearlie said.

"They probably wore masks and didn't think it was necessary," Smoke said. "But hopefully, some of the wounded may have heard or seen something that will help us as we track the bastards down."

Cal shook his head as he followed Smoke down the rise toward the wrecked train.

"I gotta tell you, Smoke," he said, his voice low. "I ain't lookin' forward to this job."

Smoke nodded. He knew the boy had probably never seen anything like what they were about to experience down below, and truth to tell, he wasn't much looking forward to dealing with this many casualties either.

16

Hammer and his men, their horses loaded down with rifles, handguns, and the personal property of the men they'd robbed on the train, made their way up slopes still partially covered with snow toward the higher elevations of the hills around the ambush site.

Bull Bannion twisted in his saddle and looked at the rail behind them. "We're leaving a pretty easy trail for a posse to follow, Hammer," he said.

"Don't worry about it, Bull," Hammer replied, glancing at the sky, which was full of dark, roiling clouds. "Looks to me like we got us a spring storm coming 'fore too long. By the time it clears enough for a party to catch up with us, we'll be across the border and back in Noyes."

Bull shivered in his heavy overcoat. "Yeah, an' with the temperature being so cold for this time of year, it'll probably be snow rather than rain."

"That should take care of any tracks we leave," Hammer said. "And judging by the number of Pinkertons on that train, I don't expect the railroad men are gonna have too many security people left to take off after us anyhow."

"So, you're plannin' on headin' straight on back to Noyes?" Bull asked as he pulled his coat tighter around him to ward off the blast of frigid air coming from the north.

"That's right. We need to lay low for a couple of days, but I plan to come right back here within the week," Hammer replied.

"How come?"

"Think about it, son. We just destroyed the entire payroll for the railroad workers back there. They ain't gonna take kindly to being told there won't be no pay this week."

"So?"

Hammer sighed. Bull was dumber than a stump for sure. "Well, Bull, they're gonna have to send another train right away, just as soon as they can get those tracks fixed. I thought when they do, we might just set up another ambush, maybe a mite further back up the line, and see if this time we can get the money outta the safe without burning it up."

"But Boss, won't they be expectin' us to do that very thing?"

Hammer shook his head. "No, I 'spect they'll think we took off for parts unknown, especially if they follow the direction of our tracks and see we headed back across the border, But even if they do, where are they gonna get another carload of guards so fast?" he asked. "Pinkerton men don't exactly grow on trees around here."

"Maybe they'll just use railroad workers as guards," Bull offered.

"Yeah, you're probably right, Bull. But railroad workers ain't exactly experienced gunmen, now are they? Once we blow up that car and commence to shootin', my guess is they'll hightail it for the nearest cover, leaving the safe to us."

Bull nodded at this expression of wisdom from his boss. "So, I guess that means we're gonna be camping out tonight in this storm that's fixing to hit."

"That's right, since there's no way we can make it all

the way back to Noyes today. Once we get far enough away from the tracks and back in these thick woods, we'll fix us a big fire and pitch our tents real close to it. This time of year the storm shouldn't last overly long."

"I hope you're right, Boss, 'cause I don't relish sitting through a real winter norther out in the open." Bull said, shivering in his coat.

Hammer grinned. "Just keep thinking of fifty thousand dollars, Bull," he said. "That ought'a warm you up better than a campfire."

As soon as the outlaws were out of sight, Smoke and his men came down off the hillock overlooking the railroad tracks and approached the wreckage site.

"Jesus!" Louis whispered at the number of bodies lying scattered on the ground.

They got down off their horses and began to move among the dead and wounded. Their horses snorted and shied at the smell of so much blood and at the sight of so many horses and men torn apart by the explosions.

When the group would find men still alive, the boys would try to make them comfortable, covering them with blankets against the cold and telling them help was on the way.

If the men weren't too badly injured, they would move them over closer to the pile of boards that was all that was left of the boxcar to get them out of the wind and elements, for Smoke had told them a storm was on the way and they needed to get the men under cover if at all possible.

The final tally was eighteen dead, six injured so badly it was doubtful if they would survive, and five with non-life-threatening wounds.

When they had done all they could to stop the bleeding and get the wounded covered, Smoke asked Cal to start a fire near where the men lay to give them some warmth and to get some coffee brewing. The more seriously wounded he gave small drinks of water and whiskey mixed together to help ease their pain.

While Cal and Pearlie gave the others coffee when it was ready, Smoke and Louis stood nearby, smoking cigars as they drank some coffee in tin mugs, cradling the mugs in their hands to keep them warm.

Louis glanced back over his shoulder at the bodies lying dead all around them. "I've seen a lot of bad men in my time out West, Smoke, but I don't know as I've ever seen anyone who could do this and just ride away as if nothing had happened," he said, a look of deep disgust on his face.

"I know what you mean, Louis," Smoke said, his expression grim as he sipped his coffee. It burned all the way down, and made his already upset stomach burn like it was on fire.

He took a deep breath, trying to get the stench of burnt flesh out of his throat, and turned to look at the dead bodies. "I want you all to remember this sight when we finally catch up with the men that did this, 'cause I do not intend to give them any quarter or mercy." He turned his eyes to Louis. "And if any of you have any reservations about what I'm going to do, you'd better head on back to the rail yard with Van Horne and the wounded men when he gets here."

Louis shook his head. "Don't worry about me, Smoke. Whatever you've got planned for the bastards that did this is too good for them." Louis's cultured face had turned grim and his eyes looked like those of a hawk, black and ferocious and unforgiving.

Smoke's lips curled in a savage grin of anticipation. "Just remember you said that, pal, when the blood starts to flow and the outlaws' bodies start to pile up."

Within an hour, Van Horne showed up with ten covered wagons and a doctor and nurse, along with ten hard-looking men, to take care of the dead and wounded.

As the doctor and nurse began to examine and care for the wounded, Van Horne and the other men moved among the dead bodies of the Pinkerton agents who'd been killed by the outlaws.

Two of the men helping put the bodies in a wagon stopped and bent over, vomiting on the cold ground in response to the carnage around them. Many of the dead were in pieces; body parts blown off by the force of the explosions that tore the train apart. Blood was everywhere, staining the mounds of snow scarlet, and the smell of burning flesh was making everyone edgy and nervous.

Van Horne, a man not unused to violence, stood looking around with tears in his eyes. "I cannot imagine the depth of evil of the men who did this," he muttered, shaking his head as the stack of bodies in the wagon grew higher.

He turned to Smoke and Louis, who stood next to him with Cal and Pearlie behind them. "The railroad will offer a ten-thousand-dollar bonus to you and your men if you capture or kill the bastards responsible for this outrage, Smoke," he said, his voice low and grim.

Smoke glanced at the others, who all shook their heads. "No, Bill, that's not necessary. My men and I will track the sons of bitches down for you and do whatever is necessary to bring them to justice without any thought of reward or payment," Smoke said, his voice equally serious.

"Yes, Bill," Louis agreed. "There are some things money cannot buy, and justice for the dead is one of them."

"Thank you, men," Van Horne said with feeling, shaking each of their hands in turn.

From over near where the wounded lay, the doctor raised his head and called, "Mr. Van Horne, one of the men wants to talk to you."

The group walked over and stood next to the man the doctor was kneeling next to.

It was Albert Knowles, the chief detective assigned to head the Pinkerton contingent on the train. His left leg was lying at a funny angle and there were cuts and smoke burns on his face and hands.

Van Horne squatted next to him. "Albert, how are you doing?" he asked gently, smoothing Knowles's hair back with his ham-sized hand.

Knowles grimaced as he tried to shift position. "I'm all right, Mr. Van Horne," he said, his eyes moving over to the wagon being filled with dead bodies. "At least, I'm in better shape than most of my men," he added in a strangled, hoarse voice full of remorse.

"Don't blame yourself for this, Al," Van Horne said. "There was nothing you could have done against an attack like this."

"No, Mr. Van Horne, I'm afraid I *am* to blame for this," Knowles said, his voice filled with self-disgust.

"How's that, Al?" Van Horne asked. "How can you possibly blame yourself for this atrocity?"

"I think I recognized the voice of the leader of the men who blew up the train," Knowles said, his eyes shifting around, unable to meet Van Horne's.

"Oh?"

"Yes, sir. While I was eating lunch at a saloon in town, a man approached me and told me he was an ex-marshal from down Fort Smith way. We got to talking and he asked a lot of questions about the security arrangements on the payroll trains." Knowles sighed. "I didn't think much about it, and he did it in such a way as not to arouse my suspicions, but I can see now he was pumping me for information on where my men would be stationed on the train to use against us."

"What was his name?" Van Horne asked grimly.

"He said his name was John Brody, but I doubt he was telling the truth," Knowles said. He went on to describe the man he'd talked to in detail, as only an experienced detective could.

Van Horne had started to shake his head when Smoke spoke up. "Bill, doesn't that sound a lot like that man who came up to us the other day while we were in town eating, who inquired about a security job?"

Van Horne snapped his fingers. "Damn, Smoke, I think you're right." He pursed his lips, thinking back to that day. "Now what was his name?" he said, almost to himself.

"He didn't give a name, as I recollect," Louis said. He glanced at Smoke. "But I think Smoke had him pegged from the get-go."

Smoke nodded. "That's right. He sure as hell didn't look like he'd spent much time using his hands for manual labor, and he wore his side arm like a man who knew how to use it, tied down low on his hip."

"Well, whatever the hell his name is and wherever he goes to try and hide, I want him brought down," Van Horne said. "One way or another!"

17

Hammer and his men rode hard for the rest of the day to put as much distance between them and the railroad as they could, until just before dusk they came to a large lake.

The edges of the lake were still rimmed with ice, with large patches out away from shore showing brilliant blue water where the ice was beginning to melt. About twenty yards from shore, the dead body of a large elk floated in an open hole in the ice where he'd evidently fallen through the ice pack.

"Looky there, Hammer," Bull said, pointing to the elk. "That sumbitch must weight over a thousand pounds."

"Yeah, an' that elk meat would taste mighty good if we cooked it over a fire," Sam Johnson, one of the gang members said, licking his lips at the thought.

Hammer glanced around. The place where they'd stopped had a good cover of trees growing by the edge of the lake, and was moderately well protected from the frigid north wind blowing across the lake toward them.

"That's a good idea, Sam," he said. "Why don't you see if you and the boys can get a rope around his horns and drag him into shore. We'll make camp here and see about cooking up some hot food."

"It's 'bout time," Shorty Wallace observed as he sat shivering in his saddle, his coyote-fur coat pulled tight around his shoulders. "I'm 'bout frozen clear through."

Hammer grinned. "Good. Then a little work pulling that elk in will warm you up, Shorty," he said. "Go on, get to it so we can eat 'fore it gets dark."

"You think that ice will hold a hoss?" Shorty asked as he tried to figure out a way to get the elk to shore.

Hammer laughed. "Well, it sure as hell didn't hold that elk, did it, Shorty?"

"Yeah, an' if you fall in that water, you'll be frozen solid 'fore we can get you out," Bull added, shaking his head at the thought.

By the time Shorty and Sam and a couple of other gang members had managed to rope and drag the elk to shore using long ropes tied to their saddle horns, Bull had a roaring fire going in the center of the copse of trees they were camping in.

Coffee had been brewed in several pots, and the men were mixing it with generous dollops of whiskey and brandy to ward off the chill as the temperature continued to fall and large, wet flakes of snow began to drift downward from the dark clouds overhead.

The wind, instead of dying at dusk as it usually did, was freshening as the storm built to its full force and the snowfall intensified.

"Damn," a half-breed Indian named Spotted Dog said, rubbing his hands together in front of the fire. "I thought Minnesota was cold, but this land is even worse."

"Shit," Jerry Barnes said, edging closer to the fire and turning his back to it to warm up his rear. "I thought Injuns don't feel the cold like us white men do."

Spotted Dog laughed. "That's right, Jerry, they don't. But I'm only half-Indian, and my white half is freezing its balls off."

"Well, why don't you squat over that there fire, Dog?" Sanchez asked, laughing. "That'll warm them *cojones* right up for you."

Shorty looked up from where he was working on the elk with a long-bladed skinning knife. "Damn, Hammer. This beast is near frozen solid. I can't hardly cut no steaks off'n it with this knife."

Hammer shook his head in disgust. "Dog, go on over there an' show Shorty how to skin an elk."

"Yeah, Dog," Jerry Barnes said. "It's just like scalpin' a man, only you got to cut deeper."

Spotted Dog glared at Barnes, who had only a fringe of hair around the side of his head, the top being completely bald. "There are times when I'm tempted to try scalping you, Jerry, but with the sparseness of your hair, I figure it would be a waste of time."

With that parting shot, which made the other men around the fire laugh, Spotted Dog stepped over to the elk and with expert flicks of his wrist, stripped the skin off and cut several large steaks off the back strap. "The trick to cutting meat, Shorty," Dog said as he held up the bloody steaks, "is to have a knife that's sharper than your thumb."

Soon, the charred meat was being cut up and passed out among the men, who were eating it with large plates of pinto beans and hard biscuits that had to be dunked in their coffee before they could be chewed.

As the men ate, they also drank a great deal of whiskey, trying to get warm. Before long, they were all in a festive, half-drunk mood, and were all talking about how they planned to spend the money they'd stolen from the train.

Smoke and Louis and Cal and Pearlie lay on their stomachs, peering through binoculars over a ridge at the outlaws' camp two hundred yards away. They'd laid their ground blankets down so the dampness of the ground wouldn't get their clothes wet, a sure way to freeze to death in this weather.

The snow was falling heavier now, and the brims of their hats and their shoulders were becoming covered with ice. Though the others were shivering from the cold, Smoke didn't even notice it, the fires of vengeance burning in his gut keeping him warm.

"I make it about thirty men, give or take a couple," Smoke said, speaking in a low voice even though he knew the snow and wind would muffle any sounds they made.

"Me too," Louis said, peering through his own set of binoculars.

"I wonder why they've made that fire so big," Pearlie whispered from his position next to Smoke. "It's like they ain't afraid of nobody seein' it."

"They probably think that since they killed most of the Pinkertons, there ain't nobody on their trail yet," Cal said, his voice quivering from the chattering of his teeth.

"You're right, Cal," Smoke said. "That and the storm that's come up to cover their tracks gives them a false sense of safety. They probably have no idea that the Chinaman who saw the robbery would have gotten us on their trail so fast."

Louis glanced at Smoke. "You planning on hitting them tonight?" he asked.

Smoke thought about it for a moment and then he nodded, his eyes flashing in the reflected light from the campfire down the slope. "Yes, but not just yet. Let's pull back a mile or so and build us a fire. We'll eat and feed the horses and get warm and wait until just before dawn to attack. That way the sentries, if they bother to post them, will be tired enough that they won't be effective."

They followed him as he eased back off the ridge and got up on his mount. He walked the horse away from the outlaws' camp for a half hour and found a good spot for a camp, nestled in a thick grove of tall pines and maple trees in a small depression surrounded by heavy boulders that would hide the light from their campfire.

As he dismounted, he told Cal and Pearlie, "Gather up as many pinecones as you can carry. They'll light easy and burn hot to get the wet wood going for our fire."

While the boys were gathering pinecones and sticks of wood, Smoke set about making coffee and fixing a camp supper that would give them the energy they were going to need later on that night. Louis saw to the horses, getting them covered with blankets and setting out piles of grain for them to eat. Once the fire was going, he would melt some snow for them to drink.

After they'd eaten and filled their bellies with plenty of hot coffee, Smoke showed them how to gather tree limbs covered with pine needles and lay them in piles up against the trunks of some of the larger pine trees. They put their ground blankets down, crawled into their sleeping blankets near the fire, and pulled the tree limbs over them. The pine needles on the limbs kept both the snow and the cold away from them, and they slept snug as bugs in rugs.

At almost exactly three in the morning, Smoke came awake. Years of living in the High Lonesome had helped him develop an internal alarm clock that rarely failed to waken him whenever he wanted.

He crawled out from under his blankets and pine limbs to find almost two feet of snow had fallen. He threw some pinecones on the red-hot embers of the fire and prepared another large pot of coffee before waking the others.

By the time Louis and Cal and Pearlie were up and awake, he was sitting next to a roaring fire, sipping steaming hot coffee from his mug and planning his next move.

As Louis filled their mugs, he glanced over at Smoke. "All right, Smoke, what's our next move?"

Smoke spoke while staring at the fire. "There's too many of them to just go into their camp with our guns blazing. We could probably get most of them, but sure as hell they'd manage to get a couple of us before we finished them off."

"So, what should we do?" Pearlie asked. "Maybe we could surround them and shoot down into their camp from a distance," he offered.

Louis shook his head. "No, son, it's too dark for accurate fire, and even then, there's so many of them that they'd be able to mount an attack on us before we could get them all."

Smoke looked up at them, his eyes full of reflected flames from the campfire, his grin fierce. "You're right Louis, so here's what we're going to do, men . . ."

Cal and Pearlie and Louis squatted down on their haunches next to the fire and listened as Smoke outlined his plan of attack.

Squatty Lyons was leaning back against the bole of a ponderosa pine, his arms crossed over his chest and his chin tucked into the collar of his rawhide coat against the north wind. "Damn that Hammer for giving me the dog watch," he mumbled to himself, his teeth chattering against the cold. "You don't see him out here in the dead of night freezing near to death keeping watch when no one's within a hundred miles of us," he complained to the night air.

He glanced over at the long line of horses tied one after the other to a rope strung between two trees as he fumbled in his coat and tried to keep his hands from shaking while he built himself a cigarette. Hammer had told him it was his responsibility to keep watch on the horses during the night. "Huh, as if someone's gonna sneak up here in the middle of nowhere an' steal 'em," he growled, sticking the cigarette into the corner of his mouth and pulling out a lucifer to light it with.

Suddenly, he sat up straighter and reached for the new Winchester he had between his legs when he saw a shadow moving over near the horse string. "What the . . ." he began to say when he felt a sharp sting followed by the sensation of someone dragging ice across his throat.

He had time to turn his head and see a hulking figure behind him before the blood from his severed throat gushed into his mouth and choked him. His eyes opened wide as the Winchester fell from his hands and he toppled over onto his face in the snow at his feet.

"*Adios,* pond scum," Louis whispered to the dead man before he moved silently off looking for another sentry. Louis fought the nausea the killing had caused in his stomach. He was used to standing face-to-face with men he was up against, and the thought of sneaking up on a man and killing him from behind went against his grain. Of course, these dirty bastards deserved no mercy, he told himself, and he steeled his conscience for the next man he was going to kill.

Cal and Pearlie, watching from behind some nearby bushes, moved to the rope holding the horses when they saw the guard fall. A quick flick of Cal's knife at one end and of Pearlie's at the other, and the rope parted. Being careful riot to spook the animals into whinnying, Pearlie and Cal took the ends of the rope and slowly led the horses away from the camp and deeper into the forest.

On the other side of the camp, Roy Woodson was walking in small circles and flapping his arms against his chest trying to keep warm as he kept watch over the packs and supplies that'd been stacked there earlier. He'd left his rifle sitting on the ground leaning up against one of the packs so he could put his hands in the pockets of his coat to keep them warm.

He turned rapidly, his heart beating fast as he heard a small splash from the edge of the nearby lake. He peered into the gloom at the ghostly whiteness of the ice and snow, wishing like hell the moon were out so he could see what had made the sound.

He whirled back around at the sound of a soft voice behind him. "Hey, did you forget this?" Smoke asked, holding the forgotten Winchester in his hands as he walked toward Roy.

Roy opened his mouth to shout for help, and Smoke swung the rifle as hard as he could. The front sight on the barrel tore through Roy's cheek, knocked three of his teeth out, and snapped his jaw to the side, dislocating it. Roy fell as if he'd been poleaxed, unconscious before he hit the ground.

Smoke crouched and waited to see if anyone had heard the sound of the sentry hitting the ground. When there was no response, he straightened up and moved over to the stack of supplies. He took two sticks of dynamite out of his coat pocket and placed them under the stack of packs and boxes and supplies the man had been guarding.

Striking a lucifer on his pants leg, he lit the two-minute fuse. As he moved toward the campfire in the niiddle of camp, he gave a low whistle that sounded remarkably like the call of a night hawk, the signal to the others they had two minutes to get clear of the explosion.

As he walked quickly by the embers of the campfire, he reached out and dumped the contents of a cardboard box into the coals, along with a burlap sack full of pinecones, and kept moving, making no sound at all. It was as if he were walking on cotton, he was so silent.

A sleepy voice from a pile of blankets near the fire mumbled, "Roy, is that you?"

Smoke grunted what might have been an answer, but he didn't slow down until he was fifty yards from the camp.

A low whistle from off to the side alerted him to the position Louis and Cal and Pearlie had staked out while waiting for him.

He moved to join them, and Cal handed him his Henry repeating rifle. The four men settled down behind the trunk of a large pine tree that had been felled by lightning, and aimed their rifles across its bark.

"Remember, fire only until your rifles are empty, and then hightail it out of here towards the horses," Smoke said, never taking his eyes off the campfire that was now burning brightly from the pinecones.

Twenty seconds later, the dynamite among the supplies exploded with a tremendous roar, shredding the outlaws' supplies and gear and extra ammunition and blowing it into the night sky in a huge fireball.

Shouts and screams of fear and pain rang out as men were literally blown out of their sleeping bags by the force of the explosion.

Dark figures could be seen outlined in the firelight as they scrambled for their boots and weapons, shouting at each other, trying to figure out what had happened.

Suddenly, the boxful of ten gauge OO-buckshot shells Smoke had put into the fire began to explode, sending molten balls of lead in every direction, rending flesh and bone like a buzz saw as they ripped into the outlaws.

"Now," Smoke said quietly, and the four of them began to fire into the crowded camp as fast as they could pull their triggers and jack new shells into their firing chambers.

More screams of pain rang out as the outlaws dropped like flies from the onslaught of .44-caliber rifle bullets spraying into their midst. Dark figures could be seen crawling and scrambling on hands and knees trying to find cover from the withering rifle fire.

As Cal fired his last bullet, Pearlie grabbed him by the collar and jerked him to his feet. "Come on, Cal boy, 'less you want to be left behind!" he urged.

The four men jogged to their horses tied a dozen yards away, and swung up into their saddles just as answering fire from the camp began to whine over their heads and slap into nearby trees.

"Shag your mounts, boys," Smoke said as he leaned over his saddle horn and put the spurs to his horse. "It's about to get real exciting around here before too long!"

As they rode off into the night, they took the time to scatter the outlaws' horses ahead of them. Few if any of the animals would be able to be tracked down by the men they'd attacked.

Once they were out of rifle range, Smoke slowed his horse and stopped long enough to take out a handful of cigars and pass them around to the others. As they all lit up, he said simply, "A good night's work, men."

Louis nodded. "There's at least of few of those treacherous bastards who won't be killing any more men again," he said.

"Amen to that, Louis," Smoke replied, drawing the smoke from his cigar into his lungs.

Cal coughed a couple of times getting his cigar lit, and then he looked back toward the outlaws' camp. "That'll teach you sorry sons of bitches," he muttered, remembering the dead men at the train wreck.

18

When he heard the sound of their attackers' horses riding off into the darkness, Hammer came out from behind the tree he'd hidden behind and surveyed the damage to their camp. Blood was running down his face from a wound on his forehead where a slug from a shotgun shell had creased his skin, and he had a hole in his trouser leg where a piece of wood from the dynamite explosion had torn through it, barely missing his thigh.

Four men lay dead near the campfire where the exploding shotgun shells had torn them apart. Two more had died in the explosion of the dynamite that had destroyed all of their supplies and extra ammunition, and Bull walked up telling him the two sentries were also dead.

"Eight men dead," Hammer said, talking to himself as he took stock. "That leaves us with twenty-one, twenty-two counting me."

"An' some of them are wounded," Bull said, glancing around the ruined camp, "though none so bad they can't ride."

One of his men, named Little Joe Calhoun, got up off the ground and dusted snow off his britches. "You think they'll be coming back soon, Boss?" he asked. His face was scorched black and he was limping from a flesh wound in his right leg, blood slowly oozing onto his boot.

Hammer thought about it for a few moments, then shook his head. "Not tonight, Little Joe. There must not be too many of them in the party or they would've finished what they started." He glanced around at his men, who were slowly coming out of hiding, some nursing superficial wounds, others miraculously untouched. "This has more the feel of a lightning raid to me." He clamped his jaws shut tight when he realized his voice was shaking from the fear and terror he'd felt during the onslaught earlier.

Shorty Wallace came running into the camp. "They've scattered the hosses, Boss. It'll take hours to try and round 'em up."

Hammer sniffed at the acrid smell coming from Shorty, and realized the man had shit his pants. He turned away to get away from the smell and considered his options, which weren't very many as he figured it.

"No, we're not gonna try for the horses, men."

"But what're we gonna do then, Boss?" Bull asked. "Just sit around here and wait for them to hit us again?"

"No," Hammer replied, looking off to the south. "We're gonna start walking as fast as we can toward the border."

"Walking?" Spotted Dog asked. "But Hammer," he argued, "the snow's almost two feet deep."

"That's all right," Hammer replied. "I figure it's less than ten miles to the border and only another five to Noyes. We've got at least another three or four hours until daylight, and on foot we won't leave much of a trail if we're careful. We should be across the border just after sunup if we make tracks now and don't hang around here jawin' about it all night."

"What good's being across the border gonna do, Boss?" Bull asked,

"If the men who're after us are Canadian lawmen, they won't be able to cross the border to come after us, at least not legally, an' if we can get to Noyes, the sheriff there will swear we were there during the time of the train robbery, so we'll be safe."

"I don't relish walkin' no ten miles in these boots," Juan Sanchez said.

Hammer shrugged as he bent to pick up a Winchester rifle he'd stolen from one of the dead Pinkerton men. "Then sit here on your ass, Juan, and you can give our regards to those bastards when they come back here to finish the job they started."

Juan gave a lopsided grin. "Well, when you put it that way, I guess walking ain't so bad after all."

"Leave everything behind except your weapons and let's make tracks," Hammer said.

Bull gave a sarcastic laugh. "Hell, there ain't nothin' left 'ceptin' our saddles, an' we sure as hell don't need those." He rubbed his hands together and added, "One good thing, walking ten miles in this weather is gonna keep us warm at any rate."

"Now, follow me, men," Hammer said, glancing at the sky, from which snow continued to fall. "And walk in single file so the snow will cover our tracks. That should give us a few more hours while the men who attacked us try and figure out which way we went."

His men picked up their weapons and strung out in a line behind Hammer as he began walking rapidly to the south, cursing under his breath the bastards that'd killed his men and messed up his plans for a leisurely ride to Noyes.

As he walked, he silently gave thanks that he'd kept the bag full of money in his blankets with him instead of packing it with the other supplies, or it'd be ashes by now.

Back at their camp, Smoke and his men sat near the fire, warming up after their raid. Cal had made more coffee, and they were drinking it and eating the last of the food they'd fixed the night before. Louis passed around a small bottle of brandy he had in his saddlebags.

"Here you go, boys, add a little of this to the coffee. It'll warm your insides a bit."

"What are we gonna do now, Smoke?" Pearlie asked as he poured a tablespoon of brandy into his coffee. "Go back and hit 'em again?"

"No," Smoke said, a thoughtful look in his eyes as he recalled the number of Winchesters he'd seen stacked around the fire when he ran through the enemies' camp. "They're pretty well armed, and even counting the men we killed, they've still got us outnumbered over five to one."

"Yes, and without any food or supplies left, they are going to be getting awfully hungry before too long, especially in this cold weather," Louis said.

"We scattered their mounts pretty good," Cal said, "so they won't be going nowhere until they can manage to gather 'em back up."

Smoke grinned. "Which we don't intend to let them do, Cal. We'll keep them on foot and let them get good and hungry before we go after them again. By tomorrow afternoon, I think they'll be softened up enough for us to take another shot at them."

He dumped his coffee out into the fire. "I don't think they'll venture out into the darkness for the rest of the night, not knowing how close we are, so let's get a few hours sleep so we'll be fresh and ready for them tomorrow morning."

Smoke woke up just after sunup, and stoked the coals from the campfire into a fire large enough to cook them some breakfast. The storm had abated, and there were only isolated snowflakes falling gently on a soft breeze.

As they filled up on fatback and beans and biscuits

made fresh by Pearlie, they discussed their plan of attack against the outlaws.

"First, we'll find out what the bastards are up to," Smoke said as he chewed the crunchy bacon he'd put between two halves of a biscuit. "I suspect they'll be scattered out trying to run down their horses. If that's the case, we should be able to take out a few more of them from a distance without too much trouble."

"What if they're still bunched up in their camp?" Cal asked.

"Then we'll surround them and use our long guns to pick them off one at a time until they decide to surrender," Louis said.

"That's right, Louis," Smoke agreed. "We should be all right if they try to mount a counterattack since we'll have our horses and they'll still be on foot. But one way or another, they're going to be in our custody by this afternoon, or they're going to be dead."

When they were finished with breakfast, Cal and Pearlie struck the camp while Smoke and Louis got extra ammunition off the packhorses and made sure all of the rifles and pistols were fully loaded.

Once they were ready, Smoke took the lead and they moved out toward the outlaws' camp, keeping a close watch to make sure they didn't come up on any of them unexpectedly.

As they breasted the rise where they'd observed the enemy camp the night before, Smoke and Louis took out their binoculars and took a long look at the deserted camp below.

"That's strange," Louis said as he swept the area with his binoculars. "I don't see any sign of life in the camp."

"You're right, Louis," Smoke said. "I see several bodies lying where they fell, but there's no sign of other men in the area."

Pearlie shook his head, a disgusted look on his face.

"They didn't even bother to bury their dead," he said angrily.

"I guess they figure coyotes and wolves need to eat same as worms," Louis said dryly.

"You think they might be out lookin' for their mounts?" Cal asked.

Smoke shook his head. "No, I don't think so, Cal. We would've seen them on our way here if that were the case, since we scattered the horses toward our camp."

"Maybe they're hiding in the woods nearby," Pearlie offered. "Just waiting for us to show ourselves so they can ambush us."

Smoke nodded. "That's possible." He sat up in his saddle and looked all around the camp through his glasses, but could see no sign of the outlaws.

"I guess we'll have to split up and check out the area on all sides of the camp, but I want you to go slow and be very careful. If you see any sign of them, fire off a shot and the rest of us will come running," Smoke said.

The four men each took off in separate directions, walking their horses slowly with their guns in their hands, ready in case of an ambush.

Two hours later, they met up at the outlaws' camp, having seen no sign of the outlaws.

Smoke got down off his horse and walked slowly around the perimeter of the camp, bending over and staring at the ground as he walked.

After a while, he straightened up and looked off to the south. "Look here," he said, squatting and pointing at the fresh layer of snow.

"I don't see anything," Louis said as he peered over Smoke's shoulder.

"This snow is an inch or so shallower than the surrounding snow is," Smoke said. He stood back up. "And the depression seems to run toward the south."

"What's that mean, Smoke?" Pearlie asked, staring in the same direction as Smoke.

"I think the outlaws took off walking to the south, and they walked in single file hoping the snow would cover their tracks," he answered. "But the depression their feet caused in the snow caused the new snow to be several inches shallower than the surrounding snowfall."

"How long ago?" Louis asked.

"From the depth of the snow, I'd say they've got five or six hours on us at least," Smoke said.

"Why would they head south?" Cal asked. "There ain't nothing that way for miles and miles."

Smoke glanced at him, his eyes thoughtful. "Nothing except the Canadian border," he said.

"Well, they can't have gone far on foot," Pearlie said, grinning.

Louis shook his head as he made a mental calculation. "The average man can walk at two to four miles an hour, Pearlie. That means if they've been going steady for five or six hours, they could have made ten to fifteen miles . . . farther if they're hurrying."

"It'd be hard to keep up that pace in this weather and with no food or warm drinks," Smoke said. "But you're right, Louis, they could be pretty close to the border by now."

"What difference does that make to us?" Cal asked.

Smoke grinned. "None, Cal. They're probably figuring we're Canadian authorities and won't be able to cross the border after them, and that's where they've made a big mistake, one that's going to cost them either their freedom or their lives, depending on how stupid they are."

He turned toward his horse. "Now, let's mount up and see just how far they've gotten."

"I hope they get frostbite on their feet," Cal said. "It'd serve 'em right."

Smoke grinned. "Frostbite's the least of their worries, Cal. I'm planning on giving them some lead poisoning to worry about."

19

Hammer and his men had made better time than they'd figured, both the cold weather and fear spurring them on to push themselves as hard as possible. They stopped only once, to build a small fire and fix a couple of pots of hot coffee to drink to help ward off the cold. Hammer wouldn't let them stop long enough to cook any food, and he didn't even let them rest to enjoy the coffee, but made them put it in canteens to drink as they walked.

They passed the Canadian border an hour or so after dawn, and were within a mile of the outskirts of the town of Noyes when they heard hoofbeats coming up fast behind them.

Hammer looked over his shoulder and saw four men on horseback bearing down on them in the distance, rifles in their hands.

He glanced around, and saw a line of boulders over near a small draw containing a tiny stream of water off to their right.

"Spread out, men," he called, jacking a shell into the firing chamber of his Winchester. "Take cover in that draw over there."

As the men dove over the banks of the stream and lined up with their rifles pointing toward the approaching men, bullets began to pock the dirt and snow around them as the horsemen fired on them.

Hammer and his men began to return fire, causing two of the men chasing them to rein in, jump down off their mounts, and take cover behind some boulders in the open spaces near them. The other two split up, going in opposite directions as they rode in a flanking maneuver to either side of the outlaws.

"Shit!" Hammer exclaimed, knowing that soon they'd be taking fire from behind as well as in front. Without horses of their own, they were trapped like rats in a barn full of cats.

"Bull," he shouted, "take half the men and get them on the opposite side of the stream. They're coming around behind us!"

Bull spat out a curse word and shouted at some of the men to join him on the opposite bank of the stream.

The two men in front of the outlaws lay on their stomachs, firing over the rocks and not giving the gang a suitable target to shoot at as they rained shell after shell on the trapped men.

Hammer fired a couple of quick shots, but knew there was almost no chance of hitting their attackers since all he could see was the tops of their heads.

"Maybe we should rush them," Jerry Barnes yelled from his place down the line to Hammer's right.

Hammer shook his head. He's as dumb as Bull, he thought. "You go right ahead, Jerry," he called back, "and I'll be right behind you."

Jerry stared at him for a moment, and then he turned back to the front and continued shooting, wasting valuable ammunition without even coming close to the men firing at them. He did manage to hit the rocks a time or two, hut the slugs ricocheted harmlessly off to the side.

* * *

Smoke and Louis, after leaving Cal and Pearlie to attack from the front, made their way around the outlaws' position to either side, staying just out of rifle range, riding bent low over their saddle horns.

Twenty minutes later, they were behind the gang, and took positions on the ground in a small depression as they aimed and fired into the draw.

Two of the outlaws screamed and collapsed under their fire as Smoke and Louis began to find the range, the dead outlaws rolling down the sides of the draw and out of sight.

"I wonder how many we'll have to kill before they decide it's time to give up," Louis said, a fierce grin on his face as he levered the rifle and fired as fast as he could.

"It wouldn't bother me if they never gave up and we killed all of the pond scum," Smoke said. "That'd save us the trouble of having to take them back to Winnipeg to stand trial before they're hung."

Smoke was about to fire again when he heard a shot from behind him and Louis, and he turned to see five men riding out toward them from the town off in the distance. All of the men were holding rifles and they were aimed straight at Smoke and Louis.

"Put down your weapons," the man in the lead shouted as he peered down the barrel of his Winchester.

Smoke got to his feet and ran crouched over toward the horsemen, noticing the man who'd shouted had a tin star on his chest.

As Smoke got closer to him, the man lowered the barrel of his rifle until it pointed at Smoke's chest. Smoke lowered his rifle and held his hands out in plain sight away from his sides, but he didn't put the rifle down.

"What the hell's going on here?" the sheriff asked, scowling down at Smoke.

"I'm Smoke Jensen," Smoke said. "And my friends and I have tracked those men all the way from Canada. They held up a train there and killed almost twenty Pinkerton agents."

The sheriff's eyes narrowed as he stared over Smoke's shoulders at the men in the draw, who'd quit firing at his arrival. "You got some papers saying you're a lawman, or a warrant or wanted sheet on those men?" he asked finally, after thinking it over for a couple of minutes.

"I'm not a lawman," Smoke said. "I was hired by the railroad to bring these men in."

"Well, we'll see about that," the sheriff said. "I'm Sheriff Luke McCain, and Noyes there is my town," he said, pointing over his shoulder at the town nearby.

"Tell your friends to cease firing and to throw down their weapons, Mr. Jensen."

Smoke looked back over his shoulder at the outlaws. "What about them?" he asked in frustration. "If we throw down our guns, what's to keep them from rushing us?"

"I'll take care of them, you just do what I say!" McCain ordered, raising the barrel of his rifle until it pointed at Smoke's head.

Smoke turned and yelled, "Cal, Pearlie, Louis, stop firing and put down your weapons. This is the sheriff."

McCain, once he'd seen Smoke's men comply, said, "Keep an eye on this one, boys. I'm gonna ride up there and take those men in the draw into custody."

"You be careful, now, Sheriff," one of his deputies warned. "They're liable to blow you outta the saddle if you ride straight on in there."

"Not likely," McCain said. "Not with all of us out here on horseback and them on foot."

He spurred his horse forward until he got to the draw where the outlaws were still lying in cover.

Hammer grinned. "Luke, it's good to see you."

"Keep your mouth shut and do what I say," McCain said in a low voice so no one else could hear. "And maybe we'll all get out of this alive. You and your men put your guns down and pretend you don't know me. I'm going to have to arrest you and take you to jail."

"What?" Hammer asked, gripping his rifle tighter as his face turned red. "Why don't you just shoot hell outta those hombres and let us go on our way?"

McCain shook his head. "Don't be a damned fool, Hammer. There're too many witnesses around. Those deputies of mine aren't in on this with us. Just do what I say and don't worry. I've got the judge in my pocket, but we have to play this out like it's real."

Hammer's lips curled into a smile. "You wouldn't be trying to fool me, would you, Luke?" he asked.

"Not a chance, Hammer. You got too much on me for me to try that. Now do what I say and everything will he all right, as long as you and your men keep your heads."

"All right, Luke, but if you try to double-cross me, you'll live to regret it."

Luke's eyes got hard. "Hey, pal, if you want I can just leave you and your men here and let those fellas behind me pick you off one by one . . . how would that be? Then I wouldn't have to put my ass on the line trying to save yours."

Hammer glanced over Luke's shoulder at Smoke and Louis, standing near Luke's deputies a hundred yards away, and he shook his head. "No, all in all, I think I'd rather go with you and your men."

"Then shut the hell up and put your weapons down and climb outta that draw," Luke ordered, turning his back on Hammer and walking his mount away.

Hammer turned to his men and gave the order to drop their guns and come with him. "And," he added, scowling, "keep your mouths shut and let me do all the talking or we'll end up swinging from a rope!"

"But Boss," Bull argued, "he said he was gonna put us in jail."

"Bull," Hammer said, his voice harsh, "you say one

more word and you won't go to jail, 'cause I'll kill you where you stand!"

An hour and a half later, with all of Hammer's men crowded into the small jail cells in Noyes, Sheriff Luke McCain had a meeting with Smoke and his men and Hammer in his office.

Luke sat canted back in his swivel chair behind his desk, while Hammer and Smoke sat in straight-backed chairs in front of the desk. Louis and Cal and Pearlie stood nearby, with two of Luke's deputies keeping watch on them. All of their guns had been confiscated on Luke's orders—until he could get the stories straight, he'd said.

"Now, Mr. Jensen," he began, "tell me your side of the story."

Smoke glanced at Hammer, and if looks could kill, Hammer would have fallen over dead. "This bastard and his men robbed a payroll train near Winnipeg, Canada, yesterday. In so doing, they killed or severely injured over twenty-five Pinkerton agents who'd been hired as security on the train. My men and I were hired by William Cornelius Van Horne to track them down and bring them to justice."

Luke nodded, and then he turned his attention to Hammer. "Mr. Hammerick, what have you got to say for yourself?"

Hammer shook his head, trying his best to look innocent. "Me and my men don't know nothing 'bout no train robbery. We were up in Canada mining for gold, and once we'd cashed out our ore, we were on the way back here when this man and his friends ambushed us. They killed eight of my friends in Canada last night and ran off all our horses." He shrugged. "So, we began walking as fast as we could trying to get back here to Minnesota, where we hoped to find some lawman to protect us from these killers." He paused and stared at Smoke. "And then they attacked us again right outside your town and killed two more of my men while we were trying to hide from them." He looked back at McCain. "Personally, I think you should arrest Jensen and his men for murder, instead of bothering us innocent miners who ain't done nothing wrong."

Smoke snorted. He glanced over at a canvas bag sitting on a nearby desk. "What about that money you found on them?" Smoke asked the sheriff.

Luke looked at Hammer, his eyebrows raised. "Yes, what about the money, Mr. Hammerick?"

Hammer grinned insolently. "I told you, we sold our ore and that's the money we got for it. It's my guess these men found out about it and were trying to rob us of it when we managed to sneak off in the middle of the night and escape from them."

"I'm told there's fifty thousand dollars in that sack, and all of it in new bills," Smoke said, this time addressing Hammer. "Are you trying to get us to believe you were paid in brand-new currency for your gold?"

Hammer shrugged again. "That's what the assayer's office gave us. I don't know anything about where he got it from or if it's new bills or old. All me and my men cared about was getting paid for our ore and heading back down south to get away from the cold up there."

Smoke got to his feet, went over to the bag, and pulled out several stacks of bills. "And these burn marks on some of the bills," he said, "how do you explain that?"

Hammer's eyes narrowed. 'That happened when you and your men blew up my camp with dynamite. We were lucky to save the money from the fire you started." He looked over at McCain. "You can backtrack us to our camp, Sheriff, and you'll see I'm telling the truth. There's plenty of evidence of the dynamite explosion there, along with eight dead men these men killed last night."

Smoke shook his head and went back to his seat. "He's lying through his teeth, Sheriff. If you'll wire Winnipeg, you can get the straight story from Mr. Van Horne," Smoke said, glaring at Hammer.

Hammer leaned forward, speaking earnestly to McCain. "What will that prove, Sheriff?" he asked. "I don't know, but maybe these men here were hired to find the train robbers, and maybe they made an honest mistake and attacked my men and me thinking we were the ones." He smiled slyly. "But why don't you ask Mr. Jensen here if he or his men actually saw us rob this train or if he's just guessing about who did it."

"What about that, Mr. Jensen?" Luke asked. "Did you see this man or any of his companions rob the train?"

Smoke shook his head. "No, sir, we didn't," he said through tight lips.

"There, you see, Sheriff? He has no proof that me and my men were even involved in a train robbery."

"Oh, I wouldn't say that, Mr. Hammerick," Smoke said, smiling. "There was a witness. A man you wounded but left alive who will testify that he knows you and recognized you at the robbery site."

"There couldn't be!" Hammer exclaimed. "We wore . . . " he began, and then he stopped himself and clamped his mouth shut before he could implicate himself anymore.

Smoke laughed at the man's gaff. "You were about to say you wore masks, weren't you, Hammerick?" he asked.

Hammer shut his lips tight, his face flaming red.

"Well, the fact is you did wear masks," Smoke said, "but the lead Pinkerton detective, Albert Knowles, recognized your voice and your clothes from a conversation you had with him the day before the robbery and he's willing to testify to that in court."

Luke sighed and shook his head at Hammer. "Well, that changes things, Mr. Hammerick. I find Mr. Jensen's story to have enough substance to hold you and your men here until I can check out the facts for myself."

"How about you just put them in our custody and let us take them back to Winnipeg to stand trial?" Smoke asked.

"I can't do that, Mr. Jensen," Luke said. "First, I'll have to wire this Van Horne fellow, and then, if he backs your story, we'll have to go before Judge Harlan Fitzpatrick here in Noyes to see if Mr. Hammerick and his men will be tried here or in Canada."

"But that could take days," Smoke argued. "And my men and I have to be back in Winnipeg as soon as possible."

Luke shrugged. "You're welcome to leave, Mr. Jensen, and if the judge says they can be sent back to Canada to stand trial, I'm sure the Canadian government can send some lawmen down here to collect them."

Smoke looked over his shoulder at Louis, who just shrugged. "It won't hurt to give them a couple of days," Louis said. "I know I can use the rest."

"All right," Smoke agreed. "We'll get some rooms in a hotel and wait for you to contact Mr. Van Horne, and then we'll see what happens."

As he got to his feet, Smoke saw Hammer smirking at McCain. "Don't get your hopes up, killer," Smoke said. "I promised Van Horne I'd see you dead or in jail, and if truth be told, I'd just as soon it be dead." He paused and stared into the sheriff's eyes. "And that goes for anyone who stands in my way too."

"Are you threatening me, Mr. Jensen?" McCain asked with some heat.

"No, sir, not if you're just doing your job. But something smells funny here, and it's not just these men."

20

Smoke and his friends left the sheriff's office and took their horses to the livery stable, where they arranged for them to be fed and curried and taken care of for a few days.

As they left the livery, Louis had a thoughtful expression on his face, and Smoke noticed him glancing toward the sheriff's office as they walked down the street toward the town's only hotel.

"What's on your mind, Louis?" Smoke asked.

"I was just thinking how strange our conversation with the sheriff was," he answered. "He seemed to be leaning over backwards to take Hammerick's side in all this."

Smoke realized Louis had the same doubts he did. Both of their instincts were trying to tell them something, and Smoke had found over the years that he should trust his instincts.

Sheriff McCain had acted a little strange in their meeting, but in the beginning Smoke had just put it down to the fact that they were all strangers to the sheriff, nothing more. Now that he found Louis had the same suspicions, he wasn't so sure that was all it was.

"You may be right, Louis, but I guess we'll just have

to wait and see what the judge says after they contact Bill and he verifies our story."

"When you men get through taking about how strange the sheriff was, do you think we could find someplace to eat?" Pearlie asked. "My stomach's done shrunk up to the size of a walnut, it's been so long since it's been fed."

Smoke laughed. "Sure, Pearlie. We wouldn't want you fainting from hunger out here in the middle of Main Street, now would we?"

Pearlie lifted his feet from the muck and mud in the middle of the street. "Hell, Smoke, if'n I did faint, I'd probably drown in this here mud."

They stopped at a small restaurant with MA'S DINER over the door, and went in to take a table in the corner so Smoke could watch the door, as was his habit.

"Three things I've learned over my many years out West," Louis said after they'd given their orders to a rather rotund woman wearing a gravy-stained apron who had a dusting of flour in her hair and on her cheeks.

"What's that, Louis?" Cal asked, eager to glean some knowledge from a man as well traveled and as cultured as Louis Longmont was.

Louis held up his hand and raised one finger at a time as he spoke his words of wisdom: "One, never get in a shooting match with Smoke Jensen; two, never play cards with a man who uses the name of a city as his first name; and three, never eat in a place called Ma's."

Smoke and Cal and Pearlie laughed, enjoying the first peace and quiet they'd had since they set off on the trail of the train robbers. Cal stretched his neck and let his shoulders relax, enjoying the feeling of not having to worry about some outlaw drawing a bead between his shoulder blades.

* * *

After their meal, which even Louis had to admit was quite good, though he put it down to the fact they were all about half-starved to death, they walked down the street to a small, two-story hotel named WINSTON'S.

Smoke took three rooms on the second floor facing the street, another precaution he'd learned over the years. The second floor made it harder for someone to sneak up on them or fire through an open window, and the windows facing the street let him monitor what was going on in town without exposing him to gunfire from an adversary.

Over at the jail, McCain held up his hand when Hammer argued about having to spend the night locked up with his men. "Now, hold on, Hammer," Luke said. "First off, I don't want Jensen getting suspicious about us having an arrangement. I don't want him trying to telegraph any U.S. marshals until after we've seen the judge and gotten things fixed up."

Hammer sullenly agreed McCain was probably right, though he did insist on the sheriff leaving the cell door unlocked and their guns out where they could get to them if Jensen or his men tried anything during the night.

McCain told him not to worry about that, and that he was going to have a deputy keep watch on Jensen's hotel rooms through the night.

"Now, I'm gonna take five thousand dollars of your money and pay a little visit to Judge Fitzpatrick over at the courthouse," Luke said.

"Five thousand dollars?" Hammer blurted out. "Hell, back where I come from, you could buy an entire town for that much money."

Luke shook his head, disgust on his face. "Listen, Hammer. You and your men did kill over twenty Pinkerton agents in cold blood. That's a lot for a judge to overlook, even one whose nose is always in a bottle. He and I are both gonna catch a lot of heat on this when you and your men end up walking out of here free and clear. I'm sure he won't think it's too much money when the federal marshals and the circuit court judge ream his ass out for finding for you in the upcoming trial, so pay him the money and keep your mouth shut!"

"You haven't said what your share is gonna be yet," Hammer said warily, his eyes narrowed and suspicious.

McCain smiled. "I think five will do me nicely, and at that you're getting a bargain."

"But that only leaves me and my men a little over two thousand dollars each, and we did all the work," Hammer argued from his jail cell.

"Yeah, well, I could always let Jensen and his men have another go at you," McCain said. "If he managed to kill most of your men, your share would be even bigger, Hammer, is that what you want?"

Hammer looked down at his feet and shook his head.

"And don't forget, it was you and your men who killed a lot of Pinkertons and then managed to let yourselves be followed to my town," Luke said, his voice hard. "Just be glad you'll be walking out of here and able to rob another train rather than taking a short trip on a rope followed by a long dirt nap."

"All right, all right," Hammer said, tired of arguing with the sheriff. After all, he reasoned to himself, there was time enough after Jensen and his men had been taken care of to see about making a better deal. Hell, they'd killed over twenty men to get that money. Another couple, like a judge and a sheriff, wouldn't be too hard.

The next morning, after McCain had visited Judge Fitzpatrick at his home the previous night and given him more money than he could make in two years on the bench, the sheriff summoned Smoke and his friends from the hotel. He walked with them over to the county courthouse, and ushered them into Judge Harlan Fitzpatrick's courtroom at precisely nine o'clock in the morning.

Of the outlaws, only Hammerick was present in the courtroom when they entered. He was being watched over by one of the deputies from the day before.

After a moment, the judge entered from his chambers and proceeded to take his seat behind a high desk in the front of the room.

A bailiff advised everyone to rise and said the county court was now in order.

After everyone took their seats again, Louis leaned over and whispered into Smoke's ear. "Look at the judge's red nose and take a whiff. I can smell the whiskey on his breath all the way back here."

Smoke nodded and whispered back, "It sure looks like he drank his breakfast, that's for sure."

The judge cleared his throat, and then he went into a coughing fit that turned his face red and made the veins on the side of his neck bulge out. For a moment, Smoke was afraid he was going to go into a fit of apoplexy right in front of them and die before he could hear the case.

"This court will come to order," Fitzpatrick said in a gravelly voice once he'd gotten control of his breath. He dropped his eyes to a sheet of paper in front of him and studied it.

After a moment, he looked up over the half-glasses perched on the end of his bulbous, vein-lined nose. "The sheriff has provided me with a telegram from a Mr. William Cornelius Van Horne, who is in charge of the Canadian Pacific Railroad. This telegram does say there was a train robbery in which many Pinkerton agents were killed and that you"—he cut his eyes to

Smoke—"Mr. Jensen, and your companions were hired to apprehend the perpetrators of said robbery."

Smoke turned his head and looked into Hammerick's eyes, as if to say, "Got you."

"However," the judge went on in his deep voice, "the telegram does not state the name of any of the robbers, and the description given of the leader of said band of thieves could fit most any man here."

"Your Honor," Smoke said, standing up and addressing the judge.

"Yes, Mr. Jensen? You have a statement you'd like to make to the court?"

"Yes, sir," Smoke answered. "Mr. Van Horne's message doesn't give a name because until we caught up with the robbers we did not know any of their names. However, there is a Pinkerton agent who can make a full identification of Mr. Hammerick here as the leader of the outlaws."

Judge Fitzpatrick cleared his throat again and made a show of looking out at the courtroom over his spectacles. "And is this witness here in the court ready to make such an identification?" he asked. "If he is, let him come forward and be heard."

"No, Your Honor," Smoke said. "The Pinkerton agent, a Mr. Albert Knowles, was rather severely injured in the attack on the train, and will not be able to travel for several weeks at least."

The judge pursed his lips and pretended to contemplate this turn of events. After a few moments, he spoke. "And you yourself and your companions were not witnesses to this alleged train robbery, and therefore cannot say with absolute certainty that Mr. Hammerick and his associates were the men who committed this dastardly crime?"

Smoke hesitated. This was not going well at all. Finally, he answered, "No, Your Honor, but—"

The judge banged his gavel on his desk, cutting Smoke off before he could explain. "Well, then." The judge shook his head sadly, as if he were performing an arduous task against his will. "In that case, I see no alternative but to postpone this hearing until such time as this Mr. Knowles can be brought down here to make his identification." The judge paused, and then he added, "I will reset the preliminary hearing for one month from today, at which time the circuit court judge and any necessary federal marshals can be present for the hearing."

"But Your Honor—" Smoke again began.

The judge banged his gavel again. "The court has ruled," he said quickly, staring at Smoke intently. Suddenly, the judge's face paled and his eyes changed, as if seeing Smoke for the first time. He shook his head, got ponderously to his feet, and gathered his robes around him and disappeared through the door to his chambers with as much dignity as a man half-inebriated could manage.

The sheriff looked over at Smoke and shrugged his shoulders as he got to his feet and approached him. "I'm sorry about that, Jensen," he said. "I'll try to keep Hammerick and his men locked up until you can get your witness here, but I don't know if the judge will allow it. He may release them on bail until the time of the trial."

Smoke just shook his head, his eyes boring into McCain's. "Well, we can't wait around here for a month, so I guess we'll head on back to Canada and see what we can do about getting Mr. Knowles back here in time for the trial."

"I think that would be best, Jensen," Luke said. "And I'll make sure that Hammerick and his men aren't released until you've left town, just so there won't be any . . . uh, altercations or disagreements."

"But you will make sure they stay here in town until we get back, won't you, Sheriff?" Louis asked suspiciously.

"Oh, I'm sure Judge Fitzpatrick will set bail high enough to insure they show up for the trial," Luke said, smiling a completely insincere smile.

"I hope so, Sheriff," Smoke said, his voice hard, "because as soon as we get back to Winnipeg, I'm going to make sure the governor of Minnesota as well as the U.S. marshals' office is notified of what happened here today."

"That's certainly your right, Mr. Jensen," the sheriff said, though there was an element of uncertainty and fear lurking behind his eyes at Smoke's threat.

"And we'll also make sure the Pinkertons know where to find the men who killed so many of their agents," Louis added, staring at the sheriff. "And I'll tell you one thing, Sheriff McCain, I sure as hell wouldn't want to have the entire Pinkerton organization mad at me. Those boys are known to play rough, if you get my meaning."

McCain looked nervously over his shoulder at Hammerick, and then he nodded his head. "I certainly do get your meaning, Mr. Longmont, and I'll be sure to pass it along to the judge just as soon as I can."

"Be sure that you do, Sheriff," Louis said. He turned abruptly, and he and Smoke and the boys started to walk out of the courtroom. Then Louis stopped and turned. "Because if something happens and those men aren't here to stand trial next month, I wouldn't give even odds on a bet that you or the judge live to see the summer."

As McCain started to protest this attitude, Louis smiled and held up his hand. "No threat, Sheriff, just stating the plain facts."

As they saddled up their horses at the livery, Smoke said, "The more I see of this town, the more I can't wait to leave it."

Louis looked at him over his saddle. "You think the sheriff and judge are in cahoots with the outlaws?" he asked.

"I wouldn't go that far yet," Smoke answered. "But then again, I wouldn't be too surprised to find out that was the case either."

21

After Smoke and his men left their hotel and went to the livery to get their horses, Sheriff McCain followed them at a distance to make sure they left town, and to make sure they didn't stop at the telegraph office to send any telegrams to the U.S. marshals' office.

Once he was sure they were on their way, he stopped back by the jail and picked up Hammer, and they headed for the judge's chambers to thank him for what he'd done in court.

When they entered, they found Judge Fitzpatrick leaning back in his chair, sipping from a glass of amber liquid, an almost empty bottle of bourbon on the desk in front of him. The judge's eyes were unfocused, and his thoughts seemed to be a thousand miles away.

In spite of the fact that the judge was clearly well on the way to being drunk, he had a worried look on his face, and a small sheen of sweat covered his brow in spite of the coolness of the room.

"Hey, Judge," Luke called as they took seats in front of his desk. "Why the frown? Everything went just as we'd planned it, and Jensen and his men have already left town."

Fitzpatrick turned bloodshot, bleary eyes on the two men sitting in front of him. He gave a sad, half grin and sighed heavily. "Dear Luke, you have no idea what you've done, do you, dear boy," he asked grimly.

"What do you mean, Judge?" Luke asked, plainly nonplussed by the judge's attitude. He'd thought everything went extremely well in the courtroom and that by the time Jensen and his friends returned from Canada, it would all be over.

Fitzpatrick leaned forward and slowly refilled his glass from the bottle on his desk. Then he sat staring at the liquor as he slowly swirled it around in the glass. Finally, he looked up, and Luke had the irrational thought that the judge was about to cry, so mournful was his expression.

"Why didn't you tell me one of the men we were going up against was Smoke Jensen?" he asked.

Luke shrugged. "I didn't think it mattered who it was as long as you made sure the letter of the law was on our side," he replied. And then, after a moment when the judge didn't say anything, he added, "And I did tell you one of the men's names was Jensen, don't you remember?"

The judge nodded slowly. "Yes, but you didn't say his first name was Smoke," he said in a voice so low McCain could barely hear him.

McCain asked, "What does that matter, and just who is this Smoke Jensen anyway that he's got you so spooked?"

The judge grinned again, but there was no mirth in his smile. McCain thought it had the appearance of the smile on a corpse that the undertaker fixes before a funeral.

"Let me tell you men a story," the judge began, his eyes staring into his drink as if he might find some solace there, "and then maybe you'll understand why I'm not jumping with joy about the fact that I took five thousand dollars to betray my robes."

He hesitated and shook his head, "In fact, I doubt very seriously if I'll live long enough to spend a tenth of it."

McCain looked at Hammer and shrugged, wondering what was going on.

"What are you talking about, Judge Fitzpatrick?" Hammer asked. "This Jensen fellow is just another of those old coots they call mountain men that like to live up in the mountains and kill beaver and such for a living."

Fitzpatrick snorted and downed his drink, immediately pouring himself another one. "You couldn't be more wrong, Mr. Hammerick." The judge leaned back and held his glass with both hands, resting it on his paunch as he slowly rocked in his swivel chair.

"Now, as I said, let me tell you a story, and then maybe you'll understand." He hesitated and stared at the ceiling for a moment, as if gathering his memories.

"Many years ago," he began, "I was just out of law school and my first job was working in a small town in Idaho named Rico. It was mainly a mining camp, and I kept myself busy filing claims for miners and settling disputes over who filed first and elementary things like that. Then one day, two men drifted into town, one older and the other barely out of his teens. Their names were Preacher and Smoke Jensen. I was in a bar, just making conversation, and asked them why they'd come to Rico, since they didn't look like miners. The young one, Smoke, said they were looking for the men who'd killed and robbed his brother and then killed his father when he went looking for them."

The judge paused in his tale to take a sip of whiskey, and to take a cigar out of the wooden box on his desk and light it. And then, with smoke trailing from his nostrils, he continued. "Well, I didn't have much to say to that since at that time Rico was plumb full of outlaws and brigands, and the old man named Preacher asked me where the nearest general store was. I told him we didn't have a store, but there was a trading post down the street a ways and that I'd be glad to point it out to him.

"After a while, we finished our drinks and he and the young fellow got on their horses and rode down the street, me walking alongside to show them the way. When we got there, I pointed the place out to them and stopped to build myself a cigarette, and the damnedest thing happened . . ."

Smoke and Preacher dismounted in front of the combination trading post and saloon. As was his custom, Smoke slipped the thongs from the hammers of his Colts as soon as his boots hit dirt.

They had bought their supplies and turned to leave when the hum of conversation suddenly died. Two rough-dressed and unshaven men, both wearing guns, blocked the door.

"Who owns that horse out there?" one demanded, a snarl in his voice, trouble in his manner. "The one with the SJ brand?"

Smoke laid his purchases on the counter. "I do," he said quietly.

"Which way'd you ride in from?"

Preacher had slipped to his right, his left hand covering the hammer of his Henry, concealing the click as he thumbed it back.

Smoke faced the men, his right hand hanging loose by his side. His left hand was just inches from his left-hand gun. "Who wants to know—and why?"

No one in the dusty building moved or spoke.

"Pike's my name," the bigger and uglier of the pair said. "And I say you came through my diggin's yesterday and stole my dust."

"And I say you're a liar," Smoke told him.

Pike grinned nastily, his right hand hovering near

the butt of his pistol. "Why . . . you little pup. I think I'll shoot your ears off."

"Why don't you try? I'm tired of hearing you shoot your mouth off."

Pike looked puzzled for a few seconds; bewilderment crossed his features. No one had ever talked to him in this manner. Pike was big, strong, and a bully. "I think I'll just kill you for that."

Pike and his partner reached for their guns.

Four shots boomed in the low-ceilinged room, four shots so closely spaced they seemed as one thunderous roar. Dust and bird droppings fell from the ceiling. Pike and his friend were slammed out the open doorway. One fell off the rough porch, dying in the dirt street. Pike, with two holes in his chest, died with his back against a support pole, his eyes still open, unbelieving. Neither had managed to pull a pistol more than halfway out of leather.

All eyes in the black-powder-filled and dusty, smoky room moved to the young man standing by the bar, a Colt in each hand. "Good God!" a man whispered in awe. "I never even seen him draw."

Preacher moved the muzzle of his Henry to cover the men at the tables. The bartender put his hands slowly on the bar, indicating he wanted no trouble.

"We'll be leaving now," Smoke said, holstering his Colts and picking up his purchases from the counter. He walked out the door slowly.

Smoke stepped over the sprawled, dead legs of Pike and walked past his dead partner in the shooting.

"What are we 'posed to do with the bodies?" a man asked Preacher.

"Bury 'em."

"What's the kid's name?"

"Smoke."

* * *

The judge let his eyes settle on Haminerick for a moment as he took a long drag from his cigar. "Anyway," he continued through a cloud of blue smoke swirling around his head, "that was the first time I met the man named Smoke Jensen. A few days later, I went to visit a friend in a nearby town, and I heard how everyone was talking about how a friend of Preacher's told Smoke that two men, Haywood and Thompson, who claimed to be Pike's brother, had tracked him and Preacher and were in town waiting for Smoke to show up . . .

Smoke walked down the rutted street an hour before sunset, the sun at his back——the way he had planned it. Thompson and Haywood were in a big tent at the end of the street, which served as a saloon and cafe. Preacher had pointed them out earlier and asked if Smoke needed his help. Smoke said no. The refusal came as no surprise.

As Smoke walked down the street a man glanced up, spotted him, then hurried quickly inside.

Smoke felt no animosity toward the men in the tent saloon, no anger, no hatred. But they'd come here after him, so let the dance begin, he thought.

Smoke stopped fifty feet from the tent. "Haywood! Thompson! You want to see me?"

The two men pushed back the tent flap and stepped out, both angling to get a better look at the man they had tracked. "You the kid called Smoke?" one said.

"I am."

"Pike was my brother," the heavier of the pair said. "And Shorty was my pal."

"You can't do anything about your family, but you should choose your friends more carefully," Smoke told him.

"They was just a-funnin' with you," Thompson said.

"You weren't there. You don't know what happened."

"You callin' me a liar?"

"If that's the way you want to take it."

Thompson's face colored with anger, his hand moving closer to the .44 in his belt. "You take that back or make your play."

"There is no need for this," Smoke said.

The second man began cursing Smoke as he stood tensely, legs spread wide, body bent at the waist. "You're a damned thief. You stolt their gold and then kilt 'em."

"I don't want to have to kill you," Smoke said.

"The kid's yellow!" Haywood yelled. Then he grabbed for his gun.

Haywood touched the butt of his gun just as two loud gunshots blasted in the dusty street. The .36-caliber balls struck Haywood in the chest, one nicking his heart. He dropped to the dirt, dying. Before he closed his eyes, and death relieved him of the shocking pain by pulling him into a long sleep, two more shots thundered. He had a dark vision of Thompson spinning in the street. Then Haywood died.

Thompson was on one knee, his left hand holding his shattered right elbow. His leg was bloody. Smoke had knocked his gun from his hand, and then shot him in the leg.

"Pike was your brother," Smoke told the man. "So I can understand why you came after me. But you were wrong. I'll let you live. But stay with mining. If I ever see you again, I'll kill you on sight."

The young man turned, putting his back to the dead and bloody pair. He walked slowly up the street, his high-heeled Spanish riding boots pocking the air with dusty puddles.*

* * *

* The Last Mountain Man

When the judge paused in his story, Hammer cleared his throat and asked, "You mind if I have a shot of that whiskey, Judge?"

Fitzpatrick grinned and shook his head. "No, not at all, Mr. Haminerick. How about you, Luke? You want a taste too?"

Luke didn't answer, but just reached out and poured him and Hammer drinks, emptying the bottle.

"Not to worry, there's plenty more where that came from," the judge said, and got another bottle out of his desk drawer and placed it on the desk between them. "I have a feeling we're all going to need another one soon," he said as he refilled his glass yet again.

"Anyway," the judge went on, "after Smoke shot and killed Pike, his friend, and Haywood, and wounded Pike's brother, Thompson, he and Preacher went after the other men who had killed Smoke's brother and stolen the Confederates' gold. They rode on over to La Plaza de los Leones, the Plaza of the Lions. It was there that they trapped a man named Casey in a line shack with some of his friends. The way I hear it, Smoke and Preacher burned them out and captured Casey. Smoke took him to the outskirts of the town and hung him on a telegraph pole for the entire town to see."

McCain almost choked on his drink. "He just hung him? No triall or anything?"

The judge took his cigar out of his mouth and stared at the half-inch-long ash on the end before scraping it off into an ashtray. "Yes, Luke, but you've got to realize that's the way it was done in those days. That town would never of hanged one of their own on the word of Smoke Jensen." He snorted. "Like as not, they'd of hanged Smoke and Preacher instead. Anyway, after that, the sheriff of that town put out a flyer on Smoke, accusing him of murder. Had a ten-thousand-dollar reward on it too."

"Did Smoke and Preacher go into hiding?" asked Hammer, thinking that would have been what he would have done.

"With a ten-thousand-dollar reward on his head?" McCain said. "He must've, 'cause most men would turn in their mother for that kind of money."

"No, sir, he didn't," the judge replied. "Seems Preacher advised it, but Smoke said he had one more call to make. I didn't see this, you understand, but a man who was there told me all about it shortly after it happened. They rode on over to Oreodelphia, looking for a man named Ackerman. But, and this is the funny part, they didn't go after him right at first. Smoke and Preacher sat around doing nothing for two or three days. You see, gentlemen, Smoke was smart, as well as fast with his guns. He wanted Ackerman to get plenty nervous. He did, and finally came gunning for Smoke with a bunch of men who rode for his brand . . ."

At the edge of town, Ackerman, a bull of a man, with small, mean eyes and a cruel slit for a mouth, slowed his horse to a walk. Ackerman and his hands rode down the street, six abreast.

Preacher and Smoke were on their feet. Preacher stuffed his mouth full of chewing tobacco. Both men had slipped the thongs from the hammers of their Colts. Preacher wore two Colts, .44's. One in a holster, the other stuck behind his belt. The old mountain man and the young gunfighter stood six feet apart on the boardwalk.

The sheriff closed his office door and walked into the empty cell area. He sat down and began a game of checkers with his deputy. He wanted no part of this blood feud, no part at all.

Ackerman and his men wheeled their horses to face

the men on the boardwalk. "I hear tell you boys is lookin' for me. If so, here I am."

"News to me," Smoke said, "What's your name?"

"You know who I am, kid. Ackerman."

"Oh, yeah!" Smoke grinned. "You're the man who helped kill my brother by shooting him in the back. Then you stole the gold he was guarding."

Inside the hotel, pressed against the wall, the desk clerk listened intently, his mouth open in anticipation of gunfire.

"You're a liar. I didn't shoot your brother; that was Potter and his bunch."

"You stood and watched it. Then you stole the gold."

"It was war, kid."

"But you were on the same side," Smoke said. "So that not only makes you a killer, it makes you a traitor and a coward."

"I'll kill you for sayin' that!"

"You'll burn in hell a long time before I'm dead," Smoke told him.

Ackerman grabbed for his pistol. The street exploded in gunfire and black-powder fumes. Horses screamed and bucked in fear. One rider was thrown to the dust by his lunging mustang. Smoke took the men on the left, Preacher the men on the right side. The battle lasted no more than ten to twelve seconds. When the noise ended and the gun smoke cleared, five men lay in the street, two of them dead. Two more would die from their wounds. One was shot in the side—he would live. Ackerman had been shot three times: once in the belly, once in the chest, and one ball had taken him in the side of the face as the muzzle of the .36 had lifted with each blast. Still, Ackerman sat in his saddle, dead. The big man finally leaned to one side and toppled from his horse, one boot hanging in the stirrup. The horse shied, and then it began walking down the dusty street, dragging Ackerman, leaving a bloody trail.

Preacher spat into the street. "Damn near swallowed my chaw."

"I never seen a draw that fast," a man said from his storefront. "It was a blur."

"The editor of the local paper walked up to stand next to the man who told me this story, where he'd been standing watching the show," the judge said. "He watched the old man and the young gunfighter walk down the street. He said he'd truly seen it all. The old man had killed one man, wounded another. The young man had killed four men, as calmly as picking his teeth.

"'What's that young man's name?' the editor asked him.

"'Smoke Jensen,' the man said. 'But he's not a man, he's a devil.'"

The judge finished his story and drained his glass, his face pale at the memory of such a dangerous young man.

McCain watched the judge finish his drink, and he felt nauseated in the pit of his stomach. He could tell Jensen was a dangerous man, that was evident from the way he handled himself, but he'd had no idea he was crazy as well. He would have to be to have done half the things the judge had said he had.

He glanced at Hammer, whose face was as pale as the judge's. I don't blame him, McCain thought. That's not a man you want on your trail with blood on his mind.

22

Hammer drained his drink and glanced over at Luke McCain, who had a thoughtful expression on his face. "So, Judge," Hammer said, trying to appear nonchalant. "I appreciate your story about this Smoke Jensen and what a tough hombre he was, but what was your point in telling us all this?" He smirked, trying not to show how afraid he was.

The judge smiled sadly at Hammer. "Do you know how old Jensen was when all this happened?" he asked.

When Luke and Hammer both shook their heads, the judge chuckled, though there was little mirth in his face. "He was only eighteen years old," he said. "And I remember thinking to myself I'd never seen eyes so cold except on a diamondback rattlesnake."

Luke and Hammer remained silent, their eyes fixed on the judge.

"And my point in telling you this, Mr. Hammerick, was to let you know that you've got us all in a hell of a mess."

"Why didn't you say something when I came to you and we made our plans on how to handle this?" Luke asked.

The judge shook his head. "I'd forgotten all about

it," he answered. "After all, that was over thirty years ago, and Jensen is a rather common name."

"So, how do you know this Jensen is the same one in your story?" Hammer asked, hoping the judge was mistaken.

"I said Jensen is a common name, Mr. Hammerick, but Smoke is definitely not."

The judge sighed, and put his empty glass down and stubbed out his cigar. "But it really only came back to me when Jensen stared at me at the end of the trial and said he'd be back. When I looked into those eyes as black as obsidian, I knew I was looking at death incarnate." The judge looked at his empty glass, as if wishing it were full so he could drain it again and put the thought of those eyes out of his mind.

"I think you're overreacting, Judge," Hammer said, trying once again to put up a brave front, though he felt as if his insides were full of ice.

The judge shook his head. "No, Hammer. The story I told you illustrates that Smoke Jensen is a man who neither forgets nor forgives. When he finds out you and your men were set free and that Luke and I were in this with you, he will come after all of us, and God help us, he'll kill us all as sure as the winter up here brings snow."

"Maybe we'll get him first when he comes," Hammer said, though his voice was uncertain and he felt as if his bowels were turning to water.

The judge shook his head again. "If you think any of us has the slightest chance against such a man when he's on the prod for us, then you are sadly mistaken, my boy," the judge said with conviction. "But even if by chance you or Luke get lucky and do finish him before he kills all of us, by then it won't matter. Jensen will have already contacted the governor and the U.S. marshals, so even if by some fluke of luck you do survive his attack, there will be a price on all of our heads that will make us a target for every bounty hunter in these territories."

"So, what do you propose?" Hammer said, sweat beginning to form on his brow. He had a wild urge to get up and bolt from the courthouse and run as far and as fast as he could in any direction as long as it was away from Smoke Jensen.

"Your only chance, and Luke's and my only chance, is if you and your men go after Smoke Jensen and kill him and his companions before they find out you've been released and he has cause to contact the governor and the marshals. Then, and only then, will we be safe."

"But Judge," Luke argued, "you just said we wouldn't stand a chance against Jensen. So why are you recommending we go looking for him?"

"I said you could not defeat him once he's on your trail and looking for you, Luke. I think the only chance anyone has of killing Smoke Jensen is if he doesn't know they're after him. If he's not expecting an attack, perhaps he can be ambushed and killed before he's on his guard."

Hammer interrupted. "But Judge, Jensen and his men are going up into the Canadian wilderness to survey for the railroad. There's no telling where they'll be or even if me and my men can find them."

The judge held up his hand. "Yes, there is a way, Mr. Hammerick. When you survey for a railroad, you leave trail marks to show the men coming behind you where to lay the tracks. Jensen and his men will be leaving a trail even a child could follow."

He looked back and forth between McCain and Hammer. "All you and your men will have to do is stay clear of the railroad authorities so you won't be identified before you can find and eliminate Jensen and his men."

Hammer nodded slowly, thinking it through. "Yeah, and while we're up there, I'll make sure to take care of that Knowles fellow who's the only witness to my being at the robbery site."

"Good thinking," the judge said. "If there are no witnesses against you, then Luke and I will not have to explain why we let you out of jail."

Hammer got to his feet. "If I hurry, maybe my men and I can catch them before they get back to Winnipeg."

The judge held up his hand. "No, give them a good lead. It'll be much better if they're killed in the Canadian wilderness rather than on the trail back to Winnipeg. That way, if you're careful, you can blame it on the Indians or some other brigands up there and no suspicion will fall on you."

"Also," Luke added, "you need to take care of this Knowles man first so that if Jensen does call the governor, he won't have a witness who can testify against you."

Hammer glanced at McCain. "So, I take it you're not planning on coming with us up to Canada?"

Luke shook his head. "No. Inasmuch as you got yourself and the judge and me into this mess, I think it's only right you should get us out of it on your own."

Hammer smiled evilly. "That will be my pleasure"

The judge smiled, and reached over to pour them all fresh drinks. "In that case, I think we should drink to a successful conclusion to all our troubles."

Smoke and his friends took their time riding back to Winnipeg. They were still tired after the long, hard ride to catch up with Hammer and his men, and decided an extra day or two on the journey back wouldn't make any difference to Van Horne.

When they finally arrived in Winnipeg, they went immediately to see Van Horne, only to find he'd already left town. He was pushing his tracklaying laborers harder than he ever had and according to the men still in Winnipeg, he was managing to stay only a few miles behind the surveyors as they blazed a trail through very heavily wooded countryside.

"How far out of town has he managed to lay the tracks?" Smoke asked.

"Close to twenty miles already," the man answered.

Smoke looked at Louis. "Twenty miles? That'll take us several days to catch up with them on horseback," he said, dreading even another day in the saddle without resting first.

The station man smiled and shook his head. "Oh, Mr. Jensen, there's no need for you to try and follow him on horseback. With the tracks laid, we can send you by train with no problem. Hell, we have to go back and forth almost every day with supplies for the laborers anyway."

"But what about our horses and equipment?" Pearlie asked, looking at Smoke. "We're gonna need 'em when we catch up with Wilson and his crew."

The station man answered with a negligent wave of his hand. "That's no problem either, my friends. We'll just attach an extra boxcar to the train, and your animals and supplies can be carried along with you. When you reach the end of the track, you can talk with Mr. Van Horne and then be on your way to join up with Tom Wilson and the other surveyors up ahead."

"When's the next train leaving?" Smoke asked.

"Yeah, and do we have time to eat first?" Pearlie added, rubbing his stomach.

The man pursed his lips and glanced at the pocket watch he pulled from his vest. "Sure, I'll tell the cook to fix you up something right away, and by the time you're done eating, the train should be loaded up and ready to go."

"You boys go on over to the cook tent," Smoke said. "I'm going to drop by the hospital tent and see how Albert Knowles is doing and let him know what happened in Noyes."

Louis and the boys headed for the cook tent, while Smoke made his way over to the tent where injured workers were kept until they healed enough to be put back on the line. Knowles had elected to stay there rather than in town so he could better supervise his few remaining men in their guard duties, and to be on site when the replacement agents he'd sent for arrived in Winnipeg.

Smoke pulled back the tent flaps and walked down the aisle between the rows of beds, amazed at how many men were in the tent recovering from injuries suffered while laying track or blasting rocks from the rail bed. "This must be a hard life for these men," he muttered to himself. "And they sure as hell don't get paid enough for the dangers they face every day."

When he got to the end of the aisle, he saw Albert Knowles, his broken left leg propped up on a wooden device that kept it elevated so the swelling would stay down while he healed. Most of his burns were scabbed over, and Smoke was glad to see there was no sign of infection, the thing that killed most men with bad burns.

"Hey, Albert," Smoke called, giving the man a nod of his head.

"Why, Smoke. When did you get back?" Knowles asked, putting an extra pillow behind his back so he could sit up and talk better.

"Just a little while ago," Smoke answered.

"Did you catch those sons of bitches that killed my men?" Knowles asked, his smile fading.

Smoke nodded. "Yes. We had to kill a few, but the rest are in custody in Noyes, Minnesota."

"Noyes?" Knowles asked. "Why the hell did they head down that way?"

Smoke shrugged. "I don't really know, unless they were trying to get across the border thinking we wouldn't be able to go after them there."

"But you fooled 'em, huh?"

Smoke smiled. "Yeah. Anyway, the sheriff and judge down there promised to hold them for at least a month, until you're well enough to go down there and make a positive identification of the leader, a man named Hammerick."

"So that's the bastard's name, huh?"

"Yes, and he's as hard a case as I've ever come across," Smoke said. "It won't be any loss when you identify him and he and his men are hanged."

Knowles patted his broken leg. "Good. The doc says another two or three weeks and I'll be able to travel. I'll see if Van Horne will arrange for me to go part of the way down there by train, so I should be able to be there within a month if there are no complications."

Smoke reached over and shook his hand. "Well, I'll be seeing you, Albert. You take care of yourself, and let me know what happens at the trial."

"I will, Smoke, and thanks for what you did for my men and me."

"Think nothing of it. Those men deserve what they're going to get. I just wish I could be there to see it happen when they hit the end of their ropes."

Smoke turned and went to the cook tent, hoping he'd have time to eat before the train got ready.

As it turned out, Smoke had just finished his meal when the station man came into the cook tent and told them the train was loaded and ready to leave. Just as he'd promised, their horses and supplies were loaded in a boxcar that'd been added to the train.

As they boarded the short train, Pearlie looked at the almost empty passenger car. "Good, there's plenty of empty seats," he said. "I think I'll take me a short nap to help me digest my food."

"When did you ever need any help digestin' your food, Pearlie?" Cal asked, grinning.

"Well, I don't often get steaks as thick and as good as the railroad cook fixed us," Pearlie said defensively. "Especially if you're doin' the cookin', Cal."

"Huh, I never heard you complain when I cooked," Cal said. "You always had your mouth too full to even speak, let alone complain."

"That's 'cause the bellyaches always came later," Pearlie rejoined, "when you weren't around."

"A nap sounds good to mc too," Louis said, interrupting the argument between Cal and Pearlie.

"Yeah, it might be good if we all got some sleep," Smoke said. "I have a feeling once we join up with Tom Wilson and the mountain men, we're gonna be working from daylight to dark most every day."

"That's right," Louis said. "And the country we're going to he surveying is among the wildest in North America, from what I heard around the rail yard."

"It's hard to believe it's any wilder than the High Lonesome north of Colorado," Pearlie said, covering a wide yawn with the back of his hand.

"Well," Smoke said, "the country's about the same, but since the Rocky Mountains in Canada are so much farther north, the weather is even worse than in Colorado."

"I find that hard to imagine," Cal said, remembering some of the winters they'd spent up in the mountains with Smoke in the past.

As the train pulled out of the station on its two- or three-hour journey, the four men stretched out on seats in the car, pulled their hats down over their eyes, and dropped off to sleep before the train got up to full speed.

23

The men were so tired that they had to be woken up when the train finally reached the end of the tracks. Van Horne himself performed the task, standing in the front of the car and banging a knife against the side of a bottle of fine brandy.

When the bell-like tones brought the men to their feet, he had a Chinese boy pour generous drinks into brandy snifters for them all, then sat among them, demanding to be told in detail of their exploits on the trail of the train robbers.

Smoke left the telling of the tale to Louis, who was much the better speaker, and he had Van Horne in stitches laughing at how Smoke had blown up the outlaws' supplies and then killed them by dropping shotgun shells into their campfire.

His expression sobered when he heard how the sheriff and judge had acted as if Smoke and the rest of them were the criminals instead of the outlaws.

"Those dumb sons of bitches," Van Horne exclaimed. "Just wait until I get back to camp. I'm going to wire the governor of Minnesota, who by the way is a personal friend of mine, as well as the United States marshals' office in Grand Forks, and see if I can't light a fire under those boys."

He sniffed and adjusted his vest. "They'll be sorry they ever messed with William Cornelius Van Horne before I'm done with them."

Smoke and the others had to laugh at Van Horne's expressions of rage, and soon they had him laughing too, and pouring more brandy into their glasses.

"Whoa there, partner," Smoke said after the second glass, when Van Horne tried to fill his glass for the third time. "You keep that up and we won't be able to sit a saddle when we head on up ahead to join Tom Wilson and his crew."

"Nonsense," Van Horne said, continuing to pour. "You'll spend the night here with me, of course. I've got my private rail car at the head of the tracks. You boys have been on the trail almost continuously. It's time you had a good night's sleep and some decent food."

"Did you say food?" Pearlie asked, even though it had been a mere three hours since his last meal back in Winnipeg.

Van Horne laughed. He'd forgotten Pearlie's penchant for fine food, and lots of it. "Yes, Pearlie. In addition to bringing my private car with me whenever I'm out laying track, I also bring my own private chef along as well."

He reached down and patted his more-than-ample stomach. "As you can well see, I believe in living as well as one can, no matter the circumstances or the geography."

"How about them copper bathtubs?" Cal asked. He looked at Pearlie and sniffed elaborately. "Some of us could use a bath and another go-round with that brush and soap we used on the way up here."

Van Horne nodded, smiling. "Yes, I think hot baths and a good shave will make all of you feel better," he said, and after a moment's hesitation, added with a grin, "as well as making those who sit near you more comfortable as well."

When they got out of the passenger car and walked up the tracks toward Van Horne's private cars, Smoke was amazed at the number of men he saw working alongside the tracks up ahead. He figured there must have been several thousand men stretched for almost a mile on either side of the tracks, emptying fist-sized chunks of gravel from a rail car onto the ground to be a base for the tracks.

Two other cars contained large wooden ties, which Van Horne said were being cut a few miles over and brought to the building site by wagons, and iron rails. Up ahead of these men were even more men cutting down trees, blasting boulders and rocks into fist-sized pieces, and generally transforming a heavily wooded area into a flat road upon which the men behind would lay the tracks.

Van Horne followed Smoke's gaze, saying proudly, "We can make between three and five miles a day, weather permitting, if the terrain isn't too hilly and we don't have to cross too many rivers."

"Damn," Pearlie said, his eyes wide, "I'll bet Wilson and his men don't do much more than that."

Van Horne grinned. "You're correct, Pearlie," he said. "In fact, we usually manage to stay just a few miles behind him."

"That's amazing," Louis said.

"Well, of course, he's doing the really hard work of finding a suitable path for the tracks, and sometimes he'll have to backtrack for miles if he comes to an area that cannot be tunneled through or swung around, and I've got the benefit of thousands of men, each doing one particular job, so we can move very fast indeed."

After an evening of fine conversation with Van Horne, wherein he told them of some of his exploits building other railroads in the past, and an even finer dinner, the boys were treated to steaming hot baths, and finally, exhausted, they went to sleep in his sleeping car.

Just before he fell asleep, Pearlie asked the Chinese attendant to put more wood in the potbellied stove at the end of the car. "I've been cold for so long, I don't hardly remember what it's like to feel warm," he mumbled as his eyes closed.

They awoke the next morning to a sumptuous breakfast of eggs, bacon, thinly sliced fried steak, flapjacks, and, with Smoke wondering where in the world Van Horne got it at this time of year, freshly squeezed orange juice.

As he finished his third cup of coffee topped off with a cigarette, Smoke thanked Van Horne for being such a gracious host, and he and the men prepared to leave.

Van Horne escorted them out to their horses, and showed them how Wilson was marking the trail he was leaving for Van Horne's tracklayers to follow.

"See how he not only blazes the trees to either side of the trail," Van Horne said. "He also has several rolls of bright red cloth that he ties high up in trees on either side, so the trail will be easy to find."

"Thanks, Bill," Smoke said. "We shouldn't have too much trouble locating him."

"Just be sure to give him a signal when you get close," Van Horne said. "Tom's been out here in the wilderness many times, and he's been known to shoot first and ask questions later if he feels his men are being threatened."

"Will do," Smoke said, and after they'd all shook Van Horne's hand, he and his friends hit the trail.

24

Much refreshed by their rest with Van Horne, Smoke and his men set off along the trail ahead of the tracks that had been blazed by Tom Wilson and his crew. Even though the air was chilly and carried a hint of frost, the sky was clear and there were no signs of any spring storms in the offing.

As Van Horne had said, it was remarkably easy to follow the blaze marks and the swatches of red cloth tied to nearby trees along the way. As they rode, Smoke would occasionally check his compass, and he found they were heading generally north by north-west, along the route discovered and advocated by Fleming back in 1877. Of course, Fleming wasn't trying to find a level course a train could follow, so they occasionally had to deviate from his path due to natural obstructions he had ignored on his journey.

Soon, they came to the edge of a large lake, and Smoke consulted the rather crude map Wilson had given him weeks before. "This must be Lake Manitoba," Smoke said.

"I don't understand it," Louis said as he rode his horse to the very edge of the lake. "The blaze marks lead right up to the water's edge."

"You don't suppose he means for Van Horne to build a bridge across this lake, do you?" Pearlie asked.

"I suppose so, but it looks like an awfully long way for a bridge to be built," Smoke answered, scratching his head. "And I just can't imagine how men could stand to work in water that's just a few degrees above freezing."

"Hold on a minute," Cal called from off to the left. "Here's a note under this red cloth on this tree. You want me to pull it out and read it?"

Smoke nodded, and Cal stretched up in his stirrups and pulled out the paper, which was encased in waxed paper to prevent it from getting wet in case of rain. He unfolded the paper and read to himself for a moment, his lips moving as he scanned the letter. "Oh," he said, refolding the letter. "Wilson is giving Van Horne a choice, it says here."

"Well, go on, Cal boy, tell us what it says," Pearlie said impatiently.

"Wilson says it's only about a mile across the lake and it's not very deep, and that it's another fifteen miles to go southwest and cut around the lake. I guess he's leaving it up to Van Horne whether to build the bridge or to detour around the lake the longer way."

Cal stuck the note back under the red cloth and turned back to Smoke. "What do you want to do, Smoke?"

"Well," Smoke said, grinning, "unless you want these horses to swim us a mile across a lake where there's almost more ice than water, I guess we'll take the route around the lake."

As they turned their horses to the southwest, Pearlie said, "If it's really fifteen miles around the lake, that's gonna take us another day or two to catch up with Wilson and the others."

Smoke glanced at the terrain they'd be going though, which was fairly heavily wooded, though, thankfully, flat without much slope. "Yes, I think you're right, Pearlie." He looked up at the clear sky overhead. "However, with the moon out tonight, if it doesn't cloud in, we may be able to ride pretty late and make up five or six hours on them."

"Smoke," Pearlie said, "if we're gonna be riding half the night, I suggest we take our nooning now."

"Oh, hungry, are you?" Louis asked, smiling, for he knew Pearlie was always hungry.

"It's not that," Pearlie argued, his face red. "It's just I think we need to give the horses a rest if we're gonna be working 'em all night."

Smoke and Cal both laughed, seeing through Pearlie's excuse. "All right, I guess you're right, Pearlie. Let's make a short camp here and let the horses eat."

Cal glanced at the lake, a dozen yards away. "Smoke, you think there might be fish in that lake?"

"I don't see why not," Smoke replied.

"Fried lake trout would sure go down nice for lunch," Pearlie said.

"But we didn't bring any fishing poles," Louis said, though the sound of fresh fish appealed to him too.

"Oh, Smoke don't need no fishin' poles, Louis," Cal said. "Last year, up in the mountains above Big Rock, he showed us how the mountain men caught their fish."

"Well," Louis said, stepping down off his horse. "This I've got to see."

"Come on, Louis, I'll make a mountain man out of you yet," Smoke said. "Boys, take care of our horses and get a fire and some mountain-man coffee going while I show Louis how to catch our lunch."

Smoke walked among the birch and maple and ash trees near the water's edge until he found a fairly straight young tree that was about two inches in diameter. He pulled out his knife and with a couple of swings, cut the tree down and skinned off the small branches. He then whittled a sharp point onto the end and walked over to the lake. He moved down the bank until he came to where a maple was leaning out over the water.

"The shadow of the tree makes you able to see down into the water better," Smoke said as he squatted down on his haunches. "It cuts the reflection from the sun and sky. In fact, you can sometimes see shore birds standing in shallow water with their wings held out to make a similar shade," he added. He looked back at Louis. "Squat down," he said. "Otherwise, the fish will see your shadow and it'll spook 'em."

A few minutes later, Smoke struck out with the homemade spear and brought it out of the water with a three-pound lake trout wiggling on the end.

"Hey, that's great," Louis said. "Can I try it?"

"Sure, but remember, the water distorts your vision. You have to aim a little bit under where you think the fish is or you'll miss it."

Sure enough, it took Louis three or four tries before he got the hang of it. But the lake was full of fish and since the water was so cold, they were moving slowly. In no time at all, Smoke had a pan full of fish filets cooking in bacon grease on the fire.

As Louis sampled the fish, he smacked his lips and moaned, rolling his eyes. "Smoke, I've never tasted anything better than this."

"I wouldn't tell Andre that," Smoke said, smiling.

Louis assumed a horrified look, "Oh, heavens, no. The man would quit instantly were I to admit anyone else could cook as well as he."

"Course," Smoke said, "there's something about eating food cooked outdoors over a campfire that makes whatever it is seem to taste even better. You'd probably turn your nose up at these fish if you'd ordered them in a fancy restaurant."

"Oh, I'll agree the location has something to do with it," Louis said, "but these fish would meet with anyone's approval in any restaurant in the world, no matter how fancy."

When they finished eating, and Cal and Pearlie had washed the plates and coffeepot out, Smoke said, "Now, unless you think you need an after-lunch nap, Pearlie, we can be on our way."

Pearlie blushed. "No, I think I'll be all right for a while, Smoke."

"I wished you hadn't put the idea in his head, Smoke," Cal said, grinning. "Now he'll be dozing in his saddle an' we'll have to stop ever so often to pick him up when he falls on his butt."

"That'll be the day," Pearlie retorted, smiling at the picture Cal painted.

"So I guess you're saying you can stay awake then, at least until dinnertime anyway," Cal said, swinging up into his saddle.

Pearlie took a swat at the young man with his hat, but missed.

They rode as hard as they could push the horses through the rough terrain, Smoke electing to hold off stopping for supper until just past ten o'clock that night. The half-moon cast enough light so that they could easily follow Wilson's blaze marks, and other than stopping for a quick pot of coffee and to let the horses rest, they continued riding until late that night.

Smoke decided to stop after Cal had fallen asleep in the saddle twice and almost fallen off his horse, much to the delight of Pearlie, who teased him unmercifully about being the one who almost fell off his horse.

"All right, men," Smoke finally said. "Enough is enough. Let's make camp, eat, and get some sleep. Dawn's gonna come awfully early."

"Thank God," Louis said, getting down off his horse and rubbing his buttocks with both hands. "I didn't realize how sitting in my saloon all day had made me unused to the saddle. I think my blisters have blisters on them."

"I still got some of that liniment Bear Tooth gave

me," Pearlie said, a malicious grin on his face. "Want to give it a try?"

Louis shook his head quickly. "No, thanks, Pearlie. I saw how it affected you, so I'd just as soon live with my blisters if you don't mind."

"I may be too sleepy to eat, Smoke," Cal said. "Mind if I just crawl into my blankets now?"

"Hang on for a little while, Cal," Smoke said. "You need to put some food in your stomach. I wrapped up some of the fish from lunch, so it won't take long to heat them over the fire."

As Pearlie got the fire going and Louis made sure the horses were fed and watered, Smoke threw some fish on a skillet and began to heat it over the fire.

While they were eating, Smoke suddenly cocked his head to the side and held perfectly still, his fork halfway to his mouth.

Louis, noting his actions, whispered, "What is it, Smoke? You hear something?"

"Keep on eating, boys," Smoke said, putting his plate down on the ground. "Just act like nothing's wrong. I'm gonna take a look-see around."

Seconds later, Smoke melted into the darkness and slipped away.

A few minutes later, a tall, dark figure walked into the camp, a rifle cradled in his arms. "Yo, the camp," he called softly, and Tom Wilson moved into the light cast by the campfire.

"Hey, Mr. Wilson," Pearlie called. "Where'd you come from?"

Wilson put his rifle down and squatted next to the fire, warming his hands. "I made my camp just about a half mile up ahead. I smelled your fire and then I saw the glow."

He glanced at Louis. "You boys should post a guard when you camp. If I'd been an Indian, you'd all be dead."

Smoke moved out of the darkness behind Wilson

and walked into the light, his rifle cocked and ready. "Oh, I don't know about that, Tom. I heard you coming ten minutes ago."

Wilson, startled by Smoke's sudden appearance behind him, grinned. "But I didn't make no noise."

"You made enough for these old mountain-man ears to hear you."

"Would you like some lake trout?" Louis said to forestall any further arguments.

"Why, yes, thank you kindly. I'm kind'a tired of beans and fatback."

After Louis prepared a plate of fish for Wilson, Smoke asked, "Where are the rest of your crew?"

"Oh, they're camped about a mile ahead," Wilson said, hungrily devouring the fish on his plate.

"But you said your camp was only a half mile away," Smoke said. "Don't you camp with your men?"

Wilson shook his head, his mouth too full to answer for a moment. "No, not usually," he said. "It's my habit to camp by myself, especially out in the wild."

"Why is that, Tom?" Louis asked.

Wilson shrugged. "I don't know. I guess it's just my contrary nature. I cannot stand to spend too much time around other people, and working with them all day is just about all I can stand." He drained his coffee cup and stood up. "So at night, after we eat, I usually make my camp a little ways off from the others."

He touched his fur cap with his right hand. "Thanks for the grub, gentlemen. I'll see you in the morning and we can all have breakfast together."

After he'd left, Louis shook his head. "What a strange man."

Smoke smiled. "Oh, he's not so strange, Louis. He is a mountain man, after all. The main reason men come up to the mountains is they value their solitude."

"But Bear Tooth and Red Bingham are partners

and spend time together, just like Bobcat Bill and Rattlesnake Bob," Pearlie said.

"Yes," Smoke said, "but those men are the exceptions, and they didn't team up until they were quite old. For many years, all of them rode and camped alone. It's the mountain-man way to distrust others, even other mountain men."

He looked over and saw that Cal was slumped in front of the fire, his plate on his lap, fast asleep. He chuckled and shook the boy awake.

"Now, let's hit the blankets, boys."

"I can't believe you woke me up just to tell me to go back to sleep," Cal said grumpily.

"If I had let you sleep sitting up like that, Cal," Smoke explained, 'you would be so stove up in the morning you couldn't sit a saddle."

"Oh," Cal mumbled as he crawled beneath his blankets. "Thanks."

"Don't mention it," Smoke said, pulling the edge of the blanket up a little to cover the boy's ears.

25

There was only one doctor in the town of Winnipeg. After Hammer told his men to split up and go to several different saloons to eat their lunch, or in most cases to drink it, so that so many men traveling together wouldn't arouse suspicion, he went to the doctor's office and entered.

Doctor Mack Freeman had his office in an old Victorian-style mansion on the outskirts of town, and he used several of the extra bedrooms as patient rooms for men recovering from injuries or sicknesses.

A lady wearing the white dress and dark blue apron of a nurse met Hammer in the foyer.

"I'm sorry, sir," she said. "The doctor has been called away on an emergency. If you're ill, you may have a long wait to be seen."

"Oh, I'm not sick," Hammer said, holding his hat in his hands. He rarely dealt with women other than of the dance-hall variety, and he didn't quite know how to act when speaking to a lady.

He kept his head down and mumbled, "I'm here to visit a friend I heard had suffered an injury working on the railroad a while back. A Mr. Albert Knowles."

The woman pursed her lips and frowned. "I'm afraid I don't recognize that name, but most of the railroad employees stay out at the clinic at the rail yard if they need to be kept under observation."

"So, Mr. Knowles isn't here then?" Hammer said, disappointed. He'd gotten himself all fired up to kill the man on sight, and now he was going to have to wait.

"I'm afraid not, but if you want, you're more than welcome to call back later and ask the doctor."

Hammer put his hat on and tipped it to the nurse, trying to control his impatience. "I'm sure that won't be necessary, ma'am. I'll just ride on over to the rail yard and check there."

Hammer left the doctor's house and went to the saloon where he'd left Bull and a few of his other men. He entered and walked directly to their table.

"You done him already?" Bull asked, looking over Hammer's shoulder to see if there were any lawmen on his trail in case they had to leave in a hurry.

"No, damn it!" Hammer exclaimed. "The son of a bitch is evidently in a tent for injured workers over at the rail yard," he added, signaling the waiter to bring him a glass of whiskey and some food.

Bull pursed his lips, thinking. "That ain't gonna be easy, Boss. Going out there, you're liable to run into some of the men on that train that might recognize you."

Hammer sighed. He was getting tired of having to do all the thinking for his men, but the alternative was to have men smart enough to perhaps challenge his leadership. "I know that, Bull," he said, trying to hide his disgust at having to discuss the obvious. "So what I'm gonna do is wait until nightfall, and then I'm gonna sneak into the tent and put a bullet through Knowles's head."

"But Boss, don't you think a knife might be better, seeing as how a gun might wake up the whole place and bring the guards running?" Bull asked innocently.

Hammer started to utter a sharp reply, and then he

realized Bull was right. Damn, he thought, even a blind hog will find an acorn once in a while. He smiled and patted Bull on the shoulder. "You know Bull, you're right. A knife will do just fine."

Just before midnight, after having his men set up camp north of the rail yard so they could get an early start going after Smoke Jensen, Hammer pulled the collar of his coat up around his neck, pulled the brim of his hat down low over his eyes, and walked through the darkness toward the rail yard at the end of town.

Once there, he stopped a man walking back from town who was carrying an almost empty bottle of whiskey and who looked drunk enough not to remember his face. "Say, friend," Hammer said. "Can you tell me which tent is the one where they keep the injured workers?"

The man grunted and swayed on his feet as he looked around. After a moment, he pointed to a tent off to one side that had a single lamp burning just inside the doorway.

"Thanks," Hammer said, and immediately walked toward the clinic tent.

When he got to the doorway, he slipped a large-bladed skinning knife from his right boot and held it under the lapel of his coat.

Pushing the canvas flap of the doorway open, he eased inside and looked around. At a small desk just inside the doorway, a young man sat with his head down resting on his crossed arms. He was evidently asleep on the job. Hammer grinned, but just to make sure he wouldn't be interrupted in case the man woke up, he stepped behind the man and brought the steel hilt of the knife down hard on the back of the man's head, knocking him off his chair to lie stunned and groaning on the floor.

Hammer took the lamp from its hook near the

door, turned the wick down low to lower the flame, and carried it in front of him as he walked among the beds in the clinic.

A couple of men moaned as he passed and laid their arms over their eyes against the light, but no one challenged him on his journey to the end bed.

He recognized Knowles's face and moved toward the bed. The light woke Knowles up, and he shaded his eyes against the light, smacked his lips a couple of times as he caine awake, and asked in a low voice, "Yes, Doctor?"

Hammer set the light down on the small table next to Knowles's bed, keeping it between them so Knowles couldn't see his face. He leaned over the bed, putting his left palm over Knowles's mouth, and put his face close to the injured man's. "I ain't no doctor, Knowles. Remember me?" he asked.

Knowles's eyes widened and he reached up to try and grab Hammer's hand over his mouth, but Hammer slammed the point of the knife into Knowles's throat, pushing it in all the way to the hilt.

Knowles strangled and gurgled once or twice, and then blood spurted out over Hammer's hand and the light went out of Knowles's eyes and he died, drowning in his own blood with his good leg doing a little dance under the covers.

Hammer wiped the blood on his knife and hand off on Knowles's sheet, and then he slipped the knife back down into his boot and strolled calmly out of the tent, whistling softly to himself.

That's one less problem to worry about, he thought as he made his way to where he'd left his horse. *Now, all we have to do is kill Jensen and his men and we don't have a thing to worry about.*

As he rode north along the blazed trail by the side of the tracks that had already been laid, he considered how best to accomplish his goal of killing Jensen and the men who rode with him.

First, he reasoned to himself, we have to find them, but that won't be hard if we just follow this here trail. Then all we have to do is keep out of sight until Jensen and his men are off all alone. Then we ride down in force and pump them full of lead.

"Hah," he said aloud to the back of his horse's head. "I'll show that chicken-shit judge who's the baddest hombre around, and it sure as hell ain't Smoke Jensen."

26

Over breakfast the next morning in Wilson's camp, Smoke and his men had a reunion with the four mountain men he'd convinced to come to Canada for a new adventure.

As Bear Tooth put away an impressive number of eggs and flapjacks, he said to Smoke, "Damn but I'm glad you're back, young'un."

Smoke smiled. Only a mountain man who was old enough to be his father would call him a "young'un." "Why's that, Bear?" Smoke asked, doing a fair job on the flapjacks himself.

Bear Tooth inclined his head toward Wilson, who was sitting nearby staring at them over the rim of his coffee mug. As usual, especially early in the morning, Wilson's face was serious, without a trace of a smile or good humor anywhere on it.

"That damned Wilson is plumb near workin' us to death out here."

Almost as if it pained him, Wilson cracked a small smile as Bear Tooth continued. "He looks like a mountain man an' he dresses like a mountain man, but he sure as hell don't work like no mountain man," Bear Tooth groused, scowling at the weakness of the coffee as he took a drink of the brew that for almost anyone else would be considered too strong by half.

"What do you mean?" Smoke asked, winking at Wilson where Bear couldn't see.

"Hell, a real mountain man knows he has to git up with the birds 'fore dawn and git his traps run an' such. But we also know that come noon, a body's natural tendency is to take a after-noonin' nap. After all, ain't nothin' happenin' during the middle of the day. Even critters as dumb as beavers an' foxes know the middle of the day is for sleepin', or at least lyin' around takin' it easy."

He looked around and grinned when Red Bingham, Bobcat Bill, and Rattlesnake Bob all nodded their heads in agreement. "You know we ain't lazy, Smoke, but ol' Tom over there he don't allow hardly no time fer a noon nap at all. He's got us up an' pushin' through the bush from dawn to dusk," he said grumpily.

"An' then some," agreed Red, snorting at the idea of a civilized man not taking a break in the middle of the day like most folks with any sense knew was only right. "A man can't hardly digest his food traipsin' around the wilderness with a full stomach like that."

Smoke looked at Bear's ample gut, hanging over his buckskin trousers. "Yeah, Bear, I can see ol' Tom's damn near working all the fat off you." He grinned. "It's a good thing I got back here to slow him down 'fore you wasted away to a mere two hundred pounds or so."

Bear glanced down and grinned, showing dark yellow stubs of teeth worn down by years of no dental care. "Well, now, Smoke boy, I got to admit I ain't got no grouse comin' 'bout the quality nor the quantity of the food he serves," Bear said.

"'Ceptin' the coffee, dagnabbit," Red added. "He just won't hardly make it strong enough to be fit for a man to drink. He uses way too much water."

"Yeah!" Bobcat added with emphasis. "We been

tellin' the man if'n you don't need a knife to cut it, it ain't near strong enough."

Tom laughed and shook his head as he got to his feet. "Speaking of work, gentlemen," he said. "If you're through stuffing your faces full of my terrible coffee, how about we get the dishes washed and put away and see if we can't blaze a couple of miles today, or do you want to petition Smoke for an after-breakfast nap too?"

Bear stroked his beard, smiling as his eyes twinkled. "Now, I ain't never considered no after-breakfast nap, but if you insist, Tom . . ."

"Off your asses and on your feet!" Tom yelled, pretending to be angry. "Before I take my boot to your hides!"

Bear shook his head and struggled to his feet, groaning and giving Smoke an injured look. "See . . . see how the man abuses us, Smoke?"

While the other men were breaking camp, Tom gestured Smoke over to show him his map. "See here, Smoke," he said, pointing to the map. "Fleming went on across Lake Manitoba, using handmade rafts according to his journal. But since we had to blaze an alternate trail for Van Horne in case he didn't want to bother with a bridge, we've come on south and then back north around the lower edge of the lake. Now we're gonna head for the lower end of Lake Winnipegosis, where we'll turn west again and head for Fort Edmonton."

"What are these lines here?" Smoke asked, pointing to two divergent lines running approximately east and west, one up near Fort Edmonton and the other lower and running more north and south.

"That lower line there is the South Saskatchewan River and the upper one is the North Saskatchewan River. We'll have to find a good fording place to cross the south branch, but we'll stay south of the north branch and with any luck won't have to cross it," Wilson explained. "In any event, neither of them is much of a river till the spring thaws bring all that glacier water rushing down 'em. Then they can get a bit hairy."

"I see by the map that once we've reached Fort Edmonton, we'll start running into the Rocky Mountains again," Smoke observed.

Wilson nodded, his face grim. "Yes, and that's gonna be really tough going. It may be spring everywhere else, but up this far north, it'll still be winter for another couple of months." Wilson stroked his short beard with his hand as he peered at the map over Smoke's shoulders. "We're gonna be up to our asses in snow, and the horses are going to need more feed and rest after struggling through the snowpack."

"I meant to ask you about that," Smoke said. "Why are we cutting so far north? Wouldn't it be easier going if we kept as far south as possible?"

"It'd be easier going until we reached the Rockies," Wilson explained. "See this little X up here on the map?"

Smoke nodded.

"That's a place Fleming named Yellow Head Pass. His journal isn't too specific about the slopes on the way up to the pass, so it'll be up to us to find out if they're too steep for a locomotive to make the grade."

"And if they are?" Smoke asked.

"Then we either go north to Smoky River Pass, or south and try Athabasca Pass, or Howse Pass, or even farther south to Kicking Horse Pass if we have to," Wilson said.

"Why not try the southern ones first?" Smoke asked.

"Because all the southern ones have large mountains we'd have to go around to get to them. As you can see by this line here," he said, moving his finger along the map, "the Athabasca River runs almost straight through to the Yellow Head Pass, and over the years it's created a river valley that I hope will be easier going for a train than winding back and forth around five or six big mountains."

Smoke shrugged and grinned. "Well, I can see you've thought all this out pretty well, Tom."

Wilson shook his head. "I don't know, Smoke. The whole idea of trying to build a railroad through this country is crazy, if you ask me." He looked around at the wilderness surrounding them and the massive snow-covered peaks of the northern Rockies in the distance. "After all, who the hell is going to ride on it anyway?"

"You mean Van Horne hasn't given you his dream speech yet?" Smoke asked.

"No, why?"

"It seems Van Horne and his partner and boss, James Hill, have this dream of bringing in thousands of Eastern tourists and visitors to see the wilderness without having to endure any hardships."

"You're not serious?" Wilson asked, his face a mask of disbelief.

"Well, *they* certainly are," Smoke said. "They intend to build big hotels all along the railway routes to house these pilgrims, and make millions of dollars off the fools who decide to take these trips."

"But what about the Stony Indians, and the highway-men and robbers who infest these regions?" Wilson asked. "Do you think they'll refund the pilgrims' money if they end up getting scalped on their trips?"

Smoke laughed. "Who knows, Tom? Like I said, this is Bill Van Horne and James Hill's dream, not mine. I'm like you, just the hired help who's supposed to make it happen."

Wilson shook his head and folded up his map. He got to his feet and moved toward his horse. "I guess you're right, Smoke. They hired us to do a job for them, not to second-guess their plans.'

He climbed into the saddle. "Head 'em up, boys, and move 'em out," he called, and jerked the head of his horse around and pointed it north toward Lake Winnipegosis.

27

Smoke soon discovered the way Wilson liked to work his crew, and he approved of its stark simplicity. While Wilson and the three men from the railroad he had with him, the two McCardell brothers and Frank McCabe, traveled right down the path outlined by Fleming in 1877, he would send out the other members of the team in oblique directions on either side of his middle path.

That way, if Wilson ran into an obstruction that he thought would be too big or severe for the railroad men laying the track to overcome, he would call the other teams back to join him, and would discuss with them what the terrain they'd been over was like. This saved him time, as he rarely had to backtrack if his way was blocked.

The only problem that Smoke could see was that the team's members were separated for much of the day, each smaller team traveling on its own through admittedly hostile territory.

When they broke for lunch the first day, Smoke decided to bring his concerns up to Wilson. As they sat leaning back against pine trees with their plates of food on their laps, Smoke looked over at Tom, who was sitting next to him. "Tom, I've been meaning to ask you about the way we're splitting up the crew during the day."

Wilson returned his gaze and smiled. "You think it'd be safer if we all rode together, huh?" he asked, showing Smoke he'd thought about the dangers as well.

Smoke shrugged. "Tom, this is your country, so I'm not about to tell you how to run a crew, but the thought had crossed my mind that if we were to come under attack by hostiles, either Indians or highwaymen, it might be better to be traveling as a group."

Wilson nodded as he chewed on some deer meat they'd killed the day before. "You're right, of course," Wilson said. "But with Van Horne pushing us so hard, staying just a handful of miles behind us, I'm under some pressure to move as fast as possible."

He paused to drink some coffee and stare at the peaks of the mountains off to their left. "Now, I'm not going to let that make me put my men at risk, no, sir. But right now, we're at least a few days away from Indian territory, at least according to everything I've read in the journals of the men who've traveled across this land before."

Smoke grinned. "Well, I hope the Stony Indians have read those journals, Tom, so they'll know where they're supposed to be."

Wilson laughed in return. "I know, Smoke, I'm taking a slight chance, but I promise you when we get past the Winnipegosis, I'll bring the crew back together and make sure we all travel with our guns loose."

Louis, who was sitting nearby and had listened in on the conversation, spoke up. "Of course, there's one other way to look at it, Tom."

Wilson turned to look at Louis. "Yes?"

"If we're traveling all together and we run into an Indian ambush, we are in real trouble. But if we're divided into three different teams and one of the teams stumbles across the Indians, the other two teams have the option of either running like hell or coming to the first team's aid."

Wilson laughed. "You're right, Louis. In some aspects it would be better that way."

Smoke grinned. "Course, it'd be a mite tough on the team that got jumped," he said.

Louis put on his poker face, hiding his smile. "Well, the odds of being on that team are one in three. In poker, that'd be a good bet."

"If you're betting chips, that's a good bet," Wilson said. "If you're betting your life, the odds are still too high."

He got to his feet with a wry grin on his face. "Well, gentlemen, I'm glad we had this little chat," he said sarcastically. "You've convinced me that no matter how I lead this expedition, I'm damned if I do and damned if I don't."

"Hey," Smoke said, smiling and shrugging, "no one ever said being in charge was easy."

"You got that right, Smoke," Wilson said, and chuckled as he went to wash his plate.

When they'd finished with their nooning, Wilson sent the four mountain men off to the right toward the edge of Lake Winnipegosis, ignoring Bear Tooth's wide yawns hinting at the need of a nap, and he sent Smoke and his three men off to the left, while he and his men took the middle course.

"Remember," he cautioned the men before they took off, "don't get more'n a couple of miles off the course so we don't get too far separated. Keep checking your compasses so you'll stay on line with the other teams."

The mountain men smirked at this advice, thinking anyone who needed to use a compass to find their way in the wilderness had no business being there in the first place.

* * *

About two hours later, while riding through some very heavy undergrowth near the edge of the lake, Bobcat told the others to hold on a minute while he took a squat and relieved himself of the lunch they'd eaten.

He pulled his horse over to the side out of sight of the others and got down off his mount, ignoring their taunts about being an old man who couldn't control his bowels until dinnertime.

Bobcat threw his horse's reins over a tree limb and moved off into some bushes. He'd just lowered his trousers and was squatting down when he realized he'd moved into the middle of a wild berry bush.

While he squatted, he reached over and began to pick a few of the wild strawberries, popping them into his mouth and enjoying the bittersweet taste of the berries.

Just as he finished his business and wiped himself with a couple of leaves, he heard a thrashing off behind him in the brush.

"Uh-oh," he muttered, knowing he was in trouble as soon as he heard the high-pitched grunting from a few feet to the side and a much lower-pitched growl from a bit farther off.

"Damn-nation," he muttered, "it's a baby grizzly or my name's not Bobcat Bill."

He knew he had to get out of there fast, for there's nothing worse than getting mixed up with a grizzly momma when she's got a cub nearby to guard.

As he began to run toward his horse, the cub scampered out of the bushes right in front of Bobcat, and he stumbled over the small animal, making it squeal in terror as they both rolled on the ground.

"Shit!" he exclaimed, knowing he was in for it now, his rifle still in its rifle boot on his horse twenty yards away.

Bobcat jumped to his feet and drew the wide-bladed skinning knife from his boot just as two thousand pounds of furious momma grizzly charged him from the side.

Bobcat crouched and whistled shrilly as loud as he could, both to try and scare the grizzly off and to call to his friends for help.

Seconds later, the grizzly was on him, swatting and batting at him with claws as long as his fingers. The first swipe sliced four furrows across his chest three inches deep and knocked him flat on his back, blood pouring from his wounds.

Bobcat held the knife out in front of him in his left hand while he clawed for his pistol with his right.

The grizzly roared and stood on her hind legs, shaking her muzzle and flinging saliva in all directions as she bellowed her anger.

Just as she pounced on him, Bobcat got his Walker Colt out and got off two shots into her chest, which had no more effect than a bee sting on the massive beast.

When she landed on top of him, wrapping her long arms around his chest and trying to get his head into her wide open mouth, Bobcat grunted in terror and pain and stuck his knife into her throat as hard as he could while ducking his chin into his chest and trying to protect his head from being crushed like a pecan.

Ignoring the knife wound, she chomped furiously at his head, her fangs slipping over the surface and taking half his scalp off with the first bite.

Bobcat fainted just before three shots rang out, blowing the back of the grizzly's head off and dropping her on top of him.

Minutes later, his friends rolled the bear off Bobcat and knelt next to him, trying to stop the bleeding from his head and chest.

Bear Tooth applied pressure with his hands and yelled, "Red, cut some chunks of fat off that bitch and hand 'em to me, quick."

While Red Bingham sliced open the skin of the bear and cut off thick chunks of fat to make a compress, Rattlesnake held his Henry up in the air and fired off several shots in quick succession.

Once that was done, he squatted next to Bear and helped him hold the pieces of fat tight against Bobcat's wounds, slowing the flow of blood clown to a trickle.

Red moved over, grabbed the large flap of scalp hanging loose, and pushed it back against Bobcat's head, as if hoping it would stick there.

"Goddamn, Red," Bear growled as the bleeding slowed, "What the hell are you doin'?"

Rattlesnake grinned sourly. "Maybe he thinks that scalp'll take root there and begin to grow again."

"Won't hurt to try," Red said gamely, still holding the scalp pressed down tight. "At least, it'll slow the bleedin' a mite."

By the time the other teams had come to help, Bobcat was conscious again. He lay propped up against a fallen log, his teeth clamped shut tight against the pain. Mountain men, like Indians, put great store in not showing pain at any time, but it was all Bobcat could do not to scream from the agony in his chest and head.

Wilson and his men arrived just minutes before Smoke and his friends galloped up to the attack site.

"Holy Jesus," Thomas McCardell whispered, crossing himself in the Catholic manner.

Frank McCabe turned from the gruesome sight and bent over, his hands on his knees, doing his best not to vomit into the snow on the ground.

Smoke squatted down next to the mountain men, taking stock of what they'd done. By necessity, all mountain men became fairly good at emergency treatment of wounds, or they didn't survive long in the outback.

"How's the bleeding?" Smoke asked.

"Pretty nigh stopped now," Bear said, though he kept a tight grip on the fat he had plastered to Bobcat's chest.

"And his head?" Smoke asked.

"He's lost some hair, but it don't feel like the bones are crushed," Red answered from where he was holding Bobcat's scalp tight against his skull.

"Good," Smoke said, smiling grimly, "then he won't have no brains leaking out all over the ground."

Bobcat's pale lips turned up in a half grin. "Thank God fer that, otherwise I'd be as dumb as Bear here," he said, his voice tight against the pain.

Louis leaned down and held out his brandy bottle. "How about some of this, Bobcat?" he asked. "It'll help with the pain."

Bobcat grinned weakly. "What pain?" he croaked, and passed out again.

"Try to get some of that down him," Smoke told Louis, and he stood up and moved over next to Tom Wilson.

Wilson was digging in one of the boxes on the back of a packhorse as Smoke walked up. "He gonna make it?" Wilson asked as he pulled a long stick out with a funny-looking round tube on the end of it.

"Well, he's lost a lot of blood, but the bleeding's stopped right now. If we can get him to a doctor soon, he should pull through," Smoke said. "The trouble is, I don't think he can stand to be moved by horseback."

"Don't worry about that," Wilson said. "I'm fixing to call for help."

"How—" Smoke started to ask, until Wilson stepped off to the side, struck a lucifer on his pants leg, and held it to the two-inch fuse on the bottom of the tube. Then he quickly bent over, stuck the stick in the ground, and stepped back.

Seconds later, the fuse ignited the gunpowder in the tube and it flew into the air, bursting overhead into a bright red explosion of color high in the sky.

"The Chinese make these for us," Wilson said. "Red is a signal for Van Horne to send help as fast as he can."

"How will we know he saw the signal?" Smoke asked, just as a green explosion in the distance occurred high in the air.

Wilson smiled. "That means he got the message and help is on the way. He should be here in a couple of hours with a doctor and a wagon and some men with guns in case they're needed."

Smoke smiled. "I'm glad to see you and Van Horne thought of everything."

Wilson pulled a heavy blanket out of another box on the packhorse. "Now, let's see if we can keep Bobcat warm until the cavalry arrives," he said.

As he moved to cover Bobcat with the blanket, he glanced over his shoulder at McCabe. "Frank, get us a fire going and heat some water for coffee. I think we could all use some."

"Yes, sir, Tom," Frank said. "I'll cook up some beans and bacon too, just in case anyone's hungry."

28

Hammer Hammerick and his men were following Wilson's blazed trail, going slow and being careful so they wouldn't come upon the surveying party unawares, when suddenly, from not more than a couple of miles ahead, they heard a volley of shots ring out, shattering the stillness of the wilderness.

Hammer's hand went to the butt of his pistol as his horse shied and crow-hopped at the sudden barking explosions up ahead.

"Damn," Bull said, holding his horse's reins tight as it shied also. "You think they seen us, Boss?" he asked, looking around quickly to see where the shots were coming from.

After he'd gotten his horse under control, Hammer shook his head, his expression thoughtful. "No, Bull. Them shots are too far away to be aimed at us."

Little Joe Calhoun rode up next to Hammer, his face pale in the frigid air, his Colt in his hand and his eyes wide. "You think maybe they ran into Injuns?"

Hammer held up his hand and waited a moment, listening for more shots. When there were no more guns being fired, he shook his head. "Not unless there were just a couple of 'em," he answered. "If they was under Injun attack, there'd be a lot more firin' than that."

Suddenly, in the air above their heads, a bright red explosion occurred, sending flaming red shards arching across the sky to slowly fall to earth.

"Holy shit!" Bull exclaimed. "Would you look at that?" he asked, pointing at the bright display above their heads as it spread across the sky.

"What the hell's that, Boss?" Juan Sanchez asked as he stared skyward.

"How the hell should I know?" Hammer answered, as bewildered as his men by the explosion.

"Hey, Boss, looky there!" Jimmy Breslin hollered from the rear of the column of men.

Hammer looked behind him and saw another explosion of green colors spread across the sky behind them.

"That looks like it's comin' from back where the tracks are bein' laid," Shorty Wallace said as he stared at the sky behind them.

Hammer thought for a moment, and then he snapped his fingers. "Hell, boys, it must be some kind'a signal from the surveying crew to Van Horne's men behind us."

"What kind'a signal?" Bull asked, as if Hammer would know what was going on.

Hammer shook his head. "Don't know, but my guess is the boys up front run into some kind'a trouble and they're asking for help from the men back behind us."

"Oh," Bull said, as if that explained everything. "What are we gonna do?"

Hammer sighed. The burden of leading this group of idiots was becoming almost more than he could stand. "I guess the smart thing to do would be to mosey on off this trail and get ourselves hid until we see the lay of the land. If Van Horne is gonna be sendin' some men up here to help the others out, we sure as hell don't want 'em to see us."

Hammer jerked his horse's head to the side, and led his men off the blazed trail and deeper into the woods off to the side. "We'll move on off a couple of miles and set ourselves down and wait and see what happens," he said to Bull. "Leave Spotted Dog close enough to the trail to watch it, but tell him to stay outta sight and not let himself be seen," he ordered.

Bull pulled his horse back to talk to Spotted Dog, while the rest of the men followed Hammer away from the trail.

While Wilson and the others waited for Van Horne and the doctor to arrive, keeping Bobcat warm under blankets and giving him coffee laced with Louis's brandy to give him energy to fight the shock of his injuries, Bear Tooth and Red and Rattlesnake walked over to the dead grizzly bear.

Two of them grabbed it by its fur and turned the body over onto its back. "Well, would you look at that?" Bear said, pointing to the carcass.

Embedded in the bear's throat all the way up to the hilt was Bobcat's skinning knife.

"Why," Rattlesnake said, squatting down next to the body, "that beast was more dead than alive when we shot her." He glanced over at Bobcat. "That hairy old beaver done kilt the bear with his knife whilst she was in the middle of trying to eat his head off."

Red Bingham shook his head. "I ain't never heard of such an act, a man killin' a crazed momma grizzly with only his knife before."

"Come on, boys," Bear said, pulling out his own knife. "Let's skin this critter and cure it up for Bobcat to wear. After all, the crazy ol' coot deserves it after what he managed to do."

They'd just finished skinning the bear when Van

Horne arrived in a wagon with a doctor and ten additional men on horseback, all carrying rifles and shotguns.

He jumped out of the wagon, followed closely by the doctor, who immediately knelt and began to take care of Bobcat's wounds, pouring carbolic acid over them to prevent infection and beginning to suture them up, with Bobcat, who was well on his way to being drunker than a skunk, laughing and calling for more brandy.

After Van Horne made sure Bobcat was being well taken care of, he motioned for Smoke and Tom Wilson to join him off to the side, with Louis and Cal and Pearlie standing nearby.

"I've got some bad news, men," he said.

"What's that, Bill?" Tom Wilson asked, wondering what could be worse than one of his men being chewed up by a grizzly.

"Albert Knowles was killed last night while he slept in the medical tent in Winnipeg."

"What?" Smoke asked, remembering how well the man looked when he talked to him.

"Yes. Someone snuck into the tent in the middle of the night, slugged the male attendant on duty, and cut Albert's throat," Van Horne said, his eyes sad and angry at the same time.

Smoke slammed his fist into his palm. "It could only be one man who'd do that," he said. "Hammerick is the only one who had anything to fear from Knowles."

Van Horne nodded. "I agree," he said. "As soon as I found out about his death this morning, I wired the sheriff over at Noyes to see if they were still in jail."

"A dollar will get you five they're not," Louis said, disgust in his voice.

"You're right, Louis," Van Horne said. "The sheriff said the judge released them on bail a week ago, and they haven't been seen since."

"The son of a bitch barely waited for us to leave

town before he set them free," Smoke said, his voice hard and tight. "And now a good man's dead because of it."

"That's not all of the bad news, Smoke," Van Horne said, a troubled expression on his face.

"What else?" Smoke asked.

"On our way out here, while we were following Tom's blazed trail, we found evidence of a lot of horses following the same trail. The prints were fresh and didn't have any snow buildup in them, and since it snowed last night, they must've been made sometime today."

Tom glanced around at the heavy woods surrounding them. "But we haven't seen anyone, Bill."

Smoke smiled grimly. "And you won't, Tom, not until they decide to attack us," he said. "It's got to be Hammerick and his gang. They managed to kill one witness to their crimes, and now they've come to get rid of me and my men to put them out of danger of being hung."

"Well, I won't have that," Van Horne said angrily. "I'll leave these men here with you for protection," he said, but Smoke shook his head.

"No, Bill, that's not the way to handle this."

"Why not, Smoke?" he asked, puzzled at Smoke's refusal of help.

"Because if there are too many men around, Hammerick will just sit back and bide his time until he can catch us alone, and then he'll strike." Smoke shook his head again. "And I'm not going to live looking back over my shoulder and waiting for the son of a bitch to come after me."

"What are you gonna do, Smoke?" Tom asked.

Smoke bared his teeth in a savage grin. "Why, I'm going after him, of course."

"But according to your report, he has over twenty men riding with him," Van Horne said. "It'll be suicide for you to try and go up against that many by yourself."

"No, it's the right thing to do. Hammer won't be expecting me to come after him alone, so when I make my move, he won't be ready for it."

"You mean when *we* go after him, don't you, Smoke?" Louis asked, his eyes flashing.

Again Smoke shook his head. "Not this time, Louis, old friend. I'll stand a better chance and be able to move quicker and faster if I'm alone." He cut his eyes at Cal and Pearlie, who had angry expressions on their faces. "And besides, Sally would cut my throat if I let anything happen to Cal or Pearlie while she wasn't here."

"But Smoke," Pearlie began, until Smoke cut him off.

"This is the way it's got to be, son," he said, not unkindly. "It'll be safer for me this way, and Tom still needs your help in the surveying in case of Indian attack."

Tom nodded, his face sober. "I agree with Smoke," he said. "One man has a better chance out in the wild against a larger force 'cause he can maneuver faster and hit and run better than a group of men, no matter how good."

"If that's the way you want it," Van Horne said, though it was clear he didn't like the idea.

Louis spoke up. "Bill, when you get back to Winnipeg, could you do me a favor?"

"Sure, Louis. What is it?"

"Would you wire the sheriff and Judge Harlan Fitzpatrick in Noyes that no matter what happens to Smoke, I will be paying them a personal visit when this is over to discuss their actions in this matter."

Van Horne felt the hair stir on the back of his neck at the anger and hatred in Louis's face, and he was glad he would never have cause for it to be directed at him.

"Certainly, Louis," he said. "Anything else?"

"You can tell them Pearlie and me'll be there too,"

Cal said, "and you can add that they shouldn't make any long-range plans!"

"At least, not any plans that require them to be breathin' to carry 'em out!" Pearlie added.

29

When Van Horne readied the wagon to take Bobcat back to Winnipeg, Rattlesnake offered to stay with Tom and the others, but they all knew his heart was with his partner, so they made him ride back in the wagon with Bobcat.

After Van Horne and his men had left, Tom said, "Until you tell us it's safe and the threat of the outlaws is past, we'll all ride together while doing our surveying. Louis, you and the boys will ride out front, and Bear, you and Red will bring up the rear. The McCardells and Frank McCabe and I will do the actual surveying, with the rest of you acting as guards so we can't be snuck up on."

"That's a good plan," Smoke said. He moved over to his horse, took an extra rifle boot off the packhorse, and added it to the one already on his mount. He put his Henry in one boot, and a short-barreled ten-gauge express shotgun in the other.

While Smoke checked his pistol loads, Louis glanced over at Tom Wilson. "Tom, you got any more of those signal rockets left?" he asked.

"Sure, Louis," Tom said, grabbing a couple off his packhorse and handing them to Louis.

"If somehow you get your back up against a wall,

old friend," Louis said as he passed the rockets over to Smoke, "fire one of these off and we'll come running."

"I don't expect that to happen, pal," Smoke said, smiling at he took the rockets. He stuck them in his saddlebags next to a handful of dynamite sticks he'd taken off the packhorse earlier.

"It's what we don't expect that can get us killed, partner," Louis said.

Smoke swung up into the saddle and smiled. "Don't be concerned if you hear some explosions and gunfire tonight, men," he said. "I plan to have a busy night."

It was almost dusk by the time Spotted Dog rode up into the outlaws' camp. Hammer had a small fire going between a couple of large rocks so it couldn't be seen from a distance, and the men were drinking coffee and whiskey and standing as close to the meager flames as they could to try and keep warm.

Spotted Dog hailed the camp so he wouldn't be shot coming in, and jumped down off his horse and hurried over to the fire. "Give me some coffee, quick," he said, his teeth chattering. "I'm 'bout froze clear through."

Hammer handed him a steaming mug, and while Dog warmed his hands on the cup and inhaled the steam, Hammer asked, "Well? What did you find out?"

"The surveying crew had a man injured somehow," Dog said. "I watched when the men who'd come from back down the trail returned with a couple of men in a wagon. One was covered with blankets that had blood on 'em, an' the other was sitting next to him, like he was a friend or something."

"So, Van Horne and his men have all gone back down the trail?" Hammer asked.

"It seemed so. At least they had the same number of riders they had when they went up the trial."

"So, Smoke Jensen and his men didn't get any reinforcements, huh?" Hammer asked, a thoughtful expression on his face.

"I guess not, Boss, an' now they got two less men than they had before up there," Spotted Dog said.

Hammer looked up as snow began to fall and the wind picked up. "Looks like we got us another spring storm brewin'," he said, smiling.

"How come that makes you so happy, Boss?" Bull asked, wrapping his coat tight around him.

"The storm will give us good cover to attack the surveying camp," Hammer said. "While they're sitting around a fire trying to keep warm, we'll ride in and blow them all to hell."

Smoke, who was lying on his belly twenty yards away behind a fallen log, smiled when he heard this. He'd cut Spotted Dog's tracks earlier and followed the half-breed all the way to the outlaws' camp without being seen.

Now, as he lay there and the snow began to fall, he considered his options and how he was going to play things . . .

As the gang broke camp and mounted up, Smoke ran silently to his horse and jumped up into the saddle. He knew his greatest ally in the upcoming battle would be fear, and he planned to create as much fear and confssion as he could in the men up ahead.

Hammer moved his men slowly through the forest toward where he figured the surveyors' camp would be. The men walked their horses in single file so as to make as little noise going through the brush as they could.

Smoke rode parallel to the outlaws until he was a little

ahead of them, and then he got down off his horse and squatted behind some bushes near where they would pass.

As the outlaws filed by, Smoke pulled out his bowie knife and held it ready at his side.

When the last man in line approached, Smoke leapt out of hiding and jumped up on the man's horse behind him, wrapping his left arm around his mouth and jerking his head back, exposing his throat. Smoke's blade sliced through veins and arteries and tissue like a hot knife through butter, and then he let the man fall to the side. He hadn't made a sound, so far.

Sam Johnson was riding next to last in the line. When he felt and then saw a horse's head moving up next to his leg, he half-turned to tell Jack McGraw to slow down and stop crowding him.

"Hey, Jack," he began, and then he saw fierce eyes staring out at him from under an unfamiliar hat. "What the . . . he said as the man swung his right arm at him. A burning pain speared his chest, and he looked down and saw a stream of black blood spurting from a hole in the front of his coat. "Oh, shit," he moaned, and then he toppled off his horse and onto the snow.

Smoke reached down and grabbed Johnson's horse's tail, and tied the reins of the horse he was riding to the other's tail. As the two horses followed those in front, Smoke jumped down and jogged along the trail toward the next man in line.

He did this four times until the last four horses in the line were empty and walking with tails tied to reins of the horses behind them.

Smoke finally stopped and waited for the horses to get almost out of sight, and then he whistled sharply and turned around and ran back to where he'd left his horse tied to a tree.

Jerry Barnes heard the whistle behind him and turned in his saddle, expecting to see one of the gang behind him. Instead, he saw the dim outlines of four horses with empty saddles following him down the trail.

"Jesus!" he whispered, and he drew his pistol and yelled, "Hey, Boss, you'd better come look at this!"

Minutes later, the men were gathered around the horses, all talking excitedly among themselves. "Keep it down," Hammer cautioned, not wanting the sound of their voices to warn Jensen and his men up ahead.

He walked his horse next to one of the empty saddles and reached out and touched a black stain on the side. When he put his hand in front of his face and smelled it, he frowned. It was blood.

He looked angrily at Barnes. "How could somebody kill four men right behind you and you not hear it?" he growled.

Barnes, who now had a sheen of sweat on his forehead, just shrugged. "I don't know, Boss. There weren't no sound to hear is all I can say."

Hammer drew his gun and eared back the hammer. "Spread out, men. It's got to be Jensen and he's right in the area. Find him and kill him," he ordered.

The men all pulled out rifles and shotguns and pistols and moved off in different directions, just as Smoke had wanted them to do. With any luck, he'd have them shooting each other in the dark before it was all over.

As two men approached the tree Smoke had his horse behind, he leaned out and aimed the express gun at them. He let go with both barrels from a distance of less than twenty feet. The shotgun exploded with a roar, blowing flame and molten slugs from the twin barrels that shredded the men in front of him and tore them from their saddles. They never even heard the shot that killed them.

As soon as he pulled the triggers, Smoke leaned low over his saddle horn and spurred his horse away from the area, knowing what was going to happen.

Within seconds, eight guns opened fire from the darkness around him, aiming at the muzzle flash of his shotgun and the sounds of the shots.

Luckily, by this time, Smoke was already gone from the place, and the shots hit the tree he had been behind but missed him by dozens of yards.

Two other outlaws weren't so lucky. Directly in the line of fire, they screamed as their friends' bullets tore into their chests and killed them instantly.

As Smoke rode off, the snow stopped as quickly as it had begun and a full moon peeked through scattering clouds, bathing the forest in a ghostly light.

"There he goes!" Juan Sanchez shouted when the moonlight revealed a fleeing figure among the trees.

Juan and three other men who were nearby began to fire as they spurred their horses after the dark man up ahead.

Smoke jerked his Palouse around a clump of trees, and reached up as he passed beneath a large oak tree. He grabbed a low-lying limb and let his horse's momentum swing him up onto the branch. He leaned back against the trunk of the tree and drew his pistols, earing back the hammers.

His horse, when Smoke's weight lifted out of the saddle, slowed and came to a stop thirty yards from the tree.

As Sanchez and his three companions rode toward the horse, they slowed when they saw the saddle was empty.

"Where the hell is he?" Sanchez hollered, sweeping the area with the barrel of his gun.

"Right behind you, boys," Smoke said softly.

As the men jerked around in their saddles, Smoke let loose with both handguns, firing so fast it almost seemed like one long continuous burst of gunfire.

The four men were slammed out of their saddles and were dead before they hit the ground.

Smoke's pistols were empty, and he needed his rifle

in the rifle boot on his horse. He gave a low whistle, and the horse picked up its head and moved slowly back until it was under the tree. Smoke lowered himself into the saddle just as several gunshots rang out and bullets tore bark off the oak behind him.

Smoke jerked his Henry from its boot and spurred his horse into a dead run, whirling around the tree and heading straight for the outlaws who'd fired on him.

Surprised that their quarry was attacking them instead of running away, three men hurried their shots, and Smoke could hear the buzzing of slugs as they passed over his head and to the side.

Shooting from the waist without taking the time to aim, Smoke fired and jacked the loading lever and fired, again and again, until the three men flopped off their mounts and fell dead in the snow.

As he passed them, Smoke threw his empty Colts into his saddlebags, grabbed two more he had there still fully loaded, and stuffed one into his right-hand holster and the other under his belt in front.

When he got to the dead men's horses, Smoke reined his own mount in, fished a cigar from his breast pocket, and lit it with a lucifer.

As he puffed it into life, a shotgun roared from off to his left and he felt the tug in his coat as buckshot shredded the back of it, burning furrows of white-hot pain across his shoulder blades.

The force of the blow almost unseated him, but Smoke fell forward over his saddle horn and kicked his horse forward just as more shots rang out, barely missing him as he fled.

Three more men pulled onto the trail behind him, firing as they rode, some of the bullets coming uncomfortably close to Smoke's head.

As he rode, he reached down into his saddlebag and pulled out a stick of dynamite. Holding the fuse to the tip of his cigar until it caught, he twisted in the saddle and flipped it at the men behind him.

The dynamite went off just as their horses straddled it. The explosion blew men and horses into thousands of pieces, which rained down together in a bloody mix of horseflesh and human tissue for several seconds.

Hammer and Bull and Spotted Dog were the only members of the gang left alive. They'd survived this long because after Hammer sent his men searching for Jensen, he'd signaled the two to follow him while he rode in the opposite direction. He'd remembered the story the judge had told about Jensen and how tough he was, and he wanted to see if his men could take care of Jensen before he tried it himself.

Now, as he peered into the forest in front of him, the filtered moonlight revealed a solitary figure moving slowly toward him, the glowing tip of a cigar between his teeth.

"Bull," Hammer whispered, "you move on off to the right. Dog, you take off to the left. When he gets between you, we'll have him cornered and we can all let go at the same time. He won't stand a chance."

Smoke, whose eyes were as sharp as an eagle's, saw the shadows up ahead as they parted and spread out to his right and his left. He grinned as he moved his horse into the shadows cast by a large ponderosa pine tree, and he slipped out of his saddle.

He pulled the Henry out and steadied the barrel against the trunk of the tree while he took careful aim at the figure to his right. He aimed low, intending to wound rather than kill. Slowly, breathing out and holding it, he caressed the trigger. The Henry exploded and bucked and a second later, a horrible scream rang throughout the forest.

"Oh, Jesus!" Spotted Dog yelled as he toppled from his saddle, "I'm gutshot! Help me, Boss, please, I don't want to die . . . help me!"

Smoke was glad to hear the man call for his boss. That meant Hammerick was still alive and wasn't one of the men he'd already killed.

"You hear that, Hammerick?" Smoke yelled from behind the tree. "Your man is calling for you. Are you going to help him or just let him die?"

"Shut up, Jensen, you bastard!" Hammerick yelled from up ahead.

While Hammer was talking, Smoke took off his hat and hung it from a short branch on the pine tree. Then he took his cigar and wedged it just under the hat behind a piece of bark. Once that was done, he got down on his hands and knees, crawled ten yards away from the tree, and lay on his belly, his Henry aimed out to his left, waiting.

"Did you hear me, Jensen?" Hammer yelled again. "I'm coming to kill you!"

Smoke didn't answer Hammer's taunt; he just waited.

Two minutes later, a shot rang out from Smoke's left and the slug tore his hat off the tree.

Aiming just above the muzzle flash, Smoke squeezed the trigger of the Henry. Like an echo to the gunshot, a scream rang out and a huge figure stumbled out from next to a tree, fired his gun two more times, hitting nothing but air, and then fell onto his face. Bull was dead.

Smoke stood up and retrieved his cigar, and was bending over to pick up his hat when Hammer fired from twenty feet away. His bullets took Smoke in the left shoulder and tore a chunk of flesh from his chest, spinning him around and up against his horse, the Henry flying from his grasp.

As he sank to his knees, Smoke grabbed his saddlebags and pulled them down with him onto the ground.

"How'd you like that, Jensen, you asshole?" Hammer yelled gleefully. "1 thought you were tough, mountain man!" he said scornfully as he walked toward where Smoke lay on the ground.

Unable to get to his pistols, Smoke eased the rocket from the saddlebags and positioned it pointing toward the dark shape approaching him. He would only get one chance, so he had to make it right.

Smoke let his head flop down next to the fuse, his eyes squinting along the length of the rocket, taking aim.

"Don't try and play possum on me, Jensen," Hammer growled, raising his pistol and pointing it at Smoke. "I know you ain't dead yet."

"You got that right, killer," Smoke muttered, and he moved his head to touch the fuse with the end of his cigar.

As Hammer grinned, his teeth glowing in the moonlight, he eased back the hammer on his pistol.

With a sudden *whoosh*, the rocket ignited and streaked toward Hammer like lightning.

Hammer's eyes opened wide and he grunted as the rocket struck him in the middle of his gut, doubling him over and knocking him two steps backward.

He straightened up and stared down at his stomach, where the rocket was buried halfway into his abdomen.

He had time to say, "Oh, shit!" before the rocket exploded, sending Hammer to hell in a heartbeat.

30

EPILOGUE

Three months later, his arm and chest healed and their work for the Canadian Pacific Railroad completed, Smoke, Louis, Cal, and Pearlie rode into the town of Noyes, Minnesota.

Accompanying them were two U.S. marshals and four deputy marshals.

As they came abreast of the sheriff's office, Luke McCain stepped out, a cup of coffee in his hand. His face paled when he saw the marshal badges on the chests of the men with Smoke, and his hand dropped near the butt of his pistol.

"Please, Luke," Smoke said, his teeth bared in a grin of anticipation, "go for your gun and give me the satisfaction of putting a bullet through that badge that you've dishonored that you wear on your chest."

McCain thought about it for a moment, then smiled ruefully and held his hands up. "Sorry, Jensen, I won't give you that pleasure."

Smoke shrugged. "Then I guess I'll just have to be content to watch you hang."

"Hang?" McCain asked as one of the deputy marshals

took his guns. "But all I did was let some men outta jail. I didn't kill nobody."

"No, Mr. McCain, you didn't," the U.S. marshal said, "but the men you let out of jail did, and that makes you what the law calls an accessory."

"And the punishment for an accessory is the same as for the man who pulled the trigger," Louis said with satisfaction. "Hanging from a rope until you are dead."

As they turned their horses toward the courthouse, Smoke could see a wide figure outlined in the window of the judge's chambers.

When they got in front of the building, they heard a shot ring out from behind the window. Smoke looked at the others and turned his horse's head south toward Colorado and Sally. "I guess our job here is done, men," he said, and they all rode south toward home.

AUTHOR'S NOTE

William Cornelius Van Horne was born on February 3, 1843. In 1881 he was asked to be general manager of the Canadian Pacific Railway. His contract was to connect British Columbia to the rest of Canada by building the Trans Canada Railway, at the time the most ambitious project in the world. Van Horne started the railroad in 1882, and completed the project three years later when Donald Smith drove the last spike at Craigellachie, B.C. on November 7, 1885.

He started work in Winnipeg and worked west from there, making about three miles every day, crossing over six hundred miles of mountains in the process.

In the first year alone, over 1500 miles of track was laid. In 1888, Van Horne was named president of the CPR, and was also appointed chairman of the board.

He was awarded a knighthood for his achievements, and spent the last twenty-five years of his life on Ministers Island, which he had purchased. He died on September 11, 1915, in Montreal, and was buried in his hometown of Joliet, Illinois.

In 1882, guided by a Stony Indian, Canadian Pacific Railroad packer (i.e. trailsman) Tom Wilson was the first white man to see Lake Louise. He named it

Emerald Lake (later to be named Lake Louise after the daughter of Queen Victoria).

In 1883, railway workers William McCardell, Thomas McCardell, and Frank McCabe discovered hot springs (known today as the Cave and Basin) at the foot of Sulphur Mountain, near Banff.

In 1888, the original log-framed Banff Springs Hotel was opened for business by the CPR.

In 1889, Van Horne and the CPR brought in Swiss guides to the Rockies to lead tourists to the summits of the mountains.

TREK OF
THE MOUNTAIN
MAN

1

William Pike, known to one and all as Bill, stood up in his stirrups and stretched his neck and back, groaning with pleasure as the knots and kinks in his muscles relaxed. It had been a long ride from Corpus Christi, Texas, to the Rocky Mountains of Colorado.

He sat back against the cantle of his saddle and turned to look at the nine men riding with him. They were a disreputable and dangerous-looking lot. Most had beards, some grown to cover knife or bullet scars, others just worn because of the lack of hot water while riding the owlhoot trail.

Pike and his men thought of themselves as Regulators—a fancy term for bounty hunters that shot first and asked questions later. They were fresh from the infamous Nueces Strip, a corridor of land stretching from Corpus Christi down to the Mexican border. They'd made a good living there, killing or capturing the Mexican *bandidos* who came up from Mexico looking for easy pickings among the many settlers coming to the area from the East. That had all come to a grinding halt when the Texas Rangers sent in a man named McNally and a corps of other Rangers every bit as tough and ruthless as Pike and his Regulators. Suddenly, the pickings were as slim as the twelve-inch stiletto Pike carried in his boot. The *bandidos* began to shy away from the area, and the other robbers and rapists and footpads were of such a small danger they carried very low prices on their heads.

Looking for a new territory to ply their trade, Pike and his men had ridden to Utah, home of many outlaws trying to hide from John Law. There he'd come upon what he thought to be a golden opportunity— a wanted poster offering a king's ransom for one man, a man who lived in Colorado.

Pike turned his glance from his men to stare down the ridge on which he'd stopped his mount.

"Hey, Bill," Rufus Gordon called from the rear of the line of men.

"Yeah, Rufe, whatta ya want?" Pike answered without looking back.

"You said once we got to Colorado, you'd tell us why you brung us here. How about it?"

Pike nodded. He guessed it was about time to let the men in on it. He reached inside his coat and pulled out a yellowed, wrinkled paper. He unfolded it and held it up for the men to see. "This here wanted poster is gonna make us rich, boys," he said, his grin exposing blackened, crooked teeth under his handlebar mustache.

"What's it say, Bill?" Gordon asked. "I can't read it from back here."

Hank Snow, a stone killer who was himself wanted for murder and rape in three states, laughed out loud. "Hell, Rufe, you couldn't read it if'n it were in your hands."

He was referring to the fact that Rufus Gordon carried a sawed-off ten-gauge shotgun in a holster on his hip instead of a pistol because he was so nearsighted he couldn't see anyone more than a few feet away from him.

"That's a lie an' you know it, Hank," Gordon replied. "I can read as good as you any day."

"That's not sayin' much," Blackie Johnson sneered.
"Hank never learned to read neither."

Pike cleared his throat to get his men's attention.
"Well, here's what this poster says, boys." He read
aloud:

WANTED
DEAD OR ALIVE
THE OUTLAW AND MURDERER
KIRBY "SMOKE" JENSEN
$10,000.00 REWARD
Contact the Sheriff at Bury, Idaho Territory

"Ten thousand greenbacks, boys," Pike continued.
"That's nothing to sneeze at."

"Hell," Gordon said, counting on his fingers, "that's
. . . uh . . . exactly how much is that for each of us, Bill?"

"That is one thousand dollars apiece, gentlemen,"
Bill answered.

Hank Snow shifted the chaw of tobacco from one
cheek to the other, leaned over, and spat a stream of
brown juice at a horned toad sitting on a rock watching the men. "That's if none of us gets killed 'fore we
collect it," Snow said around the tobacco. "More if a
couple of us catch a lead pill."

"Hank, the poster's fer one man, not a whole gang,"
Gordon argued. "How's one man gonna stand up to
us, the meanest, baddest gents west of the Pecos?"

Snow looked at Gordon and spat again, his eyes as
black as the beard on his cheeks. "Yore forgittin'
somethin', Rufe," he said in a low voice. "Ten grand
on one man's head must mean he ain't no pilgrim hisself." He turned his gaze to Pike. "What'd this *hombre*
do to make hisself so valuable, Bill?"

"Yeah," Gordon added, "what did the sheriff up
there tell ya?"

"I didn't exactly talk to the sheriff, boys," Pike said. "I
didn't want nobody else to know we was after this Jensen

feller. I got my information, along with this wanted poster, from a miner I met in a saloon up in Utah."

"Well," Snow said, "we're waitin'."

"This miner said he was in Bury, Idaho Territory, a few years back when some gents named Stratton, Potter, an' Richards rode into town with a gang of outlaws. He said there were 'bout twenty or so of 'em all told. A little later, this Jensen, along with a bunch of old mountain men, surrounded the town and told all of the miners and townsfolk to get outta town. They'd come for the gang."

"What'd the gang do to get Jensen an' the mountain men all riled up?" Blackie asked.

Pike grinned. "Nothin' much. Just killed Jensen's wife an' baby boy, an' stole all the gold he'd spent a year minin'."

"So Jensen an' his gang rode into town an' shot up the other feller's gang?" Snow asked.

Pike shook his head. "Nope. The old miner said all of the folks in town gathered on the ridges overlooking Bury and sat an' watched as Jensen rode into town alone to face down the gang."

"You mean one man went up against over twenty outlaws by hisself?" Gordon asked.

Pike nodded. "Yep. The miner says it was like a war down there, an' when it was over, Smoke Jensen was the last man standing."*

"Jesus," Gordon said. "I can see why he's worth ten thousand dollars."

Pike scowled. "I didn't say it was gonna be easy, boys. But a thousand dollars apiece is more'n we made in a year down on the Nueces Strip."

"You're forgettin' one thing, Bill," Snow said. "How the hell are we gonna find one man in these mountains?"

*Return of the Mountain Man

Pike grinned and pointed over his shoulder down the ridge. "Easy. That there's Smoke Jensen's ranch, the Sugarloaf. I hear he's given up his guns and turned into a peaceable gentleman rancher. I figger we'll ride in and surround the place. Kill any son of a bitch that makes a move toward a gun. This poster says he's wanted dead or alive, so it's just as easy, maybe easier, to kill the bastard."

Blackie Johnson cleared his throat. "Uh, Bill. That there wanted poster don't say nothin' 'bout no ranch hands being wanted dead or alive."

Hank Snow laughed and slapped his thigh. "Hell, Blackie," he called as he punched brass into his six-gun. "You weren't so particular who you killed down Corpus way last year."

"That was different," Blackie growled back at Snow. "Them was Mexicans up from Mexico, an' you know a Mexican's just a little better'n an Injun."

"Don't worry about it, Blackie," Bill Pike said. "We won't kill nobody unless they draw down on us first."

His men began loading their shotguns and rifles while they looked down on the Sugarloaf, thinking this was going to be the easiest money they'd ever earned.

"He'll most likely have a woman with him, so we'll take her too an' have some fun with her tonight," Pike said.

When Blackie started to speak, Pike held up his hand. "Now, go easy Blackie. We won't kill her, just work her a little bit to have us some fun."

Blackie scowled but held his tongue, not wanting to be labeled a sissy by these tough men. He remembered how Whitey Jenkins had been brutally beaten down near Harlingen when he'd objected to Hank raping a young girl in her teens who they'd come upon on the road back to Corpus Christi.

Hank had cut the girl up pretty bad, and then he'd beaten Jenkins within an inch of his life. None of the men had stood up for Jenkins, with most saying he'd deserved what he got for being such a sissy about what Hank had done. Blackie didn't intend to make the same mistake.

Once the men were ready, Pike held up his hand and yelled, "Let's ride, boys!"

The ten men, loaded for bear, spurred their mounts down the ridge toward Smoke Jensen's ranch. As they rode, holding out six-shooters, rifles, and shotguns, Pike grinned as he thought about how they were going to kill Jensen and all his hands and take his woman for their pleasure. . . .

2

"You cold-mouthed son of a flea-bag good-for-nothin' . . . !" Pearlie yelled, struggling to hold on as his horse bucked and tried to swallow his head in the chill morning air.

Cal looked up from the morning fire, staring through steam rising off his coffee, and laughed. "Hey, Pearlie. When are you gonna learn to walk that hoss of yours around a little bit 'fore you try and mount him?" he hollered.

Pearlie held on to the saddle horn with one hand and the reins with another as his horse crow-hopped and danced around the cowboys' camp.

Smoke Jensen smiled as he screwed a cigarette into his face and bent over a match. He tipped smoke out of his nostrils, and watched as Pearlie finally regained some control over his mount and walked it toward the fire.

"Maybe he just needs a little coffee," Smoke offered while he took the blackened coffeepot off the coals and poured a cupful for Pearlie.

Pearlie jumped down out of the saddle, gave his horse a baleful look, and flicked the reins over a limb of one of the numerous cottonwood trees that lined the stream where they'd camped the night before.

He was still muttering to himself when he gratefully

accepted the cup of steaming brew from Smoke and took a deep draught.

Cal winked at Smoke and approached them. "Say, Pearlie," he said, trying to suppress a grin. "I know a man who's right handy with horses over at Big Rock. He could probably train that mount of your'n so he wouldn't do that every morning when you get on him."

Pearlie glared at Cal over the rim of his cup, his eyes flat and his expression black. "Cal, you know there ain't nobody in Big Rock knows any more 'bout horseflesh than I do," Pearlie said in an even voice.

Cal cut his eyes over at Cold, the name Pearlie had given his horse when it became evident he was extremely cold-mouthed in the morning and would buck for five to ten minutes the first time Pearlie got on him every day.

"Oh, yeah," Cal replied, now openly grinning. "I can see how well-trained Cold is."

Pearlie set his cup down and began to make himself a cigarette out of his fixin's.

"Just because that broken-down old nag of yours doesn't have enough spirit to buck, don't mean he's any better trained than Cold," he said.

Cal looked at Smoke and rolled his eyes. Smoke was used to this byplay between Cal and Pearlie, and would've been worried if it ever stopped. He knew the two would each put their lives on the line for each other without a second thought.

Smoke took a final drag of his cigarette and threw the butt in the fire. "If you two children are through jawing at each other," he said, "we've still got some beeves to move."

"Yes, sir," Cal said, dumping his coffee on the hot coals of the fire and beginning to put the dishes from their breakfast away. "I'll be ready in a few minutes." He looked over his shoulder and grinned. "After all, I don't have to spend a lot of time gettin' my mount ready to ride."

They were moving a small herd of fifty or so heifers south from the Sugarloaf to a distant neighbor's spread. The neighbor, a man by the name of Wiley, had made the mistake of buying some cattle from a seller who'd gotten them in south Texas the year before. Wiley's herd had been almost completely wiped out by Mexican tick fever carried by the Texas cattle.

When Sally, Smoke's wife, heard about the Wileys' plight from the man's wife one day in the general store in Big Rock, she'd immediately offered to stake them to a new starter herd.

"But Mrs. Jensen," the woman had said with tears in her eyes, "we don't have no money to buy a new herd with right now. In fact, Sam's been talking about heading back East to try and get a stake to start over."

"Don't you worry about paying us for the herd, Mrs. Wiley," Sally had said. "There'll be plenty of time to talk about that after you've built the herd up enough to sell some to market."

"But you don't hardly know us at all," Mrs. Wiley said.

"You're our neighbors," Sally answered. "That's all I need to know."

So now, in the final days of autumn before the winter snows would come to the Colorado high country, Smoke and the boys were making good on Sally's promise and driving the young beeves to the Wiley ranch.

As they got mounted up, Pearlie held up a coin. "Call it, Cal," he said.

"We ain't flippin' no coin for the drag position today, Pearlie. I rode it all day yesterday an' my throat is plumb raw from all the dust I ate."

The drag position on a trail drive, riding at the rear of the herd to round up stragglers, is the worst possible place to be. A moving herd of cattle throws up a lot of dust in the air, most of which is breathed in by the drag rider.

"Hey, Cal," Pearlie argued. "As the youngest man

on the team, you're supposed to ride drag every day. I think I'm bein' right nice to give you a chance to win the point position by flippin' for it."

"But I always lose!" Cal complained.

"It ain't my fault you the unluckiest man in Colorado," Pearlie countered.

"Oh, all right," Cal said. "I call tails."

Pearlie held out his left hand and flipped a coin. He caught it and turned it over onto the back of his right hand. "Heads," he said shortly, and spurred his horse toward the front of the herd.

As Pearly rode past, Smoke said, "Don't you ever feel guilty, cheating Cal like that?"

"Why?" Pearlie asked, his face a mask of innocence as he slowed his horse to a stop in front of Smoke. "What do you mean?"

Smoke shook his head. "I know all about those two coins you had made by the blacksmith in town. One with two heads and one with two tails."

Pearlie looked over his shoulder to see if Cal had heard what Smoke said. The boy was already fifty yards away and fast disappearing in the dust cloud that rose behind the herd. "You gonna tell Cal, Smoke?"

"No. The boy is a grown man now, and he's got to learn to find these things out for himself. It's not up to me to teach him how not to be cheated . . . especially by his best friend."

Pearlie got a pained expression on his face. "Aw, Smoke, I ain't exactly *cheatin'* Cal," he said, though it was clear he wasn't proud of what he'd done.

Smoke shrugged and smiled. "If it's not cheating, what exactly would you call it, Pearlie?"

Pearlie opened his mouth to reply, stopped, and just hung his head as he rode off toward the rear of the herd to change places with Cal.

Smoke was proud of him. Both of the young men were far more to him than just hired hands. In fact, both he and Sally felt as if the two were members of their family, and treated them accordingly.

As one of the beeves bolted from the herd and ran past Smoke, he pulled his rope off his saddle horn, let out a four-foot section, and whirled it in a circle as he spurred his horse, Joker, after the errant animal. Time to quit daydreaming and get to work, he thought, exulting in being back on the trail after a summer of working around the ranch.

Smoke had come to the high country of Colorado almost twenty years before with his father from Missouri to make a new life for them. Here they'd met up with an old mountain man named Preacher, who took both the pilgrims, as he called them, under his wing and taught them the facts of life on the frontier.

After Smoke's father was killed, Smoke rode with Preacher for many years, learning all the experienced mountain man could teach him about the mountains he so loved. It wasn't long before Smoke himself became one of the region's most famous mountain men, becoming a legend in his own time among that strange breed of men who had no use for civilization and its trappings.

After outlaws killed his wife and son, Smoke and Preacher tracked them down to Idaho and Smoke killed every one of the sons of bitches in face-to-face combat. This put him on the owlhoot trail for a time and he was a wanted man, until some federal marshals found out the truth and got him a pardon from the governor.

It was shortly after that when Smoke met up with a schoolteacher named Sally Reynolds and married her. They moved to the area where they lived now and founded their ranch, the Sugarloaf. Smoke had stayed on the right side of the law ever since.

Once the herd was bedded down for the night, Smoke and the boys made camp near a stream so they'd have water for cooking, though it was much too cold for bathing.

As they sat around the fire, eating beans and fat-back bacon cooked in a skillet, Smoke reached in a paper sack and took out a handful of biscuits Sally had prepared for them before they left the Sugarloaf.

He pitched a couple to Cal and to Pearlie and kept some for himself.

Pearlie used the biscuit to sop up some of the juice from the bacon and popped it in his mouth. He closed his eyes and moaned at the excellent taste. "Boy, Smoke, these sinkers Miss Sally made are sure tasty," he said.

Smoke nodded, too busy eating to reply.

Cal glanced over at Pearlie. "How would you know how good they taste, Pearlie? You're such a chowhound you don't even chew 'em 'fore you swallow 'em."

Pearlie grinned back at Cal, bacon juice running down his chin. "You don't have to chew these, Cal boy, they plumb melt in your mouth."

He took a deep drink of his boiled coffee, glanced down at his empty plate, and then looked over at Smoke, a wistful look in his eyes.

"You don't happen to have any of them bear sign Miss Sally made, do you?"

Sally Jensen was famous for miles around for the quality of the sweet doughnuts she baked that were called bear sign by mountain people. Pearlie was one of her most ardent admirers and had been known to eat an entire batch of bear sign on his own and then clamor for more.

Smoke looked in the paper sack. He reached in and pulled out two bear sign and held them up. "I see there's two left," he said, keeping his face serious.

He pitched one to Cal and kept one for himself. "Sorry, Pearlie, but if I remember correctly, you had a mite more than your share at our nooning today."

Pearlie's face looked panicked. "Smoke, you know

you can't do that to me. You and Cal wouldn't eat those bear sign in front of me without sharin', would you?"

Cal winked at Smoke. "I know, Pearlie," he said slyly. "Why don't we flip a coin for the last one?"

Pearlie smiled quickly, and then his face fell and he hung his head. "I knowed I shouldn't have told you 'bout those two-sided coins, Cal."

Smoke laughed and threw his bear sign to Pearlie. "Here you go, Pearlie. You can have mine."

"But don't you want it?" Pearlie asked, though he made no effort to return the pastry.

Smoke shook his head. "No." He patted his stomach. "Sally's been after me to lose some weight so she won't have to spend all winter letting out my britches."

Pearlie laughed. Smoke was anything but over-weight. Standing a little over six feet tall, with shoulders as wide as an ax handle, a stomach that looked like a washboard, and arms as big around as Pearlie's neck and as hard as granite, he certainly didn't need to lose weight. Pearlie knew it was simply Smoke's way of letting him have the bear sign without any argument.

Pearlie sighed. "I just can't do it, Smoke," he said, tearing the bear sign in half and throwing part of it back to Smoke. "But I will let you share it with me," he added, popping his half in his mouth before he could change his mind.

Smoke took the bear sign and dunked it in his coffee cup. "I agree with you, Pearlie," he said after devouring the doughnut. "Sally is the best cook in the territory."

"In the territory, hell," Pearlie added as he bent to light a cigarette off a burning stick from the fire. "She's the best cook in the world!"

3

Bill Pike held up his hand to slow his riders as they crossed several large pastures while moving toward the log cabin in the distance.

When the riders had slowed their mounts to a walk, Rufus Gordon pulled up next to Pike. "What's goin' on, Bill?" he asked.

Pike gave him a look. "I'm thinkin', Rufe," he answered. "Somthin' you don't know nothin' about."

Gordon pushed his hat back on his head and scratched his forehead with the barrel of a .44 pistol he was carrying. "What's there to think about, Bill? I thought we was gonna head on into Jensen's ranch and blow hell out of him."

Pike reined his horse in. "That's just it, Rufe. Does it look like anybody's workin' this here ranch?"

Gordon and the other men looked around. There were numerous cattle and some horses milling around in the fenced-in pastures between them and the cabin on the horizon, but no cowboys or other workers were present.

Gordon pursed his lips. "Now that you mention it, Bill, it do look a mite slow fer a workin' ranch."

"And what does that tell you, Rufe?"

"Uh, I dunno, Boss. You're the brains of this outfit."

Pike nodded. "Yeah, and don't you forget it. Now, what I think is that either Jensen is in that cabin, or he is somewhere else on the ranch outta sight."

"So, what's that mean?" Gordon asked, his brows knit in puzzlement.

"It means we don't want to go riding in all hell-bent for leather and warn him we're coming if he's in the cabin. Nope. We're gonna ride in nice and slow, like we've just come to pay a nice visit."

"But what if'n he comes outta that cabin blastin' away with his six-killers?" Gordon asked.

"Then, we'll cut him down like autumn wheat," Pike replied. He stood up in his stirrups to get a better look at the area around the cabin. He saw it was surrounded on three sides by heavy forest, though none of the trees were within a hundred yards of the house.

He nodded, talking low to himself. "Yeah, that Jensen is a careful feller all right. He's cut the trees back away from the cabin to give himself a clear field of fire in all directions so nobody can't sneak up on him when he's there."

Pike saw another building fifty or so yards from the cabin that had the look of a bunkhouse to it.

"And he's smart enough to keep the bunkhouse close so his men will be nearby in case he needs 'em," he mumbled to himself. "This ain't gonna be no easy hombre to corral," he said out loud to the men in his group. "He's careful and he's smart."

"What do you want us to do, Bill?" Gordon asked.

"Rufe, you take two men with you and ride on around to the left there and come up to the cabin from over there," he said, pointing to the trees off to the cabin's left side.

"Blackie, you take two men and circle off to the right and do the same thing. The rest of you come with me and we'll head straight on in toward the cabin. That way, if Jensen's in there and he sees us comin', he won't have no place to go to."

* * *

Sally Jensen was in the kitchen, frying some chicken for the ranch hands to eat for lunch when they got back from Big Rock. She'd sent them in to get some fencing supplies to have on hand for the upcoming winter season. The heavy snows of the high country always played havoc with their fences, and much of the winter season was spent repairing the ravages of the storms that came through the high valleys.

Though she and Smoke didn't have many employees, the few they had were well paid and treated as friends rather than employees. There were six men besides Cal and Pearlie that were full-time workers, and a dozen more who'd come in and help out part-time when it was calving season or if some beeves needed to be moved to market.

Four of the men were in Big Rock, and the other two were working on the walls of the bunkhouse, filling up holes so the winter winds wouldn't whistle through while they were sleeping.

Sam Curry stood up from the board he was sawing and stretched his back. "I'm going outside for a smoke, Will," he said. "You want me to see if Miss Sally has any coffee hot 'fore I come back?"

Will Bagby took some square-headed nails out of his mouth and nodded. "Yep, that'd be right nice, Sam," he answered. "That north wind is already startin' to get a mite chilly."

Curry laughed. "Hell, this is like summer compared to a month from now when you'll be freezin' your *cojones* off."

He fished the canvas sack containing his tobacco out of his shirt pocket, and was just taking one of his papers out of its packet when he stepped out of the bunkhouse to find four men on horses coming up the trail from the north pasture.

Curry, who knew just about everyone in the county, didn't recognize the men, and furthermore, he didn't like the look of them either. The had the look of trouble written on their faces, and the way they wore their guns tied down low on their hips let Curry know they weren't ordinary cowhands looking for work.

He'd left his own pistol on a peg in the bunkhouse, and it was too late to go for it now, so he just gave a low whistle as a signal to Will that there was possible trouble brewing.

"Howdy, gents," Sam said, nodding his head at the four men while he continued to build himself a cigarette. "What can I do for you?"

Bill Pike's eyes drifted down, and he saw the man standing in front of him wasn't wearing a side arm. "Howdy, mister," he said, smiling and trying not to look dangerous. "We're looking for a Mr. Smoke Jensen, and we was told this was his ranch. Is he around?"

Curry stalled for time. "Uh, what do you want to see Smoke about?"

Pike tried to keep his voice neutral and unthreatening. "Why, I don't think that's any of your business, sir," he said, smiling widely.

Suddenly, Will Bagby stepped from the bunkhouse door with a twelve-gauge shotgun cradled in his arms. "Well," he said, keeping his eyes on the men with Pike, "we work for Mr. Jensen. So if you don't want to state your business, you'll just have to ride on back to town," Bagby finished.

Pike's smile faded and he began to frown. "That's not very friendly, mister, pulling an express gun on us like that."

Pike's eyes raised and he stared behind Curry and Bagby, and then he nodded once.

A shot rang out and a hole as big as a fist appeared in Bagby's chest as the bullet Rufus Gordon fired into his back came out. Bagby flopped forward, blood pouring from his mouth and nostrils.

Curry yelled, "You bastards!" and bent to try to grab Will's shotgun.

Pike calmly drew his pistol and shot him in the face, blowing him backward up against the bunkhouse wall.

The door to the log cabin slammed open and a beautiful, dark-haired, hazel-eyed woman appeared on the porch. She was holding a sawed-off ten-gauge shotgun in her right hand and a short-barreled, silver pistol in her left hand.

"Hold on there!" she yelled, her eyes wide with horror as she saw her friends lying dead on the ground. "Drop those guns or I'll blow you to hell!" she said.

Rufus Gordon laughed and began to move his pistol toward her. She fired without aiming, and the pistol along with two of Gordon's fingers flew through the air.

"Ow . . . God damn!" Gordon yelled, bending over and cradling his right hand up against his belly to stop the bleeding. "She blowed my goddamn fingers off!" he moaned, tears of pain in his eyes.

As Pike's gun hand began to move, Sally eared back the twin hammers on the ten-gauge and smiled grimly at him. "Just twitch, mister, and give me a reason to scatter your guts all over my front yard," she said menacingly.

Pike, who'd rarely ever feared a man, and never a woman, felt his guts turn to ice and knew he was as close to dying as he'd ever been in his life. He let go of his pistol and let it swing down to hang by the trigger guard on his trigger finger.

Sally shook her head. "That won't do, mister. My husband invented the border shift. Just drop the pistol on the ground."

Pike smiled, though he had to force his lips to move. "Would your husband be Smoke Jensen, ma'am?" he asked.

Sally didn't answer, but turned her attention to the other men riding with Pike. "Now, all of you. Unbutton those gunbelts and let them drop."

Pike noticed some movement behind the woman

out of the corner of his eye, but he kept his gaze fixed on her face so she wouldn't be warned.

Spreading his arms wide to get her attention, Pike said, "We don't want no trouble, ma'am. We just wanted to talk to Smoke about some business," he said, trying to keep his voice level.

Sally's eyes flicked to the two dead men lying next to the bunkhouse.

Before she had a chance to respond, Blackie Johnson stepped up to her from around the corner of the cabin and stuck his pistol in her back. "Drop that scattergun, little lady," he growled.

Sally's finger tightened on the triggers of the shotgun, and for a moment, Pike thought she was going to fire anyway. He felt his bowels rumble at the thought of what ten gauge buckshot would do to him, before her face fell and she lowered the two guns to the porch and raised her hands.

Pike grinned with relief and stepped down off his horse. "Check out the cabin, Blackie," he said as he bent and picked up his pistol and held it pointed at the woman.

Blackie entered the door and returned a moment later. "All clear, Boss," he said, holstering his pistol. "There ain't nobody else around."

Pike walked up to the woman and backhanded her with his left hand, snapping her head back and drawing blood from her full, red lips.

"Now, unless you want to end up like your men over there, tell us where your husband is, Mrs. Jensen," he snarled.

Sally sucked the blood off her lips, grinned, and spat directly into Pike's face. "You'll find out soon enough, you coward," she said evenly, showing not the slightest trace of fear. She looked again at the dead men and smiled grimly. "In fact, his face will be the last thing you ever see when he finds out what you've done and comes to kill you."

"You talk big for someone who's lookin' down the

barrel of a six-gun, lady," Pike said, admiring her courage in spite of his frustration at not being able to cower her.

"I've looked down the barrel of guns before, mister," she replied, "and I'm still here, which is more than you'll be able to say after Smoke gets through with you."

Pike took a deep breath as he looked around the ranch. "Well, I guess he's not here, so our best bet is to take his woman and hightail it off his home territory, boys," Pike said to his men.

"Where're we going, Boss?" Blackie asked.

Pike's eyes went to the mountains in the distance. "Let's head on up into the high country. We'll leave Jensen a note telling him if he wants to see his woman alive again, he'll come up there to talk to us."

He looked back at Sally. "Tie her up good and tight and put her on a horse while I write Mr. Smoke Jensen a note," he said.

While his men tied Sally's arms behind her and saddled up one of the horses in the nearby corral, Pike wrote a note to Smoke, and then he pinned it to Sam Curry's shirt.

Blackie, who was watching him, asked, "Why don't you leave it in the cabin, Boss?"

Pike grinned maliciously. "'Cause I've got other plans for the house," he said.

Once the men had Sally up on the horse and had bandaged Rufus Gordon's right hand, Pike went into the cabin. He stripped the sheets off the bed and piled them in the middle of the kitchen floor, poured kerosene on them from the lanterns, and then put a match to the pile of cloth.

By the time he was on his horse and they'd ridden out into the pasture toward the distant mountains, bright orange flames were licking the roof of the cabin sending clouds of dark smoke into the overcast sky.

Sally glanced back over her shoulder, tears of loss and frustration in her eyes.

4

Peg Jackson, owner of the general store in Big Rock along with her husband, Ed, checked the list in her hand for a final time while Emmit Walsh looked on.

"Well, Emmit," Peg said, "I think we've gotten just about all of the things Sally sent you into town for, with the exception of the gingham cloth she wanted. Just tell her I'm expecting that in on the next shipment from Colorado Springs and it ought to be here next week."

"Yes, ma'am," Emmit said as he filled his arms with some of the packages of foodstuffs and canned goods Sally Jensen had asked him to get from the store.

"You want Ed to help you load those things?" Peg asked.

Emmit shook his head. "No, ma'am, thank you. I can handle it."

He carried the bags out to the buckboard parked in front of the store where the other men from the Sugarloaf were waiting for him.

The back of the buckboard was stuffed with bales of wire, stacks of fence posts, buckets of nails, four salt-lick blocks, and other sundry ranching necessities they'd picked up from the feed store down the street.

"That about got it?" Josey McComb, another of the hired hands, asked.

"Yep," Emmit replied.

Monte Carson, sheriff of Big Rock, ambled by, taking a stroll down the boardwalk. He was, as usual, smoking his pipe and sending clouds of evil-smelling smoke into the chilly autumn air.

He stepped over to the buckboard and stopped to lean his arms on the sides of the wagon. "Looks like Smoke's gonna have you boys busy doing some fencing 'fore the winter snows come," he observed cheerfully.

When Emmit and Josey nodded, Carson added, "Well, don't let Smoke work you too hard."

Emmit laughed. "Oh, Smoke's not there right now, Sheriff. He and Cal and Pearlie are taking some beeves over to the Wiley spread to help them out after all their cattle died of tick fever. It's Miss Sally that's being the slave driver. I've never seen a woman work so hard to make a place look good."

Carson grinned. "Yeah, Sally Jensen is a perfectionist all right, but they've got a right nice place to show for it."

"You can say that again," Josey said. "She's even got us putting little wooden tags with numbers on 'em on the beeves' ears so we'll know when each one of 'em drops their calves. She keeps it all in a little book up at the cabin."

"That's what you get for working for an ex-schoolmarm," Carson said, shaking his head. "Teachers like to keep things neat and orderly."

"I don't mind," Emmit said. "The Jensens are about the nicest folks I've ever worked for, and the food is the best in the area."

Carson nodded. "Especially those bear sign Sally's so famous for, huh?"

"Stop it, Sheriff," Josey said. "You're makin' my mouth water just thinkin' 'bout 'em."

Carson tapped out his pipe on the side of the buckboard, put it in his shirt pocket, and moved back to the boardwalk. "Well, see ya later, boys," he called, waving over his shoulder.

"See ya, Sheriff," they answered, and Emmit jumped up on the hurricane deck of the wagon and slapped the horses with the reins to get them started back toward the Sugarloaf.

Josey and the other two cowboys followed on their horses, singing old campfire tunes as Josey played on his mouth-harp.

As they passed the city limits sign, Emmit pulled out his pocket watch. "Looks like we'll be back home just in time for lunch."

"I sure hope Miss Sally has that fried chicken ready when we get there," Josey said.

When the buckboard crested a small rise about ten miles from the Sugarloaf, Emmit jerked back on the reins. "Oh, shit!" he called.

"What is it?" Josey asked, letting his horse come up even with Emmit.

"Looky there," Emmit said, pointing up ahead.

Josey followed his gesture and saw a large cloud of black smoke rising and spreading across the sky.

"Damn!" he exclaimed. "That looks like it's comin' from the cabin area."

"Josey," Emmit said, "you hightail it on back to town and get the sheriff and anyone else you can find an' bring 'em out to the Sugarloaf. Tell 'em it looks like Miss Sally's in trouble."

"Jim," he said to one of the cowboys as he jumped down off the buckboard, "give me your mount an' you bring the buckboard on along. I'm gonna ride as fast as I can to see if'n there's anything I can do until we get some help."

He swung up onto Jim's saddle and whipped the horse with the reins as he dug his spurs into its flanks. "Giddy up, hoss!" he yelled as he and the other cowboy bent over their mounts' necks and raced toward the ranch.

Monte Carson was in his office, sitting leaned back in his chair with his feet up on his desk, enjoying his fifth cup of coffee of the morning, when Josey burst through his door.

When the door burst open and slammed back against the wall, the noise startled Carson so much he jumped and spilled coffee all down his shirt.

"God damn!" he yelped, and hurriedly brushed at the scalding liquid as it burned his chest.

"Sheriff, you got to come quick!" Josey McComb yelled. "There's a big fire out at the Sugarloaf."

Carson stopped fussing with his shirt and stared at Josey. "What?" he asked.

"On the way out to the ranch we saw a big cloud of smoke coming from the area of the cabin," Josey said, still breathing hard from his ride into town.

"Is Sally all right?" Carson asked as he grabbed his hat off a rack next to the door.

"Don't know, Sheriff. Emmit told me to get back here an' get some help to come out to the ranch."

Carson ran out of the door and stopped on the boardwalk. "You go on over to the general store and get Ed and Peg! I'll get Doc Spalding and anyone else I can find!"

As Monte Carson ran down the street toward Dr. Colton Spalding's office, his heart was filled with dread to think that something might have happened to Sally Jensen. Smoke and Sally were his closest friends in Big Rock, and were responsible for him being sheriff.

Before he came to Big Rock, Carson had been a well-known gunfighter, though he had never ridden the owlhoot trail.

A local rancher, with plans to take over the county,

had hired Carson to be the sheriff of Fontana, a town just down the road from Smoke's Sugarloaf spread. Carson went along with the man's plans for a while, till he couldn't stomach the rapings and killings any longer. He put his foot down and let it be known that Fontana was going to be run in a law-abiding manner from then on.

The rancher, Tilden Franklin, sent a bunch of riders in to teach the upstart sheriff a lesson. The men killed Carson's two deputies and seriously wounded Carson, taking over the town. In retaliation, Smoke founded the town of Big Rock, and he and his band of aging gunfighters cleaned house in Fontana.

When the fracas was over, Smoke offered the job of sheriff of Big Rock to Monte Carson. Monte married a grass widow and settled into the job like he was born to it. Neither Smoke nor the citizens of Big Rock ever had cause to regret his taking the job.

Monte Carson knew he owed the Jensens a debt he could never repay, and he'd be damned if he was going to let anything happen to Sally while Smoke was away.

Louis Longmont, owner of Longmont's Saloon, was sitting at his usual table, sipping on a china cup filled with his favorite chicory-flavored coffee. Even though it was still mid-morning, he was playing poker with three trail hands who'd come to town the previous night. The game had been going on for over twelve hours, and showed no signs of stopping anytime soon. He was in the process of what he called teaching amateurs the laws of chance.

Louis was a lean, hawk-faced man, with strong, slender hands and long fingers, nails carefully manicured, hands clean. He had jet-black hair and a black pencil-thin mustache. He was, as usual, dressed in a black suit, with white shirt and dark ascot—something he'd picked up on a trip to England some years back. He wore low-heeled boots, and a pistol hung in tied-down leather on his right side. It was not for show, for Louis was snake-quick with a short gun and was a feared, deadly gunhand when pushed.

Louis was not an evil man. He had never hired his gun out for money. And while he could make a deck of cards do almost anything, he did not cheat at poker. He did not have to cheat. He was possessed of a phenomenal memory and could tell you the odds of filling any type of poker hand, and was one of the first to use the new method of card counting.

He was just past forty years of age. He had come to the West as a very small boy, with his parents, arriving from Louisiana. His parents had died in a shantytown fire, leaving the boy to cope as best he could.

He had coped quite well, plying his innate intelligence and willingness to take a chance into a fortune. He owned a large ranch up in Wyoming Territory, several businesses in San Francisco, and a hefty chunk of a railroad.

Though it was a mystery to many why Longmont stayed with the hard life he had chosen, his best friend Smoke Jensen thought he understood. Once, Louis had said to him, "Smoke, I would miss my life every bit as much as you would miss the dry-mouthed moment before the draw, the challenge of facing and besting those miscreants who would kill you or others, and the so-called loneliness of the owlhoot trail."

Sometimes Louis joked that he would like to draw against Smoke someday, just to see who was faster. Smoke allowed as how it would be close, but that he would win. "You see, Louis, you're just too civilized," he had told him on many occasions. "Your mind is distracted by visions of operas, fine foods and wines, and the odds of your winning the match. Also, your fatal flaw is that you can almost always see the good in the lowest creatures God ever made, and you refuse to believe that anyone is pure evil and without hope of redemption."

When Louis laughed at this description of himself, Smoke would continue. "Me, on the other hand, when some snake-scum draws down on me and wants to dance, the only thing I have on my mind is teaching him that when you dance, someone has to pay the band. My mind is clear and focused on only one problem, how to put that stump-sucker across his horse toes-down."

Louis had tried his best not to take all of the cowhands' money during the long night, though it would have been relatively easy for him. He knew the men had worked over three months on the trail to amass the money they were now risking in the poker game, and he had no desire to take all of it from them. However, he didn't mind taking enough to pay for his time and to teach the men that poker wasn't really a game of chance so much as a game of skill.

The man across the table from him raised Louis's bet. Louis was considering whether to let the man have the pot so he'd be able to stay in the game a while longer, or whether he should just go on and clean him out so he could go home and get some sleep, when Monte Carson and Doc Spalding rushed through the batwings as if their pants were on fire.

Louis turned his head and raised his eyebrows in question. It wasn't like Monte to get so riled up this early in the morning.

"Louis," Carson said, rushing over to the table. "There's a fire out at the Sugarloaf. Emmit says it looks like it might be the house, and Sally's there alone."

Without a second thought, Louis flipped his cards onto the table. "I'm out of the game, gentlemen."

As he stood up, the man across the table scowled. "You can't leave now," he growled. "You got to give me a chance to win my money back."

"It took you twelve hours to lose it, pilgrim," Louis said

as he scooped the money in front of him into his pocket. "How long do you think it'd take you to win it back?"

"That ain't the point," the man said, jumping to his feet with his hand next to the butt of his pistol.

Before he could blink, Louis had drawn his Colt and cocked it and had the barrel inches from the man's nose. "You might want to reconsider your words, mister," Louis said in a low voice. "I'm in a bit of a hurry, so either pull that hog-leg and go to work, or shut up and sit down."

The man gulped and sat down, his face pale and sweating.

Louis smiled and holstered his weapon. "Andre," he called to his French chef. "Fix these men anything they want to eat and put it on my bill," he said, and then he whirled around and raced out of the saloon behind Carson and the doctor.

When he got on his horse, Louis noticed it looked like half the town was in the street heading out toward the Sugarloaf. The Jensens were well liked in Big Rock and the citizens were on their way to help.

5

By the time Sheriff Monte Carson and Louis Longmont and the rest of the people from Big Rock
arrived at the Sugarloaf, Smoke and Sally's cabin had
burned to the ground.

Monte got off his horse and walked over to where
Emmit Walsh and Jim Sanders were standing over
the bodies of Will Bagby and Sam Curry, lying next
to the bunkhouse. Their hats were in their hands
and expressions of sorrow were on their faces.

Doc Spalding ran over, and knelt down next to the
bodies and examined them for a moment, taking
note of the gunshot wounds. He glanced up at
Emmit and then over at the smoldering ruins of the
cabin. "Any sign of Sally, boys?" he asked, dreading
the answer.

Emmit shook his head. "No, sir. We even checked
the bunkhouse just to make sure she wasn't in there."

Monte followed his gaze toward the pile of smoking logs and wood where the cabin used to stand. "I
guess we're gonna have to comb through the rubble
to see if Sally's in there somewhere."

Louis walked up, stood next to Monte, and stared
down at the bodies. He noticed a piece of paper

stuck on the front of Sam's shirt. He pointed his finger. "You might want to take a look at that, Monte," he said.

Monte bent down and took the paper, holding it up so he could read it. "Smoke Jensen," he read out loud, "we got your wife. Come to Pueblo one week from today and go to one of the saloons. Come alone if you ever want to see her alive again. If you bring the law, you'll find pieces of her scattered all over the mountains."

Monte glanced at Louis. "Son of a bitch!" he said, his voice tight with anger. "They've taken Sally."

"Is there a signature on the paper?" Louis asked.

Monte nodded. "Yeah, it's signed W. Pike."

"W. Pike? Have you ever heard Smoke mention that name, Monte?" Louis asked, his expression puzzled.

Monte shook his head. "Not that I remember."

Doc Spalding stood up. "Sam Curry wasn't armed, Monte," he said, "but it looks like Will had a shotgun." He inclined his head toward the scattergun lying next to Will's body.

"Sam never wore a gun, Sheriff," Emmit said. "He kept one in his saddlebags in case of snakes or wolves or such, but he didn't believe in wearing one."

"It looks like Will was shot in the back, Monte, and Sam was shot in the face," Doc Spalding said.

Monte shook his head. "Bastards gunned them down without giving them a chance."

Louis looked at Emmit. "When was Smoke due to arrive at the Wileys' ranch?" he asked. Everyone in town was aware of the Jensens' charitable gift to the Wileys, and a couple of other ranchers had donated some cattle for Smoke to add to the ones he was taking there.

"He should be gettin' there today sometime," Emmit answered.

Louis looked at Monte. "We'd better head on over there and let Smoke know what's happened," he said. "Maybe he'll know who this Pike is and why he'd want to do this."

"I'll take care of the bodies and see that they get a proper burial," Doc Spalding said.

Ed Jackson stepped forward. "Tell Smoke the people of Big Rock will take care of cleaning up the cabin. We'll save whatever we can."

Monte and Louis swung up into their saddles. "Peg, would you let my wife know where I'm goin'?" Monte said. He and his wife lived a short way out of town on a small spread, and she wouldn't have heard what was going on yet.

"Sure, Monte. Ed and I'll go by there on our way back to town."

"Just a minute, Sheriff," Emmit said, and he ran over to the corral behind the bunkhouse. He returned a few minutes later with two horses with dally ropes on their halters. "Take these broncs with you. That way you can change hosses when yours get tired."

Monte and Louis each took a dally rope in their hands, and jerked their horses' heads around and put the spurs to them, heading off toward the Wiley ranch. It would normally be a two- or three-day ride, but if they pushed it and used the extra horses, they could make it in a day and a half.

Smoke and Cal and Pearlie pushed the beeves they were herding over a crest above a valley, and looked down at the Wiley ranch in the distance. It wasn't a particularly large spread, just big enough for Mr. and Mrs. Wiley and one hired hand to run by themselves.

Cal moved up from the drag position on the herd next to Smoke. "Jiminy, what's that smell?" he asked, wrinkling his nose up at the smell of charred and burning flesh.

Smoke pointed off to the side of one of the Wileys' pastures. A large pile of what looked like cattle was being burned. "Mr. Wiley is burning the carcasses of his cattle that died from tick fever," he said. "That's about the only way to stop the fever from infecting other cattle he puts on the ranch."

"That's good," Cal said, taking off his hat and slapping dust off his clothes. "I'd sure hate to drive these beeves all this way and have them take sick too."

Smoke looked up as a light dusting of snow began to fall from dark clouds overhead. "The cold weather and snow will help too," he said. "It should kill off any ticks that still have the disease before they can make the new cattle sick."

Pearlie rode over to join Smoke and Cal. "You two gonna sit here jawin' all day, or are we gonna get these beeves down to the Wileys?"

Smoke laughed. "What's your hurry, Pearlie?" he asked.

"It's time for lunch, Smoke, an' I'm so hungry my stomach thinks my throat's been cut."

As they moved the cattle down the ridge toward the valley, Mr. Wiley and his hired hand saw them coming, and got on their horses and rode out to help them bring the herd in.

Bill Wiley shut the gate on his north pasture behind the last of the beeves, dusted his hands off on his britches, and turned to Smoke and the boys. "Come on up to the house, men. Martha oughta have lunch ready by now."

Smoke drew a startled look from Pearlie when he said, "We don't want to impose, Mr. Wiley."

"Don't be silly, and please call me Bill. When I saw you boys up on the ridge, I told Martha to cook us up a couple of turkeys I trapped this fall."

"Turkeys?" Pearlie said, almost drooling at the thought of a turkey dinner.

"Yep, with all the fixin's," Wiley said.

6

Snow began to fall from dark, ominous-looking clouds and the temperature started to fall. Sally, riding near the front of the band of outlaws, shivered and felt her hands begin to grow numb.

Bill Pike looked at her, noticing for the first time she was only wearing a relatively thin housedress. Her heavier clothes and coats had been in the cabin they'd burned, and none of the men had thought to get something more suitable for Sally to travel in before the house was torched.

Pike reached behind his saddle and pulled a yellow poncho out of his saddlebags. Even though it was thin, it was made of oilcloth and would keep the worst of the wind and snow off the woman. He kneed his horse over next to Sally's and prepared to drape it over her head and shoulders.

Sally glanced at him, her eyes flat and emotionless. "Since you're being so thoughtful, would you mind loosening my hands?" she asked.

Pike glanced at her hands, and saw that they were pale and almost blue from lack of circulation. Though he wasn't sure just yet what he was going to end up doing with this woman of Smoke Jenson's, he wasn't totally heartless.

He slipped a long-bladed knife from a scabbard in his boot and sliced through the ropes binding Sally's hands behind her back. Holding the knife point in front of Sally's face as she rubbed her hands trying to get feeling back in them, he growled, "I'm gonna leave your hands untied, Mrs. Jensen. But I'm warnin' you, if you try to run or cause any other trouble, we'll catch you, an' then I'll use this knife on your face so even Smoke won't ever want to look at you again."

Sally looked at the knife. "Point taken," she said in an even tone, showing no fear.

"What?" Pike asked, not understanding the term.

"I understand what you're saying," Sally said, carefully not promising not to try and escape.

"That's good," Pike said, "'Cause my problem is with Smoke, not you, an' I'd hate to have to hurt you."

Sally's eyes narrowed. "What problem do you have with my husband, Mr. Pike?" she asked.

Pike gave her a nasty grin as he put the knife back in its scabbard. "That's none of your business, Mrs. Jensen."

"I think it *is* my business, Mr. Pike. After all, when a woman's husband has to kill a man, it's only right she should know why he had to do it."

Pike threw back his head and laughed. "I think you got it backward, little lady. Smoke ain't gonna kill me, I'm gonna kill him."

Sally smiled sweetly and shook her head, her eyes sad. "Do you have any idea how many men before you have said that, Mr. Pike, and how many men are dead because they underestimated Smoke Jensen?"

Pike's expression darkened, and he clamped his jaws shut tight and spurred his horse on up ahead of Sally so he wouldn't have to talk to her anymore.

He rode up next to Rufus Gordon, who was riding bent over with his ruined hand pressed tight against his belly. Gordon glanced at him and then back over his shoulder at Sally. "I'm hurtin' awful bad, Bill," he groaned.

Pike nodded. "I know, Rufe. We'll get you some laudanum when we get to Canyon City. We got to pass through there on the way to Pueblo."

Gordon cut his eyes back to Sally. "And when the time comes, I want to be the one to kill her, Bill. I owe her for what she done to my hand."

Bill grinned. "Maybe you ought to thank her instead, Rufe. From where I sit, it looks like she coulda put that bullet in your brain just as easily as in your hand."

"That don't matter, Bill. She damn near shot my hand off an' I'm gonna make her pay!"

Pike's eyes got hard and his expression soured. "You'll do exactly what I tell you to do and nothing else, Rufe!" he snarled back. "I'm still head man of this outfit, and I'll tell you what you can do and what you can't do. Got me?"

Gordon's eyes fell. "Yeah. I ain't tryin' to cross you, Bill."

"That's good, Rufe, 'cause what that lady did to you ain't nothin' to what I'll do to you if you ever try to go against me."

After they finished the turkey dinner, Mr. Wiley and Smoke and the boys went out on Wiley's porch for coffee and smokes. While Wiley filled an old corncob pipe with black tobacco, Smoke and Cal and Pearlie all built themselves cigarettes.

Wiley stood at the porch rail and watched as the snow became thicker. "I think it'd be best if you men spent the night here, Smoke," he said. "There ain't no use in you trying to get started tonight with this storm brewing."

Smoke took a drag on his cigarette and chased it with some of Mrs. Wiley's excellent coffee as he stared out into the early evening snowfall. "We wouldn't want to put you and Martha out, Bill," he said.

Wiley waved his pipe in the air. "Don't be silly, Smoke," he said. "It won't be any trouble at all, and you and the boys can start out fresh in the morning after a good breakfast."

At the mention of food, Pearlie's ears perked up. "That sounds good to me, Smoke," he said, licking his lips.

"Any time somebody mentions food it sounds good to you, Pearlie," Cal said, laughing.

Smoke and Wiley joined in the laughter, and Smoke said, "We'll accept your hospitality, Bill, but only if Martha will let Pearlie and Cal do the dishes after we eat."

"That's a deal," Wiley said.

The storm broke during the night, and the day dawned with clear skies and the temperature just above freezing. After a hearty breakfast of scrambled hens' eggs, deer sausage, and biscuits almost as good as Sally made, Smoke and Bill Wilcy went out on the porch to finish their coffee while Cal and Pearlie helped Martha Wiley clean up the kitchen dishes.

As they sat there, smoking and drinking coffee, Smoke's sharp eyes saw two figures appear on the ridge above the Wileys' valley.

"Looks like you have company coming," Smoke said.

Wiley got to his feet and walked over to the edge of the porch. "Must be something important," he said. "The poor bastards must've ridden all night through that storm to get here."

Smoke stepped into the house and got his binoculars out of his saddlebags. When he put them to his eyes, he was startled to recognize the riders as Monte Carson and Louis Longmont.

"Damn!" he muttered to himself, his heart racing. The presence of his two best friends way out here could only mean serious trouble back home. His mouth grew dry and his stomach churned at the thought that maybe something had happened to Sally.

Bill Wiley stuck his head back in the door to the house. "We got company coming, Martha. Better put on some more coffee and fix up some more breakfast."

Smoke jumped off the porch and ran through ankle-deep snow to meet Monte and Louis in the front yard.

"What's wrong?" he asked, not waiting for them to get off their horses.

Monte and Louis looked at each other, neither wanting to be the one to break the news to their friend.

Finally, Louis spoke. "Someone attacked the Sugarloaf, Smoke. They killed Sam Curry and Will Bagby, burnt your house down, and took Sally with them."

Smoke stopped dead in his tracks. "Are you sure they took her?"

Monte and Louis climbed stiffly down off their horses. Snow and ice were packed on their hats and shoulders. "Yeah," Monte said, reaching in his pocket. "They left this note."

As he handed the note to Smoke, Bill Wiley came out of the house and took their horses' reins. "You men get on in the house 'fore you freeze to death out here. I'll have my hand take care of your horses."

Minutes later, while Monte and Louis warmed up by eating breakfast and drinking several cups of coffee, they explained what had happened at the Sugarloaf to a rapt audience.

When they finished, Smoke read the note for the fifth time, trying to remember if he'd ever crossed paths with anyone named W. Pike.

"You have any idea why this Pike fellow would do such a thing, Smoke?" Monte asked. He knew Smoke had made a lot of enemies in his many years on the frontier.

Smoke started to shake his head, and then he remembered a day long ago when he and Preacher rode into Rico. . . .

Smoke and Preacher dismounted in front of the combination trading post and saloon. As was his custom, Smoke slipped the thongs from the hammers of his Colts as soon as his boots hit dirt.

They bought their supplies, and had turned to leave when the hum of conversation suddenly died. Two rough-dressed and unshaven men, both wearing guns, blocked the door.

"Who owns that horse out there?" one demanded, a snarl in his voice, trouble in his manner. "The one with the SJ brand?"

Smoke laid his purchases on the counter. "I do," he said quietly.

"Which way'd you ride in from?"

Preacher had slipped to his right, his left hand covering the hammer of his Henry, concealing the click as he thumbed it back.

Smoke faced the men, his right hand hanging loose by his side. His left hand was just inches from his left-hand gun. "Who wants to know—and why?"

No one in the dusty building moved or spoke.

"Pike's my name," the bigger and uglier of the pair said. "And I say you came through my diggin's yesterday and stole my dust."

"And I say you're a liar," Smoke told him.

Pike grinned nastily, his right hand hovering near the butt of his pistol. "Why . . . you little pup. I think I'll shoot your ears off."

"Why don't you try? I'm tired of hearing you shoot your mouth off."

Pike looked puzzled for a few seconds; bewilderment crossed his features. No one had ever talked to him in this manner. Pike was big, strong, and a bully. "I think I'll just kill you for that."

Pike and his partner reached for their guns.

Four shots boomed in the low-ceilinged room, four shots so closely spaced they seemed as one thunderous roar. Dust and birds' droppings fell from the ceiling. Pike and his friend were slammed out the open doorway. One fell off the rough porch, dying in the dirt street. Pike, with two holes in his chest, died with his back against a support pole, his eyes still open, unbelieving. Neither had managed to pull a pistol more than halfway out of leather.

All eyes in the black-powder-filled and dusty, smoky room moved to the young man standing by the bar, a Colt in each hand. "Good God!" a man whispered in awe. "I never even seen him draw."

Preacher moved the muzzle of his Henry to cover the men at the tables. The bartender put his hands slowly on the bar, indicating he wanted no trouble.

"We'll be leaving now," Smoke said, holstering his Colts and picking up his purchases from the counter. He walked out the door slowly.

Smoke stepped over the sprawled, dead legs of Pike, and walked past his dead partner in the shooting.

"What are we 'posed to do with the bodies?" a man asked Preacher.

"Bury 'em."

"What's the kid's name?"

"Smoke."

A few days later, in a nearby town, a friend of Preacher's told Smoke that two men, Haywood and Thompson, who claimed to be Pike's half brother, had tracked him and Preacher and were in town waiting for Smoke.

Smoke walked down the rutted street an hour before sunset, the sun at his back—the way he had planned it. Thompson and Haywood were in a big tent at the end of the street, which served as saloon and cafe. Preacher had pointed them out earlier and asked if Smoke needed his help. Smoke said no. The refusal came as no surprise.

As he walked down the street, a man glanced up, spotted him, then hurried quickly inside.

Smoke felt no animosity toward the men in the tent saloon—no anger, no hatred. But they'd come here after him, so let the dance begin, he thought.

Smoke stopped fifty feet from the tent. "Haywood! Thompson! You want to see me?"

The two men pushed back the tent flap and stepped out, both angling to get a better look at the man they had tracked. "You the kid called Smoke?" one said.

"I am."

"Pike was my brother," the heavier of the pair said. "And Shorty was my pal."

"You should choose your friends more carefully," Smoke told him.

"They was just a-funnin' with you," Thompson said.

"You weren't there. You don't know what happened."

"You callin' me a liar?"

"If that's the way you want to take it."

Thompson's face colored with anger, his hand moving closer to the .44 in his belt. "You take that back or make your play."

"There is no need for this," Smoke said.

The second man began cursing Smoke as he stood tensely, legs spread wide, body bent at the waist. "You're a damned thief. You stolt their gold and then kilt 'em."

"I don't want to have to kill you," Smoke said.

"The kid's yellow!" Haywood yelled. Then he grabbed for his gun.

Haywood touched the butt of his gun just as two loud gunshots blasted in the dusty street. The .36-caliber balls struck Haywood in the chest, one nicking his heart. He dropped to the dirt, dying. Before he closed his eyes, and death relieved him of the shocking pain by pulling him into a long sleep, two more shots thundered. He had a dark vision of Thompson spinning in the street. Then Haywood died.

Thompson was on one knee, his left hand holding his shattered right elbow. His leg was bloody. Smoke had knocked his gun from his hand, and then he'd shot him in the leg.

"Pike was your brother," Smoke told the man. "So I can understand why you came after me. But you were wrong. I'll let you live. But stay with mining. If I ever see you again, I'll kill you."

The young man turned, putting his back to the dead and bloody pair. He walked slowly up the street, his high-heeled Spanish riding boots pocking the air with dusty puddles.*

*The Last Mountain Man

7

Monte Carson, noting the faraway look in Smoke's eyes, shook him gently by the shoulder. "Smoke, are you all right?" he asked.

Smoke's eyes cleared and he shook his head. "Uh, yeah, Monte. I was just remembering a time long ago when Preacher and I went up against some men." He glanced around the table. "One of them I killed was named Pike."

"Do you think this W. Pike who kidnapped Sally is related to the man you killed?" Louis Longmont asked.

Smoke shrugged. "I don't know, Louis." He thought for a moment. "There was another man there, named Thompson, who said he was Pike's half brother."

"Did you drill him too, Smoke?" Cal asked.

Smoke shook his head. "No. As I remember, after I shot him in the arm and the leg, most of the fight went out of him, so I let him live."

Louis shook his head. "You know better than that, Smoke," he said.

Smoke's eyes met Louis's. "I was only in my teens at the time, Louis. I hadn't learned yet not to ever leave a man alive who has reason to come after you later."

Bill Wiley, standing over at the counter next to his wife, Martha, cleared his throat. "Gentlemen, I ain't exactly an expert in all this, but I think we're getting off the point here. It don't matter why this galoot took Smoke's wife. The question is, what are we gonna do about it?"

Smoke glanced over at Wiley, a sad expression on his face. "There is no *we*, Bill. Pike, whoever he is, made it clear in his letter that I was to come after him alone. I can't risk any harm coming to Sally by charging up to Pueblo with a posse, even if they are my best friends."

"But Smoke," Pearlie said. "You can't go after them alone. They're sure to be waitin' for you along the trail. You wouldn't stand a chance."

Smoke ignored Pearlie and asked Monte, "Did you check out the tracks around the cabin, Monte? Any idea of how many men were riding with Pike?"

Monte nodded. "Louis and I both took a look, Smoke. It wasn't real clear, but it looked like between eight and twelve different tracks in the area."

Smoke got to his feet. "Well, they probably didn't know where I was, or they would've come up here to get me, so that gives me a slight edge. I can be in Pueblo a couple of days ahead of the deadline, before they're expecting me."

"So could Monte and I, Smoke," Louis said.

Smoke shook his head. "No, it's too dangerous, Louis. Both you and Monte are too well known around Big Rock. If this Pike sent a couple of men to look the town over before attacking the Sugarloaf, they might have seen you around."

"That don't apply to Cal and me," Pearlie said. "We been with you the whole time, so they couldn't have seen us."

Louis nodded. "Pearlie's right, Smoke. Having a couple of extra guns around just might give you the edge you need to save Sally."

"I agree, Smoke," Monte said. "If, God forbid, they

do manage to get the drop on you, there'd still be Cal and Pearlie there to maybe save Sally."

Smoke thought for a moment, and then he slowly nodded. "You're right, as usual, Louis, and saving Sally is the most important thing to think about."

He stepped over to his saddlebags and pulled out a wrinkled map of Colorado. Spreading it on the table, he bent over it. "See here, if they head straight for Pueblo from the Sugarloaf, they're going to have to go through Canyon City first."

He looked at Louis. "Louis, I need to borrow some of that cash you always carry. I didn't bring much with me when I left the Sugarloaf."

Louis grinned and pulled a large, black wallet from his coat pocket. He pulled out a wad of greenbacks and handed it to Smoke. "There ought to be about five thousand dollars there, Smoke, give or take a hundred."

Smoke handed the bills to Pearlie. "I need for you to get me some supplies in Canyon City. Things I'm gonna need to take on this gang of Pike's."

He asked Martha if he could get a sheet of paper and a pencil, which she quickly pulled from a kitchen drawer and handed to him. While he made a list of the things he wanted Pearlie and Cal to buy, he asked Bill Wiley, "Bill, do you happen to have any dynamite or a long gun of any kind handy?"

Wiley nodded. "Got all the dynamite you'll need, Smoke. We use it to clear stumps out when we cut wood. As for the long gun, the only thing I have is an old Sharps buffalo rifle my daddy used when we first started this ranch."

Smoke grinned. "That'll do just fine, Bill. They don't make 'em any better than the Sharps."

He handed the list to Pearlie, who asked, "What do you want us to do after we get this stuff, Smoke?"

"Just hang around town and keep your eyes open," Smoke answered. "I don't think they'll dare take Sally into town, but if these men have been on the trail for a while, I doubt if they'll pass up the chance to visit a saloon if they get a chance. I need you two to try and find out just how many men we'll be going up against and to get some idea of how good they are." He paused, and then he added, "But I don't want you or Cal to try anything that will make them notice you."

"What are you gonna do, Smoke?" Monte asked.

"I'm going to try and cut their trail before they get to Canyon City. It shouldn't be too hard, with the recent snowfalls."

"And then what?" Louis asked.

Smoke grinned, but it was a terrible grin without a trace of humor in it. "I'm going to follow them and keep a close eye on them. If I get a chance, I'll go in and take Sally away from them. If not, I'll bide my time until they get to Pueblo and make their camp. Sooner or later, they'll let their guard down enough for me to make my move."

While Bill Wiley got the Sharps and dynamite together, Smoke put his saddlebags on his horse. When Wiley came outside, Smoke packed the dynamite on one of the extra horses Louis and Monte had used, along with the Sharps and a bag of extra ammunition for it, and some .44 cartridges for Smoke's pistols and the Winchester rifle he always carried with him.

"I don't know if this'll be of any help, Smoke," Wiley said, handing him a short-barreled ten-gauge shotgun and a couple of boxes of shells, "but if you get in close, this thing will blow a barn door down."

"Much obliged, Bill," Smoke said, adding the shotgun and shells to the packhorse.

Martha Wiley came out of the house and handed Smoke another sack. "I've put some fried turkey, fatback, beans, and a handful of biscuits in there for you Smoke. You're going to need some good food up in those mountains when the snows come."

"Thank you kindly, Martha," Smoke said as he swung up into the saddle. He tipped his hat.

"And if you need another gun, I'm at your service too," Bill said.

"I'll let you know, Bill." Smoke looked around at his friends, realizing that with the odds he was going up against, this might be the last time he saw them. "See you later," he said, and then he put the spurs to his horse and took off toward the distant mountains, pulling the packhorse behind him.

Pearlie slapped Cal on the shoulder. "We'd better git movin' too, Cal."

"Just a minute, Pearlie, and I'll fix you up a sack of food for your journey," Martha Wiley said, rushing back into the house.

Cal grinned. "Better make it two sacks, Mrs. Wiley. You've seen how he puts it away."

Louis stepped over to Pearlie. "There's a telegraph in Pueblo, Pearlie. If things look like they're going badly, wire me at Big Rock and I'll come running."

Monte nodded. "*We'll* come running."

8

At mid-afternoon of their first day on the trail, snow again began falling from low-hanging, dark clouds. The air became so cold and so dark that Bill Pike decided to make camp and build a fire before he and his men froze to death in their saddles.

They were still in the foothills of the mountains, and were not making as good a time as he'd hoped, though he knew that the foul weather would bother anyone who was trying to follow them as much as it was slowing his men.

He held up his hand, signaling the men riding behind him to stop. "Rufe, tell the men to make camp here," he said, moving his horse off the trail and under a stand of tall ponderosa pine trees nearby.

Sally, who'd been riding with her head down to keep the blowing snow out of her eyes, glanced up as the man holding the reins to her horse jerked it to a stop.

The man had a deformed right arm, with what appeared to Sally to be a frozen right elbow. His right leg hung out straight from the side of his horse, and was affixed with two wooden braces with leather straps that ran from his upper thigh down to his ankle. She'd noticed that he continually stared at her with hate-filled eyes, though she had no idea why since she hadn't heard him open his mouth the entire journey.

"Are we making camp here?" she asked the strangely silent man.

He merely grunted, and awkwardly swung his right leg over his saddle and hopped to the ground.

Bill Pike tied his horse's reins to one of the pine trees, and then he walked over to help Sally down off her horse. "Come on down, Mrs. Jensen," he said in a not-unkind voice. "We're gonna make a fire to get some of the chill out of our bones and heat up some food."

Pretending to be more helpless than she was, Sally let him take her elbow as she got down off her horse. She figured if he thought she was a helpless female, it would improve her chances of escape later.

She did not have to fake her shivering, however, since the poncho she was wearing did little to keep her warm. Since she'd been taken without a hat or gloves, her hands and ears felt numb and tingly, almost in the first stages of frostbite.

As the flames of the campfire rose, casting an orange glow over the gloom of the copse of trees they were under, she moved as close as she could, holding her hands out almost in the flames to heat some life back into them.

Shortly, Bill Pike handed her a steaming tin cup filled with dark boiled coffee. "Sorry," he said, inclining his head in a short bow. "We ain't got no sugar nor milk."

"That's okay," Sally said, gratefully downing half the cup to get some heat into her stomach. "I take it black."

"Humph!" the man with the crooked arm snorted from across the fire, where he sat nursing his coffee and staring at Sally with grim eyes.

She glanced at Pike. "What is wrong with that man over there?" she asked. "He looks like he wants to kill me."

Pike laughed shortly. "Well, he probably does, Mrs. Jensen, an' you can't hardly blame him. It were your husband who ruined his arm and his leg for him."

"Smoke did that?" Sally asked.

"Yep."

"When did this happen?"

Pike chuckled again. "More'n twenty year ago."

Sally finished her coffee and handed the cup back to Pike. "And he's just now getting around to doing something about it?"

"Well, it seems old Zeke there spent some time in a prison over at Yuma . . . for rape and murder," Pike said, staring at Sally with flat eyes. "And he said the whole time he was doin' it to that woman, he was plannin' in his mind what he'd do to Smoke Jensen's woman if he ever got the chance."

Sally shook her head. "That poor man."

"What?" Pike asked, astounded at her reaction.

"Yes. To be eaten up with hatred for all those years must have made his life miserable." She hesitated, and then she looked Pike in the eye. "But I do know one thing. If Smoke did that to him, then he deserved it, because Smoke Jensen never shot a man except in self-defense or that he needed shooting."

Pike's expression turned sour. "I'll be sure an' let Zeke know that," he said.

"What is his last name?" Sally asked.

"Thompson. Zeke Thompson," Pike replied. "He's my half brother."

Sally nodded. "So that's why you attacked my men and burned my house down. To avenge Mr. Thompson's wounds."

"No, not really," Pike answered. "I don't give a damn about Zeke. Never did like him much anyway."

"But then why?"

"'Cause, right before Jensen shot Thompson, he shot and killed my full brother, Ethan Pike. I didn't know about it till Zeke got outta prison a year or so ago and looked me up. When I found out, I decided to make things right and to make Smoke Jensen pay for what he done."

"So, your heart's filled with hate also," Sally said, giving Pike a look of pity.

He shrugged. "No. I didn't particularly like my brother Ethan either, but there are just some things a man's gotta do, an' killin' the man who kilt his kin is one of them."

Sally smiled back at Pike. "Could I have another cup of coffee, please?" she asked.

"Sure," Pike said. "Wouldn't want you to freeze to death 'fore the boys have had a chance to help keep you warm tonight."

As he handed her the cup, Sally, her face showing no fear whatsoever, said in a casual voice, "So, that's how it's going to be, is it?"

Pike shrugged. "It's been a long time since the boys have seen a woman as pretty as you, Mrs. Jensen. It'd be a shame to disappoint them."

Sally took a drink of her coffee and nodded. "I can understand that, but. . . ."

"But what?" Pike asked, wondering why this woman wasn't cowering with fear and begging for her life.

"It's just that I thought you said you wanted revenge on Smoke Jensen."

"Yeah, we do," Pike agreed.

"Raping and killing me out here in the wilderness wouldn't be near as satisfying as waiting until you have Smoke Jensen prisoner and then doing it in front of him, don't you think?" Sally said, her voice still as calm as if she were discussing the weather.

Pike threw his head back and laughed. "You're just hoping that Jensen will get the best of us and save you before that happens."

Sally looked at him, her eyes wide and innocent. "Well, of course I am, Mr. Pike. But that doesn't change the fact that if you want the ultimate revenge on Smoke Jensen, that would be the way to do it."

Pike sipped his coffee and stroked his mustache, thinking for a few minutes. Finally, he looked back over at Sally. "I'll tell you one thing, Mrs. Jensen, you've got sand."

"Well," Sally said, "what do you think about my idea?"

"I think you're right. If Smoke truly loves you, I can't think of anything that'd make him suffer more than to see my men take you on right in front of him." He nodded to himself, as if the whole thing had been his idea. "So, I guess that's the way it's gonna be."

Sally looked around the fire at the men sitting there, drinking coffee or whiskey and staring at her with hungry eyes. "I don't know, Mr. Pike," she said easily. "It looks like your men may have other ideas."

Pike straightened and puffed out his chest. "My men do what I tell them to do, Mrs. Jensen. Don't you worry none about that."

"I hope so," Sally said under her breath, waiting to see how things would turn out.

Blackie Johnson, who was the group's designated cook since he was the only one present who could make biscuits that were at all edible, finished frying several large slabs of fatback bacon. He took a large knife and sliced the slabs up while they were still sizzling in the pan. "Meat's ready," he called, and stood back as the men rushed over with tin plates in their hands to help themselves to the bacon, some beans he had cooking in a pot on the fire, and more coffee.

Johnson took it upon himself to fix a plate of food for Sally and take it to her. "Here you go, Mrs. Jensen," he said, his eyes not quite meeting hers.

Sally sensed this man was different from the rest, not quite as coarse and rough. Even his voice was cultured, as if he'd actually gone to school some.

Sally took the plate, searching Johnson's face as she said, "Thank you."

"You're welcome," he replied.

"Would you tell me your name?" she asked as she began to eat.

"Uh, Zechariah Johnson," he replied. "But most of the men call me Blackie."

Sally cocked her head and looked at him with appraising eyes. "Forgive me for saying so, Mr. Johnson," she said, "but you don't look like you belong with these other men."

He gave a half smirk and shook his head. "Don't let me being polite fool you, Mrs. Jensen. I am no better than the rest of the gang."

"But you speak as though you've had some education," Sally replied.

He nodded. "Yes, ma'am. I finished high school, and even had a year of college back in Ohio. I wanted to be a veterinarian."

"What happened to change your mind?"

He shrugged. "I came upon this man beating a team of horses that couldn't pull a wagon he had loaded too heavy, and when he refused to quit hitting them, I hit him."

"That's understandable," Sally said.

"Yeah, but it seems I hit him too hard. When I saw he was dead, I hightailed it out of town and headed West." He smiled, but it had more sadness in it than mirth. "I've been on the owlhoot trail ever since."

Just then, the man named Zeke Thompson stepped around the fire and shoved Blackie aside. "Don't you go tryin' to get this bitch into your blankets tonight, Johnson," he growled in a husky, whiskey-roughened voice. "She belongs to me first, an' if'n there's anything left when I'm done, you can have it."

Pike moved behind Thompson and grabbed him by the shoulder and spun him around. "Shut your pie-hole, Zeke!" he said in a loud voice, his eyes blazing. "Ain't nobody touching Mrs. Jensen until I say so."

Zeke, who was wearing a pistol on his right hip with the handle facing forward for a cross-handed draw, let his left hand move toward his belly. "That ain't what we planned, Bill, an' you know it."

Quick as a flash, Pike's pistol was in his hand and the barrel was pressed up against the underside of Thompson's chin. "Now, Zeke, you just calm down and try an' remember who's the ramrod of this gang," Pike said in a voice loud enough for all the men to hear. "Any time you think you can do a better job, you're welcome to try and take over," he added, locking eyes with Thompson.

Thompson blinked and looked down. "Aw, you know that ain't it, Bill. I just wanted to teach this uppity slut a lesson."

"You'll get your chance, Zeke, but not until I say it's time." He glanced over his shoulder as he eased the hammer down on his Colt and put it back in his holster. "And that goes for the rest of you too. Mrs. Jensen will be left alone until I give the word. Anybody who touches her will have to answer to me."

Sally, watching this byplay, thought she saw a small smile curl Blackie Johnson's lips. She made a mental note that he might turn out to be a valuable ally when it came time for her to attempt to escape.

"If you're through eating, Mrs. Jensen, it might be better if you turned in for the night," Pike said. He leaned close and whispered so no one else could hear. "I want to get you out of sight so the men can quit thinking about what they're all thinking about."

Sally nodded and got up off the ground. She followed Pike over to where he'd fixed a couple of blankets on top of a groundsheet under a pine tree. "I'm gonna put you over here next to me so nobody will mess with you," he said.

Sally eyed him. "Does that include you, Mr. Pike?" she asked.

He grinned. "Oh, it's not that I wouldn't like to, Mrs. Jensen, but I gave you my word nothing will happen until we have captured your husband, an' that's the way it's gonna be."

"Good night then, Mr. Pike," Sally said, and she crawled beneath the blankets and pulled them up under her chin.

9

While Cal and Pearlie headed north by northeast toward the small town of Canyon, Smoke took off on a more directly eastern direction, hoping to cut across the trail the kidnappers would have to take to travel from the Sugarloaf to get to Canyon City and then Pueblo.

Fall was rapidly changing to winter as chilly winds flowed from Canada down into the area of the Rocky Mountains, occasionally accompanied by glowering skies, overhanging clouds, and intermittent snow flurries. Smoke hoped the snow continued, for it would help him track the band of men who held his wife prisoner.

He would have to cross the Sangre de Cristo Mountains to get to Pueblo, but that would be no problem for Smoke, who knew most of the mountains in Colorado Territory as well as he knew the pastures and features of the Sugarloaf.

It took him almost twenty-four hours of continual riding to arrive at the small village of Silver Cliff, a town built up to supply the many miners in the area with food and mining utensils and such. Like most mining towns, Silver Cliff consisted mainly of saloons, gambling parlors, and a couple of general stores, along with a ramshackle hotel for the miners to stay in when they visited the town to buy supplies and blow off steam from their isolation the rest of the year.

All but asleep on his horse after his long journey, Smoke decided he wouldn't be much good to Sally when he found the kidnappers unless he was rested, so he got a room in the hotel and asked the proprietor if a hot bath was available.

The man chuckled. "Yeah, we got a bathtub, mister, but it ain't used much this time of year. Most of the miners don't bathe much between September and April."

Smoke nodded. He knew how that went. When he'd lived up in the mountains with Preacher years before, the man had told him it was plumb unhealthy to bathe more than once or twice a year.

"How long will it take you to get the water heated?" Smoke asked.

"Oh, 'bout an hour, if I crank up the stove now."

"Is there any place in town that serves good food while I wait?"

"That depends on what you mean by good," the man answered with a straight face. "If you mean can you eat it without getting' poisoned, yeah, there is. If you mean does it taste good, well, that's a different story."

Smoke laughed. He liked this man, who seemed to have a good sense of humor, which was sometimes rare in a mining town where everyone usually seemed to be eaten up with gold fever.

The man came out from behind his counter and walked to the front door. He leaned out and pointed down the muddy main street toward a small clapboard building at the edge of town, sandwiched in between what appeared to be a whorehouse and a saloon. "That there is called Ma's Place, though if the old lady who runs it was ever a mother, I'll eat my hat."

Smoke glanced at the big Regulator clock that hung on the wall behind the counter. "I'll be back in an hour for that bath," he said.

"I'll have the water hot enough to take the feathers off a chicken by then," the man promised.

Smoke walked down the roughshod lumber along the street that served as a boardwalk until he was across from the building with the sign on it that read MA'S PLACE. Seeing no help for it, he hopped across the mud puddles still rimmed with ice that covered the middle of Main Street and entered the eating establishment.

True to the hotel man's word, almost every table was taken up by miners and workers eager to have some cooking that they hadn't done themselves for a change.

A portly woman in an apron, with hair that hadn't seen a comb in some time, walked up to Smoke. "Table, mister?" she asked.

The only empty table was in the center of the room. Since his gunfighting days, Smoke had made it a practice never to sit with his back to a door or window or where someone could sit behind him. He glanced over at the corner table and saw that the four men sitting there were finished eating and were talking and smoking over final cups of coffee.

He nodded his head toward them. "If it's all the same to you, I'll wait until that table is unoccupied," he said.

Ma looked over at the table, and then she stared back at Smoke. Her eyes fell to how he wore his twin holsters low on his hips, the left-hand gun butt-first and the right hand one butt-back. "Oh, so it's like that, is it?" she asked, a knowing look on her face.

Smoke shrugged.

She grinned and stuck out her hand. "My name's Ellie May, but everyone around here just calls me Ma."

He took her hand. "I'm Smoke Jensen," he said.

Her eyes widened a bit, showing that even here in this backwater town she'd heard the name before. "I'll see what I can do, Mr. Jensen."

"Just Smoke," he said.

She smiled back over her shoulder, revealing teeth that showed it'd been as long since she'd seen a dentist as it had since she'd been to a hairdresser.

She went over to the table, leaned over, and said something to the men in a low voice. As all their heads turned to stare at Smoke, he nodded at them in friendly greeting.

They hurriedly got to their feet, picked up their coffee cups, and moved to the center table, leaving theirs vacant.

As he walked past them, Smoke tipped his hat. "Much obliged, gentlemen," he said.

One of the men put out his hand and touched Smoke's arm. "Is it true, Mr. Jensen, that you've kilt over a hundred men?" he asked.

Smoke took a deep breath and stopped to look down at the man. "I don't know, mister. I don't keep count," he answered. "Putting a number on a man's life trivializes killing. And killing is never trivial."

Smoke turned his back and walked to take a seat at the vacant table by the window, with his back to the corner. Questions like that used to make him angry, but as he got older and more famous, he got used to it. Ever since he'd been featured in several of Erastus Beadle's dime novels, it had only gotten worse.

Ma walked over. "What'll it be, Smoke?" she asked. "It's a little late for breakfast and a mite early for lunch."

Smoke smiled. "How about we compromise? Some eggs, a couple of flapjacks, and a small steak on the side would be excellent."

"Elk steak or beef steak?" she asked. "I've got both."

"Elk, please."

She nodded. "And to drink? I've got some fresh milk just brought in an hour ago."

Smoke's mouth watered. He'd drunk so much coffee on the trail his gut was burning. "That would be great, Ma."

"It'll be right out."

While Smoke waited for his food, he built himself a cigarette. More to keep himself awake than because he felt the urge for one.

As he bent over the lucifer to light it, he noticed the men he'd talked to at the table stop on their way out of the café and talk to a couple of young boys at the far side of the room.

One was dressed in black shirt and trousers and had a black leather vest on with silver conchos around the edges as decoration. Smoke noticed he wore a brace of pearl-handled Colt Peacemakers on his hips and had them tied down low on his leg.

When the boy, who couldn't have been more than eighteen or nineteen, stared over at him, Smoke knew there was going to be trouble. Damn, he thought, I knew I shouldn't have given my right name.

Ma appeared from the kitchen with a tall glass of milk in one hand and a platter of biscuits in the other. She put them on Smoke's table. "Here you go, Smoke. You can nibble on these till that steak is done. Won't be long."

Smoke cut his eyes toward the far table. "Who is that at that table over there, Ma?" he asked.

She looked, and then she frowned when she looked back at Smoke. "That there is trouble," she said. "Trouble with a capital T. He calls himself the Silver Kid, and he's always going around trying to pick fights with someone so he can show how fast he is with those six-guns on his hips."

"And his friend?"

"Oh, he's Buck Johansson. He follows the other one around like a lapdog, trying to act as tough as his friend, but he ain't near as mean as he tries to make out."

While Smoke was listening to Ma, he heard a chair scrape back from across the room and saw the Silver Kid approaching out of the corner of his eye. "Better get on back in the kitchen, Ma. I think there's going to be trouble."

Before she could reply, the Silver Kid brushed her aside and stood in front of Smoke with his hands on his hips. "I just can't hardly believe it, boys," he said, talking loud so everyone in the room could hear him. "The great Smoke Jensen drinking milk like a little bitty baby."

Smoke leaned back, loosening the hammer thong on his right-hand Colt under the table and straightening out his right leg so he could draw faster if he needed to. "And you are?" he asked.

"I'm known as the Silver Kid," the boy answered, letting his chest puff out a little.

Smoke noticed the Kid's friend standing behind him and a little off to one side, sweat tricking down his face. He clearly wanted no part of this.

Smoke reached out and took a deep drink of the milk, using his left hand. He smiled. "That's funny," he said. "I've never heard of you."

The Kid blushed. "Well, everbody's gonna know my name after I kill Smoke Jensen," he said, his voice cracking on the word *kill*.

Smoke smiled, slowly shaking his head. "How old are you, son?" he asked, not unkindly.

"Uh, I'm almost nineteen," the boy answered, making his voice lower this time.

Smoke nodded. "That's a good age. It'd be a shame if you don't live to see it."

The Kid grinned insolently. "Oh, I'll live to see it, Jensen. It's you that's gonna die today."

At these words, the men at the surrounding tables all got up and moved out of the line of fire.

Smoke shrugged. "Maybe," he said. "But let me show you something first. All right?"

The Kid looked puzzled. "Show me what?" he asked, his right hand hanging next to the butt of his pistol, his fingers twitching.

Smoke got to his feet and faced the boy, his hands out in front of him at waist level. "Hold your hands like this," he said.

"Why?"

"Just do it," Smoke said. "I won't hurt you."

The Kid blushed and did as Smoke asked, his hands out a foot or so apart.

Smoke clapped his hands together. "Now, do that," he said, a half smile on his face. "As fast as you can."

The Kid smirked and slapped his hands together with a loud snap.

"Now," Smoke said, his hands still out in front of him. "Do it again, faster this time."

The Kid did it, but this time, so fast no one saw his hands move, Smoke drew his right-hand Colt and had it out and cocked so that the boy's hands clapped on it.

"Jesus!" the Johansson boy breathed. "I never even saw him clear leather."

The Kid's face paled at the speed of Smoke's draw. "You want to try it one more time?" Smoke asked, holstering his Colt.

The Kid nodded and spread his hands, closer together this time.

Smoke nodded and the boy moved, but this time Smoke drew his left-hand gun and had it between the Kid's hands before they could come together.

Now it was the Kid's face that had sweat trickling down off his forehead.

"I have an idea," Smoke said as he holstered his Colt for a second time. "Why don't you boys join me and I'll buy you some breakfast?"

Buck Johansson nodded and slapped the Kid on the shoulder. "Gee, that'd be great, Mr. Jensen."

Smoke sat back down. "Call me Smoke, Buck."

The two boys took seats at Smoke's table and everyone else went back to their eating.

Ma came out of the kitchen with a large platter with

Smoke's food on it and gave him a wink as she put it on the table.

"I think we're gonna need some more eggs and steak, Ma. These are growing boys and they need some good grub," Smoke said.

The Kid grinned. "Golly, Smoke, I ain't never seen nobody as fast as that before."

Smoke began to dig into his food. "Fast is over-rated, Kid," he said. "Accuracy is what counts when you're facing a man that wants to kill you. Being able to put that first bullet where it'll do the most good is what keeps a man forked-end-down instead of the other way around."

The rest of the breakfast was spent with the boys asking Smoke questions about what it was like in the "old" days, something that made Smoke laugh, and at the same time made him wish he was twenty years younger and still back up in the mountains with Preacher.

Still, he did his best around mouthfuls of food to give the boys some idea of what it'd been like back when white men were as rare in the High Lonesome as hen's teeth.

He told them of Preacher, a man who'd spent his entire adult life living alone in the mountains until he took Smoke under his wing as his "adopted" son, and had them laughing until they cried at tales of Puma Buck, Beartooth, Powder Pete, and Deadhead, men who lived life to the fullest and still had time to laugh at the vagaries of life in the mountains of Colorado Territory.

At one point, the Silver Kid asked Smoke if he ever kept in touch with the old men and if many of them were still alive.

Smoke's face grew sad at the question. "I still see a few of the younger ones, boys," he said, "though most are in their seventies or eighties. Unfortunately, their way of life has just about passed away with the ones who've died. There are just too many people around now, and the Indians who still live in the mountains have been so corrupted by the white man's ways that it just isn't the same anymore."

When they finished eating, he got up and shook the boys' hands. "Let me give you some advice, boys," he said. "Killing a man, taking from him all that he has or ever will have, is not something to wish for. Once you've done that, you'll never be the same. You can live with it if it's forced on you and you don't have a choice in the matter. But if you go out looking for it for no good reason other than to build a reputation, it sours something deep inside and you'll regret it for the rest of your lives. You'll be as dead inside as that man you planted in Boot Hill."

10

When Smoke pulled a wad of cash out of his pocket and peeled a couple of bills off the top to give to Ma for their breakfast, he didn't notice a group of four men sitting at a nearby table watching.

One of the men, a hard case named Jeremiah Jones, punched the man next to him with his elbow. "Hey, Willy, would you look at the size of that man's stash?" he said, his eyes wide.

Willy Boatman, Bob Causey, and Sam Bottoms, Jones's partners in a failed mining venture, had been in the surrounding mountains for almost a year and had little to show for their efforts. They'd come to Colorado Territory expecting to find gold lying around for the taking, with very little knowledge of how and where to dig for it.

Desperate now, down to their last few dollars, and unable to find anyone who would stake them to another try, they'd been talking about trying to rob a store or a bank, but had as little knowledge about that as they did about how to go about finding honest work.

Willy nodded, his eyes hard. "How about we follow him and see if maybe he'll agree to share some of that with us?" he said, chuckling at his wit.

"Sure," Bob Causey agreed, "we shouldn't have no problems with it bein' four agin one."

Smoke walked back to the hotel, with the four men following a short distance behind.

"Is my bath ready?" he asked the proprietor when he entered the hotel lobby.

"Sure is, mister," he said. "I got that water so hot you can take a steam bath if you want to."

Smoke handed him a dollar. "Thanks for your trouble," he said. "I'll leave my things in my room while I bathe. Could you have a boy take my horses over to the livery and get them some grain and a good rubdown?"

"Sure thing, Mr. Jensen," the proprietor answered, taking a key from the rack behind the counter. "Your room is 312, up on the third floor. Same floor as the bath."

Neither man noticed the man standing just inside the door listening as the proprietor told Smoke his room number.

Smoke dropped his saddlebags and the larger bag containing his supplies and extra weapons on his bed, locked the door, and went looking for the bathtub down the hall.

Smoke found the room and tested the water in the tub with his hand. True to the proprietor's word, the water was steaming hot, and there was a pile of towels, a bar of soap, and a bath brush on a chair next to it ready for his use.

Smoke stripped out of his clothes, hanging them along with his gunbelt on a peg on the wall next to the door. Out of longtime habit, he took one of his Colts from its holster and placed it under one of the towels, then slipped into the hot water, sighing with relief as the heat began to loosen muscles stiff from a day and night of constant riding.

He leaned his head back against the tub and closed his eyes, luxuriating in the feeling of a hot bath.

* * *

Jeremiah Jones took out his pistol and quietly knocked on the door to Room 312. When there was no answer, he tried the doorknob and found it locked. "Damn," he muttered under his breath.

"I told you he was gonna take a bath," Bottoms said.

"We could kick the door in," Causey offered.

"Naw," Jones answered. "He's probably got his money with him anyway. Let's just go find him and git it."

They eased down the hall, walking on tiptoes so as not to warn Smoke of their approach. When they got to the room with a hand-painted sign on it that read BATH, Jones held his gun out in front of him and opened the door.

At the sound of the door opening, Smoke opened his eyes and sat up in the tub, letting his right hand hang over the side next to the pile of towels.

He smiled when he saw the hard-looking men enter, each with a pistol in their hands. "Sorry, gentlemen," Smoke said easily, with no fear in his eyes. "This bath is already spoken for."

"Shut your mouth, asshole," Jones growled. "We didn't come for no bath."

Smoke wrinkled his nose at the men's ripe odor. "I can see that, though it might be a good idea for you all to take one," Smoke said, his fingers inching under the towel slowly. "You all smell like you've been sleeping with skunks."

Jones's face flushed red at the insult. "Where's the money, sumbitch?" he asked, relaxing a little when he saw Smoke's gunbelt hanging on the peg next to the door. He didn't notice that one of the pistols was missing.

"Oh, you mean my money?" Smoke asked, planning in his mind the order in which he was going to kill the four men.

"No, I mean our money," Jones replied, letting his eyes roam over Smoke's clothes on the peg.

Suddenly, from the hall behind the men, a voice called out, "Drop them guns and get your hands in the air!"

As the men turned to look over their shoulders, Smoke pulled his .44 out from under the towel.

When all four of the men pointed their guns at the unseen voice, Smoke let the hammer down just as he heard a series of shots from the hall.

Smoke shot Jones in the side of the head, the bullet entering just above his ear and blowing half his head and all of his brains all over the men standing behind him.

Causey and Bottoms, still standing out in the hallway, both were hit at the same time, one in the chest and the other right between the eyes. As they danced backward under the impact of the slugs, falling with arms flung out onto their backs, Smoke fired a second time and shot Boatman in the neck.

The man whirled around, both hands at his throat trying to stem the flow of blood from his ruined windpipe. He gurgled and choked, dropped to his knees, and died swallowing his own blood within seconds.

Smoke stood up, still holding his Colt out in front of him until he found out who was in the hall.

A young man's grinning face appeared in the doorway. It was the Silver Kid. "Howdy, Smoke," he said, his eyes still glittering with the excitement of the gunfight, his silver-plated Peacemaker pistol still smoking.

Smoke shook his head and smiled. "Mighty glad to see you, Kid," he said, putting his pistol down and wrapping himself in one of the large hotel towels as he stepped out of the bathtub.

"After you left Ma's Place," the Kid said, "I noticed these galoots following you. I figured they might be up to no good, so I trailed along to see what they were up to."

Smoke nodded as he dried off. "I'm sure glad you did."

"When I saw them at the door, I thought they had the drop on you, so I drew down on 'em," the Kid said.

Smoke raised his eyebrows. "That was mighty brave of you, Kid, to take on four men by yourself."

The Kid shrugged. "I didn't have no choice, Smoke." He grinned sheepishly. "I didn't know you had that six-killer with you in the bathtub."

"Still, it was a very courageous thing for you to do, Kid. Not many men would take on four armed desperados to help out a stranger."

"Hell, Smoke, you ain't a stranger, you're my friend," the Kid said, blushing a bright red.

"You've got that right, Kid."

Just then the proprietor ran up the hallway, a shotgun in his hands. He stood there, the shotgun hanging in his hands as he stared openmouthed at the dead bodies littering the hallway and the blood pooling on the wooden floor.

Smoke looked at him. "Say, after you get someone to haul this trash away, would you heat me up some more water? This batch has gotten kind of cold."

Cal and Pearlie rode into Canyon City in the middle of a snowstorm. Snow and ice piled on their shoulders and ice rimmed Pearlie's mustache as they rode with heads down against the north wind down the main street of the small town high in the Sangre de Cristo Mountains.

Pearlie reined his horse to a stop inside the livery stable on the edge of town and they both got down out of their saddles. A young boy grabbed the reins. "Good thing you men got to town when you did," he said as he helped them get the saddles off their mounts. "Looks like it's gonna get a mite cold later tonight."

Cal glanced at Pearlie. "Yeah, good thing we got here while it's still warm," he said with a sour smile.

Pearlie handed the boy a couple of dollars. "See that the horses get a good rub and plenty of grain."

"Yes, sir!" the boy said, unaccustomed to being paid so well.

"Is there a good hotel in town where we can get some food and a place to stay?" Pearlie asked.

"Yes, sir. The Palace is about the bestest in town. It's a mite expensive, but it's got the best food an' it's even got a saloon right next door."

Cal, who was standing in the doorway looking at the town, thought from the looks of the place that just about every building in town was next to one saloon or another, since saloons seemed to be in great abundance.

"Thanks," Pearlie said to the boy, handing him another couple of coins for his trouble.

"Why don't you head on over there," the boy said. "I'll bring your bags an' such after I see to your hosses."

Twenty minutes later, Cal and Pearlie were sitting in a large dining room ordering steaks and fried potatoes. "And bring us a large pot of coffee," Pearlie added after giving their orders to the waiter. "We need something to get the chill out of our bones."

The waiter, evidently used to this kind of weather, glanced out the window. "Oh, this ain't cold, mister," he said, grinning. "It ain't too much below zero out there yet. Just wait till we get a real storm."

After the waiter went off to get their food, Cal wrapped his arms around his shoulders and shivered. "You know, Pearlie, livin' down low like we do at the Sugarloaf, I'd 'bout near forgot how cold it gets in the mountains."

Pearlie nodded. "I ain't been this cold since Smoke took us up into the High Lonesome a couple of years ago to show us how he and Preacher used to live."

"It's funny how the cold never seemed to bother Smoke none," Cal said.

"I guess his blood must've gotten thick after all those years he spent up there with Preacher an' the other mountain men," Pearlie said.

The waiter reappeared with a pot of coffee and two thick mugs. "You boys want sugar an' milk?" he asked.

Pearlie shook his head, but Cal nodded.

"The steaks'll be right out, but here's some home-made bread and some strawberry preserves for you to get started on."

Pearlie cut a big slice of bread and spread a thick helping of preserves on it. After he took a huge bite, he rolled his eyes. "Boy, that hits the spot."

"Is it as good as Miss Sally's?" Cal asked, fixing his own slice.

"Of course not, Cal. You know nobody's as good a cook as Miss Sally, but it ain't all that bad neither."

After the waiter brought their meal, the boys ate and discussed their plans to buy the supplies on the list Smoke had given them.

Cal, who could read better than Pearlie, went down the list while Pearlie stuffed his face. "I can see why Smoke would want most of this stuff, like the guns an' ammo an' explosives, but some of it's a mystery to me," he said.

"Like what?" Pearlie mumbled around a mouth full of steak and potatoes.

"Well," Cal said, holding the list up to the light of the lanterns around the walls, "take, for instance, these picks and shovels and empty tin cans, and this barrel of horseshoe nails and bale of barbed wire." He looked up at Pearlie across the table. "You'd think from this Smoke was plannin' on doin' some mining or stringing up some fences or somethin'."

Pearlie shrugged and held up the empty coffeepot for the waiter to refill.

"And," Cal added, "what about the fifty tent stakes on here? You know Smoke never sleeps in no tents. He always makes a lean-to shelter out of pine branches an' such."

As Pearlie refilled their coffee mugs, he looked at Cal. "Now, Cal boy, you know whatever's on that list

Smoke made, he's got a use in mind for it, so let's just get it and worry about what he wants it for later."

They both built cigarettes and leaned back, stomachs full, and enjoyed their after-dinner smokes and coffee.

When they finished, Pearlie called the waiter back over. "You wouldn't happen to have any pie for dessert, would you?" he asked.

The waiter raised his eyebrows and stared at Pearlie's thin frame and the number of empty plates and platters on the table. "Sure, we got apple and peach pie both, but I'm darned if I know where you're gonna put it, mister. You done ate enough for four men as it is."

Pearlie grinned. "You just bring it an' I'll figure out where to put it," he said.

"Uh, which kinda pie do you want?" the astonished waiter asked.

"How about a slice of each?" Pearlie asked.

Cal motioned the waiter down and whispered, "You can't tell it, mister, but my friend there has a hollow leg. He won't stop eating until it's plumb full up to his waist."

11

Smoke was up and on the trail before dawn, feeling refreshed and rested after a good twelve-hour sleep in the hotel in Silver Cliff. He headed south out of the town toward the pass between the Crestone Peak and Deer Peak mountains. He knew that the outlaws who'd kidnapped Sally would have to travel through the pass to get to either Canyon City or Pueblo, since the mountains were too high for inexperienced men to cross this time of the year.

He hoped to get there ahead of them, but he knew it was going to be close. If they were traveling fast, they might have already gone through the pass, in which case he'd be able to pick up their trail through the snow that had been falling for the past few days.

In fact, Bill Pike had been pushing his men hard. He wanted to get to Pueblo a few days ahead of Smoke Jensen so he'd be able to pick a campsite that would be easily defended and remote enough so Jensen couldn't expect any help from the local authorities.

They'd reached the pass between Crestone and Deer Peaks the night before, and had elected to camp there until morning. Both his men and their horses were exhausted from the effort to climb up to the pass, being unused to both the thin air of the mountains and the extreme cold temperatures.

When the outlaws woke up, they were grumpy and tired and breathing heavily with even the slightest exertion. A large fire was built and Bill encouraged them to eat as much as they could to fortify them against the cold.

Joe Rutledge, called Sarge because of his stint in the Army until he'd been cashiered for stealing Army horses and selling them to settlers and Indians, moved closer to the fire and held his hands out close to the flames, trying to get them warm.

"Jesus, Bill," he complained, "I'm 'bout near freezing my balls off up in these mountains."

A couple of the other men nodded sympathetically. All of them had coats and clothes more suited to the tropical climate of south Texas and Mexico, where they'd worked for the past couple of years.

Bill, who was wearing two pair of trousers, three shirts, and a medium-heavy coat, agreed. "Yeah, I know what you mean, Sarge," he said. "I checked the map last night and we're gonna be going near Canyon City tomorrow. We'll send some men in to get some warmer clothes and more supplies when we get close enough."

Sally kept her head down to hide her smile at the outlaws' discomfort. Even though she was wearing only one set of clothes and had only a poncho to keep her warm, she was more used to the cold and wasn't particularly bothered by the temperatures.

"Well," Blackie Johnson growled, "just what do you think we should do until then?"

Pike shrugged, tired of the men's bellyaching. "I'd suggest you put on every bit of clothes you have in your saddlebags. That's about all we can do until we get some warmer clothes."

Hank Snow sat on the ground near the fire and put his boots almost into the coals. "I can't hardly feel my feet, Bill. You suppose I'm gettin' frostbite?" he asked.

Pike moved over to stand over him. "Slip them boots off and let me take a look," he said.

Sally glanced up from across the fire. "I wouldn't do that if I were you," she said, cupping her hands around her tin coffee cup to keep them warm.

Pike looked over at her, a scowl on his face. "And why not, Mrs. Jensen?"

She got to her feet and moved over to Pike. "Because, Mr. Pike, if his feet are that cold, then when he takes his boots off, they are going to swell up. He probably won't be able to get them back on then."

"What do you suggest, ma'am?" Snow asked, watching as steam rose off his boots as they heated up from the fire.

"Get your feet as warm as you can by the fire. Just before we leave, cut a couple of strips off your groundsheet and wrap them around your boots. That should keep them dry and warm enough until we stop for lunch and build another fire."

"Who said we're gonna stop for lunch?" Pike asked Sally. "I want to make Canyon City by tomorrow."

Sally glanced over at the horses, which were standing in a group with their heads down, pawing at the snow, looking for grass to eat.

"Mr. Pike, it's not up to me to tell you your business, but unless you want to walk the rest of the way to Canyon City, you're going to need to let those horses rest some. I noticed you didn't bring any grain for them to eat, and the grass up here is under two feet of snow. Also, they're not used to the air up here. If you continue to push them as hard as you have been, they'll flounder by nightfall."

He looked at her suspiciously. "Why are you trying to help us, Mrs. Jensen? Are you just trying to slow us down so your husband can catch us 'fore we get to Pueblo?"

Sally sighed. "Mr. Pike, it will do me no good if Smoke catches up to us after we've frozen to death because you've managed to kill our horses, will it?" She moved over and held out her cup to Blackie Johnson for a refill, and then she glanced back over her shoulder. "I'll tell you for a fact, Mr. Pike, a man on foot up in these mountains is as good as dead. If those horses die, you'll be frozen solid within twenty-four hours."

"She's makin' good sense, Boss," Blackie said as he filled her cup. "My hoss ain't had nothin' to eat since yesterday."

Pike reluctantly nodded. "I see what you mean, Mrs. Jensen."

He turned to the men sitting around the fire. "Rufus, you and Sarge take your shovels and dig up some of that snow so them horses can find some grass while we eat breakfast, and then we'll do the same thing when we take our nooning."

Sally smiled to herself. Though she'd been telling the men the truth, she also knew that by now Smoke was on their trail and anything she did to slow them down made it easier for him to catch up to them.

She sat down next to the fire and nursed her coffee. When she saw Bill Pike building himself a cigarette, she got an idea. "Mr. Pike, do you suppose I could have one of those?" she asked.

He raised his eyebrows in surprise. "You smoke, Mrs. Jensen?"

She shrugged. "Just occasionally, when I'm very cold," she answered.

He handed her the cigarette he'd made and began to make himself another one.

Sally took the cigarette, reached into the edge of the fire, and got a burning twig to light it with. After a couple of puffs, she blew out the twig and used the charcoal end of it to write Canyon City on the hem of her dress when the men weren't looking. After a few minutes, she stood up and began to move toward the bushes a short distance from the campfire.

"Where're you goin', Mrs. Jensen?" Pike hollered after her.

"I need to . . ." she said hesitantly, as if embarrassed.

"Oh, all right, go ahead," Pike said.

"You need some help, ma'am?" Rufus Gordon asked, grinning salaciously.

"No, thank you," Sally answered coldly. "I can manage."

Once she was out of sight in the bushes, she bent down, tore off the part of her dress with the words *Canyon City* written on it, and stuffed it in the front of her dress where it couldn't be seen.

An hour later, after both the horses and the men had eaten their fill, Pike broke camp. As the men began to get up on their horses, Sally quickly placed the piece of dress under one of the campfire stones before she got on her horse.

As Pike led his men down through the pass toward the distant Canyon City, Sally glanced back over her shoulder at the message she'd left for Smoke, hoping it wouldn't be covered by the light snow that was beginning to fall.

Later that afternoon, when Smoke got to the pass, he found the campfire cold and most of the tracks of the men covered with snow. He knew from the horse droppings there had been at least eight or more horses, but he couldn't tell which direction they'd taken down out of the pass. If they went northwest, they were heading toward Canyon City. If they went northeast, then they were going directly to Pueblo.

As he knelt by the fire, touching the coals to try and determine how far behind them he was, he noticed a scrap of gingham cloth sticking out from under one of the stones around the coals.

He pulled it out and grinned when he recognized Sally's dress cloth. He was relieved to see that she was still alive. As he examined the cloth, he noticed it had something scrawled on it. He held it up to the light and read the words "Canyon City."

He smiled and shook his head. Sally had managed to let him know where the men were headed and she'd done it right under their noses. The poor sons of bitches didn't know who they were dealing with when they took Sally prisoner, he thought.

Judging from the coldness of the coals, he figured he was at least twelve hours behind the men. Well, he'd give his horses some of the grain he'd brought along, fix himself a small fire to heat up some coffee, and have a cold breakfast. And then he'd be on his way. If he pushed it, he could make up at least four hours on the men by nightfall.

While he ate the last of the turkey Mrs. Wiley had given him and drank his coffee, Smoke hoped Cal and Pearlie were getting the supplies he'd asked for.

With any luck, they'd be ready and waiting for him when he got to Canyon City. If that were the case, then they would probably be able to catch up with the group of outlaws before they made it to Pueblo.

Smoke's jaws clenched when he thought of what he was going to do to them if they'd harmed one hair on Sally's head.

12

Cal and Pearlie awoke after a good night's sleep in the Palace Hotel. "Man," Pearlie said, glancing across the room at the other bed, where Cal was just opening his eyes. "That sure felt good to have a real feather mattress under my butt instead of cold, hard ground."

The boys, though they had plenty of cash for two rooms, were of such a nature that they hated to waste money unnecessarily. Besides, after sleeping in bunkhouses for most of their lives, they were used to someone else snoring nearby and probably wouldn't have been able to get to sleep in a quiet room.

Cal stretched and yawned. "Yeah, an' I have a feeling we better enjoy the feeling 'cause once we leave here it's gonna mean sleeping out in the snow."

Pearlie jumped out of bed and began to put his clothes on. "Time to get goin', Cal boy. I think I can hear breakfast callin' my name."

Cal rolled over and covered his head with the blankets. "You go on, Pearlie. I want to catch another few winks."

"All right, if that's the way you want it," Pearlie said as he opened the door. "But remember, after today, all we're gonna have to eat is our own cookin'."

That threat did it. Cal groaned and rolled over out

of bed. He and Pearlie were spoiled living on the Sugarloaf. Sally Jensen was one of the best cooks in the county, and Cal and Pearlie weren't used to trail food. Greasy fatback bacon and boiled beans just couldn't compare to Sally's fried chicken and mashed potatoes and corn and such.

By the time Cal got dressed and made his way to the dining room, Pearlie already had a large pot of coffee on the table along with two mugs and a jar of sugar. He knew Cal liked his coffee sweet when he could get it that way.

Just as Cal took his seat, the waiter they'd had the night before came out of the kitchen with a burly, fat man following him. "See?" the waiter said, pointing to Pearlie. "There's the man who ate all that food last night. I told you he was thin as a rail."

The fat man, who had a half-smoked cigarette dangling from the corner of his mouth, just shook his head, a look of amazement on his face.

The waiter explained, "This is our chef. After you left last night, he wouldn't believe that the person who ate two complete dinners and two desserts didn't weigh three hundred pounds."

The cook grinned and patted his more than ample stomach. "How do you do it, mister?" he asked. "If I just smell food I gain five pounds."

"Just lucky, I guess," Pearlie answered, blushing a little at the unexpected attention.

"I'll tell you one thing," Cal said. "It ain't 'cause he works it off, that's for sure."

The waiter, with the cook still watching over his shoulder, asked, "What will you have this morning?"

Pearlie stroked his chin, thought for a moment, and then he said, "I'll have half a dozen hens' eggs, a short stack of flapjacks, and some pork sausage if you have it."

Cal shrugged and said, "I'll have the same."

The waiter grinned and turned to the cook. "See, I told you so!"

* * *

While Cal and Pearlie were eating breakfast, Bill Pike and his men arrived at the outskirts of Canyon City. Pike reined in his horse and looked at the town sitting down in a small valley below them.

"We gonna git to go into town and have a few drinks and git me some laudanum for my hand?" Rufus Gordon asked.

Pike shook his head. "No, I don't think there's gonna be any drinking in town, boys. I don't want us to draw any attention to ourselves until we know for sure where Smoke Jensen is."

"But Boss," Hank Snow complained. "I ain't had a drink since we got to Colorado. And I done forgot what it's like to have a woman on my lap."

Pike glared at him. "Don't forget who's running this outfit, Hank, or it might be the last thing you ever forget."

Hank clamped his lips shut and looked down at the ground.

"Now, I'll stay out here with Mrs. Jensen. The rest of you can go into town and buy the supplies we need, and you can get yourselves a couple of bottles of whiskey if you want, but I don't want you drinking it in town. Wait until we make camp tonight. And you, Rufe, if there's a doc in town, you might wanta have him take a look at that hand. Maybe he can fix it so it don't hurt so bad."

"Anything special you want us to get in the way of supplies, Boss?" Blackie Johnson asked.

"Yeah, Blackie. Get some warm clothes and a heavy coat for Mrs. Jensen. I don't want her freezing to death 'fore we meet up with her husband."

He thought for a moment, and then he added, "And you might want to pick up some heavier coats for the rest of us too. We're gonna be going up into the mountains and it's bound to get colder the higher we get. And pick up some more ammunition, just in case Jensen brings help with him and makes a fight of it."

"You think he'll do that after you told him you'd kill his wife if he didn't come alone?" Johnson asked, glancing worriedly at Sally.

Pike pursed his lips. "I don't know." He too looked over at Sally. "What do you think, Mrs. Jensen?"

Sally smiled. "Smoke won't need any help to kill you men, and he probably won't even break a sweat doing it."

Pike threw back his head and laughed out loud. "You think he's that tough?" he asked Sally.

She nodded. "You can't imagine just how tough, but you'll find out soon enough." She looked over at the other men, sitting on their horses watching her and Pike talking. "And you men had better take some time to enjoy the town while you're there, because it is liable to be the last town you visit while you're still alive."

A couple of the men laughed, but the others just eyed her with worried looks on their faces. They weren't used to anyone not showing fear when confronted by the Pike gang, most especially women.

Pike cleared his throat. "Get on into town, boys, and get those supplies. And don't forget, I'll shoot any man who comes back here drunk."

Cal and Pearlie had finished breakfast, and were in the general store picking out the supplies Smoke had written on his list, when a group of hard-looking men walked into the room.

As the men spread out and began to gather supplies of their own, one of the men walked up to the store owner behind the counter and asked, "You got any women's clothes here?"

Cal's face got hard and his hand moved toward the butt of his pistol, until Pearlie put a hand on his arm. "Careful," he whispered.

The store owner nodded. "I got some pants and

shirts that oughta fit a woman, but I don't have no fancy dresses or nothing like that."

"Pants and shirts will be all right," the man said. He held out his hand about level with his shoulder. "She's about this tall, and she's built thin, not real heavy."

The store owner walked to a rack of clothes on one wall and began to pick out trousers, flannel shirts, and some long-handle underwear.

"Oh, an' she's gonna need a heavy coat too," the man added as the store owner piled the clothes in his arms.

Pearlie motioned to Cal with his head and walked out of the store, leaving their supplies in a pile near the counter. When they got outside, he said, "That's got to be Miss Sally he's talking about."

"Yeah, I agree," Cal said.

"Now remember," Pearlie said, "Smoke said not to do nothin' to draw attention to ourselves, so don't you go off half-cocked until Smoke gets here."

"But, we can't just let 'em ride outta town without doin' somethin'," Cal pleaded.

"We are gonna do something," Pearlie answered. "I'm gonna follow 'em and see which way they're headed and make sure Miss Sally's all right."

"But what am I supposed to do?" Cal asked.

Pearlie handed him the wad of cash Smoke had given them. "You get the rest of the supplies on the list and take it over to the hotel. Then, go to the livery and pick us out a packhorse to carry it on. Once I see where they're going, I'll come back to town and get you."

"And what if Smoke isn't here by then?" Cal asked.

"I don't know. We'll just have to figure something out when the time comes."

13

As soon as Cal moved back toward the general store, Pearlie took off at a dead run for the hotel. He knew if he was going to follow the kidnappers up into the mountains, he needed to get prepared.

Taking the steps two at a time, he ran up the stairs to the room he shared with Cal. He grabbed his saddlebags, stuffed some extra clothes into one, and put a sack of beans, a hunk of fatback bacon wrapped in waxed paper, and a small can of Arbuckle's coffee in the other side.

He started to leave the room, hesitated, and went back to the dresser and picked up his Winchester rifle and an extra box of cartridges. There was no telling what he'd run into up in the High Lonesome and he wanted to make sure he had everything he might need for the journey.

Closing the door, he again ran down the stairs and turned left out of the door toward the livery stable. He hoped the boy there had given his horse plenty of grain. He likely wouldn't have time to stop and let it graze while he was on the trail of the outlaws.

Blackie Johnson stepped up to the counter at the general store, and waited patiently while the owner totaled up their purchases. While he was waiting, he noticed a young man nearby also gathering up a load of supplies. Blackie smiled and nodded to the fellow. "Looks like you're gonna be doing some mining up in the mountains," he said companionably.

Cal, startled by the man's words and somewhat surprised at the congeniality of the outlaw, nodded. "Yeah, my partner and I plan to give it a try."

Blackie glanced out of the window at the gray day. "Mighty poor weather to be going up in the mountains," he said.

Cal shrugged and inclined his head at the pile of heavy coats and other clothing on the counter in front of the man. "Looks like that's where you're headed too," he said.

Blackie nodded. "Yeah, but we're just passing through, not planning on staying too long. We're from Texas and it don't get that cold down there."

Zeke Thompson sidled up next to Johnson and stared suspiciously at Cal. He glanced at Blackie with a frown on his face. "You gonna jaw all day or get our gear ready?"

Blackie stared back at Thompson, not giving an inch. He didn't like the man and made no pretense to. "I'll pay up when the clerk has the total ready. You got a problem with that, Zeke?" he asked, standing nose-to-nose with the man.

Zeke cut his eyes at Cal. "Don't get testy, Blackie, but there's no need to discuss our business with every stranger you meet."

Blackie reached over to the counter and picked up a bottle of whiskey Thompson had gotten off the shelf. "Here, Zeke," he said, sneering. "Pour yourself a drink. It looks like you need one."

"Damned if I don't," Thompson said, and took the bottle and limped off toward the door.

"Sorry about my friend," Blackie said to Cal, who

was watching Thompson tilt the bottle to the ceiling and take a large swallow. "He ain't too personable."

Cal nodded. "I can see why," he said. "That leg of his must ache something fierce in this cold weather. I busted a knee once when I was herding beeves, an' it still hurts in cold weather."

Blackie looked over at Thompson. "I suppose so, but my guess is he's just an asshole. He don't need no excuse to be snake-mean."

The owner of the store cleared his throat and handed Blackie a piece of paper with a list of their supplies and how much it cost. Blackie looked it over, and then he pulled out a wad of bills, counted out the correct amount, and handed it to the clerk.

"Much obliged," he said to the store owner. "Hey, boys," he called to the men who were still browsing in the store. "Come and get this stuff so we can head back to camp." He paused for a moment, and then he added, "Hank, you think you could go see if Rufus is through with that doctor? I want to make sure he doesn't stop off at any saloons before he heads on back here."

After they'd gathered up their supplies, Blackie tipped his hat to Cal. "Good luck to you with your mining, mister," he said.

"Thanks," Cal answered. "And I hope you get where you're goin' without freezing your balls off."

Blackie laughed. "Me too."

After the men in the store gathered up their order and left, Cal stepped to the door and watched them load their supplies and begin to walk their horses out of town.

A few minutes later, Pearlie could be seen riding past the store, following the men at a safe distance. He glanced over at Cal standing in the doorway and winked and tipped his hat.

Cal grinned and went back into the store, where he proceeded to fill the rest of the order Smoke had given them. When he had it all stacked up on the counter, the owner of the store shook his head as he totaled the bill. "You and your partner must be planning to do a lot of blasting with all this powder."

"Yeah, it's a mite easier than using a pick and shovel," Cal answered.

The owner laughed. "That it is. But one thing, though," he added as he counted the boxes of cartridges Cal had gotten. "I don't know as you're going to need all these shells. The Indians haven't been giving the miners any trouble for some time now."

Cal nodded grimly. "It's just that my partner and I like to be prepared for whatever may happen."

"Looks to me like you're ready for the next war," the owner said as he handed Cal the bill.

Cal counted out the correct amount from the cash Pearlie had given him. "Here you go," he said. "Do you mind if I leave this stuff here for a while until I can get me a packhorse from the livery?"

"Not at all, son, I'll just pile it over here in the corner until you come back."

In less than an hour, Cal had purchased a packhorse from the livery man, loaded up their supplies, and taken the animal back to the livery, where he unpacked the boxes and bags of powder, stakes, nails, and cartridges and piled them in the stall where the livery man had his horse stored.

"I'm gonna leave these supplies here for a day or two, if you don't mind," Cal said. "My partner's out of town for a while and when he gets back we may have to leave in a hurry."

"Don't make no never mind to me, young'un," the elderly man said. "I don't 'spect nobody will bother it none."

"Thanks," Cal said, and he went back to the hotel to wait for Smoke to come.

* * *

It was mid-afternoon and Cal was lying on the bed taking a nap when the door opened and Smoke walked in.

Cal jumped to his feet and rushed over to shake Smoke's hand. "Jiminy, I'm glad to see you, Smoke."

Smoke nodded and smiled, and Cal could see he was dead tired from his time on the trail.

"Any word on the kidnappers?" Smoke asked as he set his saddlebags on the bed.

"Yeah, there was a group of 'em here this mornin'," Cal answered. "They bought some supplies at the store an' Pearlie followed them out of town."

"They didn't have Sally with them?"

Cal shook his head. "No. They must've left a couple of men with her so nobody would see her when they came to town," Cal said.

"Which way did they go when they left town?" Smoke asked, standing by the window and staring out at the street three stories below.

"That away," Cal answered, pointing northeast.

Smoke nodded. "Then they're headed for Pueblo, like they said they were," he said.

"Smoke, you look like you could use some food and a lie-down," Cal said, worried at the tiredness in Smoke's eyes.

"Yeah, I've been pushing it pretty hard trying to catch up to them," Smoke said. "Is the food any good here?"

Cal smiled. "Pearlie thinks so."

"Pearlie would eat anything that didn't eat him first," Smoke said. "Come on, let's get some grub and then I'll get some shut-eye. If Pearlie's not back in a few hours, we'll head out on our own down the trail toward Pueblo."

They went down to the dining room and ordered some food and a large pot of coffee. While they were waiting for the food to be cooked, Smoke told Cal about his trip following the men and the note Sally had written on a piece of her dress telling him where they were headed.

Cal grinned. "Miss Sally is too smart for them galoots," he said.

"That's for sure," Smoke said, and leaned back to let the waiter put their food on the table.

14

When they finished eating, Smoke called the waiter over to the table. "Hey, partner, would you have the chef fry us up four or five chickens and wrap them up for us to take with us later?" Smoke asked.

"Uh, we don't usually . . ."

Smoke handed the man a twenty-dollar bill. "Will this take care of it?" he asked, adding, "You can keep whatever's left over for yourself."

"I'll see that it gets done, sir," the waiter said, his lips curled in a wide smile. His tip would be more than he usually made in a week.

As they walked up the stairs to their room, Cal asked, "Why'd you do that?"

Smoke looked at him. "If we're going to be following these men up in the mountains, we're not going to be able to make a fire big enough to cook on without it being seen, so I wanted us to have something we could eat cold."

"Oh," Cal said, relieved that Smoke was doing the thinking for them, because he and Pearlie would never have thought of that.

Smoke went into the room and flopped down on the bed. "Wake me up in four hours whether Pearlie's here or not."

Before Cal could answer, Smoke was snoring softly and fast asleep.

Cal woke Smoke up and they were ready to leave just before nightfall. On the way out of the hotel, Smoke told the desk clerk to tell Pearlie they were on the trail heading toward Pueblo in case he returned after they left.

By the time they got the packhorse loaded up and were on their way, it was full dark and a light snow was starting to fall. "That's good," Smoke said, staring at the dark clouds in the night sky. "The clouds and snow will keep the temperatures from falling too low in the high country."

"It'll help us track the kidnappers too," Cal observed.

Smoke nodded. "That's true, if they try to get off the trail, but I suspect they're pilgrims and will stay on the road so they don't get lost in the mountains."

"Are you familiar with this part of the Sangre de Cristo Mountains, Smoke?" Cal asked as they rode north, letting their horses find their own speed.

"Pretty much," Smoke answered. "Preacher and I used to hunt this area back in the old days pretty much. There were plenty of beaver and foxes back then, not like now when the miners have hunted them out."

"You think there are any mountain men still up here nowadays?" Cal asked.

Smoke glanced at the peaks, outlined against the evening sky in the distance. "I suppose there may be a few. Some of the younger men are left, but even they're getting on up there in age by now."

It was getting close to midnight when Smoke's horse pricked up its ears and snorted through its nose. Smoke reined to a halt and held up his hand. "Quiet, Cal. Joker smells someone coming."

Since they were heading northeast and the wind was out of the north, the smells of anyone on the trail ahead of them would be carried downwind toward them.

Smoke pulled Joker's head around and led Cal off the trail and into the heavy bushes nearby. Cal followed suit when he saw Smoke draw his pistol and sit calmly waiting for whoever was headed their way.

A few minutes later, a dark form, hunched over his horse's head, could be seen moving down the trail toward them. When he came abreast of them, Smoke spurred Joker out onto the trail.

"Holy shit!" Pearlie exclaimed at the sight of two men materializing out of the wind-driven snow in front of him.

"Evening, Pearlie," Smoke said, holstering his pistol.

"Howdy, Pearlie," Cal said.

"You boys 'bout scared me outta ten years' growth," Pearlie said, taking his hat off and using it to brush the accumulated snow and ice off his shoulders and legs.

"What news of the kidnappers?" Smoke asked.

Pearlie gestured over his shoulder. "They're camped for the night, 'bout five miles up the trail."

"And Sally?" Smoke asked, his voice hard.

"Looks like they're treatin' her all right, Smoke. I got close enough to make sure she was doin' all right, nobody botherin' her or nothin', and then I headed back this way to meet up with you and Cal."

"So they're not treating her badly then?"

Pearlie shook his head. "No. In fact, they even bought her some heavy clothes, coats and such, so she wouldn't get too cold on the trip through the mountains."

"I'll be sure and thank the bastards . . . right before I kill them," Smoke said dryly.

"You want me to lead you to 'em?" Pearlie asked.

"Do they have sentries out?" Smoke asked.

Pearlie nodded. "Yeah. Two men, one north and one south. The others are bundled up next to the largest fire I ever seen tryin' to keep from freezin'."

"Well, there's no hurry then," Smoke said, pulling Joker's head around and riding off the trail toward a group of boulders nearby. "Let's make a fire, heat some coffee, and give them time to get settled in and the sentries to get sleepy."

"A fire sounds damn good," Pearlie said. "You got any food to cook? I'm 'bout starved to death."

"No time for that," Smoke said, "but we do have some fried chicken, if you don't mind eating it cold."

"Cold, hell," Pearlie replied. "I'll eat it raw if it's all you got."

After Smoke built a hat-sized fire up next to the boulders where the light couldn't be seen from more than a few feet away, Cal filled the coffeepot with snow and melted it on the fire, adding a double handful of Arbuckle's coffee once the water was boiling. After a few minutes, the delightful aroma of fresh-boiled coffee swirled in the air.

Pearlie was so hungry that he couldn't wait for the coffee to be ready. He dug into Cal's saddlebags and pulled out one of the packets of fried chicken wrapped in waxed paper. He carried it over to the tiny fire and sat cross-legged on a stone nearby while he unwrapped the food and began to eat.

When Cal handed him a tin cup full to the brim with the strong coffee, he said, "Hey, Pearlie, save a little of that chicken for Smoke and me."

"Hand me a couple of those legs, will you?" Smoke said. He preferred the legs to the white meat since he was used to eating game birds that were almost all dark meat.

"I'll take a breast," Cal said, reaching for the package.

Pearlie, who would eat any part of a chicken except the feathers and feet, pulled the package back and handed out the meat, preferring to remain in control of the delicious food.

After he took a few bites and washed them down with the coffee, he looked over at Smoke. "This is right good chicken, but it don't compare to Miss Sally's."

Smoke nodded his agreement while he gnawed on a chicken leg and drank his coffee.

"It sure would be nice to have a handful of Miss Sally's bear sign for desert," Cal observed, his mood falling as he thought about the situation Sally was in.

"It would be even nicer to have Sally here with us now," Smoke said, his eyes moving off to the north where the outlaws were camped.

When they'd finished eating and had built cigarettes to enjoy with the last of the coffee, Smoke began to outline his plan of attack on the kidnappers.

"First thing we're going to do is find their camp. We shouldn't have to worry too much about noise since the snow will muffle the horses' hoofbeats, but we'll need to make sure anything we're carrying is tied down tight so it won't clatter when we ride up close."

"After we find 'em, what do you want us to do?" Cal asked.

"I'm going to go in close while you boys hang back. I want to make sure Sally's all right. If I see she's in no danger of being treated badly, then I'll come back out to you and we'll see if we can take out the sentries without risking any noise."

Pearlie pulled out his skinning knife and held it up so the fire reflected off the blade. "That shouldn't be a problem," he said with a dark look.

Smoke shook his head. "No, Pearlie. I want to take them alive if we can."

"Why?" Cal asked.

"Because I want to ask them some questions about

exactly where the outlaws are headed and why they decided to take her in the first place."

He pulled out his pocket watch, glanced at the time, and got to his feet. "Put out the fire, boys. It's time we get back on the trail."

It was almost midnight by the time Smoke and the boys approached the kidnappers' camp. Smoke could see and smell the huge campfire from over a mile away, so he knew they were getting close. When he saw the glow of the fire over a ridge, he told Cal and Pearlie to stay with the horses, and he got down out of the saddle and crept over the ridge on foot, keeping well off the trail and into the brush surrounding the camp.

As he got closer, he got down on his belly and crawled through the forest until he was no more than thirty yards from the fire. He counted nine bodies sprawled close to the fire, bundled up in blankets and lying on rubber groundsheets to keep dry. One of the figures was a little away from the others, and he could tell it was Sally by the long, dark hair spilling out from under the blankets, which she had up to her forehead to keep warm.

He saw a rope leading out from under the blankets that was tied to a nearby tree. Evidently the bastards had tied Sally's hand or arm to the tree to keep her from trying to escape during the night. Actually, he thought, that was a good sign. If they'd harmed her significantly, they wouldn't be worried about her being able to make an escape, so she must be in pretty good shape, considering what she'd been through.

He lay perfectly still, not moving at all. He knew from the number of bodies he counted that there were probably two sentries somewhere near the camp. He figured sooner or later they would make some movement showing him where they were. Pilgrims, in cold like this, were unable to stay perfectly still while sitting sentry duty and would eventually move around to try and keep warm.

Sure enough, in a short while, he saw the flare of a lucifer off to one side as one of the sentries lit a cigarette or cigar. He made a mental note of his location and continued to let his eyes move around the periphery of the camp, searching for the other sentry's location.

His patience was rewarded after a few minutes when a moving shadow on the other side of the camp caught his eye. The man was walking in short circles, flapping his arms to his chest to get them warm.

Smoke shook his head and grinned to himself. The men were obviously dumber than dirt. The only value of a sentry is stealth. If the enemy knows the sentry's location, then he's worthless; a fact that was either not known by these men or that was being ignored out of a sense of security or boredom.

With their positions fixed firmly in his mind, Smoke slowly crawled back away from the camp until it was safe for him to get to his feet, and then he jogged back to where he'd left Cal and Pearlie and the horses.

When he got there, he drew a crude map of the camp in the snow with a stick, marking the positions of the sentries. "Now, here's what we're going to do," he said. "Cal, you and Pearlie will ease up on the man on this side of the camp, 'cause he'll be the easiest to get to without making any noise. Once you get to him, take him down with the butt of your pistol and make sure he doesn't make any noise when he falls. Then you bring him back here and make him comfortable until I get back."

"You gonna take out the other guard by yourself?" Cal asked.

Smoke nodded. "Yeah. It's going to be a little more difficult to get to him without him hearing me because of his position, but I think I can do it. If it looks like it'll make too much noise for me to take him, I'll just come back here and we'll try to get our information from the man you two get."

He stood up and put his hands on their shoulders. "Good luck, boys, and remember, Sally's life depends on you not letting them hear you."

15

Sam Kane felt as if his feet and hands were frozen blocks of ice. Even though he'd had some experience with blue northers down in Texas, he'd never seen weather so cold as this before. He pulled the cork from his canteen with shaking hands and took a swallow of the coffee he'd filled it with earlier. It was only lukewarm now and did little to warm his insides. It was definitely time for stronger medicine to ward off the chilly night air.

Looking around to make sure Bill Pike wasn't checking on him, he pulled a small bottle of whiskey from under his coat and upended it, swallowing deeply. Almost immediately, he felt the warmth of the liquor spread through his stomach and out into his limbs. Jesus, that tasted good, he thought.

He set the whiskey down on a rock next to him, being careful not to spill any, and took out his makings. He tried to build himself a cigarette, but his hands were shaking so much he spilled more tobacco than he got in the paper. He twisted the ends of the paper and stuck the butt in his mouth. Bending over against the wind, he struck a lucifer and lit the cigarette, gratefully filling his lungs with the warm smoke.

He jumped when he thought he heard a twig break

behind him, but when he turned and looked, he saw no signs of movement.

He shook his head. Must've been the wind, he thought. The spooky darkness and cold must be getting to him for him to be so jumpy.

He finished the cigarette and flipped the butt out into the snow, grinning as it sizzled in the wetness. Leaning over, he picked up the whiskey and leaned his head back to take another drink.

He caught a movement out of the corner of his eye, and turned his head just as the butt of a pistol crashed down onto his skull. The darkness opened up in front of him and he tumbled in.

Billy Gatsby, the youngest of Bill Pike's band of raiders, was lucky. He'd been given the sentry post that was partially sheltered by a large group of boulders and was back up against the side of a hillock, so most of the north wind was blocked.

Still, he was about as cold as he could ever remember being. In spite of the fact that he had on three shirts and a heavy coat over his long handles, he was still shivering and shaking like he had the fever. Don't know why Bill thinks we have to stand sentry duty way out here in the mountains, he thought. Ain't nobody within fifty miles gonna be crazy enough to be out in this storm this time of night.

He, like Sam Kane, had filled his canteen with coffee, but he'd been smarter than Kane. When Bill wasn't looking, he'd added a generous measure of rye whiskey to the canteen before filling it with coffee. His coffee wasn't as warm as Kane's was, but it packed a helluva lot more kick than Kane's did.

The night was only half over, and Billy had already just about emptied the canteen. As he took the last swallow, he debated whether he ought to go back over to the fire and fill it up again with the coffee that'd been left warming by the fire.

He shook his head and clamped his jaw tight. No, better not do that. Bill would have a fit if he left his position just to get some coffee. Not that he was afraid of Bill Pike. Billy was young and dumb enough not to be afraid of anybody, but he figured there was no need of pissing Pike off when they stood to make such a good payday off this Jensen fellow.

He wriggled his toes inside his boots, wishing he'd put on an extra pair of socks. He could barely feel his feet and they were beginning to burn. Wondering if they were getting frostbitten, he decided to walk around a little to get the blood flowing.

Slapping his arms against his chest, he stepped out from his sheltered place among the boulders, and almost ran into a shadowy figure standing just around the corner.

He grinned for a moment, thinking at first it was Bill Pike coming to check on him. And then he realized the man was much bigger than anyone in their group.

"Son of a bitch!" he started to say, grabbing for his side arm.

The big man's fist crashed into his jaw, dislocating it and knocking out three of his front teeth as it drove him down into unconsciousness.

When Smoke got back to the horses, carrying Billy Gatsby over his shoulder, he found Cal and Pearlie sitting on their groundsheets in front of an unconscious man propped up against a boulder in a copse of pine trees.

"Did you have any trouble?" he asked as he dropped his man on the ground next to theirs.

"Naw," Pearlie drawled. "This'n was too busy

drinkin' whiskey to be payin' any attention to what he was doin'."

Smoke squatted in front of the men. "Rub a little snow on their faces and see if we can wake them up."

As Cal began to rub snow on the men's faces, he looked back over his shoulder at Smoke. "Jiminy, Smoke. This one's jaw looks like it's broken. What'd you hit him with?"

Smoke grinned. "My fist."

Cal grimaced at the misshapen appearance of the man's face. "Well, that was enough, I guess."

A few minutes later, both men sputtered and came awake. Billy was groaning and slobbering blood from his ruined mouth, while Sam just held his head in both hands and kept his mouth shut, glaring at Smoke and the boys with hate-filled eyes.

Smoke, still squatting in front of the men, said quietly, "You boys know who I am?" he asked.

Kane's eyes narrowed and he shook his head. "Nope. Never seen you before in my life," he said, his voice whiskey-rough.

"I'm Smoke Jensen," Smoke said, noticing how the men's eyes changed at the mention of his name. "And that's my wife you men kidnapped, and it was my hands you killed at my ranch."

"I don't know what you're talking about," Kane said sullenly, his eyes dropping, unable to meet Smoke's.

Smoke sighed and stood up, towering over the men. "Boys," he said calmly, "we can do this one of two ways: the hard way or the easy way, and trust me, you don't want to know what the hard way is."

Kane didn't answer, but his eyes filled with fear when he saw Pearlie take out his skinning knife and slowly rub it back and forth on his pants, his eyes fixed on Kane like a snake eyeing a rabbit.

"All right," he said grudgingly, "what do you want to know?"

"First, why did your leader pick my ranch to raid?" Smoke asked.

"He found a wanted poster on you up in Utah," Kane answered. "It offered a ten-thousand-dollar reward for you dead or alive."

Smoke snorted through his nose. "That poster's over ten years old," he said. "There isn't any price on my head anymore."

Kane glanced at Billy, lying next to him, his eyes puzzled. "Then why would he do all this?" he asked.

Smoke pursed his lips, thinking. "Tell me the names of all of the gang."

After Kane told him, Smoke nodded. "This Zeke Thompson, he any kin to Pike?"

"I reckon so. They got the same mother."

"Does he have a bum leg?" Smoke asked.

Kane nodded. "Yeah, an' his arm's messed up too."

Smoke looked at Cal and Pearlie. "It's just as I thought. Pike and Thompson are after me because I killed their brother up in Utah a while back. I shot up Thompson but let him live. My mistake, I guess."

"How about Miss Sally, you pond scum?" Pearlie asked, holding the knife in front of Kane's eyes. "Have you bastards hurt her in any way?"

Kane shook his head vigorously. "No, I swear we haven't. Bill said we couldn't do nothin' to her till he had Jensen prisoner. Then he was gonna make you watch what we did."

Smoke's hands clenched at his sides. "I hope you're telling me the truth, mister."

"Ask Billy if'n you don't believe me," Kane said.

Smoke glanced at Billy, who mumbled something they couldn't understand since he couldn't talk, then nodded his head indicating Kane was telling the truth.

Smoke took a deep breath. "In that case, I'm going to let you live . . . for a while."

"What do you mean?" Kane asked.

"I'm going to take you up the mountain a ways and let you go."

"What do you mean, let us go?" Kane asked. "You mean, without no horses or nothin'?"

"That's right," Smoke said. "If you're smart and careful, you just might be able to survive until you can find some miners who'll take mercy on you. I will leave you with a knife so you can cut some trees for shelter, but that's about it."

"But we'll freeze to death up there," Kane pleaded.

Smoke shrugged. "At least you'll have a chance to live. That's more than you gave the men you killed at my ranch."

He turned to Pearlie. "Put them on your horse. I'll take them a couple of miles up the mountain and then I'll meet you back here."

Pearlie put his skinning knife away and walked over to where the two men were propped up against a boulder. He bent over to reach down and help Billy Gatsby to his feet. Billy moaned and spat out some blood from his mouth as Pearlie grabbed him under the arms.

Just as Pearlie straightened up with the young man in his arms, Sam Kane jumped to his feet, drawing a long knife with a skinny blade from his boot. He threw his left arm around Pearlie's face and stuck the point of the knife up against his throat, whirling around until he was facing Smoke and Cal.

Billy tried to grin but stopped when he realized it hurt too much. He reached down and pulled Pearlie's pistol from his holster and stood next to them, pointing the gun at Cal and Smoke.

Smoke sighed, squaring his body so he was facing the two men full on. "Are you boys sure you want to play it out this way?" Smoke asked.

"We ain't got no choice, Jensen," Zane said. "I can't let you take us up into the mountains to freeze to death or to be eaten by wild animals."

Smoke nodded. "I guess you're right, son," he said. "It might be more humane to just kill you both now, so you'll die quick and easy."

Zane grinned nastily. "I think you're forgetting who has the upper hand here, Jensen."

Billy mumbled something through his ruined mouth that sounded like "Yeah."

Smoke shrugged and glanced at Cal, who nodded grimly.

Quick as a rattlesnake striking, Smoke and Cal drew their pistols and fired, Cal's shot coming an instant later than Smoke's.

A tiny hole appeared in Zane's forehead from the slug Smoke fired, whipping his head back and flinging him spread-eagled on his back across the boulder behind him and Pearlie.

Cal's slug took Billy in the neck, snapping it and almost taking his head off before he crumpled to the ground, dead in his boots.

Pearlie reached up and fingered the thin red line on his throat where Zane's knife slid across it after he'd been hit. Pearlie smiled. "I thought you boys was gonna jaw all night 'fore you took them pond scum out."

He glanced down at Billy, noted the wound in his neck, and then he looked back over at Cal. "You a mite off on your aim there, Cal boy. Guess we're gonna have to see that you practice a bit more in the future."

Cal smiled and nodded. "Yeah, I was aiming for his heart, but I guess I rushed the shot a little since he already had his gun drawn and pointed."

Smoke holstered his pistol. "You did mighty good, Cal, especially in knowing I wanted you to take the one with the gun instead of the one with the knife."

"Yeah," Pearlie said, a puzzled look on his face. "I didn't see you pass no signals, so how'd you know which one to shoot, Cal?"

Cal spun his gun once and let it drop into his holster. "I knew Smoke would take the harder shot, so I took the easier one." He smiled at Cal. "Besides, I didn't want to risk hitting you 'stead of that bastard there, 'cause I knew I'd never hear the end of it if I did."

Pearlie and Smoke both laughed. "You got that right," Pearlie agreed.

Smoke pulled out the large bowie knife he carried in a scabbard on his belt and walked over to the dead bodies. "I think we ought to leave a little message for Mr. Pike now that these boys have forced our hand."

16

Bill Pike woke up just as the morning sun was peeking over the mountain peaks to the east. He yawned and stretched and climbed out of his blankets, noticing the fire had burned down to just coals.

He walked over to the bundle of blankets that covered Rufus Gordon and kicked it with his boot. "Rufus, wake your lazy ass up and put some wood on that fire," he said.

Rufus groaned. "Aw, Bill, you know I can't hardly use my right hand. Get somebody else to do it."

Pike looked surprised. "I thought that doc over in Canyon City fixed your hand up pretty good."

Rufus held up his right hand, totally encased in new bandages. "He did, but the damn thing's so wrapped up I can't use my fingers."

"Must make pickin' your nose a real chore," Hank Snow called from across the fire, laughing at his own joke.

"Glad you spoke up, Hank," Bill Pike said, turning to him. "Just for that, you can get the wood for the fire 'stead of Rufe."

As Snow got slowly to his feet, grumbling about no one having a sense of humor, Pike nudged Blackie

Johnson with his boot. "Blackie, get up and fix us some coffee and breakfast 'fore it's time for lunch."

While Hank Snow got the fire going, Blackie pulled the cooking utensils out of the bag on the back of one of the packhorses and began to make coffee and prepared to fry some bacon and boil some beans. He still had some biscuits he'd cooked the night before, and put them on a pan near the fire to warm up.

The rest of the gang began to get their blankets and groundsheets folded and packed on their horses. Sally sat up in her blankets and held up her hand with the rope still tied to it. "If you'll take this off," she said to Pike, "I'll put my blankets on my horse."

Pike walked over, squatted down, and untied the knots in the rope. "Did you sleep well, Mrs. Jensen?" he asked, a slight smile on his face.

"Yes, thank you, Mr. Pike," she answered. "But I'll feel a lot better after some coffee."

Pike looked over at Blackie. "That coffee ready yet, Blackie?"

Blackie nodded, poured some into a tin mug, and brought it over to Sally. "I'll have some biscuits and bacon and beans ready in about five minutes, Mrs. Jensen," he said, his eyes narrowing at the red rash the rope had made on her wrist. "And I'll get you some lard to smooth on that rash on your wrist."

Pike scowled at Johnson. "Don't go gettin' too kindly to the lady, Blackie. It ain't gonna do you no good."

Blackie stared at Pike for a moment, and then he just shook his head and went back to the fire to finish cooking breakfast.

Pike looked around at his men. "Where the hell are Billy and Sam?" he asked.

Rufus Gordon sat up in his blankets and glanced around, and then he shrugged. "They ain't here yet, Boss."

"If those lazy bastards fell asleep on guard duty, I'm gonna kick their asses!" Pike growled.

"Hank, you and Sarge go get 'em and bring 'em back here pronto," Pike ordered.

As Snow and Rutledge walked off toward the two sentries' posts, Pike squatted down, picked a piece of bacon out of the frying pan, and began to munch on it while he waited to see what was keeping the guards.

A few minutes later, both Rutledge and Snow came running back into the camp, their faces pale and sweating in spite of the frigid temperatures of the morning air. Snow looked as if he was going to throw up.

"What is it? What's the matter with you two?" Pike asked, his brow furrowed with worry.

"You . . . you better come on over here and take a look for yourself," Snow managed as he bent over, his hands on his knees, and dry-heaved.

Pike and the other men moved through the brush to the place where Sam Kane had been stationed. Lying on a boulder was a bloody scalp, two ears, and a tongue, arranged in a grotesque parody of a face on the bloody rock.

"Jesus!" Pike said, his stomach turning until he too thought he was going to be sick.

Sally Jensen pushed a couple of the men aside and stood before the boulder, a sympathetic look on her face for the dead men. "Oh, Mr. Pike," she said quietly. "I believe you've now seen some of my husband's handiwork."

Pike whirled around and glared at her. "Ain't no white man done this!" he shouted. "It must've been Indians."

Sally shook her head. "No, Mr. Pike. I'm afraid you're mistaken."

"What do you mean?" he asked, his voice a dry croak.

"In the first place, Indians wouldn't have left the scalps or the . . . other trophies," she explained. "And in the second place, if the Indians had killed your men, why do you think they would not have come on into camp and finished the rest of you off while you were sleeping?"

Pike looked at Rutledge. "What about Billy?" he asked, his eyes wide.

Rutledge shook his head. "Worse than this. You'd better come look."

The entire group moved across the camp, breakfast forgotten, and approached the sentry post of Billy Gatsby. They found his entire head stuck on a pole in the ground, his eyes open and staring at them as if in reproach, his swollen tongue protruding from an obviously broken jaw.

Pike whirled around, grabbed Sally by the shoulders, and shouted into her face. "What kind of man is your husband?"

She smiled back, unaffected by his display of temper. "He is a man of the old school, Mr. Pike. An eye for an eye and all of that."

"But we ain't harmed you none," Pike said, his voice becoming more normal as he got control of himself.

"You kidnapped me against my will, Mr. Pike, and you killed two of our friends back at the ranch. That's enough for Smoke." She turned her head to look at Billy. "I'm afraid this is what you've all got to look forward to for what you've done."

Pike jerked his gun out and pointed it at Sally. "Then it won't make any difference if I kill you now, will it?"

Sally showed no fear. "Not in the end result perhaps. You are all going to die, that is as certain as the fact that the sun will rise tomorrow. However, the manner in which you die *will* be determined by how you treat me."

Pike gritted his teeth, pulled back the hammer on his pistol, and stuck the barrel under Sally's chin.

She stared back at him with clear eyes and did not flinch in the slightest.

Blackie Johnson stepped over and put his hand on Pike's arm. "Maybe we'd better listen to what she says, Boss. If we kill her now, we won't have any hold over Jensen to make him come to us in Pueblo."

"Blackie's right, Bill," Zeke Thompson said. "I haven't waited all these years to be cheated out of my chance at Jensen 'cause you get pissed off."

Blackie glanced back over his shoulder at Zeke. "What do you mean, waited all these years, Zeke?" he asked. "I thought this was about the reward on Jensen's head."

Thompson blushed and stammered, "It was just a figure of speech, Blackie. What I meant to say was, I been waiting for a score like this for a lotta years and I don't want to blow it now."

Pike took a deep breath and let the hammer down on his gun. He holstered it and then he pointed at Sally with his finger. "You get a second chance, Mrs. Jensen, but if that crazy husband of yours does something like this again, I'll make you suffer like you've never even dreamed of."

Sally gave him a half smile and turned and made her way back to the camp, where she calmly poured herself another cup of coffee and sat there staring at the forgotten frying pan as the bacon strips slowly turned to charcoal.

Smoke, who'd been watching the scene below from a vantage point on a ledge fifteen hundred yards up the mountain, gently let the hammer down on the Sharps buffalo rifle he was holding. When Pike had put the pistol under Sally's chin, Smoke had drawn a bead on the man's head. He'd had the trigger half-depressed when Pike lowered his gun, saving his life.

Smoke took a deep breath. He knew how close he'd

come to losing Sally, and the feeling made him weak with unaccustomed fear.

Time to back off for a while and let the situation simmer down, he thought to himself. As he moved down the mountain to where Cal and Pearlie were waiting for him, he began to make plans for his meeting with the outlaws in Pueblo and how he was going to handle it.

He knew it was going to take all of his skill to meet with Pike and not let the man get the upper hand.

The main thing he had to do was to stall the kidnappers along until he could get Sally out from under their control, which meant he'd have to leave the rest of them alive until he could figure out a way to do that without getting her killed by the desperados.

When he arrived back at the place where Cal and Pearlie were holding the horses, he put the Sharps in its rifle boot and climbed into the saddle.

"Did our little show have the desired effect?" Pearlie asked.

Smoke nodded. "It sure got them to thinking," he replied. He sat on his horse and built himself a cigarette. When he was done, he stuck the butt in the corner of his mouth, struck a lucifer on his pants leg, and lit the cigarette. As smoke trailed from his nostrils, he said, "Now, here's what we're going to do when we get to Pueblo."

When he was finished explaining his plan, they rode off after the outlaws.

17

As Pike led his men through mountain passes toward Pueblo, Colorado Territory, he began to leave two men a slight distance behind to watch their back-trail. With what had happened to Sam and Billy, he now knew Smoke Jensen was in the vicinity, and he wasn't going to take any chances of Jensen sneaking up on them while they were riding.

When they got close to the town of Pueblo, he checked a map he'd been given while in Utah by a man who used to mine the area. The man had told him of a played-out mining camp north of Pueblo up in the mountain range that had some shacks and a couple of old mine shafts that would be perfect for what Pike had in mind.

The trail from Canyon City to Pueblo followed the course of the Arkansas River as it meandered south-east through the foothills of the mountains. The map indicated that just before reaching Pueblo, Pike should turn north and circle around the city until he came to a creek named Fountain Creek, which ran straight south toward Pueblo, where it then joined the Arkansas River. The deserted mining camp would be found about five miles north of the city on the banks of the creek.

As the group of outlaws rode single file down the trail, their horses moving slowly as they plowed through knee-deep snow, Sally slowed her horse until she was abreast of Blackie Johnson. She'd picked him to talk to because of all the men in the gang he seemed the least hostile toward her.

"Mr. Johnson," she said in a low voice that couldn't be heard more than a few feet away.

Johnson looked at her and nodded, but didn't speak.

"What was that you were saying back at the camp about a wanted poster on Smoke?"

Johnson glanced up at the head of the line of men, making sure Pike couldn't hear him. "Bill has a poster we picked up in Utah that says your husband is worth ten thousand dollars, dead or alive," he answered, also speaking in a low voice.

"So," Sally said, "that's why you're riding with these men?"

Johnson gave her a look. "Mrs. Jensen, no matter what you think of us, we wouldn't be out here waiting for your husband to come so we can kill him if he didn't deserve it. Men don't get ten-thousand-dollar rewards put on them if they haven't done some pretty bad things. We're Regulators, not bandits."

Sally looked puzzled. "Well, no matter what you call yourselves, there can't be a wanted poster out on Smoke. Smoke hasn't been wanted by the law for over ten years. All of the posters were recalled years ago by the governor of the territory."

Johnson slowed his horse and stared at her. "Are you sure about that?" he asked.

Sally smiled slightly. "Of course I'm sure. Smoke is in no trouble with the law, Mr. Johnson, and hasn't been for some years." She sighed deeply. "Think about it. With that much money at stake, you would have had to stand in line behind other bounty hunters to get at Smoke if it was true. After all, we weren't exactly living in hiding in Colorado."

Johnson's eyes narrowed and he stared at Pike's back. "I'll admit, Mrs. Jensen, I've been having my doubts. I thought it might be something like that. I couldn't figure why a man with such a price on his head would be living openly on a ranch in Colorado Territory so close to Utah."

Sally gave a low laugh. "That's simple. It's because he's not wanted and hasn't been for some time."

Johnson nodded slowly. "That figures," he said, disgust in his voice. He gave Pike, riding up ahead of them, a speculative look. "Bill must have some other reason for coming after your husband, something he didn't tell us about."

Sally gave him a close look. "You really don't know what all this is about, do you?" she asked.

Johnson turned his head to look her in the eyes. "No. The only reason Pike gave us was the money we'd make if we killed Jensen. Do you have any idea what's going on?" he asked, still speaking in a low voice so those in front of and behind them couldn't hear his words.

"Yes. It seems some years ago, Smoke shot and killed Mr. Pike's brother, and he wounded his half brother, Zeke. It must have been a severe wound, resulting in the problems he now has with his arm and leg."

Johnson's lips turned white as he pressed them together. "So, all this is about him getting even with your husband for something he did to his family a long time ago?"

Sally nodded.

Johnson lifted his reins and sat up straighter in his saddle. "That son of a bitch just got Billy and Sam killed, and there isn't even going to be any money in it for us."

He rested his right hand on the butt of his pistol. "I think I'll go call him on it right now."

Sally shook her head. "No, Mr. Johnson, I wouldn't do that if I were you."

"Why not?" he asked, relaxing a little.

"Because you have no proof, other than my word, and I do not think the men will believe me."

"You're right. These stupid galoots won't want to think they've come all this way for nothing."

"And killed two innocent men and gotten two of your friends killed all because Mr. Pike and Mr. Thompson want revenge against my husband," Sally added.

"What do you suggest I do?"

"Bide your time, Mr. Johnson, bide your time. Pike will give himself away sooner or later, and then you'll have the rest of the men with you instead of against you when you confront him."

"That's sound advice, Mrs. Jensen. I'm obliged," Johnson said, taking his hand off his pistol and sitting back in his saddle.

Just before noon, Pike and his men came to the stream running north and south that he figured must be Fountain Creek. They turned north and rode for another three hours, and finally came to a collection of old, weather-beaten clapboard cabins arranged in a semicircle on the banks of the river. There were well-worn paths from each of the houses down to the water's edge and to a pit dug in the middle of the open ground in between the cabins. There were even a couple of old privies that were still standing out behind the houses and away from the stream.

Pike rode into the center of the small camp and got down off his horse. "This must be the place that old miner told us about, boys," he said. "Get your gear together and see if any of these cabins are in good enough shape to bunk down in."

He stood in the center of the open area among the

houses and stared up at the mountains that rose on steep slopes on all sides of them. "Hank, while the boys unpack our supplies, why don't you take a ride up the slope over there and see if you can find the mine entrance the old fool told us about?"

"All right, Boss," Snow said, and he jerked his reins around and walked his horse up the side of the mountain.

Sergeant Rutledge came riding up with the other man Pike had assigned to watch their backtrail. "All clear to the rear, Boss," he said. "If anyone's following us, they're staying well back and out of sight."

Pike moved to a circular area in the middle of the open area where dozens of small stones were arranged around a fire pit about two feet deep. "Sarge, take a couple of men and gather up some wood for a fire, and Blackie can fix us our noon meal while the rest of you unpack."

As the men bent to their tasks, Pike walked over to Sally and helped her down off her horse. Once she was on the ground, he untied the ropes he had around her wrists. "I'm gonna untie you, Mrs. Jensen, but I warn you again, don't try to escape or it'll go hard on you."

Sally glanced around at the surrounding mountains on all sides of them and decided to once again play the helpless female. "Why, where on earth would I go, Mr. Pike? I'd never find my way out of this wilderness by myself."

Pike gave her a long look, and for a moment Sally wondered if she'd overplayed her role.

"That's right, Mrs. Jensen," he finally said, beginning to turn away from her. "These mountains are no place for a woman on her own."

Sally bit her lip to keep from smiling. Truth was, with all Smoke had taught her about the High Lonesome over the years, she was far better equipped to deal with the wilderness than any of these flatlander pilgrims were.

She followed Pike over to where Blackie Johnson was struggling to get a fire going with wood that was wet from the snow on the ground.

She stood near him and talked out of the side of her mouth so the others wouldn't know they were communicating. "Mr. Johnson, if you'll use that little hatchet to split the wood open, you'll find it is dry on the inside and will make a much better fire," she whispered, her head turned away. "I'd start with some dry grass from up close to the trees where the snow hasn't gotten to it, and then use some pine cones on top of that. It'll make the fire start a lot easier."

"You seem to know a lot about living in the open, Mrs. Jensen," he said to her as he began to split the wood with his small ax.

Sally didn't answer, but she thought to herself, a woman learns a lot married to a mountain man, including how to outsmart galoots like this bunch.

Cal and Pearlie, who'd been keeping pace with the outlaws by riding up higher in the mountains, had been surprised when the gang had made a turn to the north and headed away from Pueblo, where they were supposed to meet with Smoke.

Smoke had circled around the men, and rode hard to get to Pueblo ahead of the man he was supposed to meet there. He wanted to be waiting for him so he wouldn't know Smoke knew where his camp was.

Cal and Pearlie, from their vantage point on a slope high above the outlaws' camp, watched the men unpack their supplies and settle into the cabins near the stream.

"Looks like they're gonna make this their camp," Pearlie said.

Cal, who'd been watching Sally as she moved

around the camp, nodded. "They seem to be treating Miss Sally all right," he observed. "At least, they're givin' her the run of the place an' not keepin' her tied up or anything."

Pearlie smiled grimly. "They'd better not do her no harm, if'n they know what's good for 'em.

"We'll watch them a mite longer an' then you can ride on into town and tell Smoke where they're stayin'," he added.

18

When Smoke followed the trail into the city of Pueblo, he was surprised at how much the town had grown. He'd been through the area years ago when he was riding with Preacher, but the town seemed to have tripled in size and population since then.

Back when he and Preacher had passed through, Pueblo had been a sleepy little village built on the bank of the Arkansas River. Now the town straddled the river and was built up all along both sides of the slowly flowing body of water. The buildings weren't too close to the edge of the river because in the spring, when the snow and ice in the mountains above and all around the city melted, the river would more than double in size and speed of flow.

There was a wooden bridge built across the narrowest part of the river that allowed the inhabitants to move back and forth along both sides of it. Back when Smoke was first here, there had only been a flat raft that a couple of men pulled back and forth by means of a rope tied to trees on either side of the river.

As Smoke rode Joker across the bridge, he noticed there was now a fort occupying the north end of town. A sign on the periphery of the fort read FORT PUEBLO, and a small group of soldiers could be seen moving about within the confines of the structure.

"They must be here to maintain order among the miners, since there hasn't been any trouble with the Indians for some years," Smoke said to the back of Joker's head, a habit he'd picked up long ago when he'd spend half a year or more without laying eyes on another white man. He'd always felt talking to a horse was less troublesome than talking to oneself when alone up in the mountains.

The town was fairly busy, what with a lot of the miners coming down from their mountain camps to gather up supplies for the winter before the snows blocked the passes down to town. Along with the miners was a conglomeration of the people that invariably congregated around men with too much money in their pockets and too little civilizing influences: prostitutes, gamblers, footpads, thieves, and other assorted rowdy characters of an unsavory nature.

Now all Smoke had to do was to pick out a saloon out of the many that lined Court Street and grab himself a table. Today was the day he was supposed to meet the man who'd kidnapped Sally, and he couldn't wait to look the bastard in the eyes.

Back at the outlaws' camp, Bill Pike finished his meal and got to his feet. He checked his watch and then he looked out over the mountains thinking. It was about time for him to head into Pueblo to meet with Smoke Jensen and discuss the present situation and how they were going to deal with it. He realized he'd gotten himself between a rock and a hard place. On the one hand, he and Zeke needed to get Smoke out of Pueblo so they could wreak their vengeance upon him for killing their kin, but on the other hand, if he brought Smoke up here now, it was likely the other members of his band of cutthroats would soon learn that there was in fact no price on Smoke's head, and there was no telling how they would react to the news that they'd come all this way without a ten-thousand-dollar payday in the offing.

If they'd killed Smoke at the ranch, it wouldn't have been as bad. He could have said anything to his men. Hell, he could have waited a day or two, pretended to go to a sheriff, and then come back and told his men that the poster had been recalled. Maybe a few would have raised a fuss. But he and Zeke could have handled that. And meanwhile, Smoke would be dead.

But now, after all this time, after all they'd been through, his men needed something more. A payday, preferably a big one.

The only way out of this quandary that Pike could see would be to put Smoke off another day, and then have Smoke meet him and Zeke somewhere else with the promise to trade Mrs. Jensen for money. Hopefully, that would put Jensen's suspicions to rest and at that meeting Zeke and Pike could kill the son of a bitch.

When Zeke got in touch with Pike with the idea of getting revenge on Smoke Jensen for killing their brother and crippling Zeke, Pike had began his search for where Smoke might be living now. As famous as Smoke was, it didn't take Pike long to discover his whereabouts in Big Rock, Colorado. He'd also discovered that Smoke Jensen had become both respectable and rich.

Thinking on this, Pike chuckled to himself, seeing a way out of his predicament. He'd have Jensen wire the bank at Big Rock and have a letter of credit wired to the bank at Pueblo for ten thousand dollars as ransom for his wife.

After he and Zeke killed Jensen, Pike would simply tell the men that they had killed Smoke, taken his body to Pueblo, and gotten the ten thousand dollars reward as he'd promised. That should satisfy the men as far as the money was concerned.

To make them even happier, once he and Zeke were done with Smoke, he would give the men Mrs. Jensen as an added prize to make up for the hardships they'd faced in the frigid weather. He could then sweeten the pot by arranging to use the men to rob some of the miners in the area and make enough money to enable them to live for years on the proceeds of this little trip.

This seemed to Pike like the best way to keep everyone happy and for him and Zeke to get the revenge they craved against Jensen.

On the way into Pueblo, he would keep a sharp lookout for a place suitable for the meeting with Jensen. It would have to be isolated and yet easy enough to describe to the man so he could find it the next day.

Pike called the men together near the fire. "Blackie," he said, "take Mrs. Jensen to one of those cabins and tie her up good and tight. We've got some business to discuss."

Blackie nodded and walked over to help Sally to her feet. He led her to the cabin he'd put his things in, and told her to lie down on the bed.

Once she was lying down, he bent over her. "Mrs. Jensen, I'm going to put some ropes on your hands and feet, but I'm not gonna tie 'em real tight so they won't dig into your skin."

Sally nodded as he wrapped the ropes around her wrists and ankles. He straightened up. "Now, you got to promise me not to try and escape, or it'll go hard on me."

Sally took a deep breath. "Thank you for you kindness, Mr. Johnson. I will promise not to try and escape right now, but I won't promise not to try later on."

Johnson gave a short laugh. "That's good enough

for me, Mrs. Jensen. I'll come in and untie you as soon as Pike's through with his talk."

He walked out the door and went over to the fire, where the other men were standing, warming their hands against the chill of the cold, mountain air.

Pike looked around at his men. "Boys, I'm going to go into Pueblo and see if Jensen showed up like I told him to in that letter we left at his ranch. If he's there, I'll get him to come back to camp with me by promising to let him go if he pays us for his wife."

"What's gonna happen when he gets here?" Hank Snow asked, picking his teeth with a stick.

Pike spread his hands. "Why, we'll kill him, of course, and then take his body to the nearest marshal's office and collect our ten thousand dollar reward."

Rufus Gordon rubbed the bandages on his ruined hand, hate filling his eyes. "And what's gonna happen to that bitch what shot off my fingers after we're done with Jensen?" he asked, letting his eyes go to the cabin where Sally was.

Pike shrugged. "I guess that'll be up to you boys. As cold as it is up here, maybe you can figure out some way for her to keep you warm for a spell."

Rufus jerked a long-bladed knife out of a scabbard on his belt and held it up. "That's fine with me, so long as I get her when everybody else is through with her. I owe her big for what she done to my hand."

"Rufe," Pike said, "personally, I don't give a damn what you do with her after we've gotten Jensen, but until that happens, she is not to be touched."

"Why not, Boss?" Sergeant Rutledge asked. "If we're gonna kill the son of a bitch anyway?"

Pike sighed. "Because I don't know if Jensen will agree to come into camp unless he sees that she is all right first. We may have to show her to him to get him in here."

Rutledge shrugged. "Oh," he said, "I never thought of that."

"That's why I do the thinking for this group, Sarge," Pike said, grinning. "Now, you boys get the camp straightened up and try and get some fires in those stoves in the cabins. I don't want to freeze my ass off tonight when I get back."

As the men left the fire and moved toward the cabins, Pike pulled Zeke to the side and explained his plan to him in low tones so no one else would overhear.

Zeke's eyes glittered with anticipated bloodlust. "I can't wait to get my hands on that bastard, Bill," he said. "I'm gonna make sure he's a long time dyin'."

"Me too, Zeke," Pike said as he swung up into his saddle and walked the horse down the trail toward Pueblo.

About halfway to the town, Pike came to a bend in Fountain Creek and saw a clearing on the other side of the stream with a ramshackle cabin in it that was leaning heavily to one side as if it were about to fall down. This is a good place to tell Jensen to meet me tomorrow, he thought. He won't have no trouble finding it, and it's far enough away from the camp so the boys won't hear any gunshots when we take Jensen out.

Going over in his mind what he was going to tell Jensen, and how much money he should ask for to make the man think the ransom demand was on the level, Pike moved down the trail toward Pueblo thinking how clever he was.

19

After walking up and down Court Street a couple of times, Smoke decided to enter a saloon named the Dog Hole. He smiled when he read the sign over the saloon, since out West *dog hole* was a generic name for any bar or saloon, especially one that was dirty or unclean. He thought it would take a man with a special sense of humor to use the term as a name for his establishment, and he looked forward to meeting him.

As was his usual custom when Smoke first pushed through the batwings, he immediately stepped to one side with his back against the wall and his right hand hanging near his pistol butt. He let his eyes become accustomed to the relatively dark room while he looked over the occupants of the fifteen or so tables scattered around the place.

He saw no familiar faces from his past, and so he walked slowly to the bar, where he took up station at the end nearest another wall. He never stood with his back to the room or where people were sitting behind him. It was a habit that had saved his life on more than one occasion and the practice had become second nature to him now.

The bartender ambled over, wiping out a glass with

a dirty-looking cloth rag, as bartenders always seemed to be doing.

"What can I getcha?" he asked, his eyes dull with boredom and disinterest.

Though Smoke was normally not a drinking man, when in such places he would order a drink so as not to stand out from the usual crowd. "A shot of whiskey with a beer chaser," Smoke answered.

When the man bent over and pulled out a bottle with no label on it, Smoke held up his hand. "I don't want that," he said in a friendly tone. "Give me some of the good stuff off that back shelf."

"It'll cost you extra," the man said sullenly.

Smoke shrugged. "That's not a problem," he said, still keeping his voice amiable.

The barman turned and took a dusty bottle off the rear shelf with a label that read OLD KENTUCKY on it. Smoke doubted if any part of the bottle or the liquor within had ever been within a thousand miles of Kentucky, but he kept his mouth shut.

The bartender pulled the cork and slapped a glass down in front of Smoke that was so dirty it was almost black.

Just as the man started to pour, Smoke put his hand over the rim of the glass. "And I'd appreciate a clean glass," he said, his voice getting a little harder this time.

The bartender raised his eyebrows. "Am I gonna have trouble with you, mister?" he asked, pulling a three foot long wooden stake that was three inches in diameter from under the bar and slapping his open palm with it.

Smoke's eyes grew flat and dangerous. "The only trouble you're going to have is trying to take a shit with that pole stuck up your ass!" Smoke growled, letting his voice grow deeper and harsher.

"Why you . . ." the barman began as he raised the large stick.

Before he got the words out or moved the pole more than a couple of inches, Smoke's pistol was drawn, cocked, and the barrel was against the man's nose.

"You want to get that glass, or do I pull this trigger and decorate the mirror behind you with what little brains you have?" Smoke asked, a grim smile on his lips.

When the barman looked into Smoke's eyes, he knew he was seconds away from death and his bladder let loose.

He groaned and glanced down at his urine-soaked trousers, and his face paled.

"What the hell's going on here?" a deep, gravely voice that had suffered too much tobacco and too many glasses of whiskey intoned from the other end of the bar.

Smoke holstered his pistol and smiled nicely at the heavyset man who was approaching behind the bar. The man had salt-and-pepper hair and a dark mustache whose ends hung down to the bottom of his chin, but his eyes were the blue of wildflowers and seemed to shine with amusement at his barman's state.

"Uh, this here man's causin' some trouble, Mr. Gooch," the bartender said, backing away from the bar but keeping his eyes on Smoke.

"That true, mister?" Gooch asked, moving between Smoke and the barman.

Smoke inclined his head at the dirty glass in front of him. "All I did was request the good whiskey and a clean glass," Smoke said. "If that is too much for this establishment, I will be happy to take my business elsewhere."

Gooch glanced at the glass, frowned, and whirled around to confront the bartender. "I've told you about this before, Jack," he said angrily. "Now, get out. You're fired."

"But . . ."

"No buts, you lazy shit. Get out and you can come back later for what I owe you."

After Jack left, holding his hands in front of his stained pants, Gooch turned back to Smoke, shaking his head. "Damn," he said. "It's the gold fever."

"Oh?" Smoke asked.

"Yeah. Every able-bodied man who's not afraid of a little work is out in the mountains digging for gold. What's left in town for me to hire are the ones too lazy to work or who are looking to steal what they need instead of earning it."

Smoke nodded. "I've seen it before," he said.

Gooch took the glass and replaced it with a clean one. As he poured the whiskey, he grinned at Smoke. "This one's on the house, 'cause of the trouble with my man, but you're gonna have to pay for the next one."

Smoke smiled. "Pour two and I'll treat you to one."

"Damn," Gooch exclaimed, "I don't get an offer like that too often."

He poured himself a drink and held up his glass to Smoke. "To happier days," he said.

"I'll drink to that," Smoke said, and took a sip of his drink while Gooch emptied his own glass in one long drink.

Smoke glanced at the sign over the bar. "I like the name of your place," he said. "It indicates an owner with a sense of humor."

Gooch grinned at him and topped off Smoke's glass and refilled his own. "My name's Homer Gooch," he said. "Growing up with a name like that, you either have to learn to be a good fighter or have a good sense of humor. I ain't much of a fighter, but I don't mind the occasional laugh at my expense."

"That's a sound philosophy," Smoke said.

Gooch stuck his hand across the bar, "And what's your handle, mister?"

Smoke shook his hand. "Smoke Jensen."

Gooch's eyes opened wide and he burst out laughing. "*The* Smoke Jensen?"

Smoke smiled back and nodded. "The only one I know of."

Gooch continued to chuckle. "Old Jack would have shit himself in addition to pissing himself if he'd known who he braced with that little stick he kept under the bar."

Smoke just grinned and took another small sip of his whiskey, following it with a drink of beer.

"What brings you to our neck of the woods, Mr. Jensen?" Gooch asked. "You're not about to try your hand at mining, are you?"

"Call me Smoke, and no, I'm not here looking for gold. I'm supposed to meet someone here today."

Gooch raised his eyebrows. "A friend?"

Smoke's smile faded. "Not exactly."

Gooch shook his head and glanced at the five-foot-long mirror behind the bar. "Well, Smoke, if it comes down to gunplay, would you try not to hit that mirror? It cost me two hundred dollars to have it shipped here from St. Louis."

Smoke laughed. "I'll do my best, Homer."

Gooch looked around the room. "I bet you'll be wanting a table in a corner so's you can keep your eye on the door. Am I right?"

"Yes," Smoke answered.

Gooch came out from behind the bar and walked over to a corner table where three men wearing the canvas pants of miners sat getting quietly drunk.

"You men are going to have to move," Gooch said. "I need this table."

One of the men glanced up, his eyes red and bloodshot. "I ain't movin' fer nobody. We was here first."

Gooch leaned down, both hands flat on the table as he stared at the man. "It's worth a free bottle of whiskey if you'll take another table," he said.

The man who'd objected jumped to his feet and looked around at his friends. "What the hell are we sittin' here for, boys. Let's do what the man says."

Gooch smiled at Smoke and waved his hand at the now empty table. "I'll send a bottle over, Smoke."

Smoke shook his head. "No, thanks, Homer. I need to keep a clear head."

Gooch winked at him. "How about I fill a whiskey bottle with sarsaparilla? It looks like whiskey but it won't get you drunk."

"Helluva good idea, Homer," Smoke said. "I'm obliged."

Gooch pointed a finger at him. "Just remember to miss the mirror and we'll call it even," he said good-naturedly.

20

Smoke settled into his chair in the saloon, sipping his sarsaparilla and smoking an occasional cigarette as he waited for Pike or one of his men to show up. He had the hammer thong on his Colts undone just in case whoever showed up started blasting instead of talking.

Smoke had no illusions; he knew Pike's ultimate desire was to see him dead, and Sally was just an instrument in that final outcome. Smoke's problem was to try and avoid killing Pike or his men until Cal and Pearlie could report back to him as to where they were keeping her. He refused to entertain any thoughts that she might already be dead or injured.

After a while, Homer Gooch walked over to his table. "Smoke, you haven't told me exactly what's going on here, but if you need some backup, I'll be over there behind the bar with a ten-gauge sawed-off express gun handy. You give the word and I'll blast shit out of anyone giving you trouble."

Smoke found he liked this man more and more. "Thanks, Homer. I don't think that will be necessary, but I appreciate the thought and the help."

Gooch nodded and made his way back behind the bar, where he leaned on it, his eyes searching the room for possible trouble. Smoke smiled to himself at the man's offer. He'd discovered over the years that once people found out who he was, they generally reacted in one of two ways: They either feared him and tended to avoid his company, or they liked what they'd heard about him and wanted to be friends and help him out if they could. Such was both the penalty and the benefit of being a celebrity among common folks.

The Dog Hole was the fourth saloon Bill Pike entered while searching for Smoke Jensen. He'd never laid eyes on the man before, but he thought he'd probably recognize him when he saw him.

He walked into the Dog Hole and stepped up to the bar. He ordered a shot of whiskey and after the heavy-set man behind the counter gave it to him, he turned and leaned back against the bar on his elbows, sipping his drink and letting his eyes roam around the room.

He knew Smoke immediately when his eyes fell on the man sitting at the corner table. Damn, he thought, he's a dangerous-looking son of a bitch. Several inches over six feet tall, with shoulders as wide as an ax handle, Smoke dressed in buckskins. He must be in his forties by now, Pike thought, but his hair is still coal black, like his eyes, and there isn't a trace of softness about his body. Muscles bulged in his forearms where they rested on the table, and his expression looked as if it were cast in stone.

"You looking for somebody, mister?" Homer Gooch asked, noticing the way Pike scanned the room with his eyes.

"Yeah, but I think I just found him," Pike answered, emptying his glass and slowly moving toward the man in the corner. He kept his hands out from his sides, well away from the pistol on his hip. From what he'd heard, Jensen was snake-quick with a short gun, and

Pike didn't intend to find out for sure when he was by himself.

As Pike walked toward Smoke, Homer Gooch got Smoke's attention and winked, pointing under the bar to indicate the shotgun was ready and waiting if Smoke got into trouble.

Pike stopped in front of Smoke's table and stared down at him. "You Jensen?" he asked, trying to make his voice low and hard.

Smoke looked up at him, a tiny smile curling the corners of his lips. "Yes. Are you Pike?" Smoke answered, his voice level and smooth without a trace of fear in it.

Pike nodded and pulled out a chair across the table from Smoke. He pushed his empty glass across the table. "How about a refill?"

"Get your own whiskey," Smoke said, all trace of good humor gone from his tone. "This isn't a social call."

Pike's face paled slightly at the insult, but he turned his head and waved to Gooch. "Another bottle of whiskey over here," he called.

After Gooch had delivered one of the cheap bottles with no label on it, Pike filled his glass and took a deep drink.

"You called this meeting, Pike," Smoke said. "Say your piece."

Pike's eyes narrowed to slits. "You're talkin' awful brave for a man who's lost his wife."

"I didn't lose her, you scum," Smoke said, leaning forward but keeping his right hand on his thigh near the butt of his pistol. "You and your men took her."

"Nevertheless," Pike said, trying to get the upper hand in the conversation, "we've got her and you don't. You want her back?"

Now Smoke smiled. He screwed the butt of a cigarette into the corner of his mouth, lit it, and tilted smoke out of his nostrils, his face hard and set. "Oh,

I'm going to get her back, Mr. Pike. There is no doubt of that. The only question is how you and your men are going to die . . . slow and painful or fast and easy."

"That ain't no way to . . ." Pike began, but Smoke interrupted him.

"Make your offer, Pike. I assume that's what you came here for."

Pike took a deep breath, trying to calm his nerves. This wasn't going at all the way he'd pictured it in his mind on the way here from the camp.

"You can have her back, unharmed and untouched, for ten thousand dollars," he said, attempting to make his voice firm and hard.

Smoke took the half-smoked butt from his lips and tapped it out in an ashtray. "That all you want?" he asked, knowing full well that it wasn't.

"I figure you can go to the bank here and have a letter of credit wired from your bank in Big Rock. Once you have the money in hand, we can make the trade and nobody has to get hurt," Pike said, his eyes shifting from the dangerous look on Smoke's face.

Smoke pretended to think the offer over for a few minutes, slowly sipping his sarsaparilla and staring at Pike.

"Oh, I know all about your reputation, Jensen," Pike said, "and if you're as good as they say you are, you may be able to take out me and my men like you're thinking you can. But"—Pike leaned forward as he spoke—"in the process of doin' all this, you wife is bound to get hurt, maybe even kilt."

"There is some truth in what you say," Smoke said, letting Pike think he was considering his offer.

"From what I hear, you won't have any trouble raisin' the money," Pike added, pouring himself another drink as he watched Smoke to see his reaction.

"The money is no problem," Smoke said. "I'm just trying to figure out how we can make the trade so everyone's happy and no one gets the idea of taking the money and not delivering my wife to me."

Pike held up his hands. "Hey, we know how dangerous you are, Jensen. And since there's only three of us, we wouldn't stand a chance against you if we went back on the deal," Pike lied.

Smoke smiled. He knew Pike had at least seven or eight men left in his gang and was lying through his teeth, but Pike didn't know he knew this.

Smoke got to his feet. "Come on with me," he said, throwing a couple of bills on the table and walking toward the door. "Homer," Smoke called, "save my table for me, would you?"

"Yes, sir," Gooch replied.

Pike hastily emptied his glass and followed.

Smoke walked down the street about fifty yards and entered a building with a sign on it that read PUEBLO BANK. He walked up to a teller and asked to see the manager.

A few minutes later, a portly man dressed in a black suit and a boiled white shirt with a string tie walked out of his office. "I'm Jedidiah Morgan," the man said. "What can I do for you gentlemen?"

Smoke handed him a piece of paper. "I'm Smoke Jensen, from Big Rock Colorado. I own the bank there. I want you to wire the bank for a letter of credit for ten thousand dollars, plus whatever fee you charge for the transfer. I'll want to pick up the money tomorrow morning."

"Why, yes, sir, Mr. Jensen," Morgan said. "That should be no problem at all."

Smoke turned on his heel without another word, walked back to the Dog Hole, and sat at his same table. Pike remained standing on the other side of the table.

"As you can see, I'll have the money tomorrow morning. How do you want to handle the trade?" Smoke asked.

"There's a small clearing about three miles up Fountain Creek. It has an old cabin in it. I'll meet you there at noon tomorrow. Bring the cash. My men will be out in the woods with your wife. Any sign of a double cross, and they'll put a bullet between her eyes 'fore you can sneeze."

"I'll need to see her and see that she's all right before I turn the money over," Smoke said.

"Of course," Pike said. "I wouldn't want you to take my word for it."

Smoke smiled. "See you tomorrow, Pike."

"So long," Pike said, tipping his hat and turning to walk out the door.

"Oh, Pike," Smoke called to his back.

Pike glanced back over his shoulder. "Yeah?"

"Best say your prayers tonight that I find Sally in perfect shape. If one hair on her head is out of place, you will find yourself begging me to kill you before I'm through with you."

Pike tried to grin as he turned and walked out the door, but his stomach knotted at the expression on Smoke's face. He was looking death in the eye as sure as he was standing there. He felt sweat break out under his armpits and on his forehead, and he began to wonder if his dead brother was worth all this trouble.

Hell, he hadn't been lying to Mrs. Jensen when he said he hadn't particularly liked the bastard any way. If it weren't for Zeke and his big mouth, he wouldn't be up here in this godforsaken frozen country worrying about getting his ass shot off.

21

A few minutes after Pike left the Dog Hole, the batwings swung open and Pearlie walked in. He took one look around the place and began to move directly toward Smoke. Evidently, his rather disheveled appearance, the way he wore his pistol tied down low on his right leg, and his determined expression worried Homer Gooch.

Homer pulled the sawed-off shotgun from under the bar and rested it on top, his eyes watching Pearlie for any false moves. Smoke grinned and waved at Homer. "It's all right, Homer," he called. "This one's a friend of mine."

Homer relaxed and put the shotgun away. He raised his eyebrows and pointed at the good bottle of whiskey Smoke had been drinking from when he first arrived.

Smoke nodded and waited for Pearlie to take a seat across the table from him. After Pearlie sat down, he looked around the room and smiled. "This place is right nice," Pearlie said, grinning. "When I saw the name on the sign outside, I thought it was gonna be a dive."

Smoke laughed. "Yeah, Mr. Gooch has quite a sense of humor," he said, also looking around.

The saloon was large and well lighted, with fresh paint on the walls, and the floor was clean and well swept. The tables were placed so that everyone had plenty of room to move around without being too crowded. In one corner, a piano sat facing the room with several bar stools in front of it. There was no one playing presently, and Smoke figured it was used mainly at night. Another thing he liked was that there were no "saloon girls" hanging around to cadge drinks from the miners who frequented the place. It was just another indication of Mr. Gooch's class.

Smoke finally looked back at Pearlie. "Did you find their camp?" he asked.

Pearlie turned his attention from the decor of the room and nodded. "Yep. Cal's got 'em all staked out now. He'll tail 'em if they try to move."

Homer stepped up to the table and put the whiskey bottle down in the center of the table along with a glass for Pearlie. He picked up the bottle of rotgut Pike had left behind and the bottle of sarsaparilla and grinned. "Wouldn't want you gentlemen to get sick drinking this horse piss," he said.

"Thanks, Homer," Smoke said. "I owe you one for all you've done."

Homer waved a hand and blushed slightly. "It's the least I could do, Smoke," he said as he moved back behind his bar.

"What about Sally?" Smoke asked. "Did you see her and is she all right?"

Pearlie nodded. "She seems right as rain, Smoke. They're camped in this clearin' that has five or six old cabins scattered around. They got her stashed in one most of the time, but they seem to be leaving her alone an' not botherin' her none. They let her out to eat with them when they have a meal, but they make her sit off to one side by herself."

Smoke's face wrinkled as he concentrated on the

mental picture Pearlie had painted. "So, they don't leave anyone in the cabin with her as a guard?"

Pearlie shook his head. "No, at least they didn't the night I watched 'em bed down. I think they must tie her up to the bed or to a post in there or somethin', 'cause when she comes out she's usually rubbing her wrists like they maybe were raw from the ropes."

Smoke nodded. "That's good for us," he said. "That'll make it easier for us to get her out of there without them realizing it and starting to throw lead around."

"I noticed that big man comin' out of here when I was comin' in," Pearlie said. "I seen him out at the camp yesterday and I think he must be head honcho out there 'cause everybody listens when he talks."

"Yeah. That's Bill Pike, brother to the Pike I killed years ago. He and his half brother named Thompson are the cause of this mess."

Pearlie leaned forward. "You know, Smoke, there's only about eight or nine of them galoots out at the camp. If you and me and Cal lined 'em up in our sights, we could probably get them all 'fore they knew what was happening."

Smoke shook his head. "No, Pearlie, I don't want to do it that way for two reasons. One, we might miss one and give him time to hurt Sally. Two, that'd be too easy for these bastards. I don't want to just kill them, I want to make their lives miserable with fear before I let the hammer down on them and end it all."

Just as Smoke finished talking, Pearlie's stomach growled loudly, causing Smoke to break out in a wide grin. "Sounds like you're a mite hungry, partner," Smoke said.

Pearlie blushed and rubbed his stomach to try and make it quit howling. "Yeah. Cal and I didn't want to risk building a fire while we watched those assholes, so about all we've had for two days has been old cold biscuits and water."

"Well, I can fix that," Smoke said. "Hey, Homer," he called, "you got a good place to eat in this town?"

Homer nodded and pointed to the left. "You bet, Smoke. The Shorthorn Diner right down the street. Has the best steaks this side of the mountains."

While Smoke and Pearlie ate their late lunch, with Pearlie of course eating enough for two men, they discussed Smoke's plans for the outlaws.

"After we finish eating, I want you to buy an extra horse with saddle and all the gear to take back up the mountain with us."

When Pearlie looked puzzled, Smoke explained, "We may need it for Sally. When I take her out of the gang's camp, I may not have time to get her horse and she'll need it to ride out on."

"What about the packhorse we got up there?" Pearlie asked around a mouthful of steak.

"It doesn't have a saddle on it, and we may need it for our supplies," Smoke answered. "Besides, we may lose a horse in the battle and it's always better to have too many horses than not enough, especially up in the High Lonesome in winter."

Pearlie nodded as he continued to stuff food into his mouth as if he hadn't eaten in weeks instead of just two days.

"Now," Smoke continued, sitting back and lighting a cigarette since he was already finished with his meal, "Pike is expecting me to meet him at noon tomorrow at a small clearing a few miles up Fountain Creek, but we're not going to wait that long. As soon as you finish your meal and get the horse for Sally, we're going to head up there and get Cal."

Pearlie pointed his fork at the remains of his steak. "Don't let me forget to take him some food with us."

Smoke smiled. "All right, but we're going to be plenty busy setting up some surprises for those bastards. I'm going to use those supplies you and Cal bought for me to set some traps on the trails around their camp and on the slopes up above it. As soon as Sally's safely away from them, we're going to show them just how stupid they were to mess with us."

Pearlie grinned as he stuffed a gravy-soaked roll into his mouth. "Damn right!" he agreed.

As he rode back toward his camp, Pike kept looking back over his shoulder. His meeting with Smoke Jensen had spooked him pretty bad. He didn't think he'd ever met anyone who looked as downright dangerous as the mountain man. He recalled stories he'd heard about Jensen back when he was tracking him down in preparation for his revenge. Stories of how he'd dealt with men who'd crossed him—stories that made a man's blood run cold.

As he thought about this, his mind went back to the bloody scalp and the pieces of Sam Kane's face that someone had left for them as a warning. Now, he had no doubt it had been done by Smoke Jensen.

He knew he was riding a thin line, and if he made one false step, Jensen would exact a terrible retribution. He was going to have to make sure he and his men were on their guard at all times, or they'd never live to spend the money Jensen was getting together.

When he finally got back to the camp, he saw Mrs. Jensen sitting near the fire, her face turned away from Hank Snow, who was standing next to her. Mrs. Jensen's expression was shocked and her face was blushing a bright red. From the stiffness of her back and neck, Pike knew something was wrong.

He got down off his horse and walked rapidly over to the couple. As he got there, Snow turned and gave him a smirk.

"What's going on here?" Pike asked.

Sally cut her eyes at him and then she looked away, as if he didn't deserve her attention.

"I was just tellin' this little lady what I plan to do to her after we kill her husband," Snow said, a husky tone to his voice.

Pike stepped around so Sally would have to look at him. "Has he been bothering you, Mrs. Jensen?" he asked in a kind voice.

"What do you think, Mr. Pike?" she asked scornfully. "He is an animal and no matter what happens to my husband, he will have to kill me before I will allow him to lay a hand on me!"

"You stupid bastard!" Pike said angrily as he moved toward Hank Snow. "Didn't I tell you to leave Mrs. Jensen alone?"

"But Boss," Snow began, a puzzled look on his face.

Before he could finish, Pike reared back and smashed him in the face with his fist, knocking him down flat onto his back.

Snow grimaced in pain and his hand went toward his gun on his hip.

Pike drew and pointed his pistol at the man's face and growled, "Go on, Hank, just give me one more reason to blow your fool head off!"

Snow slowly moved his hand away from his gun and said, "Jesus, Boss. I didn't mean nothin' by it. I was just havin' a little fun with her is all."

Pike looked up at the men who'd gathered around to see the fight. "Let this be a lesson to you," he said in a harsh voice. "I'm still the ramrod of this outfit, and anyone who crosses me is going to get this, or worse."

When no one said anything, Pike holstered his pistol and took Sally by the arm, helping her to her feet. "Why don't you go into your cabin and I'll have someone bring you some coffee, Mrs. Jensen?" he asked.

Sally gave him a slight nod. "Thank you, Mr. Pike," she said, and moved off toward the cabin they'd put her in the day before.

"What's the problem, Boss?" Rufus Gordon asked. "Why are you treatin' her with kid gloves all of a sudden?"

"Because she's worth ten thousand dollars to us, Rufe," Pike explained. "If she's hurt or messed up, Jensen ain't gonna take the bait."

"Oh," Gordon said.

"I just met with him in Pueblo," Pike said. "I convinced him we just wanted some money and we'd let her go."

"That's a good idea, Boss," Sergeant Rutledge said.

"He's gonna get the money from the bank tomorrow and meet me at a place about halfway here from Pueblo at noon."

"How much money we talkin' about?" Gordon asked.

"Ten thousand dollars," Pike answered.

"Holy shit!" Gordon whooped. "That means with the reward money, we'll be getting twenty thousand!"

Pike decided now was the time to break the bad news about the reward to the men, before they found out about it on their own.

"Uh, there's not gonna be any reward, boys," he said.

"What?" several of them exclaimed in unison.

He held up both hands. "That's right. While I was in Pueblo, I checked with the sheriff's office and found out that wanted poster was recalled some years ago."

As his men glowered at him angrily, Pike continued. "But the good news is, we're gonna be getting it anyway. The only difference is, it's gonna be comin' outta Jensen's own bank."

This last seemed to mollify the men, and Pike said, "I think this news deserves a drink, what do you say?"

The men grinned, their anger of a moment before forgotten, and they all went to get their bottles of whiskey. Any excuse for a drink was a good excuse to them.

Once they all had bottles in their hands, Pike held his up and gave a toast, "To ten thousand dollars, and what it can buy."

Gordon added, "And to the little lady over there, and all the fun we're gonna have with her after we kill her man!"

22

After Smoke and Pearlie got an extra horse and tack for Sally and some food for Cal, they proceeded northward up Fountain Creek. Smoke made sure to stay off the trail in case Pike checked his backtrail to see if he was being followed, though Smoke doubted the man bothered—from their meeting at the saloon, Smoke figured he was a mite slow when it came to thinking.

A few miles out of Pueblo, they came to the small clearing with the ramshackle shack that Pike had designated for their meeting the next day.

"Hold on a minute, Pearlie," Smoke said. "I want to check this place out a little before we head on up the mountain."

Since the clearing was on the other side of the stream, Smoke turned Joker's head toward it and gently spurred the horse out into the water. Though the current was moving fairly quickly, he found the water level to be only a couple of feet deep at this time of the year.

He glanced to the sides and saw the banks of the river were several feet higher than the water level, indicating that when the spring thaws came, the stream would turn into a raging torrent unsafe to cross at any place.

Pearlie followed him across the creek and they rode around the clearing, checking for places to set traps and such. The ground rose sharply on three sides of the clearing, with assorted boulders and outcroppings of granite at many different levels. Smoke pointed these out to Pearlie.

"Pike told me he only had two or three men with him, so I'll bet he'll have the others hidden up behind those rocks, ready to fire down on me if he gives the signal," Smoke said.

Pearlie glanced back across the creek to where the trail passed the clearing. "Yeah, Smoke. It'd have to be up there 'cause there ain't much cover on the other side of the crick," he observed.

Smoke followed his gaze and saw that the nearest heavy cover was a copse of pine trees with some low brush about four hundred yards away. Other than that, the trail was pretty much open for the next quarter mile.

Smoke smiled. The setting gave him an idea if he ended up having to meet with Pike here the next day. Of course, if things go well tonight, he thought, we'll have Sally out of their camp safe and sound and I can deal with them on my own terms after that.

A couple of hours later, Pearlie slowed his mount. "The gang's camp is about another quarter mile up the trail, Smoke, so we'd better move on up the side of the mountain to get around them in case they got some sentries out watchin' the trail."

Smoke nodded, and let Pearlie lead the way off into the bushes off to the side of the trail. He found his heart was beating faster and his mouth was dry in anticipation of seeing his wife again. Even though Pearlie had assured him Sally was all right and being treated good, he wanted to see for himself, and God help any man who'd bothered her.

It took them another hour of moving slowly through dense underbrush and ravines where melting snow had washed out the side of the mountain before they got to the place where Cal was keeping watch over the gang.

Just before riding into the area, Pearlie cupped his hands around his mouth and gave a short cry like that of a bobcat on the hunt.

Smoke smiled. "You did that pretty well, Pearlie," he said. "I couldn't tell it from the real thing."

This was a high compliment from the mountain man, and Pearlie grinned back. "I had a good teacher, Smoke. You showed Cal and me how to do all the calls of the mountain critters a couple of years back, remember?"

Smoke nodded. "Yeah, but you seem to have gotten better at it than you used to be."

Pearlie shrugged, blushing at the compliment. "Well, when Cal and I are out on the trail with the beeves at the ranch, we practice a bit." He gave a low laugh. "Hell, anything's better than having Cal sing."

Seconds later, an answering cry came from the slope just ahead of them, signaling Cal knew they were coming and wouldn't shoot them when they rode into his camp.

A few minutes later, Smoke and Pearlie, along with the extra horse for Sally, pulled into a small clearing just back from a ledge that looked down on the outlaws' camp.

Cal was there to greet them. Smoke noticed he had a bandanna tied over his horse's mouth and nose to keep it from whinnying to the horses in the camp below. Smoke nodded, pleased that Cal had remembered what he'd taught him in the past about tracking men in the High Lonesome.

Cal grinned and shook Smoke's hand. "Jiminy, but I'm glad to see you, Smoke," he said.

"Everything going all right?" Smoke asked, anxious to get a look down into the camp below the ridge.

"Yes, sir. They've been sitting around the fire and drinking all afternoon."

"Is Sally there?"

"Come on and you can see for yourself," Cal said, bending down and moving low as he moved toward the ridge.

Smoke followed, crawling the last few feet on hands and knees so they couldn't be seen from below in case any of the gang happened to look up.

Smoke eased his head over the ledge just enough to look below. He saw the outlaws sitting in various positions around a roaring fire, talking and laughing and drinking from bottles of whiskey. Off to one side, a cup of coffee in her hands, Sally was sitting by herself near the far edge of the fire. Her head was down and she looked tired, but otherwise all right.

Smoke thought his heart was going to break seeing her sitting alone and in such danger. He didn't know what he would do if he ever lost her. She was his entire reason for living, and nothing would ever be the same if something happened to take her from him.

Suddenly, he had an idea of how to make her feel better. He moved back from the ledge until he could stand up and see her through a stand of hackberry bushes. He cupped his hands around his mouth and gave the whooping call a coyote would make when calling to his mate in the wild. It was a sharp barking sound followed by a mournful wail.

At the sound, he saw Sally's back stiffen and her head come up. He was too far away to see her eyes, but he knew they were looking in his direction. In their years together, Sally had spent a lot of time with Smoke up in the mountains, and she knew his calls as well as he did. She also knew that coyotes never barked or called in the middle of the afternoon, only at dawn and dusk and in the middle of the night.

The outlaws all looked up too, and one or two of them shivered at the ghostly sound Smoke made.

Sally got to her feet and moved to the fire to refill her coffee cup from the pot sitting at the edge of the coals. As she straightened up, she briefly let her right hand cross over her heart, a sign that she'd heard and recognized Smoke's call to her.

She went back to her place and as she drank her coffee, she sat straighter and more confident now that she knew her man was nearby.

When Smoke gave the coyote call, Pike lowered his bottle and looked around, clearly spooked by the mournful cry coming from the slopes above the camp.

He got to his feet and moved slowly around the campfire, his eyes on the ledges around them, his hand hovering near his pistol butt.

"What's the matter, Boss?" Rufus Gordon said, more than a little drunk. "You're not afraid of a little ol' coyote, are you?" he asked, his voice slurred.

Pike answered with his eyes still on the mountainside. "I didn't know they had coyotes up here in the mountains," he said warily.

"Well, it can't be Indians, Boss," Sergeant Rutledge said, "The man in Canyon City said they ain't given no trouble around here in years."

"It's not Indians I'm worried about," Pike said. He took a short drink from his bottle and moved over to stand next to Sally, staring down at her.

"You hear that, Mrs. Jensen?" he asked.

She stared up at him. "Of course, Mr. Pike. It was a coyote calling to its mate. Fall is the rutting season for coyotes in the mountains," she added, hoping he didn't know anything about coyotes, which mated all year long.

"Is that so?" he asked suspiciously. "It wouldn't be your husband out there signaling to you, would it?"

Sally smiled sweetly. "Mr. Pike, if my husband were out there that close, you would already have a bullet between your eyes and would be lying flat on your back."

Pike grunted as if he didn't believe her.

Sally looked around at the men lying sprawled around the fire. "You said you met with Smoke today, Mr. Pike. Did he impress you as a man who would be afraid of a bunch of men who are so drunk they couldn't hit the side of a barn with a shotgun right now?"

Pike followed her gaze and realized she was right. His men were in no condition to fight anyone right now. He decided enough was enough.

"All right, men," he called, moving back over to the fire. "Put the liquor away and get ready for nightfall. I want two men to stay in the cabin with Mrs. Jensen tonight, just in case Jensen decides to try and take her without paying the money."

He looked up at the mountains around them, which were turning slowly darker as dusk approached. "You hear that, Jensen?" he hollered. "If you're out there and you try anything, the first thing my men are going to do is put a bullet in your wife!"

Gordon looked around at the men, who were getting worried that their boss had lost his nerve. "Boss, take it easy," he said. "It was just a coyote, that's all."

"Nevertheless," Pike said, remembering the look in Jensen's eyes when they talked in Pueblo. "We're gonna post a couple of sentries and we're gonna keep a close eye on Mrs. Jensen tonight. I don't want anything goin' wrong until we get that money tomorrow."

Gordon got clumsily to his feet and stuffed the cork back in his bottle. "Whatever you say, Boss."

As the outlaws began to get to their feet and two men escorted Sally into her cabin, Smoke moved back from the ledge. "Damn," he said, "I guess that means we don't try and get Sally out tonight."

"So, what are we gonna do?" Pearlie asked.

Smoke's eyes were hard as flint. "We're going to set up some surprises for those men back down the trail so when I meet with them tomorrow, we'll have the upper hand."

As they moved away from the ledge, he relaxed a little. "But first, I'm going to make us a fire and we're going to eat some food and drink some coffee." He smiled at Cal, who was grinning in relief. "Preacher always said you can't do battle on an empty stomach."

Pearlie looked at Cal. "We brung you some steaks and biscuits and beans from town."

"Right now, I'd settle for some rawhide to chew on I'm so hungry," Cal said.

Smoke gave a low chuckle. "Now you're starting to sound like Pearlie."

23

Smoke and the boys gathered up all their supplies and the packhorse and horse they'd brought for Sally, and they moved off down the mountain about a quarter of a mile. It was fairly easy going as the night was one of those only seen in early winter: crystal-clear skies, bright starlight, and a crescent moon shedding just enough light so the path through the high mountain forest could be easily seen.

Smoke pulled his fur-lined buckskin coat tight around him. "It's gonna get mighty chilly tonight, boys," he said. "With no cloud cover or snow, the temperature is going to drop like a stone."

Once they'd circled around the slope of the mountain so as to be away from where the outlaws might spot their campfire glow, Smoke dismounted. "Cal, see if you can find some really dry wood, the kind that doesn't make much smoke," he said.

While Smoke was arranging some stones in a small circle next to a large outcropping of boulders so the fire would be out of the wind, Pearlie got the cooking gear off the packhorse along with the food he and Smoke had gotten in Pueblo.

Before long, coffee was brewing, steaks were sizzling in one pan, day-old biscuits steaming in another, while beans were heating in a kettle. When he poured the coffee in their tin mugs, Pearlie looked at Cal and smiled as he pulled a small paper bag out of his pocket. "I brung you somethin' special, Cal, 'cause of how you had to starve yourself watchin' those outlaws."

He handed the paper bag to Cal, who immediately opened it. "Jiminy," he said, "real sugar for my coffee."

Though on the trail Cal often had to drink his coffee black, Pearlie knew he much preferred to lace it with generous amounts of sugar, changing it into what Pearlie called black syrup.

As Smoke poured coffee all around, being up in the High Lonesome brought thoughts of Puma Buck to mind. The old mountain man, a decades-long friend of Smoke's, had been killed some years earlier while helping Smoke out of a jam.

He filled Cal's cup, saying, "Remember what Puma Buck said about coffee, boys?"

"Sure do," Cal replied with a nostalgic smile. "The thing 'bout makin' good mountain coffee is it don't take near as much water as you think it do."

Pearlie chuckled at the memory. The boys had only known Puma for a short while, but had come to love him as much as Smoke did. "He also said," Pearlie added, "that coffee that wouldn't float a horseshoe wasn't worth drinkin'."

"I think them steaks are 'bout ready," Cal said, eyeing the pan with the steaks in it hungrily. "At least, they've quit moving."

Cal liked his steaks rare.

Smoke picked one of the pieces of meat out of the pan with the point of his bowie knife and placed it on a plate on Cal's lap. "You'll have to get your own biscuit and beans," he said, picking out another steak for Pearlie.

Soon, they were all chowing down, relishing the flavor of food cooked outdoors under a starry sky.

After a while, their talk turned to what Smoke proposed to do about the men who held Sally prisoner.

"You know if'n you go to that meeting with Pike carryin' ten thousand dollars, he's just gonna kill you and steal the money and then do no telling what to Miss Sally," Pearlie said around a mouthful of biscuit soaked in steak juice.

"That's right, Smoke," Cal agreed. "If what you say 'bout this hombre is true, he didn't take Sally for the money, but to draw you out where he could take you down."

Smoke nodded. "I know that's his plan, boys, but planning on killing me and actually doing it are two very different things."

"If you go in there by yourself, with eight of his men drawing down on you, how are you going to keep him from killing you, Smoke?" Cal asked. "Heck fire, you won't even be able to see most of 'em."

Smoke grinned. "Easy," he answered. "I'm going to have two aces up my sleeve."

"I take it by that you mean Cal and me?" Pearlie asked after washing down his food with a drink of coffee and glancing around to make sure he hadn't missed any tasty morsels.

"That's right, Pearlie. And when the time comes, both my life and Sally's will depend on you two doing exactly what we've planned."

Cal and Pearlie glanced at each other, sobered by this responsibility. After a moment, Pearlie inclined his head. "Then let's get down to the plannin'," he said seriously.

"All right," Smoke said. He moved off a short distance from the fire and picked up a stick. Using the flat of his hand, he smoothed out the dirt in front of where he was squatting. He drew a crude map in the dust and dirt, indicating the position of the outlaws' camp, the trail down the mountain alongside Fountain Creek, and the proposed meeting place.

"Now," he said after they'd had a chance to look at the map, "Pike and his men are going to have to head down to the meeting place at least a few hours before noon."

"Why is that, Smoke?" Cal asked, clearly puzzled about how Smoke knew what Pike was going to do.

Smoke looked at him and smiled, thinking sometimes he forgot just how young and inexperienced in such matters Cal was. "They're going to have to get there early because Pike figures I'm going to be there early to check the area out," Smoke said. "He'll also need to send a couple of men ahead to make sure I don't show up with reinforcements intending to overpower them and take Sally by force."

"So, he'll want to have his men in place a good while before you get there so you won't know where they're hiding," Pearlie observed.

"Exactly," Smoke answered. "Once they've come down the mountain from their camp to the meeting place, that will give us some time to work on the trail, both above and below the meeting place, to set some traps I have in mind for them."

"Then what're we gonna do after we've set all the traps an' such?" Cal asked.

"You and Pearlie will set up where I tell you, where you'll have a good line of fire down on the clearing where I'll be meeting with Pike and on the places where we figure his men will be stationed."

"What do we do then?" Pearlie asked.

Smoke got to his feet. "Come on, and I'll show you. We've got to set some surprises around the meeting place tonight, before they go there tomorrow morning. Once that's done, I have a feeling you'll know what I want you to do."

While Pike was in the cabin where Sally was to be kept for the night, under continuous guard, the rest of the men gathered around the fire, speaking in low tones so he couldn't hear them.

Sergeant Rutledge was angry and let everyone in the gang know it. "I think that son of a bitch Pike lied to us about the reward money just to get us to come along on this trip. You can't tell me he didn't know all along Jensen wasn't really wanted."

Rufus Gordon looked down at his ruined hand and then up at Rutledge. "So what, Sarge? He told us we'd be splittin' up ten thousand dollars, an' that's exactly what we're gonna be doin'. What the hell do you care if it's reward money or money we get from Jensen?"

"It's the principle of the thing, Rufe," Rutledge answered angrily. "Why didn't he just tell us the real plan to begin with?"

Zeke Thompson, heavily into his bottle of whiskey, glanced up from the far end of the fire. "Quit your bellyaching, Rutledge," he growled, clearly more drunk than sober. "Would you have come if Bill told you he intended to try and get the money from Jensen himself in trade for his wife?"

Hank Snow laughed sourly. "Hell, no!" He shook his head. "I don't know nobody who'd pay that kinda money to get their wife back." He hesitated and then with a chuckle, he added, "Most of the men I know would more likely pay it to get someone to take their wife away 'stead of bringin' 'em back."

Zeke nodded and took another drink. "And that's exactly why Bill kept his plan to himself. He'd been askin' around about Jensen, and he knew the man had plenty of cash and that he loved his wife more than he loved the money, but Bill knew you boys wouldn't believe that, so he made up a little story to get you here. It don't matter a damn where the money's comin' from long as you get your share, right?" he asked.

Slim Cartwright, a cattle thief and footpad from Galveston nodded his head. "I do believe Jensen's money will spend just as good as the sheriff's, boys."

Larry Jackson, nicknamed Razor because of the straight razor he carried in his boot and enjoyed using on dance hall girls, agreed. "Yeah. And the best part of the whole deal is after we kill Jensen, we get the woman too."

Blackie Johnson's head came up at that remark and he winced. He was no angel and he'd done his share of bad things, but raping and killing women wasn't one of them. Besides, he'd come to like Mrs. Jensen and he hated to think of what was going to happen to her after her husband was killed. Trouble was, he didn't have the faintest idea of what he could do to prevent it, if anything.

Sally was half-sitting and half-reclining on the bed in "her" cabin, her left wrist and ankle tied to a post, while Bill Pike was sitting across the room at a broken-down table. He was leaning back in an old handmade chair, smoking a long black cigar and drinking coffee. He'd offered a cup to Sally but she'd declined, thinking she needed a good night's sleep to be able to deal with what was going to happen the next day.

"You don't seem particularly worried about tomorrow, Mrs. Jensen," Pike said in a conversational tone of voice, sounding extremely confident.

Sally's hazel eyes stared into his, her expression bland and unconcerned. "I'm not, Mr. Pike," she answered calmly, pulling her heavy coat close around her against the chill in the room. It was so cold in the cabin they could see their breath as they talked.

Pike held the cup in both hands to gather the warmth from the scalding coffee. He cocked his head. "Oh? I would think the prospect of losing your husband might concern you, not to mention what we have planned for you afterwards," he said, trying to get a rise out of her. The calmness of her demeanor was starting to get to him and he wanted to shake her up a little.

Sally straightened up in the bed and smiled slightly, almost sadly at Pike. "Mr. Pike, when you were planning this assault on my family, did you take the time to find anything out about Smoke Jensen?"

Pike shrugged. "Well, I figured out he could afford to try and buy you back." He grinned. "I don't care a whit about the money, Mrs. Jensen, it's killing your husband that's my goal, but I need something for my men."

"You really should have paid more attention to the stories I'm sure you heard about Smoke, Mr. Pike."

"Why is that, Mrs. Jensen?"

"Then you would have learned that Smoke came out here when he was just a boy. He lived up in these mountains when there wasn't more than one white man per thousand square miles and the Indians were thicker than fleas on a hound dog. Do you have any idea why Smoke not only survived this wilderness but thrived when hundreds of other men died in the attempt?"

"I hadn't really thought much about it, Mrs. Jensen," Pike answered as if he could care less.

"You should, Mr. Pike. Smoke survived when many others didn't because he is smart, tough, and when he sets his mind to do something, heaven help those who stand in his way, be it Indians or criminals."

"Well, back then he didn't have you to worry about, did he, Mrs. Jensen. Oh, I'll agree that he might get the best of us if it were just him and us up here in the mountains. But we have you and your husband knows I'll kill you if he doesn't agree to my conditions."

Sally smiled and lay back against the wall at the head of the bed and closed her eyes. "I hope you will remember, in those seconds before Smoke cuts your heart out, that I *did* warn you, Mr. Pike," she said, and then she turned on her side with her back to him.

Pike felt his heart flutter with fear at her words and the confidence with which she spoke them. He'd never met a woman as strong and as loyal to her man as this one, and he gave a short prayer that he hadn't underestimated Smoke Jensen.

24

While Pike and his men sat around their fire drinking whiskey and telling each other lies, Smoke and the boys traveled back down the mountain toward the rendezvous place so Smoke could set up some surprises for their meeting the next day.

Once they arrived across the creek from the clearing, Smoke had Pearlie bring the packhorse across the water and into the clearing. The moon had become slightly larger over the past week and there were only ragged bunches of snow clouds to hide the brilliant starlight.

Smoke unpacked the pony carrying the supplies he'd had Pearlie and Cal buy and laid them out on the ground. He used a small hammer to break the top of the keg of horseshoe nails that had so puzzled Pearlie when he obtained them. He then opened a keg of gunpowder and laid out several empty Arbuckle's coffee cans in a row. One by one, he filled the cans with a mixture of gunpowder and horseshoe nails, and then he sealed the tops of the cans. Once that was done, he took an old white shirt of his out of his saddlebag and stuck it under his belt.

Picking up a can under each arm, he indicated Cal and Pearlie should do the same thing and for them to follow him. He walked up the steep slope at the rear of the clearing until he came to one of the larger boulders sticking out of the side of the mountain. Looking for the exact right spot, he finally stooped down and placed the can up next to the boulder where it could be seen from across the creek. He shoveled a mixture of dirt and pine needles over the can until it could barely be seen, and then he ripped off a piece of the shirt and stuck it in the dirt just over the can.

He straightened up and dusted off his hands. Looking at Cal and Pearlie he asked, "Do you think you can see that from that grove of trees where you're going to be hiding?"

Pearlie looked back across the creek and then down at the white scrap of cloth in the ground. After a few seconds, he nodded. "Yep, an' the next question you're gonna ask is can I hit it with that Sharps, ain't it?"

Smoke nodded. "Yeah, and both Sally's and my life depends on your being able to plug it dead center."

Pearlie slowly nodded. "All right, no problem. How about you, Cal?" he asked, turning to Cal.

Cal grinned. "You may be a mite faster on the draw and a little more accurate with a handgun than me, Pearlie, but you know I'm miles better'n you with a long gun." He looked up at Smoke. "Don't worry, Smoke, when you give the signal, we'll get the job done."

Smoke smiled. "I know you will, boys, or I wouldn't put Sally's life in your hands. Now all we have to do is figure out all the likely places those bastards will pick to hide in and we'll plant us some more Arbuckle's cans nearby."

They spent the next hour and a half walking around the clearing and looking at it from all angles. They found several more boulders and outcroppings of rock that looked like likely candidates for hiding places, and even put one can in front of a small group of misshapen trees and brush just in case one of the men tried to lie down in it. They even put one can on top of the roof of the small, dilapidated cabin in the clearing just in case some of the men tried to take refuge in it.

Finally, Smoke was satisfied with their efforts in the area around the clearing. "Now we get to work on the trails to and from this place," he said, leading them back across Fountain Creek.

"First, we'll go down the mountain a ways and get things ready there," he said once they were on the trail. After he was about fifty yards past the clearing, he got down off Joker, took the pick and shovel he'd had Pearlie buy off the packhorse, and began to dig up a hole in the center of the trail. While he was digging, he looked up and said, "Get me some of those tent stakes out of the pack, Cal, and bring 'em over here."

In the soft gravely sand and dirt of the mountainside, it only took him a few minutes to dig a pit two feet deep and four feet wide. He took the tent stakes from Cal and kneeled down next to the pit. One by one, he stuck them down into the ground at the bottom of the pit with their sharp ends up, until he had the entire bottom of the pit covered with sharpened stakes pointing upward. Pointing to the sides of the trail, which had thick layers of pine boughs and needles lying on the ground, he told Cal and Pearlie to gather some up and to fill in the pit, and then to scatter dirt around so it looked like a normal part of the trail.

"Jiminy, I'd hate to be ridin' the bronc that steps in that hole," Cal said, rubbing his jaw.

"The stakes are in case the hole itself doesn't break the horse's legs," Smoke said. He shook his head. "I hate like hell to do that to any animal, but sometimes when you're dealing with pond scum you have to do things you don't like.

"We'll dig a couple more of these at fifty-yard intervals

down the trail, and there are a couple of other things I want to do in between the pits," he added.

He rode down the trail with Cal and Pearlie following for another twenty yards, until he came to a place where there were trees close on either side of the trail. He got down and pulled the bail of barbed wire off the back of the packhorse along with some wire cutters.

He went to one of the trees on the left side of the trail, wrapped the barbed wire around it about six and a half feet off the ground, and twisted the ends together. Then, unrolling the barbed wire as he went, he crossed the trail and did the same thing on the other side, clipping the bale off the end as he twisted it.

Pearlie shook his head. "Damn, that's gonna take a man's head plumb off if'n he rides into it at speed."

Smoke's lips turned up in a nasty grin, but his eyes were flat and without any trace of humor at all. "That's the idea, Pearlie."

They followed him down the trail as he dug more pits and wired more trees, sometimes stepping off the trail and booby-trapping the area alongside just in case the outlaws got smart and got their horses off the trail.

At each of the pits and on each of the trees he rigged, Smoke hung a small piece of white cloth.

"Why for are you doin' that, Smoke?" Cal asked, a puzzled look on his face. "We ain't gonna have to shoot these traps to make 'em work."

Smoke cocked his head at Cal and frowned. "Come on, Cal," he said patiently. "You're smarter than that."

Cal looked over at Pearlie, who shrugged. "I ain't tellin' you, Cal boy. Figure it out for yourself."

Cal thought for a moment, and then he snapped his fingers. "I got it. If'n we're riding down the trail with them galoots on our heels, we'll know where the traps are when we see the white pieces of shirt."

Smoke smiled, this time for real, and nodded. "That's right, Cal. If our little surprises up at the clearing don't kill all of the sons of bitches, we may have to make a run for it to get Sally out of danger. This way, we won't get hurt by one of our own traps."

Finished with their preparations on the lower part of the trail, Smoke and the boys headed back up the mountain toward the outlaws' camp.

"One thing's botherin' me, Smoke," Cal said.

"What's that?"

"What if in the mornin' those galoots start to go down the trail past the clearin'. Won't they come upon our traps and know somethin's wrong?"

"Good question, Cal," Smoke said. "I'm glad to see you're thinking of things that can go wrong with our plan. That is one of the most important things to do when you're trying to trap something, figure out what may go wrong and allow the animal to escape. To keep them from finding our traps below the clearing, I'm going to be in the brush just below the clearing in the morning. If they start to ride down that way, I'll come out and tell them I got there early."

"How about the trail above the camp, Smoke?" Pearlie asked. "We can't set any traps there or they'll find them on their way down."

"I know," Smoke said. "What we're going to do tonight is find the right places for the traps and mark them with white cloth. In the morning, after the outlaws come down the trail and head to the clearing, you and Cal should have time to prepare the pits and wire up above just as we've done below before the meeting takes place."

"But why are we doing both sides of the clearing, Smoke?" Cal asked. "If we do have to make a run for it, won't we be going down the mountain toward Pueblo?"

Smoke looked at him and shrugged. "Probably, Cal, but I don't want to bet my life and Sally's life on a probably. Depending on how things break, we may have to head up the mountain instead of down. Much better to make too many traps than not enough."

"You got that right," Pearlie said, "though it plumb galls me to think we may have to run from these bastards 'stead of stayin' and fightin' it out face-to-face."

"Me too, Pearlie," Smoke said. "But my first obligation is to get Sally out of danger. Once that's done, believe me, there won't be a hole deep enough for them to crawl into to escape what I have planned for them."

It took them until almost midnight for Smoke to find and mark the various places he wanted the pits dug and the trees wired and to leave small patches of cloth on the areas for the boys to find the next day.

By then, they were all dog-tired, and Smoke insisted they go back to their camp near the outlaws and get some shut-eye. "Like Puma Buck used to say," Smoke told them, "it plumb don't make no sense to go into a battle sleepy or hungry. Two things a man don't do good on an empty stomach or on too little sleep: fight or make love to a woman. You need all your wits about you to do either one right."

The boys laughed at the old mountain man's wisdom and humor and as they rode up the trail, they asked Smoke to tell them more mountain man lore.

By the time they got to their camp, he'd told several stories of how he and Puma Buck and Preacher had pulled some tricks on the Indians that were a constant menace to mountain men in the old days.

Once at their camp, he built a very small fire and heated up some more steaks and some coffee that was quite a bit weaker than what they'd had for supper.

"Probably won't have time for breakfast in the morning, so we'd better fill our bellies now," he advised.

Pearlie grunted around a mouthful of steak. "You don't have to tell me that twice," he said.

25

Before falling asleep the night before, Smoke had set his internal alarm to awaken him before dawn. Over many years of living in the High Lonesome without alarm clocks to keep him on schedule, he'd acquired the ability to make himself awaken at just about any time he wanted. Then it had been an essential survival skill, but now it was Sally's life that depended on this ability.

He blinked awake about an hour prior to sunrise and, as was his long habit, he surveyed his surroundings carefully before moving or making a sound. The forest around his camp was very quiet. The night hunters and predators had long since found their evening meals and were preparing for a day of sleep, and the daytime hunters had yet to awaken. Even the hoot owls were quiet and had ceased asking their eternal question, "Who?"

Smoke eased out of his sleeping blankets and built a small, hat-sized fire in the corner of some boulders to heat some water for coffee. Once the water was boiling, he threw in a couple of handfuls of Arbuckle's and roused the boys.

Like Smoke, years on the trail herding cattle had taught them to come instantly awake. They drank their coffee as they broke camp, cleaning up all evidence of their presence and making sure the fire was completely out before they headed down the trail to prepare for their confrontation with Pike and his men later in the day.

A light dusting of snow had fallen during the night, so they had to stay well off the trail on their way down the mountain lest their horses' hoofprints in the snow give their presence away to the outlaws.

Once they were opposite the clearing where the meeting was to take place, Smoke had Cal and Pearlie move the horses well off the trail so they wouldn't nicker when they smelled the gang's animals, and then he showed them where to set up their line of fire into the clearing.

The copse of trees he'd picked had enough underbrush scattered around to hide their position, and there was a fallen pine log behind which they could lay and rest their rifles on for better aim.

"Remember, don't dig the pits or fix the barbed wire to the trees until you are sure all of the outlaws have moved down to the clearing area," Smoke advised. "After the two dead men we left them as a warning, Pike may be worried enough to have a man hang behind to watch their backtrail, so be careful."

As the boys nodded their understanding of his warning, Smoke put his two good pistols in Pearlie's saddlebag and took out a couple of older, less accurate weapons to put in his holsters.

"Why're you doin' that?" Cal asked.

"First thing Pike's going to do when I ride up is take my weapons," Smoke said, "and I don't want to give him my good ones."

Smoke then took a small folding knife from his saddlebags and put it in the inside of his right boot, along with a .44-caliber two-shot derringer. After he'd done this, he took his large bowie knife out of the scabbard on his belt and stuck it in the outside of his right boot, leaving it where the handle could plainly be seen.

When Cal raised his eyebrows at this, Smoke explained, "I'm leaving the big knife where they can find it in my boot," he said. "That way, they'll hopefully be satisfied they've got all my weapons and won't search any farther and find the other knife or the derringer."

Once Cal and Pearlie's weapons were laid out behind the pine log, along with extra ammunition, Smoke told them to head on up the mountain so they could prepare the other traps as soon as the gang came down.

He shook each of their hands solemnly, knowing it might well be the last time he saw them, for he was taking an awful risk in putting himself in Pike's hands. He just hoped the man would want to talk and brag and gloat before deciding to shoot him. He knew if the man were smart, he'd kill Smoke as soon as he was disarmed, but he'd never yet met an outlaw who was smart. He prayed this wouldn't be the first time.

Pike and his men began to come awake as the sun rose over the eastern peaks and warmed up the air a few degrees. Most of the men were heavy-lidded and groggy after a night of too much whiskey and too little sleep, but before long the fire was rebuilt, food and coffee prepared, and they began to feel as if they might actually survive the morning, headaches and all.

Sally woke up in the cabin to find both the men assigned to guard her fast asleep, snoring loudly. For a moment, she debated whether to try and undo her ropes and make her escape, but in the end she decided to trust in Smoke and to let things play out the way he'd planned. She was afraid if she tried to escape and was caught, it would put Pike on alert and spoil whatever Smoke had in mind for the man, so she just lay there in her bed, missing Smoke and wishing the day would hurry up and begin.

"Grub's ready," Blackie Johnson announced from his place next to the fire.

Pike looked up over the rim of his coffee mug and told Rufus Gordon to go and get Mrs. Jensen from her cabin so they could feed her.

"Why're we wastin' good food on a dead woman, Boss?" he asked, his eyes glittering with hate at the thought of the woman who'd blown half his hand off.

Pike scowled at him. "The important question you should be asking yourself, Rufe, is why are you questioning my orders all of a sudden. Are you trying to get yourself killed before we collect that ten thousand dollars of Jensen's?"

"Uh, no . . . of course not, Boss. I was just . . ."

"Shut up and get Mrs. Jensen like I told you," Pike growled grumpily. He hadn't slept well the night before. Mrs. Jensen's warnings and apparent confidence in her husband's ability had worried him much more than he'd let on to her. He'd dreamed that just as he was facing Jensen the man's face had turned into a snarling, growling mountain lion. Pike woke in a sweat just as the man/lion's long, gleaming teeth were tearing into his neck. The rest of the night had been spent tossing and turning in his blankets, his nostrils full of the sour stench of his own fear-sweat. It wasn't the booze he'd drunk the night before that was making his mood foul this morning, but the fact that the mountain man's reputation had caused him such fear.

When Rufus Gordon brought Sally out of the cabin and over to the fire, Pike noticed she looked refreshed and clear-eyed, as if she'd slept like a baby. In fact, he thought, she looked about as beautiful as any woman he'd met his entire life. He shook his head to clear such thoughts from his mind. He couldn't afford to feel anything for this woman, considering what was going to happen to her after he'd killed her husband.

"Good morning, Mrs. Jensen," he said, trying to screw his face up into an expression of confidence he didn't feel about the upcoming confrontation.

Sally smiled sweetly, as if she hadn't a care in the world. "Good morning, Mr. Pike," she replied as Blackie Johnson handed her a mug of coffee and a tin plate with two biscuits and some pieces of bacon on it.

She glanced at the sky, which had dawned clear and cloudless after the snows of the night before had blown through. "It looks to be a lovely day today," she added as she drank her coffee and split the biscuits and put the bacon between them, making sandwiches of her breakfast.

Pike glanced skyward and grunted. "You think it's a good day to die, Mrs. Jensen?" he asked, again trying to rattle her out of her good mood.

She shrugged. "Any day is a good day to die, Mr. Pike, if you've lived a full and happy life," she said agreeably. "When my time comes, whether it is today or in the future, I won't regret it because I've been lucky enough to have had everything in life I always wanted."

"Well, enjoy the dawn, Mrs. Jensen, 'cause it's probably the last one you'll ever see," Pike grunted, and he turned back to his own food and coffee, trying to ignore the burning in his gut at the thought of meeting up with Smoke Jensen later in the day.

Blackie Johnson's lips were tight and his eyes were narrow. He too didn't want to think about what the men had planned for this lady. He'd come to respect and even to like her for her courage and loyalty to her husband. He thought he'd never met anyone like her before in his life, and even mused that if he had, things might have turned out differently for him.

After a moment, Pike looked around at his men, eating and drinking their coffee. A few of the men had laced the dark brew with dollops of whiskey, the hair of the dog and all that. "Hurry up with the grub, men," he groused. "We've got to get going before long."

"What's the hurry, Boss?" Hank Snow asked. "We ain't supposed to meet up with Jensen until noon."

Pike sighed. Snow was a capable gunny and as mean as a snake, but he was also dumb as a doorknob. "Hank, we got to get there and get set up long before Jensen arrives," Pike tried to explain patiently. "Far as he knows, I've only got three men with me. I don't want him to know about the rest of you, so we got to get you hidden 'fore he gets there."

Sally lowered her head to her plate at this comment to hide her knowing smile. Pike was really dumb if he thought Smoke didn't know to the man what he was up against, she thought.

Thirty minutes later, the gang had finished breakfast, packed their gear, and were headed down the mountain trail toward the meeting place Pike had told Smoke about.

"Keep your eyes open, men," Pike warned. "Jensen might have come early hoping to surprise us, so ride with your guns loose and loaded up six and six."

As they moved down the trail, Pike kept his eyes on the ground, making sure there were no fresh tracks in the snow to indicate Jensen had been there before them.

Sally, on the other hand, noticed the small pieces of white cloth stuck on various trees and bushes along the way. She'd been with Smoke long enough to know his habits and realized this was his doing. She didn't know exactly what he had planned for Pike and his gang, but she breathed easier at this sign of her husband's presence in the area.

When they got to the clearing, Pike pointed at the

boulders and outcroppings on the slopes that rose from the edges of the area. He pointed to his men one at a time, showing them where he wanted them to station themselves so they had clear lines of fire down on the clearing.

"Keep a sharp lookout, men," he said to the ones he sent up the slope. "Don't fire unless Jensen tries something or you see something going wrong, and for God's sake, try not to hit me or any of the other men."

He went to the ramshackle cabin in the clearing and brought out an old stool and a rickety handmade chair, which he sat in the center of the open space in front of the cabin. He set Sally on the stool and had Blackie Johnson tie her hands in front of her.

"Zeke," he said, "you hide yourself in the cabin. I don't want Jensen to see you 'cause he might remember your face from the last time he seen you."

Zeke nodded, his eyes staring holes in Sally as he licked his lips. Before he moved off to the cabin, he leaned down and whispered, "I can't hardly wait till I'm done with your man, Missus, and then it'll be your turn."

"Rufus, you stay here in the clearing with me and Blackie. That scattergun you use won't be any good from more'n fifteen yards so I want you at my back."

Rufus and Blackie nodded and took up station behind the chair that Pike placed ten feet from Sally's stool. He took a seat facing her, leaned back and crossed his legs, and built himself a cigarette. He struck a lucifer on his pants leg and lit the butt, exhaling a long cloud of smoke into the chilly air.

Sally watched him, her eyes steady and unafraid as he sat and smoked. She saw a thin trickle of sweat form on his forehead and run down onto his cheek, even though the temperature was in the forties.

"You know, Mr. Pike," she said easily, "it's not to late to stop this thing you're doing. If you quit now, Smoke might even let you live."

Pike's eyes darted to her and then away, as if he didn't want her to see the fear in them. "It's gone too far to stop now, Mrs. Jensen," he replied in a low voice so his men behind him couldn't hear. "Even if I wanted to, which I don't, it's much too late."

"Do you have any family you want me to notify about your death then?" Sally asked, sounding as if she were truly concerned about it.

Pike stared at her, amazed at her faith in her husband's ability to conquer all of his men. He sighed and shook his head. "If you don't shut up with that kind of talk, Mrs. Jensen, I'll have Blackie tie a gag on you."

"All right, Mr. Pike. I'll be quiet and leave you to your thoughts," she said calmly.

26

Smoke observed the activity around the clearing from a bluff up on the mountainside a quarter of a mile down the trail through his binoculars. He saw the various positions that Pike stationed his men in, and fixed them firmly in his memory. He knew that even with Cal and Pearlie covering his back, it was going to be a close thing to get both Sally and himself out of the trap without either of them catching some lead.

He waited patiently, smoking a couple of cigarettes to help keep his nerves under control. He'd faced many such situations in the past and had never worried about his ability to come out on top, but this time the most precious thing in his life hung in the balance and his gut was in knots.

Finally, he turned his binoculars to the position Cal and Pearlie were to take, and saw the brief flash of a mirror reflecting sunlight from the copse of trees across the creek from the clearing, Pearlie's signal that they were ready for him to appear.

Smoke stubbed out his cigarette, took a deep breath, and climbed into the saddle. He pulled Joker's head around and made his way down the side of the mountain until he was on the trail so it'd look like he just came up from Pueblo.

He let Joker walk the quarter mile up the trail until he was across from the clearing. He saw Pike and the two men behind him pull their weapons at his approach. Pike and one of the men held pistols, while the other, the one with a dirty bandage on his right hand, held a sawed-off shotgun cradled in his arms, the twin barrels pointing directly at Sally.

Shit, Smoke thought, he hadn't counted on the shotgun. That was going to make it even tougher to extricate Sally unharmed from the outlaws. A man under attack that's holding a pistol often can't count on his aim being accurate, but a man with an express gun doesn't have to be dead on to do considerable damage.

Breathing slowly to slow his racing heart, Smoke walked Joker across the creek and climbed down out of the saddle, holding his hands out from his body well away from the two pistols on his belt.

"Keep her covered, boys," Pike said as he got up off his chair and holstered his gun.

He walked over to stand in front of Smoke, looking him up and down with a smirk on his face, but his forehead was covered with sweat, indicating he wasn't as sure of himself as he was trying to appear.

"Give me your weapons," Pike ordered, holding out his hand.

Smoke took his pistols out, being careful to handle them with only two fingers so as not to provoke the men holding their guns on Sally.

He handed the Colts to Pike, who stuck them in his belt. Pike's eyes roamed over Smoke's body and he spied the knife handle in his right boot.

"The pig-sticker too, Jensen," he said.

Smoke bent down, pulled the bowie knife out of his boot, and handed it butt-first to Pike, who smiled evilly.

"Thought you could put one over on old Bill, huh?" he asked, testing the razor-sharp blade with his finger.

"If I was trying to trick you, Pike," Smoke said evenly, "I wouldn't have had it sticking out in plain sight."

Pike grinned. "Nevertheless, I'm gonna have to check you to make sure you don't have anymore up your sleeves," he grunted.

Smoke held his hands out from his body and Pike moved closer. He ran his hands around Smoke's waist and up along his shirt, and then he bent and felt around the left boot, ignoring the right boot as Smoke had hoped he would do.

After a couple of minutes, Pike stepped back and moved over toward the chair in front of Sally.

"You got the money?" he asked, seemingly more at ease now that Smoke had been disarmed.

"Maybe," Smoke said, letting his eyes cut to Sally and giving her a wink where Pike couldn't see it.

"What do you mean, maybe?" Pike asked, his voice becoming hard.

"I need to see if Sally is all right before I give it to you," Smoke said.

Pike grinned. "I could just take it," he said.

Smoke's face smoothed and his eyes grew flat. "That might be harder than you think," he said, his voice as low and hard as Pike's.

"Come on, Boss," Blackie Johnson said from behind him. "Let him check her out. There's no need for any rough stuff since she ain't been hurt."

Pike's shoulders relaxed and he stepped to the side. "You're right, Blackie. No need to make this any tougher than it already is. Go on, Jensen, check her all you want," he said, spreading his arms wide.

Smoke moved over to squat in front of Sally, using his body to block the outlaws' view of her. "How are you doing, sweetheart?" he asked.

Sally smiled. "Better, now that you are here," she

said, though her voice croaked from the dryness in her throat.

Smoke leaned forward to give her a hug. As his lips moved next to her ear, he whispered. "There's a knife and a derringer in my right boot. Slip them out and hide them under your hands until I give the signal."

She gave a barely perceptible nod against his cheek and he felt her fingers dip into his boot and then withdraw.

"That's enough, Jensen," Pike called from a dozen yards away. "Let's see the money and then you can kiss her all you want."

"Take Pike and the shotgun man first," he whispered before he moved, "I'll take the other one."

"I love you," Sally whispered back, knowing that in the next few moments she might lose him forever, one way or the other.

Smoke leaned back and kissed her lightly on the lips. "I love you too, wife," he said.

He slowly stood up and turned around facing Pike. As he moved toward him, he pulled a thick wad of bills from inside his shirt just below his belt, moving slowly so as not to alarm the men holding the guns.

He waved the bills in the air to get their attention off Sally so she could open the knife and cut the ropes holding her hands without them noticing it.

Smoke and Pike moved closer, and Smoke held the wad of greenbacks out in front of him as if to give them to the outlaw when he got close enough.

Suddenly, Smoke threw the bills in Pike's face and dove to the side toward Blackie Johnson. As he swung his fist as hard as he could against the man's jaw, Smoke heard two quick pops behind him so close together they sounded almost as one report.

His fist connected with Johnson's jaw, snapping his head to the side and putting his lights out instantly.

Smoke whirled around in time to see Pike grab his stomach and double over as he toppled to the ground.

The man with the shotgun stood there, his mouth open and his eyes wide with surprise as he glanced down at the small hole in the center of his chest and watched blood spurt from the wound.

Smoke took two quick strides and jerked the express gun out of his hands just as the cabin door on the far side of the clearing splintered open and Zeke Thompson limped out, pistols in both hands firing wildly as he screamed, "Jensen, you bastard!"

Smoke dove onto his stomach as bullets pocked the sand and gravel in front of his face and let go with both barrels of the shotgun at Thompson.

Thompson was picked up off the ground and blown backward by the ten-gauge buckshot loads in the shotgun, blood coming from a dozen wounds in his chest and abdomen.

Smoke didn't wait to see if he was alive or dead, but rolled to his feet and ran in a crouch toward Sally, who still stood there with the smoking derringer held out in front of her.

The entire episode had taken only thirty seconds, but Smoke knew the men on the slopes above them would be standing up to fire momentarily.

Smoke grabbed Sally at a dead run and got her behind Joker, who was rearing his head and whinnying at the sound of gunfire and the smell of cordite that filled the air.

"There's men on the hillside," Sally yelled at him as he grabbed Joker's reins and pulled the horse along with them toward the creek. He didn't dare try to get into the saddle, but used the animal as a shield for him and Sally.

The distinctive crack of a Henry rifle came from behind them and the pommel of Joker's saddle exploded.

Then, like music to Smoke's ears, the deep, booming report of a Sharps fifty-caliber came from across the creek, followed almost instantly by an explosion on the mountainside and the high-pitched scream of a man shredded by high explosives and hundreds of horseshoe nails.

The Sharps boomed again, and was accompanied this time by the higher-pitched crack of Cal's Winchester rifle as the boys began to lay down a covering fire against the men on the slopes above them.

The outlaws managed to get off several shots, which smacked into the creek with tiny splashes as Sally and Smoke ran through the freezing water toward the forest on the other side of the trail.

Another explosion boomed from behind them, and Smoke and Sally were both hit with several horseshoe nails, though at this distance they did little damage. Joker reared and bucked against the reins as three of the nails dug into his flanks, but Smoke held onto the reins for dear life and forced him to go with them across the trail.

As soon as they were across the trail and into the thick forest of ponderosa pines on the other side, Smoke threw Sally to the ground and covered her body with his just as several shots ricocheted off the trees, sending splinters of bark flying through the air.

Sally grunted and pulled Smoke close, kissing his neck and laughing. "Oh, darling, it feels like you've gained weight," she said.

27

When they saw Smoke walking Joker up the trail toward the clearing, Pearlie and Cal lay down behind the large ponderosa pine log on the ground and rested their rifles on it, aiming at the area across Fountain Creek.

"I'm gonna draw a bead on that white cloth just beside that outcropping of boulders just above the clearing," Pearlie said. "That's the galoot that's closest to where Smoke and Sally are gonna be standin'."

Cal nodded. "What about the two men down in the clearing? It looks like one of 'em has a shotgun," Cal asked.

Pearlie shook his head. "Smoke said he an' Sally would take care of anyone in the clearing an' for us to concentrate on the men up on the ridges above 'em," Pearlie replied.

"All right," Cal said. "I'll try and take out any men who stand up off to the right when Smoke makes his move. I don't know if I can hit any of those cans of gunpowder from this distance, but I oughta be able to get close enough to make the men duck for cover," he said.

"You keep their heads down an' I'll use this buffalo gun to hit the explosives," Pearlie answered,

shoving his hat back on his head so it wouldn't interfere with his aiming. "We'll just have to trust Smoke to
do the rest."

They watched as Smoke handed his guns over to
the big man who seemed to be in charge and then
moved over to squat before Sally and give her a hug.

As Smoke stood up and pulled out his wad of greenbacks and moved toward Pike, Pearlie whispered,
"He'll make his move any minute now. Get ready."

When Pearlie saw Smoke throw the bills in Pike's
face and dive to the side, he gently squeezed the trigger on the Sharps Big Fifty, the front sight about an
inch above the white patch of cloth just next to a
group of boulders on the ridge.

The rifle butt slammed back against his shoulder,
turning him half around from the force of the recoil.
An instant later, a tremendous explosion boomed
across the valley and he could see a man blown into
the air, parts of his body twisting and whirling in the
air like candy out of a busted piñata. Clouds of white
smoke billowed into the clear air as branches from
nearby trees were shredded by hundreds of horseshoe
nails zinging through their limbs.

In spite of Smoke's assurances he would take care
of the men in the clearing, Cal kept his eyes on
Smoke and Sally to make sure it went as planned. As
soon as he saw Sally stand up and fire two quick shots
into the men and Smoke knock the other one's lights
out, he shifted his gaze to the slope above the clearing and eared back the hammer on his Winchester.

He saw a couple of heads pop up and took dead
aim at the first one, who was aiming a rifle down at
Smoke. He squeezed off a shot, hitting the man just
below his neck, and saw him flung backward, screaming as his hands dropped the rifle and grabbed at his
throat.

Cal's second shot missed, but it hit the rock in front

of the second man and showered his face with needle-like shards of granite, making him duck back down.

Two other men, slightly above these and off to the side, managed to get off a few rounds before Cal could lever another bullet into the firing chamber of the Winchester. Unable to work the gun fast enough lying down, Cal raised up on his knees and began to fire and reload and fire again as fast as he could, not trying to aim accurately but just to lay down enough lead to keep the men across the way from being able to get set when they fired.

Pearlie fired again, pocking dirt next to the white cloth of the second can of explosives. He levered another cartridge into the Sharps, adjusted his aim, and pulled the trigger again.

This time he was dead on and the can exploded, blowing a door-sized boulder into the air and shredding the man behind it into mush.

By now, Smoke and Sally had crossed the creek and made it to cover in the pine trees and brush on their side of the creek.

"Keep 'em pinned down," Pearlie said. "I'll grab the mounts and take 'em down to Sally and Smoke."

Cal didn't have time to answer. He was firing and levering and firing over and over. As soon as he saw heads rise above cover across the way, he'd fire a couple of quick shots close enough to make them duck down again.

Pearlie backed up into the brush and ran to where he'd ground-reined the horses. He jumped up into his saddle and grabbed the reins of the horse they'd gotten for Sally. As he rode down the hill through heavy underbrush, he pulled Smoke's gunbelt and holsters out of his saddlebags.

Smoke eased off Sally and took her hand. Scrabbling on hands and knees, he led her back through the brush away from the trail.

He looked up as he heard horses, and drew a breath of relief when he saw Pearlie coming toward them. He stood up just as Pearlie flipped him his belt and guns.

Smoke buckled the belt on and then he lifted Sally up into the saddle. He slapped the horse's rump to get it into a lope back up the hill, and then he swung up into the saddle on Joker and raced after her. Pearlie followed, keeping a close watch behind them to make sure none of the outlaws were trying to cross the creek and follow them.

Smoke jerked the reins, pulling Joker to a halt when he got to Cal's horse. He gave a shrill whistle, and grinned when Cal burst out of heavy brush running toward them.

"Good job, boys," he said as Cal jumped into the saddle. "Now, let's shag our mounts out of here," he yelled, and they took off down the mountain.

As they galloped down the hillside, Sally turned her head and yelled, "What about the money?"

"I'll come back for it later," he answered, not telling her he wanted to get her down to Pueblo and safety before he came back for the outlaws. He knew if he told her that, she'd resist and want to go back with him right now and finish the job. Sally could shoot and ride as well as most men, but Smoke didn't want her in any more danger. He'd almost lost her and he wasn't about to take another chance on her life, not even for ten thousand dollars.

When they'd gone far enough to cut over and ride to the trail, Smoke slowed the horses to let them catch their wind.

As they neared Pueblo, Sally asked, "What now?"

"I'm going to pay the sheriff a visit and tell him what's going on," Smoke said. "I'll leave you in his care and then Cal and Pearlie and I will ride back up the mountain and finish what we started."

Sally shook her head violently. "Not without me, you won't!"

Smoke almost flinched from the fire in her eyes. "Now, Sally, don't argue," he pleaded. "You've been through enough in the past few days. Why don't you just take it easy and let me take care of this?"

Sally took a deep breath before answering. After a moment spent collecting her thoughts, she said, "Smoke, I had to stand there and watch those bastards shoot two of our friends down in cold blood, and then put up with being taken captive and held against my will for days on end. Don't you think I have a right to be in on it when you end it?"

Smoke sighed and looked over at Cal and Pearlie for support. Pearlie shrugged. "She's got a point, Smoke," he said.

Cal nodded. "I agree, Smoke. Besides, it looks like we only got three or four of 'em back there. Probably still another four or five left. Since Sally's as good with a gun as any man I know, it wouldn't hurt to have her along."

Smoke grinned and held up his hands in surrender. "All right, I give up. But I still want to go to town and let the sheriff know what's going on, just in case some of those men circle around and get down to Pueblo before we can find them."

Sally cleared her throat. "Uh, Smoke."

"Yes, dear?" he asked.

"Do you think I'd have time to take a bath and change clothes while you talk to the sheriff? I'm filthy."

Smoke and the boys laughed out loud.

28

The afternoon sun was almost obscured by the heavy cloud of cordite and gunpowder smoke that hung over the clearing on Fountain Creek like a morning fog.

As the frigid north wind slowly pushed the smoke away, Blackie Johnson groaned and tried to sit up. Pain from his swollen jaw coursed through his head like a lightning bolt, and he moaned again as he gingerly probed his face with his hands.

He tasted blood, and spat out two teeth and ran his tongue over two others that felt as if they'd been broken in half.

Jesus, he thought groggily, what the hell did he hit me with? He knew Jensen's hands had been empty, but he'd never been hit so hard in his life before and shook his head, thinking Jensen's fists must be as hard as rocks to do so much damage so quickly.

Johnson struggled to his feet and glanced around the clearing to see if anyone else was still alive. Bill Pike was lying a few feet away from him, still doubled over with his hands covering his stomach.

Blackie squatted and gently rolled his boss over onto his back, expecting to see a pool of blood underneath him. Instead, to his amazement, Pike groaned and opened his eyes.

Pike moved his hands away from his stomach, and Blackie saw the handle of the Colt Pike had taken away from Jensen sticking up out of his belt with a lead slug imbedded in the wood of the handle.

Pike shook his head and pulled the pistol out, staring at the slug in its handle with wide eyes. "Jesus, that little derringer kicked like a mule," he said.

Blackie grunted. "I don't know, Boss. All I saw was Jensen throwing that money in the air in your face, and the next thing I know I'm waking up with a jaw that feels like it's broken in two. What happened?"

Pike gave him a sardonic grin. "You wouldn't believe it," he said. "I ain't never seen nobody move that fast in my whole life. The bastard must've slipped his wife a purse gun an' a knife when he was talking to her. After he slugged you, she shot Rufe an' me an' that's the last I remember."

"Let's go see where the hell the rest of the men are and maybe they can tell us what went on," Pike suggested.

He turned to walk to the cabin and he saw Rufus Gordon lying on his back, pink froth and bubbles coming out of his mouth as he gasped for breath like a fish out of water.

They moved quickly to his side and Pike knelt and cradled the wounded man's head in his hands. "Rufe, you still with us?" he asked.

Gordon's eyes opened and he tried to speak, but all that came out was a gurgle, followed by a moan of pain as he tried to get his breath.

The hole in his chest was still slowly oozing blood, and it was clear from the froth on his lips and the sound his breath made when he breathed that he had a lung wound.

Blackie whispered, "He's lung-shot, Boss. He ain't gonna make it."

Pike nodded, and laid Gordon's head back down on the ground and stood up. He looked around the clearing and saw Zeke Thompson sprawled on his back just in front of the cabin, bleeding from what looked like a dozen wounds in his chest, arms, and legs.

"Jesus," Pike grunted. "Look at Zeke."

Blackie nodded. "Looks like he got in the way of an express gun." He looked back at Rufus and noticed his shotgun was missing. "Probably Rufe's."

"Come on, let's see if he's still alive," Pike said, and they walked toward the wounded man.

As the moved across the clearing, a movement on the slopes above them caught Pike's eye and he crouched, drawing his pistol and pointing it upward.

"Hold on there, Boss," Hank Snow called. "It's just us."

Several of Pike's men began to appear from their hiding places on the side of the mountain above the clearing, moving slowly and looking back and forth to make sure they weren't going to be fired on again.

Pike holstered his gun and squatted next to Zeke, shaking his shoulder with his hand.

"Goddamn!" Thompson exclaimed, coming awake and grabbing for his holster with his good hand.

"Hold it, Zeke," Pike said, grabbing his arm. "It's me an' Blackie."

Thompson shook his head and pushed himself up to a sitting position in the dirt. He looked down at the numerous patches of blood on his shirt and pants and began to gingerly feel of each and every one.

"What happened, Zeke?" Pike asked. "I'm a little hazy on the details after I was shot."

Thompson didn't answer for a moment, being busy making sure none of his wounds were serious. After a few minutes, he looked up, his face a mask of hate. "Jensen threw the money in the air to distract you and then he knocked Blackie on his ass. While he was doin' that, his bitch of a wife shot you and Rufus with that little peashooter Jensen slipped her while he was hugging her."

Pike's eyes narrowed as he pictured it in his mind, again remembering how fast Jensen had moved.

"I came out of the cabin when I saw what was goin' down, both my guns blazin', and Jensen grabbed Rufus's scattergun and let me have it with both barrels." His lips curled in a sarcastic grin. "Good thing Rufe made his own loads, 'cause they must've been light. The buckshot just barely went under my skin 'stead of clear through me."

Blackie was puzzled and he frowned. "But Zeke, why didn't the rest of the men blow Jensen to hell and gone after he made his move?"

Thompson shrugged. "I don't know. Maybe you'd better ask them. That shotgun plumb knocked me on my ass, even though the loads were light, I took both barrels at one time, and it put my lights out."

"I guess I'll do that," Pike answered, standing up and turning to face the men coming down the slope.

Hank Snow was leading the way, his left arm cradled in his right hand, blood smeared on his shirt from an arm wound.

Sergeant Joe Rutledge was limping along behind him, his hand holding his right flank where a bullet had pierced his side.

Slim Cartwright was alongside Rutledge, his face covered with blood where stone splinters had peppered it and shredded the skin. Luckily, his eyes had been spared.

Pike took in their condition with a glance and then he looked back up the slope.

"Where's Johnny Wright and Razor Jackson?" he asked.

Hank Snow grimaced. "They're both still up there, Boss. Johnny looks like he's been through a meat grinder, an' all we could find of Razor is about eight pieces, none much bigger'n my hand."

"What the hell happened up there?" Pike asked, shaking his head. "How come you boys didn't take Jensen and his wife out when he started this ruckus?"

"We were too busy ducking to do much good, Boss," Snow answered. "Jensen must've had lots of help, 'cause soon as he hit Blackie and his wife shot you an' Rufe, we came under a shitload of fire from across the way over there," he said, pointing to the area where Cal and Pearlie had been lying.

"What about Johnny and Razor?" Pike asked. "How'd Jensen manage to blow 'em up like that?"

"This is how," Sergeant Rutledge said, holding up an Arbuckle's can he was carrying. "I found this over by one of the boulders we was hiding behind. It was half-buried and the spot was marked with a piece of white cloth." His eyes moved toward the place Snow had pointed out. "Jensen must've had somebody over there with a long rifle, an' when the fight started he just shot the cloth, blowing up the cans."

He put the can down and pried off the top, showing the horseshoe nails and gunpowder inside.

He looked up. "As you can see, somethin' like this explode under your feet, it'll mess up your entire day."

"How long ago did all this happen?" Pike asked, glancing at his pocket watch.

"They pulled out 'bout thirty minutes ago," Hank Snow said, "Leastways, it's been that long since they done any shooting at us."

"Then we've still got a chance to catch them and kill the sons of bitches," Zeke Thompson growled, snapping open the loading chamber on his pistol and reloading.

Pike nodded. "Sarge, you get over there where they were firing from and see if you can tell how many we're dealin' with. I'll gather up the money an' we'll take off down the mountain after 'em."

"We got the money, Boss," Blackie Johnson said. "Why not just let it go?" He glanced around at the wounded men. "After all, most of us ain't exactly in the best shape for another gunfight."

"Let 'em go, hell!" Thompson yelled. "They kilt Johnny and Razor and Rufe an' you want to let the bastards go?"

Pike held up his hand to silence Zeke and he turned to Blackie. "Son, if we let them get down to Pueblo, they're gonna go straight to the sheriff an' he'll wire every federal marshal between here and Texas. It won't be much fun tryin' to spend this money with the marshals on our asses, will it?"

Johnson hung his head. "No, I guess not."

"Then get busy loading up our mounts," Pike said forcefully. "We got some people to catch."

When they were all mounted up and ready to go, Rutledge came out of the bushes where Cal and Pearlie had been stationed. "Looks like only four horses, Boss," he said, pointing to the tracks in the snow.

"And one of them is his wife," Pike said. "So we're only goin' up against three men."

Blackie grunted. "From what I could see, Mrs. Jensen could handle herself 'bout as good as most men."

Pike nodded. "That's why we're not going to show her any mercy. She goes down just like the rest of the bastards when we catch up to 'em." He jerked his horse's head around and pointed it down the trail. "Now, let's ride!"

They spurred their mounts down the trail, Pike in the lead, followed closely by Slim Cartwright and the others in single file behind him.

They'd only gone about fifty yards when Pike's mount stepped in one of the pits Smoke and the boys had dug. The horse screamed in agony as its right leg snapped and it swallowed its head in a tumbling somersault, throwing Pike headfirst into a thick snowbank alongside the trail.

Following too close to stop or turn, Cartwright jerked his horse's reins and had him jump Pike's horse in a running leap.

He'd only managed another fifteen yards when the barbed wire Smoke had strung across the trail caught him just under the chin. The razor-sharp barbs on the wire sliced through his neck like a hot knife through butter and took his head off just under the chin.

Cartwright's body continued in the saddle for another ten yards before it toppled lifelessly off the horse and sprawled onto the trail.

"Holy shit!" Hank Snow exclaimed, jerking his horse to a halt when he saw the mess of Cartwright's head hit the trail and bounce and roll like a child's ball, leaving splotches of blood in the white snow.

The rest of the men stopped their mounts and jumped down to see if Pike was still alive. All they could see of him were his boots sticking out of the pile of snow next to the trail.

Johnson and Rutledge each grabbed a boot and yanked, pulling a sputtering Bill Pike out of the snow.

He brushed himself off and moved over to stand next to his horse, which was snorting and gasping and trying to get to its feet. He pulled his pistol out when he saw the mangled leg and put a bullet in the horse's head, ending its misery.

Johnson stepped up next to him. "You're lucky you hit that snowbank, Boss," he said, "or you'd've broken your neck."

Sergeant Rutledge moved over next to Johnson and Pike. "Looks like Jensen laid some traps along the trail, Boss. Maybe we'd better rethink our idea of chasin' him an' his friends down."

"You're right, Sarge. We're down to five men now,

an' there's no tellin' what else that bastard has waitin' for us along the trail up ahead."

"So, we're gonna give up and head back to Texas?" Johnson asked.

Pike shook his head. "Not on your life, Blackie. But we are gonna be very careful the next time we go up against Jensen and his friends."

29

As they moved down the trail toward Pueblo, every so often Smoke would have either Cal or Pearlie hang back to watch their backtrail to make sure none of the outlaws were following them. He wanted to make sure they weren't surprised before they got to the town and told the sheriff what had happened.

While he was riding, Smoke found it difficult to keep his eyes off Sally. In spite of the fact that she'd not had a chance to do her hair or to bathe while a prisoner, and though she was still dressed in the oversized men's clothing the gang had bought for her in Canyon City, he still felt she was the most beautiful woman in the world.

It was amazing to him that after all she'd been through the last couple of weeks, she seemed to be none the worse for wear. She still managed to laugh and joke with Cal and Pearlie, and in general acted as if they were out on a trip to see the country instead of fighting for their lives against a band of desperate criminals.

When they finally reached the outskirts of Pueblo and rode down along the main street toward the sheriff's office, they attracted stares from almost everyone they passed on the way. Like all mining towns in the mountains of Colorado Territory, there were few women residents other than prostitutes and a very few hardy wives of miners, none of whom even approached Sally's good looks and regal manner.

A few of the younger men on the dirt streets even whistled or gave appreciative catcalls when they saw Sally passing, acts that infuriated Cal and Pearlie, but merely amused Smoke and Sally.

When Pearlie almost went after a couple of the men, Sally laughed and calmed him down. "Take it easy, Pearlie," she said. "They don't mean any harm. It's just their way of letting off steam after being up in the mountains for a long time without female companionship."

"But Miss Sally," he said, glaring at the two miscreants with narrowed eyes, "they oughta show more respect for a lady."

Sally laughed again and looked down at the oversized men's pants and shirt and coat she was wearing. "And just how are they supposed to know what a 'lady' I am, Pearlie, dressed like this?"

Under Sally's calming influence, the group finally made it to the sheriff's office without being involved in any fights or other misadventures.

When they entered the door, they found a tall, lean man with a handlebar mustache sitting at a scarred wooden desk with his feet up on the corner. He was leaned back in his desk chair and had a cup of steaming coffee cradled in his hands.

A handmade sign on the desk informed them he was Sheriff John Ashby.

When Ashby saw Sally enter with the men, he immediately got to his feet and tipped his hat, a weather-beaten black Stetson. "Mornin', ma'am, gents," he said in a voice that had more than a little Texas twang to it.

Sally chuckled. "I can see you're not from around here, Sheriff," she said.

Ashby smiled. "No, ma'am. I came up here with my daddy a few years back from Galveston. He was seeking his fortune in the gold fields."

"Did he find it, Mr. Ashby?" Sally asked as she took a seat across from his desk.

Once she was seated, the sheriff also sat back down behind his desk. "Yes, ma'am. At least, we dug up enough gold for him to head back down to Texas and buy himself a cattle ranch over near Austin." He grinned. "But I never liked chasin' beeves around under the hot Texas sun, so I stayed up here and somehow got myself elected sheriff."

Sally nodded and Smoke spoke up. "Sheriff Ashby, we've come to report some killings up along Fountain Creek."

"'Fore we get down to business, I got some hot coffee brewin' on the stove over yonder," he said, indicating a large Franklin stove in the corner of the office. "You folks can help yourselves if you've a mind to."

"Would you like a cup, Miss Sally?" Cal asked as he headed toward the stove.

"Yes, please, Cal," she answered.

Once they all had mugs in their hands and had taken seats in front of his desk, Ashby crossed his legs and sat back in his chair. "Now, you want to tell me all about it?" he asked, his eyes centering on Smoke.

Smoke started at the beginning and told the sheriff how a band of men from Texas had gone to his ranch, killed two of his hands, and kidnapped Sally.

Ashby's eyes narrowed and he looked at Sally. "They mistreat you any, ma'am?" he asked, his voice softening with concern.

"No, not really," Sally answered. "Other than keeping me tied up at all times, they did nothing to harm me in any way."

Ashby's eyes went back to Smoke, who then told him about how he figured it was a revenge motive by

Pike and Thompson for what he'd done years before in Idaho.

"What did you say your name was?" Ashby asked.

"I didn't say, but it's Smoke Jensen," Smoke replied. "This is my wife, Sally, and my friends Cal and Pearlie."

"The Smoke Jensen?" Ashby asked, sitting forward in his chair, clearly more interested now.

"I'm the only one I know of," Smoke answered.

"Last I heard, you was livin' over near Big Rock," Ashby said. "Settled down an' livin' the quiet life."

"That's where my ranch is," Smoke said. "And my life was quiet until Pike and his men interfered in it."

Ashby pursed his lips. "You say there were 'bout ten or so of 'em?"

"That's right, Sheriff," Smoke said, "though their numbers are considerably less now."

"Oh?"

"Yes. I killed a couple of them a few days ago on the trail and I figure we got another two or three this morning."

"That still leaves five or six to deal with then," Ashby said.

"I guess that's about right," Smoke said.

"Let me get some deputies together an' you can show me where all this took place."

"Before you do that, Sheriff," Smoke said, "my wife would like to clean up a bit and we all need to eat something. Can you give us a couple of hours?"

Ashby shrugged. "Sure. It'll take me that long to find some men to deputize to go with us anyway. We'll meet back here in two hours, all right?"

After they left the sheriff's office, Smoke asked Cal and Pearlie to get them rooms in the hotel while he and Sally made a couple of stops.

He and Sally went first to the local general store,

since the town of Pueblo didn't have a woman's dress shop. In there, Sally picked out some clothes that fit her better than the ones the gang had bought. She bought some pants, boots, and several shirts that were in her size, along with a fur-lined leather coat. After that, Smoke took her to the local gunsmith's store down the street.

After browsing for a few moments, Sally picked out a Smith and Wesson .36-caliber short-barreled pistol and a gunbelt and holster in a small size for her tiny waist. Though Sally could shoot a .44 as well as any man Smoke knew, she preferred the .36-caliber with its lighter recoil.

When they got to the hotel, Smoke arranged for a hot bath for the two of them. Once the boy working for the hotel had the large tub filled with steaming hot water, Smoke shut the door and braced it closed by putting the back of a chair under the doorknob.

When he turned around, Sally was already undressed and slipping into the tub. Smoke had started to take a seat in a nearby chair to wait for Sally to finish when she smiled at him. "This tub seems big enough for two, Smoke," she said, lowering her eyes.

Smoke didn't need a second invitation. He shucked out of his buckskins and joined her, taking a long-handled brush off the wall as he walked to the tub. For the next twenty minutes, they took turns scrubbing the trail dirt off each other and generally getting reacquainted after their long absence from each other.

When the scrubbing threatened to lead to more serious play, Sally stopped him with a smile. "Why don't you wait until tonight, darling," she said. "It's been a long time since we stayed in a hotel together."

Disappointed, but looking forward to the upcoming evening, Smoke got out of the tub and then helped Sally out. She dressed in her new clothes and they went down the corridor to find Cal and Pearlie's room.

There was a note on the door that read, "Couldn't wait. We're in the hotel dining room."

Smoke and Sally laughed and went to join the boys for a late lunch.

When they got to the dining room, they found them at a table for four, with enough food in front of Pearlie to serve three people.

"I see you didn't waste any time finding the grub," Smoke said as he pulled out a chair for Sally.

"I told the cook to put on a few more steaks for you two," Pearlie said. He blushed. "I didn't know how long you were going to be, so I just told him to get them ready and keep them warm until you showed up."

Smoke called the waiter over and told him to keep bringing food out until they told him to stop.

Sheriff Ashby showed up just as the last bit of steak was consumed, and raised his eyebrows at Sally's new look. When she stood up from the table and he saw the pistol tied down low on her hip, he glanced at Smoke. "Is Missus Jensen gonna go with us?" he asked.

Smoke grinned. "You want to try and stop her, you're welcome to try."

Ashby inclined his head at her pistol. "She know how to use that?" he asked.

"Probably better than you, Sheriff," Smoke said.

The sheriff looked at Cal and Pearlie, who both nodded. "He's right, Sheriff," Pearlie said.

"Then let's shag our mounts," Ashby said. "I've got four men ready to ride up there with us an' check the place out."

30

Bill Pike led his men down the mountain, making sure to stay well off the trail that Smoke Jensen had booby-trapped. It was very slow going with the snowdrifts halfway up their mounts' legs in some areas, and they had to be careful not to let their horses break a leg on stones or gopher holes covered by the thick blanket of snow and ice that was everywhere.

As he rode, Pike looked back at his motley crew of men, ravaged by the encounter with Smoke Jensen and his friends. Hank Snow rode hunched over, his wounded left arm covered with a bandage made out of a couple of bandannas tied together; Zeke Thompson was wearing his usual scowl, still wearing his clothes with holes in them from the buckshot Smoke had peppered him with and with the balls he'd pried out of his skin with his skinning knife resting in his shirt pocket; Sergeant Joe Rutledge was riding cocked over to one side, favoring his right flank and keeping his right arm pressed tight against it to stop the bleeding; Blackie Johnson was nursing a bottle of whiskey to stop the throbbing in his swollen jaw and to ease the pain of his broken and missing teeth.

Pike shook his head. All in all, he'd made the one mistake he'd tried to avoid—underestimating Smoke

Jensen. Well, he thought, that was one error he wasn't about to make twice. His plan was to circle around Pueblo and to head back to Canyon City. There, he would use some of the ten thousand dollars Jensen had thrown in his face to hire more men for his next foray against the mountain man, and this time he would make sure to plant the bastard forked end up.

Lost in his thoughts of revenge and death, Pike almost didn't hear the hoofbeats of the men riding up the trail in front of him. When he realized there were riders coming, he raised his hand and motioned for his men to move further into the brush, out of sight and hearing of the trail.

From deep in the forest, Pike could barely make out a band of eight or nine men, heavily armed, riding up the trail toward the clearing they'd just left. That son of a bitch Jensen had gotten the sheriff of Pueblo and he'd brought a posse up the mountain after him and his men.

Once the posse was past, Pike said, "Spur them mounts, boys, 'cause Johnny Law is gonna be on our tracks 'fore long and we'd better be shut of this place by then."

"I don't know if I can ride any faster, Boss," Rutledge moaned. "My side's about to kill me."

"Then I'll leave your worthless ass behind an' let Jensen finish what he started," Pike growled, putting the spurs to his horse.

Rutledge and the others gritted their teeth and followed, all of them wincing at the pain the faster pace caused to their wounds.

Smoke led the posse, along with Cal and Pearlie and Sally, up the trail toward the clearing. He was riding point so he could help the men avoid the traps he'd set for Pike and his men. As they came to the pits, he would have Cal and Pearlie take out the stakes and fill in the holes so no one else would inadvertently injure themselves or their horses in the traps he'd laid for Pike and his men. He also clipped the barbed wire off the trees as they passed so innocent miners or trappers wouldn't be injured.

Sheriff Ashby raised his eyebrows when he saw what Smoke had done to prevent their being followed. "Looks like you play pretty rough, Jensen," he observed while Cal and Pearlie filled in one of the pits.

Smoke looked at the sheriff, his face serious. "Man takes my wife and kills my hands, Sheriff, he deserves whatever happens to him," he said.

Then, Smoke's face softened as he remembered something Preacher had once told him. "A friend of mine once said any man who sticks his hand in a bees' nest trying to steal the honey has to expect to be stung a few times," he said.

Ashby laughed. "I can't hardly argue with that sentiment or with whatever happens to kidnappers or killers."

A few hundred yards farther along, just past a bend in the trail, the posse came upon a man sprawled on his back, his head torn off and lying ten yards from his body.

One of the posse members, a young man of no more than seventeen or eighteen years who wore his twin holsters tied down low on his hips like the gunfighters he'd read about in dime novels, leaned to the side after he saw the headless man and puked his guts out, retching and choking up his lunch.

Smoke, who'd seen many such men who fancied themselves gunnies, rode up next to the boy. "It isn't much like you thought it would be, is it?" he asked gently.

The boy sleeved vomit off his lips with his arm and turned red, bloodshot eyes to Smoke. "No, sir, it ain't."

Smoke inclined his head at the dead man lying on

the ground. "Take a good look at him, son," he said, leaning forward and crossing his arms over the pommel of his saddle. "When you kill a man, you take everything he ever was or ever will be from him. It's not a thing you should do lightly, or without good reason."

"Have you kilt many men, Mr. Jensen?" the boy asked.

"Yeah, I have," Smoke answered seriously. "But none that didn't deserve it, son, so I can live with that. The question you have to ask yourself is, can you live with pictures like this in your mind for the rest of your life? If you can't, then you'd better hang them guns up right now and think about a different way of life, 'cause if you keep wearing those six-killers, sooner or later you're either going to be looking down at a man you've killed, or a man who's just killed you will be staring down at your lifeless body."

"I can't believe his friends just left him here an' didn't take the time to bury him," one of the posse said.

"Just because killers ride together doesn't mean they're friends," Smoke said, and spurred Joker on up the trail.

Further up the trail was a dead horse lying over one of the pits, its front legs broken and a bullet hole in its head.

"The clearing is just up the way a bit," Smoke said as he led the posse forward.

When they arrived opposite the clearing, Smoke led them across Fountain Creek to the site of the gunfight.

"Jesus God Almighty," one of the posse exclaimed when they saw a pack of timber wolves working on the remains of the outlaws that had been killed.

Sheriff Ashby pulled a Winchester rifle out of his saddle boot and started to take aim at the wolves. Smoke reached out and pushed the barrel of the rifle down. "Hold on, Sheriff," he said. "Wolves got to eat, same as worms. They're only doing what they have to in order to survive up here in the High Lonesome."

Smoke drew his pistol and fired a couple of shots into the air, scaring the wolves off without killing any of them.

The posse spread out and moved around the clearing and up the slopes around it, checking for bodies. When two of the men came upon what was left of the two men who'd been blown apart by the explosives, they too bent over, hands on knees, and gave up their lunch.

Sheriff Ashby shook his head at the scattered body parts lying around the area. "Like I said before, Jensen, when you go after somebody, you do it in a serious way."

Smoke was standing in the center of the clearing, his hands on his hips, staring down at the place where he'd left Pike's body. "Looks like the ringleader got away," Smoke said.

"But I shot him full in the stomach," Sally said.

Smoke nodded. "Well, I don't see any blood here where he was lying, Sally. If he was gut shot, he should've leaked some blood here and there."

"Maybe you missed, Mrs. Jensen," Sheriff Ashby said.

Smoke shook his head. "No, she hit him dead center and knocked him off his feet. The only thing I can figure is something must have deflected the bullet—either the gun he took from me and stuck in his belt or his belt buckle. Either way, he took the money I left and what was left of his gang and hightailed it somewhere else."

Pearlie, who'd been searching the area for tracks, found where the outlaws had left the trail and headed down the mountain. He gave a shrill whistle through his fingers and yelled, "Smoke, here's their tracks."

Smoke and the rest of the posse rode back across the creek and found the place where Pike and his men had left the trail and taken to the brush. It was right next to where the headless outlaw's body was lying.

"I guess after they lost this man to one of your traps, they decided the trail was not a healthy place to ride," Sheriff Ashby observed.

Smoke got down off his horse and knelt in the snow, examining the horses' tracks. "It looks like four or five horses, Sheriff, headed back down the mountain toward Pueblo," Smoke said.

"Damn!" Ashby said. "We'd better hightail it back down there."

"Ain't we gonna bury these men, Sheriff?" one of the posse asked.

"Hell, Jensen killed 'em, let him bury 'em," another posse member said.

Smoke climbed back in the saddle. "Like I said, boys, wolves and bears got to eat too. Let the bastards serve some purpose in death, 'cause they sure as hell didn't in life."

He took off down the trail, riding hard, followed by Cal and Pearlie and Sally. After a moment's hesitation, the sheriff grinned and said, "What the hell, let's go, boys!"

When they got to a fork in the trail, just outside the city limits of Pueblo, Smoke saw tracks coming out of the brush and going off on the side trail toward Canyon City.

He reined his horse to a halt and sat staring down the trail. When the sheriff and his posse arrived a couple of minutes later, Smoke pointed at the tracks.

"Looks like Pike and his men headed back toward Canyon City instead of into Pueblo, Sheriff."

Ashby frowned, shaking his head. "I don't have any jurisdiction in Canyon City, Jensen. The county line is about a mile up that trail. Past that, it's the sheriff in Canyon City's problem."

"Can you wire him to be on the lookout for them, Sheriff?" Sally asked.

"I can, if the wire's not down," he answered. "Usually, it goes down after the first heavy snowfall and we don't bother to put it back up until spring."

Smoke shook his head. "Well, I don't intend to chase them any farther right now. Me and my friends are gonna ride back up the trail and take care of some traps we set between that clearing back there and the outlaws' old camp." He looked at Sally and winked where only she could see it. "After that I'm going back to Pueblo, have a good dinner, get a good night's sleep, and worry about those bastards tomorrow."

Pearlie smiled and nodded. "That part about the good dinner sure sounds good to me."

Smoke looked at him and grinned. "You might also want to consider a bath and a change of clothes while we're there, Pearlie."

Pearlie looked surprised. "Change my clothes? Heck, I've only been wearing these for a week now. They ain't hardly used at all."

31

When they arrived at the town of Pueblo, the sheriff dismissed his posse and turned to Smoke. "Mr. Jensen, I don't know much about this Bill Pike who started this vendetta against you, but if he did all this to get back at you for something you did ten or fifteen years ago, then he must be a mighty determined fellow."

Smoke smiled grimly. "I guess you could say that, Sheriff."

"I don't have either the manpower or the budget to post guards around your hotel tonight, but if I was you, I'd sleep with one eye open. Even though Pike's tracks seemed to head toward Canyon City, he might just decide to double back and try and finish what he started while you and your friends are here in Pueblo."

"Point taken, Sheriff," Smoke said. "Believe me, we're going to be very careful until we get back home or I plant Pike and his men six feet down."

Sheriff Ashby grinned and stuck out his hand. "Well, even under the circumstances, it was nice to meet you, Jensen. I been hearing about you for some time and I must say, the stories I heard weren't exaggerated."

"Thanks, Sheriff. We'll check in with you before we leave in the morning."

"Good night, Jensen, ma'am," Ashby said, tipping his hat and turning his horse's head toward his office.

"Come on, let's get these mounts to the livery so we can get to the hotel and get some dinner and then some shut-eye," Smoke said.

At the livery, he told the boy on duty to be sure and give their horses plenty of grain and a good rubdown so they'd be fit for the trip back to Big Rock the next day.

They walked back to the hotel and found they were just in time for the evening meal.

When the waiter came to their table and saw Pearlie, he broke out in a wide grin. "I hope your appetite is good, sir," he said. "I have a bet with the cook. He says you can't possibly eat as much for supper as you did this morning for lunch."

"How much did you wager?" Pearlie asked, pleased to be the center of attention.

"My tip, sir, and since you and your friends are so generous, it amounts to a lot of money for me."

Pearlie leaned back in his chair, grinning at Cal and Smoke and Sally, who were watching the byplay with smiles on their faces. "Well, son," Pearlie said, "bring on the grub, 'cause I got a powerful appetite that needs fixin'."

"Yes, sir!" the waiter said happily. "And for the rest of you?"

Smoke nodded at Pearlie. "He's right, just keep on bringing out the food until we say we've had enough. And son," he added, "don't cook those steaks too much. Just tell the cook to throw them on the fire until they quit moving and then bring 'em out here."

When they were done with dinner, Smoke left the happy waiter a large tip so he could win more money, and they moved to the lobby. When they got to the desk clerk, Smoke asked for their keys. As the man was getting them, Smoke asked, "Has anyone been inquiring as to our presence in your hotel?"

The clerk shook his head. "Why, no, sir. Are you expecting company?"

Smoke handed the man a ten-dollar bill. "No, but if someone should happen to stop by asking for us, you haven't seen us, all right?"

"Yes, sir!" the man said, making the bill disappear in his pants pocket.

"Oh, and my friends here are going to need plenty of hot water and some strong soap for their baths," Smoke said, glancing sideways at Cal and Pearlie.

"Aw, Smoke," Cal protested. "It's too cold for a bath. I'll catch my death."

Smoke put a serious expression on his face. "If you two want to ride the trail back home with Sally and me, you'll take a bath and get some clean clothes. I don't want to have to ride the whole way home staying upwind of you fellas."

As he and Sally started to go up the stairs, Sally turned and smiled at them. "And boys, no spit baths. Put your whole body in the tub, it'll be good for you."

"Yes, ma'am," they replied, glaring at the clerk when they saw him smiling.

When Smoke and Sally got to their room and began to undress, Smoke saw Sally digging in the valise she'd bought that morning.

"What are you doing, dear?" he asked, shucking his shirt off and dropping it on the floor.

She glanced back over her shoulder. "Why, I'm looking for the nightgown I bought this morning when we were shopping for my new clothes."

Smoke grinned and moved over to put his arms around her. "Never mind," he said. "You won't be needing a nightgown to keep you warm tonight. I intend to do that all by myself."

She looked up into his eyes and pressed herself against him. "Are you sure you're up to it, sir?" she teased. "After all, you've been through a lot lately."

He pressed back against her. "I think I can manage," he said, his voice suddenly husky.

Her eyes opened wide and she moved back to look down. "Yes, I can see you're up to it after all, darling."

In the morning, Smoke and Sally were up early and dressed just as dawn was breaking. They walked down the stairs, arm in arm, intending to get breakfast before the boys woke up.

As they moved through the lobby, Smoke was surprised to find a bleary-eyed Pearlie sitting in a large chair, his Winchester across his thighs, facing the front door.

He and Sally looked at each other and then they moved over to stand next to Pearlie's chair. "Pearlie, what are you doing here?" Smoke asked.

Pearlie looked up and gave a half grin. "Cal and I wanted to make sure nobody disturbed you two. Like the sheriff said last night, there's no tellin' what that Pike feller might be up to."

"Did you sit there all night?" Sally asked.

"No, ma'am," he answered, getting to his feet. "Me an' Cal split the night up. Each of us took four-hour shifts."

Smoke put his arm around Pearlie's shoulder, touched by his concern for them. "Go on up and get Cal. It's time to eat."

Pearlie's face brightened immediately. "You don't have to tell me that twice."

After skirting the town of Pueblo, Pike and his men pushed their mounts as fast as they could toward Canyon City. He knew Smoke and whoever had been helping him would probably go to the sheriff in Pueblo and then come after them, but he didn't know if they would push the chase all the way to Canyon City or not.

Even so, he didn't plan to underestimate Smoke Jensen ever again, so he made the journey as fast as they could.

Blackie Johnson, Hank Snow, Zeke Thompson, and Sergeant Joe Rutledge didn't ask any questions along the way. They all knew the law would soon be on their trails and they too wanted to put as much distance between them and Pueblo as they possibly could.

Once they entered the city limits of Canyon City, they slowed their broncs and walked them down the main street, letting them blow a bit after being pushed so hard.

Johnson eased his horse up next to Pike's. "What's the plan now, Boss?" he asked. "We got the money from Jensen, so I guess you plan to divide it up and we can all go our separate ways, huh?"

Pike slowly turned to glare at Blackie. "You're right, Blackie, we got the money, but we didn't get Jensen, so the job ain't done yet."

"Wait a minute, Bill," Blackie protested. "We didn't sign on to this just to kill Jensen. The idea was he was wanted and we went after him in order to get the reward money. Now, we got the money and as far as I'm concerned, the job *is* over."

"Listen to me, you son of a bitch!" Pike growled, his face flushed with anger. "That bastard Jensen killed Rufe an' Johnny an' Razor an' Slim, and he most likely killed an' cut up Sam and Billy too. Now, I don't know about you, but I rode with them boys for a lotta years an' I don't intend to let Jensen go on home without his payin' for what he did."

Johnson gave a short laugh. "Jesus, Bill, what the hell are you talking about? Jensen killed those boys 'cause we stole his wife and killed two of his hands. What the blazes did you expect him to do? Thank us?"

Pike jerked his horse to a halt and turned in the saddle, pulling the edge of his coat back to uncover the butt of his pistol. "All that don't matter a damn, Blackie. The fact is Jensen is gonna be made to pay for killing our friends. Now, if you're too lily-livered to go along with that, you're welcome to ride on off." Pike paused and grinned nastily. "But I ain't dividin' up this money till that son of a bitch is in the ground."

Blackie took a deep breath, his hand itching to go for his gun, until Hank Snow moved up beside them, holding his hand up. "Hold on, boys," he said, trying to be reasonable. He looked around at the people moving up and down the boardwalks and along the street. "Try to keep it down, all right?" he said. "We don't want everybody in Canyon City to know our business, do we?"

Both Pike and Blackie realized this wasn't the time or the place for a confrontation, especially with the law back in Pueblo possibly on their trail.

Hank inclined his head toward a clapboard building just down the street. "There's a saloon just over there. What do you say to getting off these broncs an' downing a little whiskey to ward the chill off our bones while we discuss it?"

Pike and Blackie glared at each other for another moment, until Pike finally nodded and turned his horse up the street.

Once they were in the saloon and had downed several stiff drinks, the men finally persuaded Blackie to go along with them on a quest to go after Jensen.

Blackie reluctantly agreed, with the proviso that they wouldn't attempt to kill Mrs. Jensen. "After all," he reasoned, "she didn't do nothing but try to protect herself."

"I knew from the way you was hangin' around her with your tongue hangin' out, you was getting' sweet on her," Zeke said sourly.

Blackie flushed crimson at the suggestion. "That ain't so," he said heatedly. "But she didn't have nothing to do with killing your brothers nor any of our friends," he argued.

"She shot Rufe dead in the heart," Pike said, his eyes narrow.

Blackie stiffened. "Well, that's my offer," he said. "Take it or leave it."

Pike thought for a moment, and then he smiled and spread his hands. "All right. I don't really care what happens to that bitch anyway. It's Jensen an' the men who helped him shoot up our friends I want to see planted."

"Now that that's settled," Hank Snow said, "what are we gonna do about killin' Jensen? There's only the five of us left, an' I don't relish goin' up against him an' his men with just five guns."

Pike grinned and looked around the saloon. "Oh, I think we can find some men up here who'll be glad to ride with us for a share of the loot we took off Jensen. Hell," he said, "it's a lot easier than tryin' to dig gold outta these mountains in the winter."

"I hope you're not plannin' on offering them a full share of our money, since they ain't exactly been in on this from the start," Sergeant Rutledge said.

Zeke Thompson leaned forward and smiled evilly. "It don't matter too much how much we promise them," he said. "When it's all over, who's to say they're gonna survive the trip anyway?"

As the other men laughed at this suggestion of a double cross, Blackie tried to hide his displeasure. He'd done a lot of bad things in his young life, but he'd never gone against his partners. Zeke's suggestion made him think about what might be planned for him once this was all over. He knew

one thing—he was going to have to watch his own
back in the future.

"Just where are you plannin' on staging this attack
on Jensen?" Hank Snow asked. "On the trail on the
way back to his ranch?"

Pike thought for a moment. "Naw," he said finally.
"They're gonna be on their guard till they get back
home. I think it'd be better for us to take a few days
off 'fore we head out after 'em. Let 'em get good an'
settled, thinking they're all safe an' sound back home,
'fore we take 'em out."

"You don't mean for us to hang around here waiting, do you?" Blackie said. "That sheriff over in
Pueblo is bound to get word up here to be on the
lookout for us."

"No, you're right for once, Blackie," Pike said.
"We'll head on down toward Silver Cliff, get us some
partners there. As I remember, it's a mite smaller than
Canyon City an' it's on the way toward Jensen's ranch.
It'll be the perfect place to lay low for a while till we
get ready to go after him an' his men."

"Well, at least we got plenty of money to spend
while we're waitin'," Hank Snow said, grinning. "And
I'll just bet there are some women in Silver Cliff
who'll be glad to help me get rid of some of it."

32

After they'd finished eating and gotten their horses packed for the journey back to Big Rock, Smoke and the others stopped by Sheriff Ashby's office.

"We're heading back home, Sheriff," Smoke said. He handed the sheriff a piece of paper. "That's where we live, and the name of our sheriff is Monte Carson. I'd appreciate it, if you hear anything about the outlaws, you send me a message care of the sheriff."

"Will do, Mr. Jensen," Ashby said. "And if any of the boys head over to Canyon City, I'll send a note to the sheriff over there to also be on the lookout for anyone matching the gang's descriptions. With any luck, they'll be caught before you get back home."

Smoke shook his head. "I don't think it'll be that easy, Sheriff, but I do thank you for your trouble and for all the help you've been."

Ashby smiled. "It comes with the badge, Mr. Jensen." He turned to Sally and stuck out his hand. When she took it, he said, "You held up real well under difficult circumstances, ma'am. It's been a pleasure to meet you."

"Thank you, Sheriff," she said, casting her eyes at Smoke. "I had a good teacher."

* * *

As they made their way down south toward home, Smoke decided to take a trail straight through the mountains to avoid going through Canyon City. He didn't want to risk running into the outlaws while he still had Sally with them. This way would take them a couple of days longer, but there was no way the outlaws would know which way they went, so it would be almost impossible for them to set up an ambush along the way.

Even so, while they rode, Smoke took turns with the boys riding point ahead of the group, just in case there was trouble.

Sometime later, when they finally arrived in Big Rock, they were surprised to see that the town was almost deserted, the streets practically devoid of citizens.

"That's strange," Smoke said. "I wonder where everyone is today."

"Smoke," Sally said, "could we stop at the undertaker's? I want to see where Sam and Will are buried."

"Certainly, dear," Smoke said.

They had the undertaker show them the graves of their two hired hands, buried while they were gone. They all stood around the still-fresh graves and Sally led them in a prayer for their departed friends.

She then arranged with the undertaker to have fresh flowers kept on their graves in season, and she paid him to carve granite headstones for their resting places with their names and the date of their deaths on it.

Afterwards, Smoke suggested they stop off at Monte Carson's office to let him know Sally was all right and that the sheriff of Pueblo might be wiring him with news of the outlaws.

They found Sheriff Carson in his usual spot, behind

his desk with his feet up on the corner and a steaming cup of coffee in his hands.

When they entered, he jumped to his feet and immediately gave Sally a hug. "Damn but it's good to see you're all right," he said happily.

Smoke smiled at the sheriff. He knew that Sally was everyone in town's best friend and that the townspeople would be as relieved and as happy as Monte to see that she had survived her ordeal intact and unharmed.

After he finished hugging Sally, Monte shook hands with Cal and Pearlie and Smoke, telling them all how glad he was to see them back.

"I can't hardly wait to hear the story of how you got Sally away from them desperados," he said, looking at Smoke.

"Well, we've been on the trail for several days now," Smoke said. "Why don't we go on over to Longmont's and get some food under our belts and we'll tell you all about it."

"Yeah," Pearlie said, grinning. "I'm sure Louis would like to say hello too."

"Smoke," Sally said, "I'm really not too hungry just now. Why don't I go on over to the hotel and make arrangements for us to stay there while you and the sheriff visit Louis?"

Before Smoke could reply, the sheriff asked, "Hotel? Why are you gonna stay there?"

Sally looked at him, surprised at his question. "Why, don't you remember, Monte? Our cabin was burned to the ground by the outlaws."

The sheriff blushed and stammered, "Well, Sally, first of all, Louis ain't at his place right now."

"I've been meaning to ask you, Monte," Smoke said. "Where is everyone? The town looks deserted."

The sheriff got an embarrassed look on his face. "Uh, most of 'em are off working on something right now."

When he saw by their expressions his explanation really didn't answer Smoke's question, he leaned over and finished off his cup of coffee in one long drink. "I'll tell you what," he said, hitching up his pants. "Let's go on out to the Sugarloaf and then we'll talk."

Smoke looked at Sally and shrugged. "All right, Monte," he said, wondering why his friend was being so mysterious.

"Hold on a minute," Pearlie said. "I thought we were going to eat first."

Monte Carson glanced at him and gave him a wink where the others couldn't see it. "Pearlie," he said, "just this once, will you forget about your stomach for a while?"

"All right, but if I starve to death before we find some grub, you can just plant me out on the Sugarloaf somewheres. No need to buy me a fancy headstone, just put a batch of Miss Sally's bear sign in my casket an' I'll be happy."

On the way out to the Sugarloaf, Monte Carson refused to answer any more questions from the group, telling them it would all be clear to them once they got to the ranch.

As they rode up the final mile toward where their cabin used to be, Smoke saw dozens of buckboards and wagons and about thirty horses milling around their corral.

When they turned the final bend before arriving at the cabin, they saw most of the townspeople they'd come to call their friends busily engaged in building them a new house. Men and boys swarmed around the place on ladders and up on the roof, putting the final touches to a large, well-appointed log cabin with two stories on it instead of the original one.

The women of the town were busy cooking food and serving hot coffee and hot chocolate to the workers and fetching kegs of nails and spikes that were being driven into the walls.

Three large wagons stood off to one side filled with furniture, drapes, and even three trunks of clothes.

Sally put her hands to her mouth as her eyes filled with tears. "Oh, Monte," she gasped, "this is so wonderful!"

Louis Longmont, his sleeves rolled up and minus his usual trademark fancy coat, wiped his hands off on a rag and walked over to meet them.

"Howdy, folks," he said cheerfully. "We'd hoped to be finished before you got back, but we're awfully glad to see Sally is all right anyway."

Smoke jumped down off Joker and walked over to embrace his friend. "Louis, I can't believe you all have done this."

"Why not, partner?" he asked. "After all you and Sally have done for the town, we figured it was time to pay you back a little bit."

"I'm overwhelmed," Smoke said, blinking rapidly to hide the tears in his eyes.

Louis spread his arms. "Well, come on in and let me show you around your new home."

As they walked forward, the townspeople all stopped their work and clapped and yelled their hellos, the women rushing over to see how Sally was and to make her promise to tell them the "whole" story later.

Pearlie made straight for the table that was spread with fried chicken, steaks, rolls, corn, and just about every kind of pie he'd ever heard of. For Pearlie, sentimentality always came second to hunger.

By nightfall, all of the furniture and clothes were in the house and it was complete except for some minor things that Louis promised would be fixed within the week. Seeing how tired Smoke and Sally were from their long trip, everyone finally left for town, with promises to come back out to the house later in the week for a housewarming party.

Once they were alone, Smoke and Sally walked around their new home, Smoke stopping to admire the brand-new handmade gun cabinet that the owner of the local gun shop had filled with new rifles, shotguns, and pistols to replace those Smoke had lost in the fire.

He took Sally in his arms and smiled down at her. "It is good to be home, dear," he said.

"Yes," she said, wiping her eyes with the back of her hand, "it is." She took his hand and led him into the bedroom. She stood before the large double bed and handcrafted quilt that was covering it, thinking how comfortable it looked. "I think it's about time we tried out that new bed the townsfolk gave us," she said, looking at him out of the corner of her eye.

"Tired?" he asked.

She grinned and shook her head. "Not that tired," she said, laughing. "I said try it out, not go to sleep."

33

Bill Pike and his men spent almost two weeks hanging around Sliver Cliff, drinking, carousing, and getting to know some of the local toughs. Even with the inflated prices of a mining town, they couldn't manage to make a small dent in the ten thousand dollars Smoke had left for them.

Finally, Pike chose five men to make an offer to. Four accepted and one declined, not wanting to make the long journey to Big Rock no matter how much money Pike offered. It took him another day to find a fifth man to join their group, and they headed out to make their way south toward Big Rock and Smoke Jensen.

On the way, Pike avoided even the smallest towns in order to keep any word of their approach from getting back to Jensen. The men grumbled about having to camp out in the frigid weather, but Pike reminded them they were being well paid to do just that.

By the time they got to the outskirts of Big Rock, they were tired, half-frozen, and in need of more supplies, especially whiskey.

Pike decided to send one of the new men into town, figuring Jensen and his men hadn't seen his face, so it would be safe for him to go for what they needed.

He sent a man named Cutter Williams, so named because of his penchant for slicing up anyone who disagreed with him with his twelve-inch Arkansas Toothpick knife. He had bright red, almost orange hair and a full beard, grown to cover a couple of jagged scars on his face from old knife fights.

Williams rode into town with a list of needed supplies in his saddlebags, and with orders to go directly to the general store and buy the goods and leave town without talking to anyone.

Williams intended to do just that, until his horse came abreast of Longmont's Saloon, where the delicious aroma of frying steaks and liquor changed his mind. *What the hell,* he thought, *nobody in this town knows me so it oughta be safe enough. Besides,* he reasoned to himself, *what Pike don't know won't hurt him.*

He tied his horse to the hitching rail in front of the saloon and swaggered inside, moving immediately to the bar area. When he cocked his foot up on the brass rail running along the bottom of the bar, Louis Longmont, who was sitting at his usual table having his morning coffee and cigar, noticed the handle of the wicked-looking blade in Williams's boot.

Louis's experienced eyes also took in the way Williams wore his Colt pistol tied down low on his thigh, a sure sign the man wasn't a stray cowboy stopping by for a quick drink before returning to the herd.

Though Big Rock occasionally had such men passing through, Louis was on alert because of the continued threat of the men that had kidnapped Sally. He'd discussed the possibility of them coming after Smoke with the Jensens, but this man didn't fit the descriptions of any of the outlaws Smoke had given him.

Still, better to be safe than sorry, Louis told himself. Anything out of the ordinary needed to be checked out.

He sat there, sipping his coffee and letting the smoke from his cigar curl up to be scattered by the wind through the windows and door, as he observed the man at the bar.

After the redhead downed two quick whiskeys, he took his glass and moved to a table next to Louis's. When the waiter came over, he ordered a large steak, fried potatoes, and sliced peaches.

As he sat back and sipped his third whiskey, Louis looked over at him and forced his face into a friendly smile. "Howdy, mister," Louis said, nodding his head at the man.

Williams looked at him suspiciously and slowly nodded back, the barest hint of a smile on his ugly face.

"I'm the owner of this establishment," Louis said, shifting his chair around to face the man. "I notice you're new in town and if you need it, I can recommend a good place to stay the night, and I can also tell you who's hiring hands in the area if you're looking for a job."

Williams's eyes narrowed. He wasn't used to men striking up conversations with him in saloons—his face didn't invite such friendliness.

"I ain't plannin' on stayin', mister, if it's any of your concern. I'm just passin' through."

This statement really raised Louis's concern. Not many men traveled across country this time of year. The winters here were just too difficult for casual travel.

"Oh, well, then, enjoy your meal and I'm sorry I bothered you," Louis said. He raised his hand to the waiter and signaled for him to bring the man another drink. "Have a drink on me for the intrusion," Louis said, and turned back to his table.

When the waiter poured the man another whiskey,

his expression softened. "Hey, mister," Williams said, holding up the glass. "Thanks for the drink. I didn't mean to be ornery. It's just I been on the trail a long time and I ain't used to talkin' to other people much."

"That's all right," Louis said, trying not to seem too interested. "You come from up north?"

"Yeah," Williams replied, his voice starting to slur a bit from the amount of liquor he'd consumed. "I was minin' up in the Rockies till it got too cold. A man offered me a job down here an' I took it. Anything to get outta the mountains in the winter."

Louis figured he'd pressed the man all he could without raising his suspicions, so he just nodded and went back to his coffee and cigar.

After Williams finished his meal, he got up and walked unsteadily out the batwings. Louis watched him get on his horse and head down the street toward the general store.

Louis was still watching thirty minutes later when the man came out with a large burlap sack filled with supplies and headed back out of town the way he'd come in.

Once he was out of sight, Louis walked over to the general store and went inside.

Ed and Peg Jackson, the owners, were busy stacking shelves with goods that had just come in from Colorado Springs by wagon.

"Hey, Louis," Ed said, wiping his brow with the back of his sleeve. "You in need of some supplies for your restaurant? We just got some tins of tomatoes and peaches that'll get you through the winter."

Louis shook his head. "No, Ed, that's not why I'm here this time."

Ed's face looked puzzled. "What can I do for you, Louis?" he asked.

"I'm interested in that redheaded man that was just in here, and I was wondering just what he bought."

"Any particular reason?" Ed asked as Peg, wondering what was going on, joined him.

Louis shrugged. "It's probably nothing, but Smoke asked me to be on the lookout for any strangers that came to town, just in case those men who kidnapped Sally wanted another chance at him."

Ed scratched his chin. "Now let me see," he said, and then he told Louis about all the things the man had bought.

"That's strange," Louis said. "It sounds like he bought enough supplies for eight or ten men, and he told me he was traveling alone."

Ed shook his head. "That doesn't sound right, Louis. There's no way a single man could need all the food he bought. It'd go bad before he could finish half of it."

"That's what I thought. Maybe I'd better take a ride on out to the Sugarloaf and tell Smoke about this."

Ed started to untie his apron. "You need any help?"

Louis held up his hand. "No, Ed, but thanks anyway. I may just be jumping to conclusions. No need to get too worried just yet."

Louis got his horse out of the livery stable and rode as fast as he could out to Smoke's ranch.

When he got there, Sally immediately offered him breakfast.

"No, thanks, Sally," he said, "I've already eaten."

"Then, how about a cup of coffee and some of my bear sign?" she asked, pulling a dish towel off a platter covered with the doughnuts.

Louis smiled as he took off his hat. "Now, that I could go for." He hesitated. "Uh, Sally, is Smoke around?"

Her face sobered at his tone. "Yes. He and Cal and Pearlie are out in the front pasture working on some fences that needed mending."

"Maybe I'd better go get him," Louis said. "There's something I need to talk to you two about."

She held up her hand. "No need for that, Louis. Keep your seat." She walked out on the front porch and rang a large bell hanging there. When she came back in, she said, "He'll be here in a few minutes. He put that bell there so I could call him in if I needed anything or if anyone showed up who looked suspicious."

Sure enough, it wasn't five minutes before Smoke and Cal and Pearlie came galloping up to the house, pistols in their hands.

They relaxed and holstered their weapons when they saw Louis's horse tied up to the rail by the porch.

They entered the house, still breathing heavily from their rapid ride in from the pasture. "Howdy, Louis," Smoke said, his eyes going to Sally to make sure nothing was wrong.

She smiled. "Louis here has something he says he needs to talk to us about, and since the bear sign just came out of the oven, I thought you boys might like a break from working on that fence."

"Did you say bear sign?" Pearlie asked, grabbing a chair and sitting at the table, his eyes wide with anticipation.

Sally's bear sign were so famous, some neighbors had been known to ride twenty miles just to partake of them.

Sally put the platter on the table and said, "Dig in, men, while I pour some coffee all around."

Once they were eating bear sign and drinking coffee, Smoke glanced at Louis. "Well?" he said.

Between bites, Louis filled them in on what he'd seen in town and his suspicions about the redheaded stranger. "It may be nothing," he added, "but I thought you ought to know about it."

Smoke nodded gravely. "You did right, Louis. I don't believe in coincidence when it comes to pond scum like Bill Pike."

"But Smoke," Pearlie said around a mouthful of bear sign, "there weren't no redheads in that gang."

Smoke looked at him. "That means Pike has gotten some men to replace those we killed, Pearlie, so there's no telling how many men we're going up against."

"What do you want to do about it, Smoke?" Louis asked. "You know you can count on my guns, as well as any you need from town."

Smoke glanced out of the window at the darkening skies. "There's no time for that, Louis. If Pike is out there, he'll probably hit us tonight. That doesn't leave us enough time to go to town and round up any help."

"So, what's your plan?" Louis asked.

"First of all, I'm going to send the rest of the hands into town. They're not gunfighters and I don't want any more innocent men to die out here." He paused, glancing at Sally. "And I'd like you to go into town too, sweetheart."

Sally's lips pressed into a tight line. "No, sir, not on your life, Smoke," she said firmly. "I can handle a gun as well as most men and I don't intend to run away to town and leave you here to face those men by yourself."

"But . . ." Smoke began, until Sally put her hands on her hips.

"We are *not* going to argue about this, Smoke. My place is here with you and that's final."

Louis smiled and shook his head. "I think you're outgunned on this one, Smoke," he said.

Smoke slowly nodded. "I think you're right, Louis. It's easier to throw a bull in heat than to change a woman's mind once it's made up."

"I'm glad you all agree," Sally said, her face softening now that she'd won her argument. "Now, what are we going to do?"

"Cal, you round up the hands and send them into town. Tell them once they get there to tell Monte Carson what's going on. I doubt he can get here before morning, but in case they don't make their move tonight, we'll have some backup for when they do."

"Yes, sir," Cal said, jumping to his feet and running out the door to round up the hands.

"What else, Smoke?" Pearlie asked.

"First of all, Sally's going to make us lots of coffee and food in case we come under siege, and then we're going to shut this house up tighter than a drum." He glanced around, glad that the townspeople, when they'd built the house, had thought to provide wooden shutters for the windows, with small gun ports in them, that could be shut against just such an attack.

Sally nodded and got to her feet, and began to prepare huge pots of coffee and to start to cook some steaks and biscuits that could be carried in bags for nourishment when needed.

Smoke leaned forward across the table. "As soon as it gets dark, we're going to leave one man here with Sally and the rest of us are going to spread out around the house in the woods and wait. When and if they come, we'll be ready for them."

34

As dusk approached, Smoke had Pearlie take the horses up to a corral in a distant pasture to get them out of harm's way, and he closed up the house, closing all the shutters and placing rifles and shotguns next to them along with plenty of extra ammunition. Once that was done, he got an old Indian bow and quiver of arrows Cal had been trying to learn to use out of the bunkhouse. Smoke strapped the quiver on his own back.

"What do you want that old thing for?" Pearlie asked, eyeing the bow with a puzzled stare. "Don't a rifle or shotgun work better?"

"Not if you need to dispatch someone quietly and they're too far away to use a knife," Smoke answered, a deadly gleam in his eyes.

He stationed Cal in the house with Sally after pulling him to the side and telling him to make sure she didn't get hurt.

"Only way they'll get to Sally, Smoke," Cal said seriously, "is over my dead body."

Smoke then told Pearlie and Louis to take everything off their clothes that might make any noise. "Remember, sound carries a long way in cold night air," he cautioned. "The smallest clink or scrape might give your position away."

Taking his advice, Pearlie and Louis removed all bits of metal from their clothes, and tied down their holsters tight so they wouldn't slap against their thighs when they moved or get caught on any branches in the brush.

As a final measure, Smoke got out a tin of bootblack and they each smeared it on all parts of their exposed skin, making them nearly invisible in the darkness.

When they got ready to head out into the night, Sally gave each of them a canteen filled with steaming coffee, a bag of steak sandwiches, and a couple of bear sign to help ward off the chill of the night.

"One thing we got going for us," Smoke said as they walked out of the door, "is that the moon is hidden by those snow clouds. It's going to be darker than a prostitute's heart out there tonight."

"Yeah," Pearlie added, "an' colder'n a well-digger's belt buckle."

After she closed and locked the door behind them, Sally went around the house, turning down all the lanterns so there was just enough light to see to move, but not enough to make them a target from outside.

As the three men moved off into the brush, Louis looked back at the cabin, thinking how well Smoke had planned the original site when he first built it. All the trees for a hundred yards in all directions had been cut down so there was a clear line of fire from the cabin. There was no way anyone could sneak up on it unobserved and there was no cover nearby for assassins to hide behind.

Louis smiled to himself. Smoke was a good man to have on your side, he thought, and a deadly adversary to have as an enemy.

* * *

Pike and his men moved across the nearby pastures toward the ranch house. When he saw the large house silhouetted against the night sky, Pike was surprised. Since they'd burned the cabin down when they were here before, he figured Smoke and his family would be living out of the bunkhouse. He couldn't believe the cabin had been rebuilt so fast.

"Hey, Boss," Sergeant Joe Rutledge said, "the house looks dark. Maybe they're not there."

Pike put his binoculars to his eyes, and didn't like what he saw. The windows were all covered, with only small points of dim light visible in them. "They're there all right," he said. "They just got the place buttoned up tight, like maybe they're expectin' us."

"But Bill," Zeke Thompson said, "there's no way they coulda know we was comin' tonight."

Pike grunted, staring at Cutter Williams. *The fool must've given us away somehow,* he thought.

"Yeah, well, don't count on it," he said. "You men split up and circle around the house. We'll just have to come at it from all sides and hope we can get close enough to set it afire an' burn 'em out."

Blackie Johnson didn't like the sound of that. "Remember, Bill, you said we weren't gonna kill the woman."

Pike glared at him. "Not on purpose, Blackie, but if she's in there and comes out shootin', then I can't be responsible for what the men do."

"Lyin' son of a bitch," Blackie muttered under his breath as he joined the others in circling around the house.

Smoke was squatting on his haunches, leaning back against a tall pine tree, when he heard the soft sound of a horse's hooves crunching through nearby snow.

He slowly stood up, keeping his back up against the tree, and fitted an arrow into his bow.

When he saw a dark figure leaning over the neck of a horse walking through the forest, he drew the bow-string back, took careful aim, and let go.

The arrow whispered through the air and embedded itself in the man's neck with a soft thud.

"Aieeee," the man screamed, clawing at his neck to try and stop the horrible pain.

Smoke bounded through the brush, somehow not making the slightest sound, and jerked the man off his horse, sticking his bowie knife up under his ribs to pierce his heart and kill him instantly.

Someone twenty yards off through the woods let go with a shotgun, the roar echoing among the trees. Smoke dove to the ground and rolled, feeling his shirt pelted by buckshot, but the range was too far for the slugs to do any real damage.

When Smoke rolled up onto his knees, his Colt was in his hand. He fired by blind instinct at the place where he'd seen the fire belch from the shotgun, pumping off three quick rounds a couple of feet apart.

The third one struck home and he heard a grunt and then a thud as the man toppled from his horse to land on a small bush.

Circling around, Smoke eased his way toward the man he'd shot to make sure he was dead and not just wounded. He eased around a tree and saw the man, dark blood staining his right shoulder, trying to reload his shotgun.

Smoke didn't hesitate. These men who kidnapped women and hid behind them deserved no mercy. He flipped his bowie knife over to grab it by the point and flicked it at the man. It turned over the standard three times and hit the man squarely between the shoulder blades. He flopped forward without a sound. Smoke walked over, removed the knife, and wiped it off on the man's shirt before sticking it back into his scabbard.

* * *

Pearlie jumped when he heard the shotgun go off over to his right, and he felt his heart begin to beat rapidly. This was it. They were out there and on the move, he thought.

He eased the hammer back on his express gun, having chosen it because of the difficulty of aiming a rifle in the darkness.

Suddenly, the faint light of the night sky was obscured by the shadows of two men moving past him in the darkness. A slight twinkle of light showed him they had their guns out and were moving toward the house.

Pearlie, not quite as bloodthirsty as Smoke, felt he ought to give the men a chance to give themselves up. He whispered, "Drop them weapons!"

Instead of lowering their guns, the men turned toward him and he let go with both barrels, blowing the men out of their saddles and almost cutting them in two at such a close range.

As he moved past them, the coppery smell of blood and the acrid odor of cordite filled his nostrils. Before he could reload, a man on horseback charged him, firing a pistol wildly.

Pearlie dropped the shotgun and drew his pistol in one quick movement. Just as one slug tore through his coat and another grazed his neck, Pearlie returned fire. His second shot hit the man full in the chest, knocking him backward off his horse with a harsh grunt.

Hearing the gunfire in the woods, Pike screamed out as loud as he could, "Charge the house!"

Zeke Thompson bent over against the wind and struck a lucifer on his pants leg, and then he held it to the torch he was carrying. He was going to burn that bastard Smoke Jensen out of his house.

Just as he started to put the spurs to his mount, a man stepped out in front of him, his teeth gleaming whitely in the gentle light from the sky. "Don't you know a grown man shouldn't play with fire?" the cultured voice asked.

"Why you . . ." Zeke yelled as he pulled his pistol up.

The Colt in the dark man's hand exploded and Zeke felt as if he'd been kicked in the chest. The force of the gunshot rocked him back in his saddle, but he didn't fall.

He grunted with effort and looked down to see a fine stream of blood that looked black in the darkness pumping out of a hole in his chest.

"Son of a bitch!" he growled, trying to raise his pistol again.

Louis chuckled. "Leave my mother out of this," he remarked as he shot from the hip and put a bullet directly into the bridge of Zeke's nose, snapping his head back and putting out his lights forever.

Just as the moon came out from behind the clouds, Cutter Williams lit his torch and spurred his mount toward the house, yelling, "Burn the bastards out!"

Blackie Johnson, outraged by this tactic, which would surely mean the death of Mrs. Jensen, kicked his horse forward after Williams. When he saw he couldn't catch him, Blackie drew his pistol and shot him in the back, knocking him off his horse.

Sally, in the house and fixing to shoot Williams, saw what Blackie did and a small smile creased her lips. She knew he wasn't as bad as the others, she thought, lowering her rifle.

Just then, Bill Pike and Sergeant Joe Rutledge rode out of the forest toward the house, each carrying torches. When Pike saw what Blackie did, his aimed his pistol at him and fired twice, knocking Blackie to the ground.

Rutledge was almost to the front porch when the door opened and Cal stepped out, his hands full of iron. He fired from the hips with both guns, hitting

Rutledge in the chest and stomach three times before the man flopped off his horse and fell across the hitching rail in front of the house.

He looked up, his hand rising with a gun in it. "You don't have to do that," Cal said, hoping the man would drop the pistol.

Rutledge grinned through bloodstained teeth. "Yes, I do."

Cal fired once more and blew the back of Joe's head off.

Pike jerked on his reins and snapped off a shot at the man standing on the porch, grinning tightly when he saw the man go down.

Hell with this, he thought, jerking his reins around and galloping across the pasture away from the house.

Smoke ran out of the woods and over to the porch to kneel beside Cal.

Cal was doubled over, his hands pressed against his side, trying to stop the flow of blood from a wound in his flank.

"Sally, get me a hot iron!" Smoke yelled as he cradled Cal's head in his arms.

In preparation for the upcoming fight, Smoke had told Sally to keep a couple of pokers ready in the stove in case a wound needed cauterizing.

Just as Sally appeared on the porch with the iron, Pearlie and Louis came running out of the woods. Louis stood on the porch facing outward in case of another attack, both hands filled with Colts.

Pearlie squatted down next to Cal. "Damn it, Cal!" he groused, his eyes filled with worry. "You just can't seem to join in a fight without getting shot up."

Cal grinned weakly, still in shock from the bullet wound. "I didn't want to disappoint you, podnah," he croaked.

As Sally bent over and Smoke pulled the shirt back to expose the wound, Pearlie took a bear sign out of his sack. "Here, pal, chomp on this. It'll help ease the pain."

Sally, who'd been through this many times with Smoke, put the red-hot end of the poker against the bleeding hole. Cal grunted and bucked against the pain, but didn't yell.

After the hole sizzled and smoked until it was cauterized shut, Sally threw the poker aside and eased Smoke out of the way as she sat down and took Cal's head into her arms, holding him tight.

"Hold the fort, boys," Smoke growled, with one last look at Cal. "I'm going after that bastard."

He took a running jump, vaulted up on the back of Rutledge's horse, and took off after Pike.

When he was gone, Sally looked up at Pearlie. "Pearlie, would you go and check on that man lying over there?" she said, indicating the place where Blackie Johnson had fallen. "That man helped save us tonight."

Pearlie nodded and walked over to check on Blackie Johnson and see if he was still alive.

It took Smoke almost five miles to catch up to Pike. As Smoke neared the man's horse, Pike reached back and took several shots at Smoke with his pistol, missing narrowly a couple of times.

When his gun was empty, he threw it at Smoke, also missing his mark.

Smoke pulled his horse up next to Pike's and dove across the mount, knocking Pike to the ground.

When they'd both stopped rolling and tumbling across the snow, each man got to his feet, facing the other.

Pike jerked a long, thin knife from his boot and crouched in the typical knife-fighter's stance.

Smoke bared his teeth in a savage grin, pulling

out his bowie knife and beginning to circle the other man.

Suddenly, Pike dropped his knife and stood up straight, seeing something in Smoke's eyes that scared the shit out of him.

"All right, Jensen, you got me. I give up," he said, raising his hands.

Smoke slowly shook his head. "No, Pike. You don't get off that easy. I'm going to cut you into little pieces, knife or no knife."

"But you can't kill an unarmed man," Pike protested.

"Then arm yourself, coward," Smoke spat.

Reluctantly, Pike picked up his knife and moved quickly toward Smoke, slashing wildly back and forth.

Smoke leaned to the side, Pike's knife so close to him that it sliced through his shirt.

Smoke made a lightning-quick move with his hand and his bowie knife cut the tendons in Pike's right hand down to the bone, causing him to drop the knife.

Pike grabbed his right arm with his left. "All right, I'm done."

Again Smoke shook his head. "Pick up the knife, Pike," he ordered.

Pike shook his head. "No."

Smoke grinned. "You ever seen a man scalped alive, Pike. It is not a pretty sight."

"You wouldn't . . ."

"Remember your two men in the mountains, Pike?" Smoke asked. "That's how you're going to look in a few minutes."

Pike screamed in fear and frustration, grabbed the knife off the ground with his left hand, and ran at Smoke.

Smoke stepped to the side and as Pike passed he backhanded him across the throat with the edge of his Bowie knife, slicing through his larynx as if it were butter.

Pike dropped to his knees and grabbed at his throat, trying to stop the bleeding.

Smoke stepped around and squatted in front of him. "I'm going to sit here and watch you drown on your own blood, you bastard," he said.

Pike's eyes were terrified, and his last thoughts were that he wished he'd never heard of Smoke Jensen, Mountain Man.

When Smoke got back to the cabin, he found Cal inside on their bed and another man lying on their couch.

He looked at Sally. "How is Cal?"

She nodded, smiling. "He's going to be fine. The bullet tore a chunk of fat off his flank, but it didn't enter the abdomen. He'll be back at work within a week."

Smoke turned his attention to the other man. As he stood looking down at him, Sally said, "Smoke, this is Blackie Johnson. When I was being held prisoner, he treated me with respect, and tonight he helped to save our new house."

"How are his wounds?" Smoke asked, though his expression showed he didn't care so much as Sally did.

Louis looked up from bandaging Johnson's wounds. "He took one in the ribs, but it didn't hit the lung. I think he's going to be all right."

Smoke walked over to address the man on the couch. "Mr. Johnson, my wife is a pretty good judge of character. If she thinks you are worth saving, then I am not inclined to argue. You can stay here until your wounds are healed, and then you will be free to go."

Blackie's eyes shifted from Smoke to Sally and he tried to smile, though the pain caused it to be more of a grimace. "Thank you kindly, ma'am," he said.